"This is an exciting romantic suspense thriller that starts off hot and . . . from there turns up the heat and the action."

—*Midwest Book Review*

"*Stolen Fury* has a complex plot with more twists than a pretzel, a sassy independent heroine, and a lush Latin hero. What more can one ask for in a romantic suspense novel?"

—Romance Junkies

"Elisabeth Naughton can spin a tale to captivate the reader and take them for a ride."

—Coffee Time Romance

## STOLEN HEAT

"*Stolen Heat* is an awesome combination of deadly suspense, edgy action and a wonderful romance with characters that you'll laugh, cry and yell with."

—Night Owl Romance

"Ms. Naughton offers readers an intense read with nonstop action, suspense, and sizzling chemistry."

—Darque Reviews

"This book has got it all: an adventure that keeps you turning the pages, an irresistable hero, and a smoking romance."

—All About Romance

Other *Love Spell* books by Elisabeth Naughton:

**STOLEN FURY**
**STOLEN HEAT**

# STOLEN
# SEDUCTION

# ELISABETH
# NAUGHTON

LOVE SPELL  NEW YORK CITY

LOVE SPELL®

January 2010

Published by

Dorchester Publishing Co., Inc.
200 Madison Avenue
New York, NY 10016

ISBN 10: 0-505-52795-2
ISBN 13: 978-0-505-52795-0
E-ISBN: 978-1-4285-0789-0

The name "Love Spell" and its logo are trademarks of Dorchester Publishing Co., Inc.

Printed in the United States of America.

10  9  8  7  6  5  4  3  2  1

Visit us online at www.dorchesterpub.com.

*For Joan.*
*CP extraordinaire, expert at everything, my rock, my*
*sanity, my partner in all things murder and mayhem.*
*This book is dedicated to you for so many reasons, but*
*mostly because without you, it just wouldn't be.*
Thank you, J.


## ACKNOWLEDGMENTS

Every once in a while a book takes you by complete surprise. That was this book. Big thanks go out to my running partner, Connie Dingeman, for brainstorming with me back when this book was only an idea. To her husband, Lieutenant Mike Dingeman with OSP, for his wealth of knowledge and stories and for just letting me "listen." To Todd Van Hee for his medical expertise, the "Poison Lady," Luci Zahray, for answering all of my pharmacology questions and to Rita Van Hee, Tonia Wubbena and Lisa Catto for catching the little things I always miss. Thanks also to my agent, Laura Bradford, for all her hard work, my editor, Leah Hultenschmidt, for helping to make this book all it could be, and the entire crew at Dorchester for everything they do to take a manuscript from computer screen to something tangible readers can hold in their hands.

I'd also like to send a special thanks to the medical staff at the Salem Hospital who, during the production of this book, not only cared for me in my time of need but also saved my life.

And finally, I have to thank my husband, Dan. *Babe, I love you for a million different reasons, but mostly because every day you remind me why I write the books I do: because happily-ever-afters really do exist.*

# STOLEN
# SEDUCTION

# CHAPTER ONE

*Chicago, IL*

"You're trying to get my ass kicked, aren't you?"

Hailey Roarke smiled at the moody male voice echoing in her ear as she peered into the darkness. "Define *trying*," she said into the mike attached to her turtleneck.

"*Trying*," Billy Sullivan grumbled in her earpiece, the frown in his voice as obvious as his perpetual sarcasm. "As in, doing whatever the hell you can to make sure I get caught and you walk away scot-free."

Hailey flashed her light around the cement walls of the steam tunnel, no more than four feet wide and six feet tall. A dim hiss echoed all around her. Above, pipes filled with blistering hot water ran just under street level from house to house in the historic Chicago neighborhood. Trying to get his ass kicked? From where she stood, Billy had the cake job, sitting in the van running surveillance while she did the down and dirty work.

"I don't need to 'try' to kick your ass, Billy. I could do it anytime I wanted."

"Don't I know it," Billy mumbled. "No wonder you're single. Take a right at the next intersection."

She followed his directions and sucked in a breath when a rat scurried out of the shadows and ran right over her boot. "Okay, smart guy. Tell me again why we couldn't go street side. Chicago underground isn't my idea of a happening scene."

"Why, H," he said with a lilt to his voice. "You're not claustrophobic like my brother, the saint, are you?"

She ignored the jab at her ex-husband and shined her light into the shadows, looking for any signs Mickey Mouse had a friend. Or ten. "Claustrophobic? No. Rodent-phobic? Um. Yeah. Slightly."

He chuckled in her ear. "The tough girl has a weakness after all."

Hailey pursed her lips. She had a whole host of weaknesses, not that she was going to share those with Billy now.

"And the answer to your question," he added, "is because you said you didn't want anyone to know we were here. I'm just following orders, boss."

She reached a hand up to the ladder now in front of her. "Remind me to take a more active role in the planning stage next time."

"Is there going to be a next time?"

"God, I hope not."

Hailey let out a breath as she climbed the ladder in front of her and fantasized about her little apartment in Key West. Today the Keys seemed as far away as Jupiter. And she missed them more than she'd ever thought possible.

She missed her plants, which she hoped her neighbor Tonia was watering. Missed her little patio with its bistro table and two metal chairs she'd picked up at a garage sale. Missed her air-conditioning that only worked half the time, and Mr. Alanzo's snoring from next door. She even missed Rascal, the neighborhood tom who was always lurking around, wailing in the middle of the night for Mrs. Potts upstairs to open her slider so Tabitha could get out and the two could go on a lovers' tryst.

She missed it all because it was hers and not tied in any way to Roarke Resorts or her family. And because she'd worked her ass off with the Key West Police Department for everything she had. She didn't have to share it with anyone, and no one told her what to do. And if she was a little lonely because of that fact, well, she got over it. At thirty-four, she already knew she wasn't marriage material. Or Roarke Resorts material. Or detective material, either. But that was okay. She was happy with her life. At least, she had been.

Had it really been a month since she'd been home? God, it felt longer. When her father had called several weeks ago and asked her to step in for him as interim CEO for Roarke Resorts—his chain of five-star hotels up and down the East Coast—she'd immediately said no. But when he'd calmly told her it was the last thing he was ever going to ask her to do and that if she helped him, he wouldn't bother her again, she'd finally caved.

To be free of the Roarke family for good? Now that was a prize worth sacrificing her cozy little life for.

Of course, now she wondered if it had been the biggest mistake she'd ever made.

"Okay." Billy's voice turned serious in her ear, dragging her attention back to the moment. "When you get to the top you may have to jimmy the manhole cover."

She stopped inches from the ceiling, her feet perched precariously on the rungs of the old ladder, and pushed her hands against the cool metal above. The cover didn't budge. "Define . . . jimmy," she said, as she pushed again.

"I don't know. Try turning counterclockwise and pushing up at the same time."

Hailey widened her stance, then shoved hard. She grunted from the exertion, clenched her teeth and used every ounce of strength in her muscles. Just about the time she was sure there had to be a car parked on top of this thing, the cover slipped, slipped again and finally gave way.

She groaned as she pushed the cover up and off with aching arms, then hauled her body out of the steam tunnel with what little strength she had left. "Okay," she said on a deep breath when she was sitting on the ledge with her feet hanging down into the hole, "I'm through."

"Damn straight, skippy." Excitement filled Billy's voice. "What do you see?"

She shined her light up and around while her chest rose and fell with her breathing. "Stairs."

Computer keys clicked in the background, and she imagined him sitting in the back of the rented van, keying in her location on his trusty map. "Ya done good, H. You're in the pump house."

At least one part of this was going right. If he hadn't been feeding her directions, though, she'd still be lost down there in the dark. She pushed to her feet and headed up the steps. "What are the chances this door's locked?"

"How's your luck been lately?"

"Crappy."

"No bets then."

When she reached the top of the stairs, she wrapped her hand around the pump house doorknob and said a quick prayer her luck was changing. Holding her breath, she turned the knob. Metal in need of a good oiling scraped against rusty metal, and then the door gave with a soft click.

Frigid Chicago air whooshed around her as she stepped out of the pump house and quietly closed the door at her back. She hadn't bothered with a heavy coat, and the January wind whipped through her light jacket, but the cold was the least of her worries now. In a matter of minutes—she hoped—she'd be in that nice warm house across the grass. "Two doors down," she said into her mike. "I'm heading across the yard now."

"You might just be my dream woman after all," Billy teased.

Two-day-old snow crunched under her boots as she stayed in the shadows of the large spindly trees and silently made her way across the yard. In all probability they could have figured out a way for her to slink up to the house aboveground, but the chances of her being noticed in this historic neighborhood were far too great. This Roarke property had been in the family's holdings for years, and the rich old biddies who still lived on this quiet street kept a close eye out for anything unusual.

When she reached the kitchen door, she pulled out the slim pick kit from her back pocket.

"Just like we practiced, H. You can do it."

"I know, I know," she mumbled. But practicing on a dummy lock in her suite up in Lake Geneva and doing the deed in subzero temperatures in the dark was something altogether different. She ignored the chill in her fingers and the wind whipping down the back of her collar and instead focused on her task.

It took three tries, but she finally got it. The lock gave with a click, and suddenly she was moving into the industrial-size kitchen and closing the door. "Another door down," she whispered into her mike.

"I think I'm in love," Billy said. "Okay, you have twenty-four seconds before the alarm goes off."

Twenty-four seconds. Right. She knew that. But oh, man, that suddenly didn't seem long enough.

No surprise, her trusty cousin Bryan Roarke, who'd been staying at the Chicago property for the last three months, had changed the access code. She and Billy had expected that, though, and they'd gone over this part as well, so she knew how to pop the cover and where to attach the wires from the small pocket-size computer Billy had given her. As she waited for the numbers to click onto the screen, she hoped like hell she wasn't tripping a silent alarm somewhere.

When the last number appeared, she keyed in the code and waited. An eternity seemed to pass before the light turned green, signaling the system was disarmed.

She finally let out the breath she'd been holding, and for the first time noticed the sweat sliding down her temple. She wiped a hand across her brow. "Okay. Done."

"I'm serious, H. Marry me and have my babies."

She couldn't help chuckling as she tucked the computer into her pocket and turned to get a look at the kitchen. "I think that would cause some problems, don't you?"

"Nah. Rafe's remarried now. He's too busy to notice."

The room was silent but for the hum of the furnace somewhere in the depths of the old house. Hailey's eyes skipped over the stainless-steel appliances—all upgrades from the last time she'd been here as a kid—the copper pots hanging from the ceiling, the mission-style furniture and miles of black granite. "I was thinking more along the lines of your dating habits, Billy. A wife tends to get in the way of things like all-night parties and buxom beach babes."

"There is that," he said wistfully. "Listen, you're free and clear. I've got an eye out, but the housekeeper left when you were in the steam tunnel, and you said Bryan's not due back for another two hours?"

"At least. He's at some charity function downtown. Not that the man knows a thing about giving to the poor." He didn't know much about running a business, either. Bryan was in charge of the new resort being built in Lake Geneva, but the project had been horribly mismanaged. Bitterness brewed in her chest as she crossed the kitchen's hardwood floor, rounded the big old oak table she remembered eating at years ago and headed into the heart of the three-story colonial.

She really should feel something for this old house. She'd been here numerous times as a kid, had some pretty decent memories of chasing Bryan—before he'd turned into a jerk—through the third-floor suite of rooms while they pretended they were the kids in *The Lion, the Witch and the Wardrobe*. But by and large to her the monstrosity of the house was just as massive and empty as her parents' place back in Palm Beach.

Hell, it was just as massive and empty as her family in general.

Shoving that piece of emotional baggage deep into the recesses of her mind, Hailey wove through the long, elegant dining room with its Louis IV chairs, until she found herself standing in the enormous entryway looking up at the circling staircase that wound its way up three towering flights.

Where would he hide it? The terms of her eccentric father's will flitted through Hailey's mind. *The individual who collects all six statues and deciphers the code locked within will be awarded controlling interest in Roarke Resorts.*

Controlling interest. Not something she'd ever wanted, yet here she was, breaking into a house she technically owned but didn't have access to. True, the cryptic personal note her father had left for her had piqued her interest in his ludicrous will, but it was Bryan's not-so-gentle message that had driven her to Chicago tonight.

She lifted a gloved hand and gently touched her bruised cheek, winced at the sharp pain. *Man, Dad. You owe me big-time.*

She didn't bother to turn on the lights; didn't want to give any of the nosy neighbors reason to be suspicious. She skipped stairs to get to the third floor quick, paused on the landing and thought about her lazy cousin. The safe would be in his home office—to her right. Though the piece she sought was rare, monetarily it was of very little value, especially to someone like Bryan. He wasn't exactly the sharpest tack in the box, but he wouldn't be so dumb as to leave the bronze in the vault because he'd know that's the first place any of them would look.

*So where would he keep it?* Hailey rubbed a hand over her mouth. Close to him. Where he could look at it and know it was still there. Knowing Bryan, the greedy miser, probably under his frickin' pillow.

Hailey turned slowly. *Bedroom.*

Billy was humming along to some heavy metal music in her ear, and Hailey found the sharp beat oddly reassuring as she headed for the suite at the end of the hall. The door was partway open when she reached it. One look inside confirmed exactly what she'd forgotten about her no-good cousin: the man was a slob.

"How's it goin'?" Billy asked.

"Slow."

She stepped over a pair of sneakers strewn across the floor. Over dirty Jockeys and a damp towel, like he'd ripped them from his body. One glance at the expertly made bed told her Bryan's tornado had obviously blown through after the housekeeper had made up the room.

What was it with the rich that they thought everyone else was at their beck and call?

Thanking her lucky stars she'd walked away from this kind of life, Hailey checked the closet first. She was quick and efficient, but careful to put things back where she found them. When that proved useless, she moved to the bureau, dug through the nightstands, took a careful sweep of the entertainment armoire and the wet bar.

And still no sign of the bronze.

On a breath she dropped to her knees and peered under the bed. Dust bunnies and a couple of skin magazines. Not the piece she sought.

Okay, not in his bedroom suite. *Think, Hailey.* Where would he hide the damn thing?

"Oh, shit," Billy said in her earpiece. "H, crap. We've got trouble."

Her head darted up, one gloved hand braced on the mattress. "Define *trouble*."

"Bryan's back early."

Faintly, a car engine cut off, followed by the slamming of doors and footsteps and voices outside below. Hailey's heart rate jerked as she pushed up from the floor and paused to listen.

The front door opened and snapped shut. Feminine laughter and a deep chuckle echoed up the staircase. Followed by a squeal, then footsteps pounding up the steps.

*Damn, damn, damn.*

She glanced quickly around the room, contemplating her options. She tried the balcony door. It was locked. There was nowhere to hide in the closet without being seen, and the bathroom was nothing but miles of marble and glass. A shriek, followed by girlish giggling and a male growl, sounded outside the room. Something hard hit the door with a thwack.

On instinct, Hailey dropped to her stomach and wriggled under the bed. Then held her breath and hoped like hell Bryan and his latest mistress were only here to pick up something they'd forgotten.

"I'm so glad we left early," the woman crooned. "I thought I'd die if I had to listen to one more story about homeless brats."

Something about the muffled female voice was oddly familiar. Lying on her stomach with her face pressed into the dusty floor, Hailey strained to listen.

"You'd never know it by looking," Bryan said. A loud clank echoed against the floor. Glancing up through the sheer bed skirt, Hailey realized it was one of Bryan's shoes. "You seemed enraptured."

*Oh, shit.*

"Bored out of my freakin' mind is more like it."

Another shoe hit the floor, followed by two silver stilettos, which landed just in Hailey's line of sight.

*Please, God, do not let this be happening.*

"I'm sure Madeline would have fit in perfectly well," the woman said with a sarcastic lilt. "Since she's perfected boring to an art form."

Bryan's chuckle at the mention of his wife was gravelly and full of lust. Hailey's stomach rolled at what she suspected was coming next.

A shuffle of cloth, the rasp of a zipper, Bryan's belt hitting the floor with a thud. "Not you," he growled. "You're not boring at all, are you?"

"Never."

The woman gasped, and the next moment the gigantic bed dipped above. Something sharp jabbed into the back of Hailey's arm. She bit into her lip hard to keep from screaming, realized—as her eyes watered from pain—that it must have been a loose coil or sharp metal point sticking out of the box spring, and shifted to the side as soundlessly as she could. When moaning echoed from above, Hailey closed her eyes tight and pressed her forehead into the hardwood floor.

No, no, no . . . she was going to be sick. If she had to lie here and listen to these two have sex, she was seriously going to lose it.

"H," Billy whispered in her ear. "What's going on?"

"Can't . . . talk . . . now," she managed as quietly as she could, swallowing back the bile.

Slurping sounds drifted to her ears. The bed shook and jiggled. Hailey wiggled her arms around and pressed her hands against her ears so she didn't have to listen.

She was never having sex again. Not after this. She was never going to be able to look at a bed again without remembering this horrendous night.

Suddenly the mattress stopped moving. Were they done already?

"Are you going to let me see it? Tonight?"

In a moment of clarity, Hailey recognized the voice. And the burning pain in her arm slid to the wayside.

Lucy Walthers, a secretary at their main headquarters in Miami, and a woman Hailey interacted with on a weekly basis. *No way.* Lucy was screwing Bryan? She was at least ten years younger than Bryan.

"Let's not talk about that now," Bryan said.

The bed moved once. Stopped.

"Tonight, Bryan. You know I've been waiting so long." When he grunted in obvious frustration, she added in a sexy voice, "If you let me see it, I'll let you do that thing you've been begging me to let you do for months."

Silence. And then he groaned. "Yes, yes, yes. Tonight, yes."

She laughed, the bed dipped, but then the mattress stilled and her voice grew serious. "Where is it?"

"Somewhere safe. Someplace no one will find it."

"You're so clever. They all underestimated you, didn't they?"

He growled and the bed bounced once, like they'd rolled across it. "They all did. Especially Garrett. And Hailey, that bitch. She's never getting a piece of this company. I'll do whatever it takes to make sure of that."

"Whatever it takes?" the woman asked in a startled voice. "You don't mean . . ."

"That's exactly what I mean." Bryan groaned, the way a man does when he's on the edge of control.

"Bryan, wait—"

The bed picked up steam again and skin slapped above, followed by a series of grunts and groans. But Hailey barely heard it. Because at the moment, all she could focus on was the roar of her blood echoing in her ears.

Thoughts of Bryan's 'message' filtered back through Hailey's mind as she lay there, hands covering her ears.

What had her father written in that note he'd left her? *Your participation in this endeavor is a matter of life and death. You're the only one I trust.* At the time she hadn't thought he'd meant *her* life. Now she wasn't so sure.

Out of nowhere a memory from her childhood erupted in her mind, one of her many Indiana Jones adventures with Bryan in this very house.

And like a lightbulb going on, she instantly knew just where he'd hidden it.

# CHAPTER TWO

*Four hours later*

She'd passed parched two hours ago.

Hailey scanned the patrons of Players Sports Bar as she pushed the side door open and stepped into the smoky establishment. It was close to ten o'clock, three hours after she'd planned to be here. She glanced around the room, but didn't see anyone she recognized. No doubt Mr. Dark and Mysterious was long gone, but considering the way her luck was running lately, that was probably a blessing in disguise.

She found an empty table in the back corner, shrugged out of the thick winter jacket she'd changed into in the car and sat with her back against the wall so she could keep an eye on the door, just in case. Even knowing this was one of those weaknesses she'd never cop to Billy—or anyone— didn't stop her. Sure, she was flirting with danger by even being here, but no matter how many times she'd tried to talk herself out of this little pit stop on her way back to Lake Geneva, curiosity kept winning out.

A waitress came and took her order. Minutes later she was savoring the hops lingering on her tongue and the golden liquid sliding down her throat. She needed this after what she'd been through. Deserved it after what she'd had to endure.

Billy had been going nuts sitting in the van while she'd been in that house, but he was getting no sympathy from Hailey. *He* hadn't been subjected to Bryan and Lucy screwing each other blind. She shuddered at the memory. Took another long drink. And that didn't even take into account the nice gouge in her arm she'd gotten from a metal spring thanks to their little gymnastics routine. Luckily, she'd had a tetanus shot recently, but the slice still hurt like an SOB. The only good part about the whole ordeal was that she'd gotten what she'd come for.

Classic '80s rock pumped out of a jukebox at the end of the room. Pool balls clacked and thumped against bumpers. A group of twentysomething college kids were playing darts along the far wall, drinking and laughing without a care in the world. She glanced at the flat-screen TVs mounted over the bar, which were replaying the day's sports news on ESPN, as her nerves slid back to the normal range and her heart rate slowly came down.

One beer. Then she was gone. Since they'd driven two cars into the city, she and Billy had split up after she'd finally gotten out of the house. If she didn't get back to Lake Geneva soon, he'd start to worry. A little of her curiosity had been eased, seeing where Mr. Dark and Mysterious hung out after work. Enough to get her by for the next few months, at least. Tonight of all nights wasn't really the time to "bump" into him anyway.

She finished her beer and was just pulling a ten out of her pocket when the bell above the big old oak door at the front of the bar jangled. And Detective Shane Maxwell stepped inside.

Her stomach did a little flip, and her hand froze in her pocket. Though she tried to keep her pulse steady and even, it jerked back up in the triple-digit category. Just like it had when she'd met him in Key Biscayne three months ago. Just like it had when they'd danced and talked most of the night together at the wedding of her ex and his sister shortly thereafter in Puerto Rico. Just as it did whenever she thought of him, even now.

Okay, coming here had been a bad idea. Her mind hadn't been playing tricks on her all these months after all. He was just as gorgeous as he'd been back then. Tall, fit and athletic, with naturally tan skin, deep chocolate, mysterious eyes, and all that messy dark hair. Since she'd seen him in shorts and a tee on Rafe's boat in Florida, she knew the body beneath those worn jeans and that faded leather jacket was in superb shape. And just the visual was enough to make her hormones surge all over again.

Really, *really* bad idea. She was clearly still operating on an adrenaline rush from the night's activities, because she most definitely wasn't up to seeing him. Not tonight, at least.

As she was reaching for her jacket from the back of the chair, she heard the bartender's booming voice say, "Hey, copper. How 'bout a cold one?"

Sound in the bar seemed to fade into the background, and from her spot near the back hallway, she heard Shane's deep and sexy voice—a sound she knew all too well. "Mick, you read my mind."

"Long day?"

"Longer than Bonds's home-run streak."

Liquid poured, then glass clapped against the wooden bar. And the fact Hailey was zeroed in on exactly what was happening way across the room was a big ol' red flag that it was time to leave.

She grabbed her coat and turned without looking at Shane, then realized way too late she was trapped. The brick hallway led to a pay phone and the bathrooms. The side exit that spilled out into the alleyway between this building and the next was up dangerously close to the end of the bar where he was sitting. She'd slinked in easily enough earlier, when activity in the bar and attention on the Cubs scouting report on the big screen had distracted the patrons. But there was no way she was getting out that side door now without Shane seeing her.

*Shit.*

"You see the news about Blane?" the bartender asked.

"Didn't have to," Shane said. "Heard about it downtown."

"Shit, man. Dumbass rookie. Boy's set for life with the Cubs if he wants, local hometown talent and all, then goes and gets himself in trouble with that girl. What was he thinking?"

"Wasn't," Shane said, his glass clinking against the bar again. "Most of these guys aren't when there's a girl involved."

"Pride of Chicago, my ass," the bartender said with a huff. "Girl flashes her titties at him and he's toast. You think the charges'll stick?"

"Don't know," Shane answered on a sigh. "Doesn't look good for the Pride, though."

Hailey's mind spun as she tried to block out the conversation. Maybe there was a window in the bathroom. If there was, she could make her grand escape unscathed after all.

"Some new faces in here," Shane said as Hailey moved with haste toward the hall. "Those college kids back there giving you any troub—"

Whether he'd stopped talking or she'd finally just blocked out his voice, she wasn't sure. Either way, she was happy to be out of there. Hailey closed and locked the single bathroom door, then cursed when she discovered no window. Dammit, things were not going the way she'd planned, not that they ever did.

What was he doing here so late? Lisa had said he stopped by for a quick drink after his shift—usually between six and seven P.M. Not ten o'clock at night!

*Okay, so think.* She could go back out, take her chances he was too wrapped up in his conversation to notice her, or wait.

For some reason, waiting sounded a helluva lot better than facing the fire.

She paced. Sat on the closed toilet lid. Told herself she was being childish. All she had to do if he saw her was say she'd been in town for business—*which was true*—engage in a little conversation—*like she'd originally planned*—then hightail it out of here. *Easy.*

She stood and looked at her reflection in the mirror over the single sink. The makeup had done a good job covering her bruised eye and cheek, and in the dim light of the bar, she was pretty sure no one could tell she'd been knocked around recently. She pulled the band out of her hair so her curls could hide a portion of her face. Not great, but better. Dropping her hands, she lifted the sleeve of her sweater and checked the cut on the back of her arm.

The bandage Billy had slapped on in the van was bloody, but nothing fresh, which meant the bleeding had stopped. One good sign, at least. Her jaw clenched. *Idiot, Bryan.* Another reason she didn't feel guilty about what she'd done tonight.

She lowered her sweater again, rolled her shoulders and told herself to quit stalling.

She heard laughter and music, glasses clanking and the sounds of ESPN's *SportsCenter* from the bar when she stepped out into the darkened hallway. No Shane. Breathing easier, she turned and ran smack into one very hard, very familiar chest.

"You made a wrong turn at Tallahassee, Officer Roarke."

Heart thundering against her ribs, she looked up, thankful the hall was dark enough to camo her bruises, and saw that sexy lopsided almost-smile of his. What would it look like at full grin?

"I . . ." *Thump, thump, thump.* In an instant she got lost in those smoldering eyes just like she'd done three months ago. "Hi."

"Hi, yourself." Shane's voice was as soft as a whisper and as dangerous as a lover's first touch. And he was standing so close she could feel the heat radiating off his muscular body and smell the beer lingering on his tongue. "You are the last person I expected to see in Chicago in January. What are you doing here?"

Oh, man. How to answer that one?

She should really step back. She had enough problems already to last a lifetime. Her arm ached, her face hurt, and her adrenaline was suddenly back in the out-of-this-world range. But just like she'd done in Puerto Rico at that wedding, she pushed aside the rational side of her brain that said she was flirting with disaster where he was concerned. "I'm here for work. Not here. Um, in Lake Geneva, I mean. But there were a few errands I needed to run in the city."

*Liar.*

*Had she really thought seeing him tonight was a good idea?* Oh, good God. She was seriously losing it.

"Errands, like, hanging out in a dive bar all by yourself?" The sparkle in his eyes said he was baiting her and she should be careful.

And like a fool, she ignored it.

"No. That was an afterthought. Sorta." And a bad one. Her palms grew sweaty.

"An afterthought," he said, eyeing her carefully. He shot a thumb over his shoulder behind him. "Shoulda been your first thought with this crowd. What kind of business does a Key West patrol officer have up here?"

"None. I mean, a patrol officer doesn't. But I do. I'm taking a break. Leave of absence, really." Lovely. Now she couldn't even form a coherent sentence. If that wasn't a sign she needed to bail, nothing was.

"Why?"

His sister must not have filled him in on what had happened with her family, thinking he wouldn't care. And why that bothered her so much at the moment was as much of a mystery as was the fact she hadn't cut and run already.

"My father died."

"What? When?"

"Two weeks ago. Heart attack."

"Oh, jeez. I'm sorry."

She had to avert her gaze because the concern pooling in his chocolate eyes was suddenly too much to deal with. And because even though she and her father hadn't seen eye to eye recently, there'd been a time, ages ago, when they'd been close. The memory of that stayed with her, and it hurt, just a little, just beneath the breastbone, whenever she thought of never seeing him again.

"If there's anything I can do—"

She waved a hand and pulled her gaze from his strong chest. "Thanks. No. Really, I'm fine. It wasn't a complete surprise. His health hadn't been good lately. He asked me to help out with the company about six weeks ago. I'm only staying on until a new CEO can be appointed."

*Double liar.*

"So what are you doing in Lake Geneva?"

"Oh. Um. We're midway through construction on a new resort there. Unfortunately it's way behind schedule. With everything surrounding my father's funeral and such, this is the first chance I've had to get up here to check things out."

He nodded slowly, and again she had to look away because those eyes of his were just too much to deal with. They made her think of dancing and laughing and his hands on her hips, his body pressed up against hers, his breath fanning her cheek and all the incredible places they could have gone that warm night in Puerto Rico if he hadn't walked away.

Her cheeks heated at the memory, and she took a small step back to break the spell she was slipping under. She'd fantasized about him for the last three months, but the reality was, if he'd been interested, she'd have heard from him before now. The fact she hadn't was what she needed to remember. That and the fact the very *last* thing she should be thinking about right now was a guy.

"I should get going," she said.

"What? You can't leave yet. I just got here. Let me buy you a drink."

A drink? With him? And those sexy smoldering eyes? Ah, no.

"I can't," she said quickly. "I have to drive back to Wisconsin tonight before the roads freeze much more. And besides, I've reached my Cubs limit for the night. In fact, I think I've reached it until at least the play-offs."

He chuckled then, a smooth, rich sound that vibrated all the way through the floor and into her toes. "It's kind of a religion around here."

"Ah, yeah. I got that. Spring training hasn't even started."

"Pitchers report in two weeks. Can't get here soon enough."
He grinned then, and oh, man, yeah. That smile at full force
was too much. She had to glance toward the door to keep
from staring. Before she could figure out a way to say good-
bye, he touched her at the elbow. "How about coffee?"

"Oh, I—"

"Come on, don't say no. My sister Keira gave me this
espresso machine for Christmas that I haven't figured out
how to use yet. This is the perfect excuse to break it out. My
place is just around the corner."

His place? Oh, holy hell, *no*. That was a monumentally
bad idea. "I shouldn't—"

His fingers tightened on her elbow, and she looked up to
see that mischievous spark in his eyes all over again. The
same one she'd seen in Key Biscayne. The same one she'd seen
in Puerto Rico at that wedding. The same one she'd dreamed
of way longer than was smart, and which had driven her
here tonight when she should be safe in Lake Geneva right
this minute, licking her wounds. "I don't bite, Hailey. And
besides, even if I did, we both know you could kick my ass
anytime you wanted."

Their eyes held, and she felt her lips slowly curve at what
he was obviously remembering. The night he'd shown up in
Key Biscayne to find his sister. Hailey had been there and
thought he was an intruder. She'd taken him down hard to
the patio, disarmed this beefy Chicago homicide detective
and started reading him his rights before Lisa had come barreling out of the dark and announced he wasn't a peeping
Tom, but her brother.

"I guess one cup of coffee wouldn't hurt anything," she
heard herself say before she thought better of it.

His grin widened. "Quick and painless. I promise."

Her heart thumped. She seriously doubted that.

But damn if she wasn't thinking how sweet a little pain,
the likes of which only he could provide, would go along well
with some espresso.

* * *

He wasn't sure how he'd ended up walking down a windy Chicago street in the middle of January with Hailey Roarke, but Shane wasn't about to go overanalyzing anything right now. Life had thrown him a curveball when he'd stepped inside Players after work on this miserably cold day and seen her standing there, looking as hot as she'd been in Florida. He knew it was wrong—she was his new brother-in-law's ex-wife, for crap's sake—but for once in his life, he was determined to enjoy the surprise that'd dropped in his lap, no matter where it took him.

He glanced sideways at her, shivering in her puffy black jacket with the fur-trimmed hood, her curly blonde hair tumbling down to her shoulders, and had a sudden urge to wrap his arms around her and let her heat thaw him out.

That wicked attraction he'd felt for her from the first was very much at play right now. But whether she felt it remained to be seen. Obviously she felt something, right? Why else would she have ended up in his bar tonight?

"It's just up here." He led her up a flight of stairs and slipped the key in the lock. As he held the door for her and she slid by him, warmth enveloped his body and the scent of lilacs drifted toward his nose.

He closed and locked the door, flipped on the light, then slid the jacket from her shoulders. Tingles ran over his skin where he touched her, and he had to force himself to lift his hands and not get lost in her softness right there and then. Trying to keep his hormones in check, he tossed both coats on a side chair. "Make yourself comfortable."

"This is a nice place," she said as he moved into the kitchen. "Not a typical bachelor pad."

A small island separated the kitchen from the living room. He glanced up after he found the unopened espresso maker on the floor in the pantry, set it on the counter and took a quick sweep of the living room to make sure it wasn't trashed. No stray clothes on the leather couch, no soda cans on the end tables. A folded newspaper and the most recent *Sports*

*Illustrated* were the only things on the coffee table next to his remote. "Thanks. Catrine will be thrilled you said that. She picked out the furniture and all the decorative crap on the shelves."

"You mean knickknacks?"

He dragged his eyes away from her and managed to get the contraption out of the box. Then eyed the fifteen-page instruction booklet with a frown. Might as well have been in Chinese for all the good it was going to do him right now. "Is that what they're called? For some reason I can never remember that. Whatever they are, they were her suggestion. The only things I insisted on keeping were my Cubs stuff."

She chuckled, the sound so sexy it drew his attention all over again, and glanced toward artistically framed photos that hung on the walls—the frames being Catrine's idea as well. "Now those, for some reason, look like your influence. Who's Catrine? A girlfriend?"

"What? No. One of my sisters. You met her at Lisa's wedding."

"I did?"

"Yeah. Red hair, clipboard." His brow wrinkled as he turned over the bag of screws in his hand. "You couldn't miss her."

"I thought that was the wedding coordinator."

Shane huffed and mumbled, "In her dreams."

She wandered to the window, the way she moved drawing his eyes when he should be focusing on the darn coffee-maker in front of him. "Nice view. I imagine property like this has to go for a pretty penny."

"It does. It was my grandmother's place. When she died, I got it for cheap."

Realizing she was now staring at him and that those pretty blue eyes of hers were short-circuiting his brain, he darted a look back down at the instruction manual he had no desire to decipher. The only thing he wanted to look at right now was her. "How do you feel about regular coffee? I think I need a PhD in aeronautics to figure this thing out."

Hailey laughed, the sound like sweet wine that sent his nerves humming. "Regular sounds great. I've never been wild about all those designer coffees anyway."

Neither was he.

He went about his business refilling the Mr. Coffee on the opposite counter and tried not to sneak peeks at her across the room. She was wandering, checking out his books, the sports memorabilia on the shelves he'd had to argue with Catrine to keep, the family picture his mother had taken just a few weeks ago at Christmas. He thanked his lucky stars the place was clean. Mrs. Lewis was worth her weight in gold for what he paid her to clean up after him.

While she looked her fill, he pulled the fridge open, grabbed the milk jug and sniffed. Then blinked hard at the rancid smell before shoving it back in the icebox. He pawed through the cupboard, searching for some kind of snack to put out with the coffee and told himself it was time to go shopping. Again. Once a month probably wasn't cutting it. He managed to find a half-empty bag of Oreos in the back of the pantry, popped one in his mouth and figured half stale was better than nothing at all.

By the time he had the cookies on a plate, the coffee was done, so he poured two mugs, perched one precariously on the plate of cookies and took everything out to the living room.

She'd dimmed the lights and was standing near the windows again, looking down at the city's illumination and the dark lake beyond. From where he stood, the glow through the glass made her skin look richer, her hair darker, her curves that much more prominent. And watching her there, surrounded by all his things, he realized he hadn't had a woman—other than family—in his apartment in . . . hell, a long-ass time.

*She'd turned the lights down.*

He cleared his throat, which was suddenly thick from arousal, and handed her the mug when she turned. "I hope black's okay. I'm all out of milk."

"That's fine."

He set the cookies on the coffee table and watched as she brought his favorite Cubs mug to her full lips, sipped and smiled with a sexy little sigh that jacked up his hormones and supercharged his blood. She turned toward the family picture from Christmas. "I love how all the women are grinning and the men are scowling."

He scratched the back of his head. "Stressful day. Holidays basically suck in the Maxwell household."

She laughed again. Sipped. Moved down the wall to look at something else. He loved watching the way she moved, as smooth as a dancer with her long legs and slim frame, but with purpose and self-confidence. Suddenly she stopped, and her cobalt eyes grew wide. "Oh, my God. Is that . . ."

He set his mug down on the coffee table and walked up behind her, looking over her shoulder at the framed fifteen-year-old snapshot on his mantel. "Yeah, it is."

"No way." She put her mug down and reached for the frame. "How the hell did you meet Jon Bon Jovi?"

"Funny story, actually. It was years ago, as evidenced by my baby face in that shot there. I was working patrol at the time and this guy comes flying down Lake Shore Drive just as my shift's ending. I pull him over, read him the riot act, and turns out it's Jon's drummer. They'd just finished a concert at the United Center."

"How fast was he going?"

"Ninety, ninety-five."

"On Lake Shore Drive?"

"Yeah." He shoved his hands into his pockets. "It's like one in the morning, the streets are deserted, I'm convinced he's blitzed. Turns out he wasn't, just blowing off steam from the set. After a while I give him a warning, I'm too tired to deal with the paperwork anyway, and to say thanks he invites me to this party he's going to. I wasn't gonna go but . . ." He smiled, shrugged.

She flicked a look over her shoulder that was so damn sexy, he curled his fingers in his pockets to keep from reaching for her. "A warning? For ninety-five in the city?"

He shrugged again. "I plead insanity. I mean, it was Bon Jovi."

Her grin was wide and awe-filled as she turned to trace her finger over the photo. "That is so cool."

God, he loved the way she smiled. With her whole face, not just her plump, perfect lips. As he watched the shadows play across her features and toned body, he had a sudden urge to see her smile at him like that.

*Not a good idea. Remember the last time you had that urge?*

The little voice chanting in the back of his head brought reality back into sight, but he worked like hell to ignore it; was sick and tired of living his life by the push and pull of that voice even though he knew it was the only thing keeping him alive these days.

"Kinda ruined me," he added, hoping to get her looking at him again as he moved dangerously close to her.

"Why?"

His smile returned when she shifted those glittering blue eyes his way once more, the ones that looked like the Caribbean on a cool day and reminded him of what he'd wanted to do with her in Puerto Rico. "I was like twenty-three when that happened. It was just after I'd joined the department. I thought that was normal. Imagine how shocked I've been that no other rock stars have been beating down my door, intent on dragging me off to their wacked-out parties."

There it was, that sparkle in her eyes and that broad smile that showcased her tempting kiss-me lips. Only this time she was looking at him, not a piece of paper. "Wild night?"

"The wildest."

His groin tightened at the way she was studying him, and he knew he was walking a thin tightrope with her here, now, like this. Not only had it been way too freakin' long since he'd been with any woman, but she was the trigger that seemed to shut down his brain. Realizing that fact was part of the reason he'd walked away from her three months ago in Puerto Rico. An even bigger part of the reason he hadn't dragged her upstairs to his hotel room after his sister's wedding and stripped her out of that clingy black dress with his hands and teeth and toes like he'd wanted to do that whole damn day. And the only reason he hadn't contacted her since.

Her eyes slid to his lips as he moved just a fraction of an inch closer. "I should probably go," she said. But she didn't move.

"You haven't finished yet."

"Finished what?" she asked, never once looking away from his mouth.

"Your coffee."

"Oh. Right. That." A hint of disappointment edged her words, and when she licked her lips in a suggestive move that made him visualize her mouth running down his bare chest and abdomen, all the blood in his head went due south, straight into his cock.

He knew then, without a doubt, that she was feeling a little of the mind-numbing arousal he was. And hell if that didn't jack him up more and shove the rational side of his brain to the wayside.

*Don't do it.*

He rubbed his finger across her cheek and felt her tremor all the way in his feet. "I've got one question."

"Just one?"

Her need-filled voice wasn't helping. But before this went any further, he needed to know for sure. "Did you pick that bar at random, or did you know Players was my neighborhood hangout?"

"Lisa might have mentioned it. Once or twice."

"I was afraid you'd say that."

He framed her face with his hands, lowered and took her mouth like he'd wanted to do for months. Like he'd kept himself from dreaming about doing for way too long. Her lips were soft, her sigh so damn sexy, he had to force himself not to rush. He brushed his lips over hers, slowly, gently, until her sigh turned into a moan and she was opening to take him in.

Oh, man, *this* was why he hadn't kissed her in Puerto Rico. One taste and he was a goner.

He took the photo from her hand and set it back on the mantel while he slid his tongue into her mouth and tasted the sweetness of her kiss. He moved closer so their bodies were pressed up tight and her heart beat in time with his. The stand on the frame didn't catch, and the picture toppled to the floor with a thud that didn't faze either of them. And when she moaned again, he responded by threading his fingers into her curly blonde hair, tipping her head the other way and kissing her deeper.

She was tall for a woman—close to five-nine, he guessed—but perfect against him where the tips of her breasts brushed his chest and the long line of her body came into contact with his. Her hands found his elbows, his stomach, his hips, and then it was his turn to groan as her tongue slid over and around his. And when she flexed her fingers to pull him close so his growing erection was pressing into the soft curve of her belly . . . the rational side of his brain that had been telling him this was a dangerous move shut down completely.

He wished he'd ditched his gun and shoulder holster. That he'd thought to put clean sheets on his bed. That he'd had the foresight to buy condoms.

Shit. He hadn't bought condoms in over six months. Did he have any that were any good anymore?

"Maxwell," she whispered.

He found the hem of her sweater and lifted, sliding his hands along the silky smooth skin of her abdomen, up higher until his knuckles brushed her satiny bra. He groaned again, cupped the heavy mass in the palm of his hand and squeezed just enough to make her gasp.

"I want you," she whispered.

Oh, man. He wanted her, too. More than even he'd realized until right now. Her words ignited a fire in his gut, turned his blood to a roar in his ears. He shifted her body and pushed her back against the wall while he continued to kiss her like a man starved.

One hand slid to her leg at the knee, lifted so he could hook her inner thigh around his hip as he pressed himself between her legs. She gasped all over again, making him rub harder, pull back and press again. His lips found her throat and that soft, soft place just behind her ear. "Jesus, Hailey. You are so damn sweet. I want to taste every part of you. Here." He drew her earlobe into his mouth. "Here." He nipped her collarbone exposed by her V-neck sweater.

"Oh . . ."

She drew in a sharp breath that urged him on, so he pushed his hips into hers again, over and over, until he had to stop because he was on the verge of coming, just from that simple contact. He moved to sample her other collarbone.

"Maxwell . . . oh, God, this is a bad idea."

"The worst."

She ran her fingers up to his hair. "But we're going to do it anyway."

"Absolutely."

She pressed into him on a moan and kissed him harder. Did it again. And again. Until he was light-headed from the contact. Her hands went up under his shirt, to the skin of his abdomen, around to his side, and brushed the scar on the right side of his ribs.

He flinched. Reeled as her touch registered. Caught himself. Only for the split second her fingertips had feathered that scar, he wasn't in his apartment. He was in a hole-in-the-wall, rat-infested slum with a knife sticking into his side and a smoking gun in his hand.

The image was so real, he had to push back quickly to clear his head. His legs hit the arm of the sofa, crumpled and went out beneath him. And even in that instant of *oh, shit*, he tried like hell to make it look like he'd planned to take a load off, not that he'd fallen on his ass like a complete pansy.

"Maxwell—"

He held up a hand to stop her from touching him, took two deep breaths and ran a shaky hand over his face.

Bad, bad, bad idea. Just like he'd known it would be. No wonder he hadn't had a woman up here in a frickin' eon.

"Did I do something?" she asked. "Are you okay?"

"I'm fine." Or at least he would be. When he was alone. Like he always was. His heart thundered in his chest. Sweat broke out on his forehead. He'd gotten over the panic attacks a while ago, but that jolt from past to present was sometimes so overwhelming, it left him more than a little off balance, like now.

She was studying him like he'd just grown a second head, and he felt like it. Like a freak of nature. Holy shit, this was the woman he'd been fantasizing about and he couldn't even separate himself enough from then and now to . . .

He swallowed hard. Pushed that lovely thought away, and grappled for something to say. "Look. Sorry. That was . . . yeah. You were right. A bad idea. I mean, you're you and I'm . . ."

Silence settled between them. And tension, as thick as molasses, zapped the sexual energy in the room and drowned all that heady arousal.

Yeah. Now he was just making this worse. He chanced a glance at her stricken expression and realized, *Way to go, dumbass. Why don't you just slap her while you're at it?*

He raked a hand through his hair. "I'm . . . sorry," he said again, for lack of anything else to say.

"It's okay," she finally said after a lengthy silence.

But it wasn't. As she crossed her arms over her chest and glanced toward her coat, he knew it definitely wasn't all right. Goddammit, *this* was why he'd walked away from her the first time. Because when he got close to her, he stopped thinking. And when he stopped thinking, he got dangerous. And then all kinds of bad things happened.

"I should go," she said, slowly walking toward her coat, the coffee and conversation and everything else, quickly forgotten.

"Yeah." He stood. "I, uh . . ."

She pulled the door open before he could think of something that wasn't totally lame to say, but when she glanced his way, the look in her eyes stopped him cold. "Just forget I was ever here. I'm going to as soon as I walk out that door."

He stood where he was long seconds after the door slammed and her footsteps faded outside in the January chill. His heart was pumping a mile a minute, this time not from arousal or fear, but from something he'd seen in her Caribbean blue eyes just before she'd left. He recognized it because it was the same damn thing he saw every time he looked in a mirror.

Secrets. The kind that haunted a person and changed their life forever. She had one, and it was big enough to drive her to Chicago and into his arms before he'd driven her right back out again.

# CHAPTER THREE

Hailey's nerves were a jangled mess by the time she reached her rental car. She slid the key in twice before she found the ignition, then just sat with her hands gripping the steering wheel and the engine idling while she looked out into the darkness on the quiet Lincoln Park street.

Not exactly what she'd planned. All she'd wanted to do was maybe run into him. Possibly see where he hung out. Find out how he was doing. Prove to herself he wasn't as fabulous as she remembered. Going back to his apartment was her first mistake. Learning he *was* as incredible as she remembered was the second. Kissing him was the third.

Kissing? Yeah. No. That wasn't kissing. That was second base, rounding for third.

But, oh, God, that mouth. She lifted a hand to her lips, rubbed her fingers over the swollen tissue where he'd kissed her senseless. When he'd had his hands on her body, his tongue in her mouth and she'd been surrounded by all that sweet masculine scent, she'd forgotten everything else that had happened tonight.

Oh, man. She'd even forgotten her pledge that she was never having sex again. Apparently, Bryan's little sexcapade hadn't scarred her nearly as much as she thought it had.

Disgusted with herself, she frowned. The absolute *last* thing she needed right now was to get distracted by a guy. By Shane Maxwell, for crying out loud. She'd finally committed to the terms of her father's will. She needed to focus on fixing what was wrong with the Lake Geneva property, then get serious about finding those statues. Maybe when she was done and her life was back to normal and she was back at her old job in Key West . . . maybe then she could think about running into Shane again.

Reality dropped her hopeful heart into her stomach. Not likely. Not from the way he'd pushed her away. Obviously, something had turned him off in the midst of rounding second. What had he said? *You're you and I'm . . .* Yeah, she could only imagine what that meant.

A sharp sound sent her heart into her throat, and she jumped at the shrill notes playing her favorite Bon Jovi song, then let out a breath when she realized it was just her cell. "Yeah."

"Where the hell are you?" Billy's voice was edged with more than alarm; it bordered on irate. And with that clip to his words, he sounded way too much like his brother.

She put the car in gear and headed toward the freeway. "I'm on my way back right now."

"You're still in Chicago?"

"Relax, would you? Everything's fine."

"Everything *will* be fine when you get your ass back up here. This whole thing was way too close for my taste. I knew we shouldn't have taken two cars."

"We didn't want anyone to see us together, remember? And they didn't. Stop worrying."

"Where the hell have you been?"

"I stopped to get a bite to eat." A brewsky. Have one helluva make-out session. And a big ol' boot right back out the door.

"Jesus. You really know how to give a guy a coronary."

She pushed thoughts of Shane Maxwell out of her head for good, then felt her heart warm at Billy's concern. For all Billy's shortcomings, she could say this about him: when something mattered, he pulled through. "I'll be there in about an hour. Do me a favor, would you? Have a martini ready for me. It's been one helluva night."

"Will do." She heard the victory in his voice. "We need to celebrate anyway. We got exactly what we needed tonight, and no one's the wiser."

Nope. No one was. But part of her wished Bryan knew. Too bad he wouldn't ever have a clue.

Shane had never been so happy to be called back to work.

As he walked across the icy street and headed for the front walk of the mansion that had just become a crime scene, he popped two Tic Tacs into his mouth, snapped the plastic lid shut and stuffed the small box into the pocket of his jeans.

Chicago had taken a nasty hit from Mother Nature two days ago, and remnants of the storm were still evident in the cars and trees covered in snow. While being out in the sub-zero temperatures in the middle of the night wasn't usually his idea of fun, it was way better than staring at the ceiling in his bedroom, replaying what had happened with Hailey and dreaming about a bottle of hooch.

His partner for the past two years, Tony Chen, was just pulling to a stop as Shane made it to the front walk. Police vehicles were parked on the quiet street, and a handful of officers were milling around, keeping rubberneckers back. Dressed in jeans, a sweater and a light jacket, Tony slammed the car door of his sedan and gave Shane the once-over. "Well, shit, wife. You had a date."

Shane frowned. "You always lead with that. Don't you think it's getting a little old?"

Tony slid a piece of gum into his mouth and grinned. At five-eleven he was a good two inches shorter than Shane, with dark hair reminiscent of his Chinese roots, but pale, almost teal eyes that just didn't seem to fit his face. "This time I'm serious. You've got that I've-just-been-screwed look on your face, and not in a good way."

Shane flipped Tony the bird as they both headed up the front steps. "A lot you know."

Tony chuckled, took the gloves a rookie handed him when he stepped into the house. Shane did the same as the door snapped shut and the cold was left behind

The three-story brick was fronted by a wide porch and

massive columns. A tall entryway with gleaming tiles and a circular table holding a fresh display of flowers screamed of wealth. No doubt whoever lived here had bucks, but obviously that hadn't been enough to keep the grim reaper away. Not that it ever was.

They headed toward the living room, where the brunt of officers were milling around, collecting evidence. Amanda Kent, an investigator with the Cook County medical examiner's office rose from where she'd been examining the body on the far side of the room. "Chen, Maxwell. Nice of you boys to finally show up." Her gaze raked Shane. "Dismal date?"

Shane frowned at Tony. "Why the hell does everyone keep asking me that?"

"I don't know," Tony mumbled. "Maybe because you're so freakin' tense it's obvious you need to get laid."

Shane glanced back at Amanda, who held up a gloved hand in protest. "Don't look at me. My husband would kill me."

Shaking his head, Shane glanced down at the body, hoping to get things back on track. "What have we got?"

Amanda sighed. "White male. Roughly thirty-five years of age. Contusions to his neck and abdomen." The man, dressed in gray slacks and a white dress shirt covered in blood, lay on his back on the hardwood floor, staring up at the ceiling. "The attacker hit from the front. If you look at the wound here, you'll see the angle of the cut indicates it came from a horizontal direction. My guess is his attacker was probably several inches shorter than him."

"Right- or left-handed?" Tony asked.

"Right. Definitely. And I'm willing to bet he knew his attacker. There was no sign of forced entry, though the two did struggle."

Shane glanced around the room. A small table lay on its side, throw pillows littered the floor, some kind of crystal had been shattered into a hundred pieces and amber liquid puddled in the glass. "Man or woman?"

"Hard to tell at this point," Amanda said. "Could be either. But it would have to be someone pretty strong to get the upper hand. He wasn't a lightweight."

No, the guy had to be close to 190. Maybe 200 pounds. "Any evidence under his nails? Hair fibers?"

"Nothing yet. But we've just started."

"Murder weapon?" Shane asked.

Amanda shook her head. "Afraid even I'm not that good. Gotta leave something for you boys to do to earn those paychecks."

"What about time of death?" Tony asked, ignoring her joke.

"Based on body temp only? I'd say three to six hours ago. They've got the girlfriend upstairs. Says she was asleep. Didn't hear anything. Woke up alone, came down to find out where he'd gone. Found him like this."

The front door opened, and a blast of cold swept into the house.

"Look alive, boys," Amanda muttered. "Jim Hill's here. That's fast, even for him."

At the mention of the DA's pompous investigator, Shane glanced at Tony. "I'll give you my opening-day Cubs tickets if you take the girl upstairs."

Tony pinned him with a look. "And leave you alone with Hill? No way. I leave you two alone, and you'll deck him or he'll find a way to screw us on this. Either way, you wind up back on IA's hot list and I'm stuck bailing your ass out again." He nodded toward the stairs. "Lock it up. It's your turn anyway, Romeo."

Shane glared at the stairs as Amanda went back to the body. He'd much rather deal with Hill than get stuck with another hysterical female witness. The last time he'd done that? Yeah, he didn't even want to remember the last time.

"Yo, Manda," Tony said before the ME could dive back into her work. "You get an ID on the guy?"

Across the room, Amanda looked down at the clipboard in her hands. "Yeah. Let's see." She scanned the page. "Bryan

Roarke. Florida driver's license. Business card in his pocket says he's with Roarke Resorts." She glanced up. "Hey, didn't I hear Roarke Resorts was building in the Lake Geneva area?"

Shane froze with his foot on the first step.

No way this was a coincidence.

# CHAPTER FOUR

*Lake Geneva, WI*

"You've been in there for almost an hour. Hurry up, girlie-man."

Hailey pounded her fist on the bathroom door one more time. The shower was still going, and humming came from the other side of the door. At this rate, he was going to use up all the hot water. Considering the Lake Geneva resort wasn't up and running yet and this wing was the only portion of the place that *had* hot water, that wasn't completely unlikely.

"Is the coffee here yet?" Billy called from the other side of the door. "Because I'm not coming out until there's coffee. It's frickin' cold in this place!"

"Southern boy," Hailey mumbled. "Take him out of the sun, plunk him in the deep freeze and he turns into a five-year-old."

"Hey," Billy called, feigning shock. "I resent that comment."

Hailey chuckled. "Maybe if you grew some—"

"Okay, now you're just getting personal!"

A knock sounded at the door in the other room. Hailey's ears perked. "I think I hear the coffee now. You just got spared, princess."

"Very funny," Billy yelled.

One side of Hailey's mouth curled as she headed for the living area of her suite. *Suite* was a generous term. This one was close to the offices and the kitchen and was one of only a handful that had been active for a few days now. It boasted a living area, one bedroom and a veranda that overlooked the lake. It wasn't fancy, but she wasn't staying more than a few days. Since she'd gotten what she needed from Bryan last night, she could put at least one worry out of her mind. The meeting with her staff here this morning to go over the construction timeline, budget and the cause of the delays would take care of the second.

Three days max. Then she'd be back in Florida, worrying about the rest of her father's cryptic will.

She pulled the door open, expecting to see Liam, the head chef's new assistant, but instead an attractive Asian American man filled the doorway. He held up his badge. A badge she immediately recognized as being from Illinois. "Ms. Roarke? I'm Detective Chen with Chicago PD. Can I have a minute of your time?"

Chicago police?

Hailey pulled her white terry robe tighter to her chest. "What's this regarding?"

"Do you know a man by the name of Bryan Roarke?"

Oh, crap. Bryan had figured out the security system had been down last night.

Hailey kept her face neutral. "Yes, I do."

He glanced up and down the hall. "Mind if I come in? I'd really prefer not to discuss this in front of your staff."

Hailey hesitated, then realized, yeah, whatever he had to say, she didn't want said in front of her staff, either. She eased back a step. "Sure, Detective—"

"Chen." She made a move to close the door after he stepped in the room, but a hand that seemed to shoot out of nowhere stopped her. Chen gestured with his chin. "This is my partner, Detective Maxwell."

If she'd been sucker punched in the stomach, Hailey would have been less surprised. Her blood warmed at the memories from last night as Shane walked into the room—his mouth, his hands, the things he'd whispered in her ear.

Then she remembered how he'd pushed her away.

Hailey let go of the door and stepped back into the living room, trying to keep her hands from shaking. If Detective Chen noticed any sudden tension in the room, he didn't show it. She purposely didn't meet Shane's gaze. Couldn't.

"Were you in Chicago yesterday, Ms. Roarke?"

Hailey looked toward Chen. "I'm sorry. What was that?"

Chen's eerily light eyes narrowed. "Were you in Chicago yesterday?"

Though her pulse was kicking up in her chest, her brain was slowly coming back online, and the tone of Chen's question finally registered. Two Chicago detectives were standing in her living room asking her whereabouts from the day before.

She chose her words carefully, knowing if she got caught in a lie it would just make things worse. But if Bryan had squealed about her being at the house . . . If he'd lied to get her out of the way . . . "Yes, I was."

"Where about?" Chen asked. "What were you doing there?"

"I had some errands I needed to run and then got a drink."

Chen and Maxwell exchanged glances. And in the time it took for Chen to look back at her, Hailey knew something was seriously wrong.

"What's going on here?" she asked, glancing between the two. Shane still hadn't uttered a single word since stepping in the room and it didn't look like he was about to, either.

Good cop, bad cop. Oh yeah, she knew the drill.

"What's your relationship with Bryan Roarke?" Chen asked.

Hailey's spine tingled. "He's my cousin."

"He works for Roarke Resorts?"

She nodded. "He's vice president of operations for the northern region. Did Bryan do something?"

Chen widened his stance. "I'm afraid we have some bad news, Ms. Roarke. Your cousin was found dead late last night."

The floor shifted under Hailey's feet. In her mind she saw Bryan's aggressive demeanor when she'd refused to sign those papers just two days prior. She must have wobbled, because one minute she was spinning and the next Shane's big hand was wrapped tightly around her upper arm and he was easing her back to the couch.

Okay, she'd been wrong. Seeing Shane walk in the room this morning wasn't the biggest shock of her life. Hearing the news about Bryan beat that by a long shot. "Are . . . are you sure? Maybe you have the wrong person." She looked up at Chen.

"We're not wrong," Chen said flatly. "What kind of errands?"

"Um . . ." She lifted a hand to her forehead. Could she tell them the truth? No, because that would just raise a bunch of flags about how she'd gotten into the house and what she was doing there. And she couldn't risk letting Billy get involved. "Shopping," she lied. "I don't get to Chicago very often."

"Were you alone?"

"Yes." More lies. Oh, man.

"Then you went to a bar? Whereabouts?"

"Ah . . ." She looked at her bare feet. "Somewhere near Lincoln Park."

"You don't know the name of the establishment?"

"No. I asked the cabby where I could get a good burger and beer, and he took me there. I didn't pay much attention to the name."

*Liar.* She chanced a look at Shane from the corner of her eye, swallowed and looked back at her feet.

Chen made notes on a tablet in his hand. "What time was that?"

"I don't know. Nine, I guess."

"And what time did you leave?"

"Sometime after ten." Oh, man, could she sound guiltier? She'd practiced all this in her mind, just in case Bryan figured out someone had been in the house and caused a ruckus within the company. But she'd never once anticipated she'd be answering questions about her whereabouts to the police. And never, ever, because of his death.

Oh, shit. He was really dead. Her stomach rolled.

"Did anyone see you there? Can anyone vouch for your timeline?"

Vouch for her? Hold on a minute. In the midst of all the fuzz in her brain, one thing got through. Her gaze snapped to Chen. And as she focused on his pale eyes, reality dawned.

These two hadn't come here simply to relay bad news. They'd come to question her. Which meant Bryan's death hadn't been an accident. It also meant either they knew about the rocky relationship she'd had with her cousin, or they'd already found evidence she'd been in the house.

Oh, double shit. The cut on her arm. She'd worn gloves to prevent fingerprints, just in case, but her arm had bled good when she'd been stuck under that bed. She'd cleaned up what she could see, but blood could be found with a black light. And if he'd been killed between the time she'd left the house and when she'd run into Shane . . .

A lump formed in her throat, but she pushed words out and forced herself not to swallow and look guiltier than she already was. "I'm not certain. The bartender for sure. A waitress." *Shane.* She chanced a glance his way and took in his rigid jaw and tight shoulders. Why wasn't he saying anything? Did he think she was guilty? Was he ashamed of being with her? Did he think she'd run into him just so she could have an alibi?

That last thought sent her stomach swirling. She looked back at Chen. "How did he die?"

Chen glanced at the notepad in his hand. "The house is registered as a Roarke Resorts holding. Did your cousin live there permanently?"

Oh yeah, she was in deep trouble. He was avoiding her question.

She shook her head and looked at the carpet in front of her. *Play it cool. Keep your head about you and you'll do fine. You know how this works.* "No. He, ah, lives in Florida. He has a wife." She closed her eyes. Crap. Madeline. She forced her eyes open again. "He's been overseeing construction up here. But he prefers to stay in the Chicago house rather than here."

"Quite a commute, isn't it?" Chen asked.

Yeah, but that was Bryan's plan. Stay far enough away so he had an excuse for being gone a lot of the time. None of the staff would ask questions and he'd get off on easy street. It was part of the reason this resort was half a million dollars over budget and two months behind schedule. And it was also *part* of the reason she was up here now.

Her brain flicked back over the scene she'd witnessed. Paused on Lucy Walthers. Whom neither one had mentioned yet.

Shit. Should she tell them? No. Because then she'd definitely have to give up Billy. And she'd never do that.

"It is," she agreed in a quiet voice.

She couldn't help it. She flicked another look at Shane only to find his hard, dark eyes focused solely on her. He still hadn't said a word, and aside from catching her before she'd gone down like a wussy female, he hadn't touched her again. But the way he was watching her with those probing eyes set her on edge. They weren't the soft, gentle eyes they'd been last night. These were cop eyes. The kind that looked all the way through a person and decided, *Yep, she's lying.*

Hailey had to look away.

"Did you go by the house yesterday, Ms. Roarke?" Chen asked.

Her stomach clenched. Now, how was she going to answer that one?

Before Hailey could open her mouth, the phone on Chen's hip went off. He looked down at the number, scowled and flipped it open. "I need to take this. Detective Maxwell can finish things up here."

He didn't wait for an answer from her, simply lifted the phone to his ear and said, "Chen" as he strode for the exit.

Okay. Finish up. At least that meant they weren't going to arrest her. And it meant she wasn't going to have to say a word about Billy. A shot of relief raced through Hailey, as strong as any triple espresso. Until the moment the door snapped shut and she was suddenly all alone with Shane.

He stared at her with narrowed eyes. Didn't say a thing. And in the silence between them, every one of her self-doubts came rushing back.

She'd never been good enough for any man. Not for her father, not for her ex-husband, and definitely not for this burly detective she'd been thinking about for three long months. In the end, they'd all walked away from her for one reason or another.

She took in the way he was studying her. This was not a man who was interested in her anymore. Not as a woman, at least. And definitely not as a possible lover. He was here right now only because she was a suspect.

A *suspect*. Forget all that lovey-dovey crap. The only thing she needed to focus on now was figuring a way to keep her ass out of jail.

*Damn, Bryan. And damn my father, too.*

She squared her shoulders, refusing to be intimidated. And was just about to open her mouth and cut the silence when the bathroom door flew open and Billy walked out in a rush of steam and heat that poured into the room.

"Babe, I thought you said there was coffee." Her former brother-in-law was naked but for a pair of low-slung Levi's and a towel he was rubbing through his light brown hair. "You know I'm no good before nine without some caffeine."

Shane's gaze snapped from Billy's bare chest to her white terry bathrobe. And in his eyes she saw a whole lot of *What the fuck?* He knew who Billy was. And he knew Billy's reputation.

Hailey closed her eyes and blew out a long breath. Yeah. Things weren't looking up at all. And this was doing shit to keep her out of jail.

Shane's back tightened as Hailey quickly stood and turned away from him. "Billy. You remember Shane Maxwell, don't you?"

Billy halted and his head came up. Surprised, hazel eyes darted to Hailey's face, then over her shoulder to Shane.

*Yeah. You keep lookin' buddy.* Shane's jaw clenched. Billy was his sister Lisa's new brother-in-law. Technically Shane supposed that made Billy some twisted form of family. Not that he was claiming the kid, though. What little he knew of Billy Sullivan could be summed up in one word: fuckup.

In his mind's eye, Shane saw the bruises all over Hailey's face that had nearly stopped him cold when he'd stepped into the suite—the ones he hadn't noticed last night in the dim light of the bar or his apartment—her in nothing but that cotton bathrobe and this punk in front of him. And it all totaled up to one big-ass question he had no right to ask.

"Yeah. Sure." Billy looped the towel over his bare shoulder. "What brings you up here, cop?"

Hailey stepped between them, and Shane knew without even seeing her bruised face she was flashing Billy a warning. Smart girl. He was in no mood to play nice. "*Detective* Maxwell came up to ask me a few questions about the new hotel."

Billy's gaze snapped to her face. And no, Shane didn't imagine it. The kid may be a fuckup, but he was quick on the uptake. "You don't say."

"Why don't you head down to the kitchen and check on that coffee," Hailey said with way more enthusiasm than it needed. "I'll finish up here while you're gone."

Billy nodded once, flicked a look at Shane, then took two steps back toward the bedroom door. "Yeah. Lemme just grab my shirt."

He was back in a flash, pulling a plain white tee over his head, flip-flops clacking against the soles of his feet. "You guys want anything?"

"No, we're good," Hailey said quickly.

"Okay then. I'll see ya."

The door snapped shut, and silence settled over the room. Slowly, Hailey turned Shane's way again. Only this time she didn't look shocked, like she had when Tony'd told her the news about her cousin; she looked guilty.

*No frickin' way.*

She bit the inside of her lip. Eyed him warily. Waited.

And though he knew it was the absolute wrong thing to say, he couldn't seem to stop himself. "Moving from one brother to the next?"

Surprise hit first, then fire flashed in her sapphire eyes before they narrowed. "Fuck you, Maxwell."

Pow. Like he didn't deserve that one? Yeah, he'd been the one to call things quits last night, but seriously . . . Billy Sullivan? *Billy Sullivan?*

He raked a hand through his hair and pushed that damn thought right out of his head. Who the hell she screwed wasn't his concern. But if the guy was using her as a punching bag, Christ Jake, that was his business, big-time. "What happened to your face?"

She tipped her head and shot him a bored look. "I fell."

"Bullshit. Either spill it or I'll find someone who will."

Her expression never wavered, but finally realizing he wasn't backing down, she lifted a shoulder, dropped it. "Which ones?"

*Which ones?* She was letting Sullivan beat on her? On a regular basis? Oh, man, the kid was dead meat. And where was the spunky, I-don't-take-crap-from-any-guy woman he'd met in the Keys?

She dropped her crossed arms. "Oh, please. I know what you're thinking and that's not it. Have you talked to Lisa recently?"

He thought back to the last time his twin sister had called. "Last week."

"Did she tell you what happened with Pete?"

Pete was Peter Kauffman. A friend to Lisa and Rafe, and Rafe's business partner at the Odyssey Gallery. Shane had met Kauffman in Florida as well. Smart. Quick. Everybody's friend. The kind of guy—in Shane's mind—you seriously had to watch out for because you didn't know what he'd do next.

"About the trouble with his girlfriend?" Shane asked, remembering what Lisa had told him. A few weeks ago Kauffman's ex had been stalked by two guys linked to a terrorist faction in Egypt because of a scandal she'd witnessed. He didn't know the details, only that there'd been a run-in in New York, Kauffman and the girlfriend had gotten away, and the terrorist had been killed.

"Yeah." Hailey pointed at her face. "Yellow bruises. I was helping Pete with some research. Kat's 'friends' mistook me for Pete's sister. I guess they thought I might be good bargaining material."

His eyes widened. Holy shit. She'd been taken hostage. By a jihad terrorist. "What happened—"

"Nothing," she said quickly. "I got away. Bad guy got what was coming to him. End of story."

A rush of relief forced his breath out. But that relief was short-lived when he remembered what she'd said earlier. *Which ones?*

He focused back at the fresh bruise near her eye. "What about the new bruises?"

She bit her lip again.

"Don't even think about holding out on this, or your boyfriend out there's gonna be in serious trouble."

Her lips flattened. "Are you asking because you're concerned for my well-being or because you need a statement from your top suspect?"

Her beauty and killer curves almost made him forget she'd been a cop herself. "You're not a suspect." Not yet, anyway.

"But I'm a person of interest. Semantics, don't you think?"

"We're talking to everyone related to this case, not just you."

She studied him a long second. "How did he die?"

He hesitated. "We're not sure. Autopsy hasn't come in."

She knew he was lying. She could read it in those crystal blue eyes. "I'm not answering any other questions without my attorney."

His back went up. And whatever affable mood he thought they'd been working toward imploded. "That's entirely your choice. But there's no reason—"

"Yeah. There is. Now if there's nothing else, Detective, I'd appreciate it if you'd go. I have several calls I need to make. Family to notify and responsibilities to see to. If you have any other questions, have Detective Chen call my secretary and I'll cooperate in any way I can. With my lawyer. Otherwise, this conversation is over."

His eyes raked her battered face. Ran down to the V of her robe and back up again before he could stop it. She saw, and pulled the lapels together.

This was better. Keeping things professional. Not falling back into lust with her like he'd been in Florida. Or Puerto Rico. Or damn . . . in his apartment last night. She was right. She was a person of interest in their case, and he was a detective investigating a crime he knew instinctively she was somehow linked to.

Better. Easier. Definitely safer. Especially for her.

He pulled a card from his back pocket and handed it to her. "If you think of anything else, give us a call."

He stopped with one hand on the doorknob. But didn't dare look back at her. "Why didn't you just tell him you were with me last night?"

Silence.

Then quietly she said, "Why didn't you?" When he didn't answer, she added, "That's what I thought. As far as either of us is concerned, it never happened."

# CHAPTER FIVE

Hailey's hands were shaking as she reached out to grip the edge of the couch. She wasn't going to hyperventilate, dammit.

Bryan was dead. Just like her father. *Your participation is a matter of life and death. You're the only one I can trust.* A chill slid down her spine. What if her father had been trying to tell her something in that note? Was it possible his death hadn't been an accident?

Heart racing, she reached for the phone and dialed the one real friend she had in the Key West PD. Alice Hargrove answered on the second ring.

"Funny farm. What's your emergency?"

Hailey's mind spun. And because she'd been conditioned, she rattled off the first thing that came to her. "You talking to me?"

"Better, H. But you need to come up with something more original than *Taxi Driver.* And a little humor in your voice would help. A takeoff on Paris Hilton would work better. Try, 'I've lost my pink-tutu'd Taco Bell dog.'"

Hailey closed her eyes. Normally Allie's jovial personality eased whatever was bothering her. Allie's humor had made her laugh when she'd been rejected for the detectives program, when she'd been going through her divorce, even after the death of her father two weeks ago. But today it didn't do a thing to ease the sickness in her gut. "Allie, I need a favor. A big one."

Allie's tone grew serious. "What is it? And where are you?

I left a message on your home phone last night but you never called back."

"Wisconsin. I came up to check on the new resort. Allie, Bryan's dead."

"No shit?" There was a long silence, and then Allie said, "Well, not to be morbid or anything, but that isn't exactly a bad thing for you, is it?"

Hailey cringed. A little digging and Shane would figure that out as well, if he didn't already know. "I'm pretty sure he was murdered. The police were just here questioning me."

"What? Why you?"

Hailey ran her hand over her brow. The shakes were gone, thankfully. But she still felt like she might throw up. "Because I went by the house yesterday before coming up here."

"Well, technically it's your house, right? How do you know he was murdered?"

"Because they wouldn't have been here questioning my whereabouts if he hadn't been. Allie, it's not going to take them long to figure out exactly what you just said. I have motive. I had means. I have a crappy alibi."

"Whoa, whoa, whoa. Back up the train, circus-girl. What do you mean you have a crappy alibi? Where were you yesterday?"

Hailey bit her lip. She wasn't going to drag Allie into this. They were friends, but Allie was up for a promotion. And unlike Hailey, she was a damn good officer.

"That doesn't matter. Listen, I need you to do me a favor. My father was autopsied. I saw the final report, but nothing stood out to me. Can you get hold of the report and have your dad take a look at it? See if something jumps at him?"

Allie's father was the Monroe County medical examiner. If ever there was a death expert, it was James Hargrove. "You think your father didn't die of heart failure like the ME concluded? And for the record, I saw the way you changed subjects there."

Hailey ignored the last sentence and focused on the important one. "I'm not sure. A few things he said to me at the end don't make a whole lot of sense. I've got this strange feeling he was trying to tell me something. I was dealing with a lot right after his death. I didn't read the report as carefully as I could have."

"Yeah, H, I can do that, but what does this have to do with Bryan?"

"I'm not sure. It's a gut feeling. Something's not right."

"I'll say. Stinky and Denmark come to mind."

"I've never understood that saying."

"Me, either," Allie said. "I'm sure it offends someone somewhere, but I'm always offending people, so that's nothing new."

This time when Hailey smiled, she did feel marginally better. If only for a second. But her smile quickly faded. "You'll never guess who the detective was that questioned me."

"Howie D!"

Hailey couldn't help it. She chuckled. Allie's obsession with the Puerto Rican Backstreet Boy was legendary. Through Hailey's short marriage to Rafe, Allie had routinely pointed out that Rafe looked like an older, taller version of the singer. A fact that used to piss Rafe off to no end.

"No. Unfortunately. Think tall, dark and brooding Chicago detective."

"No!"

"Unfortunately, yes."

Allie whistled on her end of the phone. "What happened?"

Since Hailey had already told Allie all about Shane and their combustible chemistry, no explanation was needed. She did, however, think it wise to omit the whole make-out session in his apartment last night. "Not much. He insulted me. I insulted him. He tried to get me to confess to killing my cousin. Match made in heaven, don't you think?"

"Honey, we need to work on your man skills."

"Among other things. Look, Allie, I gotta go. I'll call you later."

"You better. I'll get in touch with my dad and get what you need." Her tone grew serious. "And, H, seriously, if you need anything else, call me. I mean it. I'm worried about you."

"Don't be. I'll be fine. But thanks."

Hailey hung up, then dialed the car service she frequently used. The door to the suite opened just as she was hanging up. Billy stepped in the room carrying two paper cups.

She rose and took the coffee he held out for her. "What did the cops want?"

She took a long swallow and felt the bitter liquid slide down her throat and warm her iced-over belly. "Nothing. Maxwell was just in the area and stopped by to say hello."

Billy's eyes narrowed. "Bullshit. I remember the way you two were all buddy-buddy at Rafe and Lisa's wedding. This wasn't a casual meet and greet."

She sipped again but didn't look away. No matter what Billy thought he knew or what he said now, she wasn't pulling him into this. One more run-in with the law and he was going to be in serious trouble. And while Hailey could handle the fallout that would cause with her ex-husband, she wouldn't let it happen because she owed their mother. Teresa Sullivan was the mother Hailey had always wished she'd had, and she was in the last stages of pancreatic cancer. If her youngest son went to jail now, before it was truly over, it would kill her. Literally.

"You don't think he'd stop by just to see me?"

"That's not why he was here."

With a frown she moved to sit in a side chair. "Some men do find me attractive."

Billy chuckled as he dropped onto the couch, slipped off his flip-flops and propped his bare feet up on the glass coffee table. "I know they do. That cop definitely does. But that's not why he was here." He glanced down into his paper cup as a wicked smile spread across his face. "He thinks the two of us are doing the nasty. And he was not thrilled with that idea."

Considering the way Shane had put the kibosh on their little lip-lock last night, Hailey seriously doubted he cared whom she did what with. "You say that like it grosses you out."

"Don't get me wrong, H, you're hot and all that. But even if there wasn't the whole ick factor because you're family, Rafe'd kick my ass. Now, your sister"—his brow lifted—"that's another story."

Hailey pinned him with a look. Her sister, Nicole, was close in age to Billy's twenty-seven, and everything Hailey wasn't. Petite, naturally tan, stunning in a you-can't-miss-me kind of way, and a total party girl. It made perfect sense Billy would find her attractive.

It was also the reason she needed him to get back to Miami and take care of that other thing she needed done *before* Nicole got home from her trip to Europe.

"I called you a car. It'll be here in a few minutes."

He eyed her over the plastic lid. And though she tried not to let her anxiety over everything she'd just learned show, he saw it. The guy was too smart for his own good. "You sure you don't need me up here?"

She shook her head. "We got what I wanted last night. The only thing I need from you is to handle that other matter we discussed."

His hazel eyes held hers longer than she liked. And her stomach tightened at the anxiety she hoped he didn't see. He was nothing like his brother, her ex. Light instead of dark, strongly resembling their father's Irish genes, while Rafe looked more like the Puerto Rican side of the family. Spontaneous where Rafe was careful. Cocky where Rafe was sure. Someone who did things his way and because of it, was usually misunderstood.

She figured that last quality was why she liked Billy so much. Yeah, he made bad choices, and more often than not it landed him in trouble, but in retrospect, he wasn't a whole lot different from her. In fact, as he studied her now with eyes that saw way too much, she realized she and Billy had way more in common than she'd ever had with Rafe.

He finally broke the stare-down, dropped his feet and

leaned forward. "What does it mean? The number on the bottom of the statue? Twenty-five. Twenty-five what?"

"I don't know." More and more she was starting to believe maybe her father *was* trying to tell her something. What if this crazy treasure hunt wasn't really all that crazy after all? Who had killed Bryan, and why? And what if the same person had had something to do with her father's death?

The phone buzzed, indicating the car was there, the sharp sound like a chain saw cutting through her thoughts.

She plastered on a smile as she and Billy said a quick good-bye. He grabbed his backpack from the bedroom and told her he'd be in touch. As the door closed, she prayed his part of their little plan went off without a hitch. Then dropped her head against the wood as soon as she was alone.

*Way to go, Hailey.*

Billy was the only person who could vouch for her true whereabouts last night and she'd just let him go. If Bryan had been murdered, then she really was in deep shit.

She turned, braced her back against the cool door and stared across the suite. She needed to get out of Chicago ASAP. Before the police figured out a reason to keep her here. Before Shane Maxwell came back and questioned her all over again. If it weren't for that meeting tomorrow morning with the Lake Geneva planning commission, she'd be on a plane right this very minute.

Something inside her said sticking around was going to be bad news, just like it had been in that bar. In each and every way she could think of.

Tony was in the car on the phone when Shane slid into the passenger seat. He pulled the door closed and glanced at the construction site. Though this part of the resort was close to being finished, there was no landscaping around the base of the building, just mounds of dirt and construction materials strewn about under a thin layer of snow.

Tony flipped his phone closed and shot a look Shane's way. "Get anything out of her?"

"Nothing more than you did."

"She say what happened to her face?"

"No." Shane's jaw clenched as he stared at the resort. And thought about what she'd admitted to—shit, being taken hostage by a jihad terrorist? Kauffman was at the top of his list of assholes to deck the next time he saw the man, right after he pounded Billy Sullivan to dust.

His brain switched over to what she hadn't admitted. "Could have been a random mugging."

"You buy that?"

"No. Do you?"

Tony perched an elbow on the windowsill and shook his head. "No way. Just making sure you don't. Girl's lying through her teeth."

Hell yeah, she was lying. Big-time. And Shane wanted to know why.

He also wanted to know what Sullivan was doing in her hotel room. The kid was in his midtwenties. She had to be at least six years older than the guy. What the hell did she see in a screwup like Sullivan? And if she was really with the loser, why the hell had her tongue been in Shane's mouth last night?

He raked a hand through his hair when he realized where his thoughts were going and tried to put the visual of the two of them naked and sweaty out of his mind.

"Son of a bitch," Tony mumbled from across the car. "You fucked her."

Shane's gaze darted his direction. "What? No, I didn't."

"Then you want to," Tony said emphatically.

Shane scoffed and shifted around so he could reach the Tic Tacs in his pocket. He needed one. Or fifty. "Get your head out of the gutter."

"I would if you didn't have yours firmly up your ass. I saw the way you two were looking at each other. She's a possible suspect, man. To a pretty nasty murder, in case you forgot. If there's something going on between the two of you, you better fucking lay it out on the table right now."

Shane glared up at the building again and tried to figure out what he could say that would make a lick of sense. No way Tony was backing down on this one. Not after the last time.

"Look, there's nothing going on between us, okay? I met her when I went to Florida to find Lisa a few months ago. That's it."

"That's it? Really? 'Cause it doesn't look like *it* from where I'm sitting."

Shane's jaw flexed. He should just come clean. Tell Tony he'd been with Hailey last night. But if he did, he'd get thrown off this case. And if Bryan Roarke's murder had happened before he'd run into Hailey . . .

"That's it," he said firmly. Decision made. "End of story."

Tony eyed him a long beat. Then slowly shook his head. "I hope so. I really do. Because you know what happened the last time you got involved with a woman wrapped up in a murder—"

"Yeah, I know," Shane said quickly. He popped a handful of Tic Tacs and reached for the seat belt. Like he needed Tony or anyone else reminding him of that fact. "Now you gonna tell me who was on the phone and why it was so damn important you left in the middle of our interview or what?"

Tony started the ignition. "That was Ramos. They just went through the surveillance tapes from the Roarke house."

"And?"

"And they want us to take a look. They've got footage of what looks to be a woman breaking in close to time of death."

Shane's eyes narrowed. "A woman? They sure?"

Tony turned onto the freeway heading south. "Pretty damn. Ramos said she looked blonde."

"Fuck," Shane muttered, glancing back out the front windshield at the sea of white.

"Not now," Tony tossed back, switching lanes. "Not ever if you're smart. And this time, Maxwell, I sure the hell hope you're smart. God knows I can't handle you any other way."

\* \* \*

Eleanor Schmidt Roarke knew she wasn't alone the second she stepped into the entryway of her Palm Beach mansion.

Only one person made that kind of noise in her house and got away with it.

Her daughter was back.

She followed the thump of Jay-Z pouring out of the back of the house and stopped in the doorway to the industrial kitchen. Across the center island was strewn lunch meat and breads, bags of potato chips and an open container of M&Ms Eleanor hadn't even known she'd had in the house. Standing near the sink with a horrified expression, Matilda, Eleanor's housekeeper, was staring at the mess and the size-two behind sticking out of the giant open refrigerator.

Nicole whipped around with half a cheesecake in her hands and stopped singing midsentence when she saw her mother. Her dark ponytail bobbed behind her.

Eyes locked on her daughter, Eleanor reached over to the Bose CD player Matilda kept in the kitchen so she could listen to her classical music, and switched it off. Silence fell over the room like a heavy dark cloud.

"You're back early," Eleanor said.

A smug smile spread across Nicole's face. "Miss me?"

Eleanor lifted one brow.

Matilda rushed over. "Miss Eleanor, I did not know—"

Eleanor held up a hand. "It's all right, Matilda. My daughter and I have things to discuss. There are packages in my car that need to come in."

"Yes, ma'am." Matilda scurried out of the room.

Nicole frowned when they were alone. "Don't punish her because you're pissed at me."

"That's not what I'm doing. And watch your tone, young lady." With a scowl, Eleanor flicked a scattering of crumbs across the granite counter to clear a place for her Valentino handbag. "We had an agreement, Nicole. You were to stay in Europe for a month."

Nicole, defiant as ever, rounded the other side of the counter and reached for a knife from the block. She hacked a quarter of the cheesecake and slid it onto a plate, then picked up a fork and took a huge—very unladylike—bite. "I got bored. So sue me."

Eleanor's blood pressure inched up, but she drew slow breaths to keep it in check. The fact her twenty-six-year-old daughter could shove whatever garbage she wanted into her mouth and still stay a svelte size two while Eleanor worked out daily and watched every morsel that went into her body so she could fit into her size-six slacks was just one of the many things she despised about motherhood. "Trust me when I say things will be better for you if you are not here."

"What does that mean?" Nicole asked around a second gigantic mouthful.

Had she actually raised this child? The girl had no social grace. Eleanor walked around the island, plucked the plate and fork from her daughter's hands and set them in the sink. "I understand your father's death has been very hard on you—"

"Oh, cut the crap, Mother." Nicole wiped her mouth with the back of her hand. "It's been as hard on me as it's been on you. There's only the two of us in this room. You don't need to play the grieving widow. I *know* who you were with the night Daddy died."

There went the blood pressure again. Eleanor calmly reached for a towel hanging on the rack and straightened it. "You're mistaken."

"No, actually, I don't think I am." Nicole snatched the bag of M&Ms and shoved a handful in her mouth. "In fact, that's part of the reason I came back," she said while chewing. "Does Hailey know? About your new man?"

Eleanor turned slowly to face her daughter. Defiance and attitude. She'd gotten it all from her father. Both her daughters had. "My decisions are not yours or Hailey's to approve. And furthermore, young lady, when I tell you to do something, I expect you to do it. You'll return to Paris immediately—"

"Like hell," Nicole flipped back, chewing.

"—and you will not utter one word to the press about your unplanned trip home."

"Oh, get a life, Mother. Do you think anyone cares I came back?"

"The entire world cares, Nicole. You've made sure of that fact." She grabbed the candy from Nicole's hands and tossed it in the garbage. "Gallivanting around at all hours of the night with those Hollywood deviants."

Nicole rolled her eyes. "They're my friends."

"No one named Star or Lakesha is a friend of the Roarkes."

"Well, maybe that's the problem. Maybe they should be."

"I will not let you speak to me that way—"

"Then how about this way." Nicole crossed the room and grabbed a bag from the floor that had been sitting next to the kitchen table. She pulled out the bronze and smacked it on the granite counter. The same bronze Eleanor had been looking for the past three days. The girl had had it with her the entire time. "Explain to me why Bryan called me yesterday in Paris and wanted to know where that silly statue was Daddy gave us all for Christmas? When he's never had any interest in it before. When, and I remember this clearly, he thought that gift was a piece of crap the night Daddy gave it to him."

Eleanor stared at the famous bronze image of seduction without blinking. God, how she hated that damn statue. And everything it represented.

"No answer?" Nicole asked. "Okay, then how about you explain to me why CNN reported this morning that Bryan had been found dead in his house in Chicago? And why it is, Mother, you don't seem a bit surprised by that fact."

Eleanor's eyes slowly lifted to her daughter. And in that instant, she realized she'd underestimated Nicole Roarke. They were very much alike, not only in appearance but in thought processes. Nicole wasn't the brainless bimbo the media made her out to be. She might not care who ran RR, but she did care where her money came from. And since she'd already whittled down a good chunk of her trust fund, it made sense she'd be paying closer attention to what went on at home than she ever had in the past.

Eleanor's eyes narrowed. "You're not upset Bryan's dead?"

"Are you?"

"What are you proposing?"

A slow smile spread across Nicole's model-perfect face. "That depends on just what it is you're willing to give me. For keeping my mouth shut, that is." She nodded at her bronze. "And for this."

Eleanor glanced back at the bronze. She itched to reach for it, but that would show her desperation, and if there was one thing she wasn't willing to do, it was be desperate. She'd vowed never to be that way again.

"Be warned, Mother. Daddy's lawyer called me, too. I know about this little game you're all playing. So you'd better make it worth my while." She leaned over the counter for emphasis. "Or I call the next person on my list."

Eleanor's gaze darted up. "You wouldn't dare."

"Watch me."

# CHAPTER SIX

A smart man would know to leave well enough alone. A smart man would know not to push his godforsaken luck. And a smart man would definitely realize when he was walking on quicksand.

But Shane Maxwell had never been particularly bright, at least not where women were concerned. He'd had his fair share of relationships—all had crashed and burned for various reasons—and when it came to commitment, he'd memorized one word in response: *run.* But there was something about *this* woman he just couldn't get out of his head. Or his chest. Whenever he thought about her, he got this stab of regret right beneath his breastbone and heard this really irritating voice in his head that screamed: *coward.*

It was that voice he hated most. The same one that had been dogging him for months. The one that had pushed its way into his head when he'd had Hailey in his apartment last night. The one that was telling him to flee now, that being here was a bad-ass idea. That only shitty things could come from getting involved again.

He stared at the darkened windows of the Roarke Lake Geneva resort and flipped the Tic Tac box open and closed in his pocket. The clock on the dash of his sedan read 11:42 P.M. She was probably asleep. Or tucked in bed, watching *The Tonight Show.* Or naked in that big, soft bed with Billy Sullivan.

That last thought propelled him out of the car and across the iced-over sidewalk toward the hotel's front doors before his better judgment kicked in. The doors were locked, just like he expected, but since he'd been sitting out in the cold for the last hour like a freakin' stalker, he knew a janitor was working the lobby. He stood there shivering in his Columbia jacket and last year's scuffed Nikes as he tapped on the glass and waited for the middle-aged man to turn off his vacuum and glance Shane's way.

When the guy finally did, Shane held up his badge and gestured toward the doors. The janitor ambled over and flicked the locks. "There a problem, Officer?"

Shane tucked his ID back in his jacket pocket and stepped into the lobby, blocking out the cold. "No. I just need a few minutes with Ms. Roarke. A couple follow-up questions from earlier today."

The man's bushy salt-and-pepper brows drew together. "Right now? Can't it wait 'til morning?"

It should. Damn if Shane didn't know why it couldn't. "No, I—"

"I heard her tell her secretary 'round five she didn't want to be bothered tonight. Had dinner delivered from some fancy restaurant earlier. Must be nice to have money like that."

Shane's muscles flexed as he thought of Billy again. And the fresh bruises on Hailey's face. Only this time he saw the two of them sitting down to a nice, romantic, secluded dinner in her room. He brushed past the janitor and headed toward the hall he'd been in this morning that led to the first-floor suites. "She can spare a few damn minutes for me."

"I can give her a call to let her know you're here," the janitor called after him.

"Don't bother," he tossed back. He wanted to surprise her. Hell, he wanted to surprise her good. Then slam his fist into Billy's face just for the fun of it.

He tamped down his temper as he reached the door to her suite. Then stood there just listening. No sound came from the other side. He knocked and waited, and still nothing.

He headed back to the lobby. The janitor was nowhere to be seen. Growing more frustrated by the minute, he reached into his pocket and pulled out his Tic Tacs. He popped a handful in his mouth, then shoved the plastic box back into his pocket. His finger flicked the lid open and closed as he thought about where she could be.

He really hoped she wasn't locked in that bedroom suite with Sullivan and hadn't heard him knocking. The fact she could be and had just ignored him sent that stabbing back to his chest. And that's when his ears registered the sound. A very faint bass pounding from somewhere in the building.

He strained to listen. It was coming from the other hallway off the main lobby.

He headed in that direction, listening as the bass grew louder, almost certain he recognized classic Bon Jovi.

He passed a series of conference rooms, an open lounging area with couches still covered in plastic wrap and glass walls that looked into what he suspected would soon be a spa. The music grew louder as he turned a long corner, then nearly tripped over his own feet at what he saw next.

Three oversize glass windows gave full view of the resort's fitness room. A series of exercise equipment that looked like they had never been used were lined up in front of the windows, facing the opposite wall and a row of flat-screen TVs. But behind all that, what was suddenly making his pulse pound was the woman dressed in nothing more than a pair of tight-fitting shorts and a black sports bra, hands taped up like a prizefighter and curly blonde ponytail flying at her back as she pounded the crap out of a punching bag hanging from the ceiling.

His throat grew thick as he watched. She didn't stop dancing, barefoot on the blue mats beneath her feet, or throwing punches in time to the heavy beat. And as the music pulsed and perspiration dripped down her temple, he had a heady vision of her naked and sweaty, pounding him all night long to the beat of that drum, not wasting her energy on that damn lucky punching bag.

The song came to an end, and she paused to catch her breath. Her creamy skin glistened under the gym's fluorescent lights. Her chest rose and fell, accentuating those perky breasts. And as his eyes drifted lower, he got a full-on visual of toned abs and a body she kept in tip-top shape.

He swallowed hard. Remembered what she'd looked like in shorts and a tank back in Florida. He'd thanked his lucky stars then he hadn't seen her in a bikini, but now couldn't stop visualizing that body in something with strings and side ties he could loosen with his teeth.

As the music shifted from nice days to life on the docks and Hailey lifted her fists again to jab at the bag, he pulled the gym's main door open and stepped inside. Sweet female sweat and just a hint of the lilac scent he always associated with her drifted toward his nose.

She didn't stop punching. Left hook, left, right again. And his blood warmed the closer he got. It wasn't until he reached the stereo and hit the power button that she stopped abruptly and whipped his way.

Surprise registered in her sapphire eyes first. Then distrust. And finally, disgust.

Okay, after their run-in earlier, he had that coming. But she'd purposely left him hanging, and he wanted answers.

She didn't say anything, but her chest rose and fell as she drew deep breaths. A bead of sweat rolled down her bruised temple, over her jaw, down the long, slender column of neck, heading straight for her breasts. Like an idiot, he watched the droplet, his body temperature growing hotter by the minute as it slid downward.

And that's when he saw the yellowing bruises. Faint traces of what she'd been through before. On her ribs, on her thighs, on the soft skin of her arms. Near a bandage by her shoulder.

"How'd you get in here?" she asked, breathless.

He forced his gaze away from her fading injuries, told himself she was fine, healthy, that whatever she'd endured, she'd survived. But the urge to coldcock whoever had done this to her was hard to overcome. And Kauffman was seriously dead meat.

"Janitor."

"Did you come to arrest me or are you just having trouble sleeping, Maxwell?"

Her voice pulled his brain away from exacting revenge, and he focused on her face. He wasn't about to tell her he didn't sleep, not much anyway. And the look in her eyes warned him her workout session hadn't done much to cool her temper. "Should I arrest you?" he asked.

She glanced past him to the windows, then looked at his face again. "Who's playing good cop tonight?"

"No one. I'm here alone."

One elegant brow lifted. "Inspector Clouseau know you're going renegade?"

The muscles around his eyes tightened with humor. "No, he doesn't. He'd tear into me if he did."

"Then why are you here?"

"'Cause I'm not done with you yet."

Her eyes never left his as she lifted her hand to mop up the sweat on her forehead. "I already told you I'm not answering any more questions without my lawyer."

"I'm not here officially, Hailey." When she opened her mouth to protest, he added, "I saw the surveillance tapes. Trust me when I say, you need a friend right now. And I may be all you've got."

Her eyes narrowed. "What do you want?"

"Answers. Unofficially," he added before she could spout off anything else about her lawyer. "But mostly to help you."

Those blue eyes of hers searched his face, and he could practically see the wheels turning in her mind. Along with a great big dose of *I-don't-think-so*.

"You want answers?" she said. "Unofficial?"

He nodded slowly, thinking she was capitulating way too quickly, but thankful he wasn't going to have to pry it out of her.

"Fine. I'll answer whatever question you've got. But you've got to take me down first. I take you down, I get to ask the questions."

She wanted to spar? With him? Here? Now? He glanced

around the mats, back at her, slicked with sweat, bruises not yet healed from her last run-in and juiced up on endorphins. Yeah, he wanted answers, but he wouldn't hurt her to get them. "I don't think that's such a good—"

"Scared?"

The look of utter confidence across her face stopped him. "No, I just—"

She took a step back and held out her hands. "How bad do you want your answers, Maxwell? Gimme your best shot."

He wasn't going to actually do this, was he?

The smug spark in her eye answered his question. Before he thought better of it, he was toeing off his shoes and sliding out of his jacket.

"The gun, too," she said as he tossed his coat on the counter along the far wall. "I don't want you to get shot again."

He glanced back at her as he removed his shoulder harness and set his firearm on the counter as well, refusing to rub the scar on his shoulder where he'd been shot three months before when he'd gone looking for his sister in Florida. Hailey had been there then as well. In fact, if it weren't for Hailey, he might not have survived.

He remembered the panic in her voice when she'd found him left for dead, and the way she'd said his name—the only time he ever remembered hearing her say his first name—how sweet and sexy it had sounded on her lips. How he'd wanted to hear her say it again. But she hadn't. Not when she'd sat with him at the hospital telling him stupid jokes when he'd been getting stitched up or when she'd kept him company on the way back to Florida. Even after they'd hung out and danced most of the night at Lisa and Rafe's wedding, weeks later, she hadn't once called him by his first name again.

Which, in retrospect, was probably a good thing. What would he have done if she had? Just because she was the first person who'd made him feel something in almost a year, didn't mean shit.

Except . . . he suddenly wanted to hear her say it. Needed to for reasons he couldn't understand.

He walked back out on the mat, dressed in his jeans and T-shirt, watching as her eyes ran over him from head to toe. His blood warmed under that heated look, and he told himself if she wanted to play this game, he'd go along, but he wouldn't hurt her. No answers were worth adding to her bruises.

"You're looking a little overconfident there, Maxwell."

"Only because I know you've got to be tired after your workout."

Her eyes sparked. "I was only warming up. Show me what you've got."

Neither of them moved. Just stared at each other. He felt like an idiot because he wasn't about to flip her to her back and pin her to the mat. When it was clear they were at a standoff, he stepped toward her. "Look, Hailey—"

She had her hand around his wrist before he even saw her move. She was quick, and her pressure-point technique worked like a charm. As his wrist numbed and pain shot up his arm, she hooked her arm under his elbow, twisted his wrist around his back and slammed him into the mat, face-first.

"That's one for me," she said, pressing his wrist into his back until his teeth knocked together from the pain. "Why did you walk away from me in Puerto Rico?"

"I didn't—"

"Nice try." She twisted his wrist up until he slapped his free hand against the mat to keep from screaming like a little girl.

"Alright! Goddammit. It was a crappy thing to do, okay?"

She let go of his wrist and stood quickly. "I know it was."

He rolled to his back, wiggled his wrist to get the blood flowing again. Then sat up slowly and studied her across the mat.

Okay, this was a surprise. He'd known she was attracted to him, but he'd figured walking away from her after the wedding instead of after he slept with her would spare her some angst. Obviously he'd thought wrong. "I saved you from getting involved with me then. You should be thanking me instead of being pissed about it."

"I am. Get up and let's go again."

That good ol' instinct of his said he should do what he'd done back then and walk away from her *now*. But that irritating voice screaming, *coward*, forced him to his feet. And as he studied her carefully, he realized she'd led with her left. Come to think of it, when she'd been pounding the crap out of that bag, she'd been using her left hand as well. "Hailey, I really just want to talk to you about what happened at your cousin's—"

"No talking. Give me your best move."

He still wasn't willing to fight her over this. He took a step forward to try to get her attention, and again she moved so fast he barely tracked it. One minute she was facing him, the next she was up close, her left arm sliding around his back, her torso twisting around and lowering so her hip hit him just beneath his center of gravity. Then all he felt was air as she threw him over her hip and he hit the mat with a resounding thud.

He groaned and rolled to his back. Okay, that one she hadn't learned at the academy. And damn, she was stronger than she looked.

"That's two for me, Maxwell." She braced her hands on her knees and leaned down toward him with a self-satisfied expression. "Is that a habit of yours, going around leading women on, or are you just a prick?"

"Leading women on? Is that what you think I did?"

"Two for two. I'd say that's *exactly* what you do. I think you like the power of it. I think you like seeing a woman get all worked up so you can drop her on her ass. Good fun, huh?"

*Shit.* "Hailey, I—"

"In case you forgot, I'm the one asking the questions. You're the one getting your butt kicked." She stepped back. "Go again."

His blood pulsed as he pushed to his feet. Okay, he'd been wrong. She was ticked about what had happened in Puerto

Rico and even more pissed about last night than he'd thought. Which meant only one thing—he'd gotten under her skin. Maybe as much as she'd gotten under his. That thought cooled him out a little. But his adrenaline surged when she charged out of nowhere, grabbed him by the shoulders, slid to the ground and kicked both legs out from under him.

He landed hard on his back, and this time saw stars. And oh, shit, there was something seriously wrong with him because he liked this. Liked having her hands on his body and loved being hurt by her.

She was on her feet before he could even catch his breath. But she was breathing hard. And she wasn't quite as solid as she tried to appear. "Go home, Maxwell. I've got better things to do than toss you to the ground all night long. And as fun as this has been, I'm not interested anymore."

She turned and got one step away before he kicked out, knocking her off balance. Her hands flew out in surprise, but before she hit the mat he was up, twisting around so he was at her front, going down with her so he took the brunt of the fall and she landed hard against his chest.

She immediately pushed off, but he rolled, pinning her beneath him. Her hands darted out, but he easily grabbed them and shackled them over her head. Then he hooked his feet around her legs so she couldn't break free and kick him in the nuts as he stared down at her enraged face.

"Let me go," she growled.

Each time she wiggled, it brought their hips into closer contact and sent more blood rushing to his groin. "Not a chance. I think a pin counts for three."

"Go to hell."

"I will. But not today. Question one. Are you sleeping with Billy Sullivan?"

"*What?*"

"I'm the one asking right now. You're answering. Yes or no."

She glared up at him. Struggled. Realized she was stuck. "No."

"You sure?"

"Is that your second question?"

*No way.* "Did Sullivan hit you?"

"No."

"Who did?"

Her jaw clenched. "Some prick in the elevator at my father's building in Miami. Wanted to send me a message to back off."

"Back off what?"

"Running the company. Everyone wants me to sign over my interest so they can get rid of me."

"Including your cousin?"

She stared at him long and hard, and he saw then why she hadn't wanted to answer his questions. No matter how she did, it was only going to make her look more guilty. "Yes."

"One more question—"

She struggled against his hold again. 'I've answered way more than three already—"

"—if you aren't sleeping with Sullivan, who are you sleeping with?"

Her eyes flared. "That's none of CPD's goddamn business!"

He tightened his grip on her hands. "You're right. It's mine. Who?"

"No one!"

"Good."

He lowered and took her mouth before she could close her lips. He wasn't tender or sweet or gentle like he'd been in his apartment. Instead he took exactly what he wanted, demanding and bruising in his kiss as his tongue dipped into her mouth and tangled with hers. She grunted and wriggled again beneath him, but all the friction did was juice him up and send his last remaining brain cells due south. His groin swelled, and he pressed into her, giving her a warning hint at what she was doing to him.

She went still. Relaxed beneath him as he changed the angle of the kiss and stroked deeper with his tongue, more insistent, more frantic, more wild as her taste filled his mouth and head and soul. And though he knew he should stop, that he was doing exactly what he said he would never do to her or any woman, he couldn't.

*You think this makes you less of a coward? Less of a failure?*

That little voice somehow cut through the sexual haze surrounding him, and when it did, he realized what the hell he was doing. He let go of her hands, braced his on the mat near her shoulders and started to push off. But as soon as his mouth and body lifted from hers, she let out a moan of frustration, flipped him to his back quickly and climbed on top of him.

Reality came crashing in. And with it, a whole helluva lot of guilt. "Hailey. Shit, I didn't mean to—"

But he didn't get to finish his apology because her mouth was suddenly on his again, only this time *she* was kissing *him* with a frantic need that was 10,000 times hotter than he'd ever imagined.

He groaned into her mouth as her tongue licked over his, knew he had minutes—maybe seconds—until one or both of them realized what a stupid move this was. His hands rushed to her hair, and he pulled the band free, letting all those gorgeous blonde waves cascade around him. He brushed her hair back, ran his fingers over her shoulder, down her sweat-slicked back, to her hips, where he grasped and pulled until she was rubbing right where he wanted her most.

*Are you trying to save her now, too?*

His brain came back online like a power grid suddenly amping up. And though he wanted nothing more than to flip Hailey to her back once more, strip her of those hot little shorts and prove to himself he could shove that goddamn voice out of his head for good by driving deep inside her, he couldn't.

He'd learned his lesson before. He couldn't help her if he got wrapped up with her any more than he already was. Which meant he needed to kill this right now and never let it happen again.

He rolled her to her back and broke the kiss. She was breathing hard and staring up at him with rank sexual hunger in her eyes. And he knew right then it was too late. He was already way more wrapped up with her than he ever had been with Julie.

He pushed off her quickly and stood, running a hand down his face as he reached into his pocket for his Tic Tacs. Not the Jameson he desperately needed. But they worked. Most of the time. He palmed five and popped them in his mouth.

She eased up slowly to her elbows and stared at him. And she knew. He didn't even have to hear the voice to know what she was thinking.

*Coward.*

Yeah, he was. But she was too important to play loose and easy with. And he still hadn't told her the real reason he was here.

He held a hand out to help her up. She stared at it a beat, then slowly slid her fingers in his and let him pull her up.

When she was on her feet in front of him, his eyes ran over her bruises again, and that guilt swept through him like a tsunami. "Did I hurt you?"

"No." The venom was gone from her voice, but she was cautious. "I'm tougher than I look."

Yeah, she was. And dammit, he didn't want her to be. He wanted her locked up safe and sound where nothing could harm her. "They have you on the house's surveillance video."

Her gaze, which had dropped to his mouth, suddenly shot back up to his eyes.

"You and someone else," he said quickly. "They found DNA in the house they think they can link back to the killer. Shit, they've got a Roarke employee saying you threatened Bryan in Miami. Hailey, what the hell's going on?"

She reached across her body and grabbed her upper arm. But didn't answer. Only stared at him until he wanted to scream.

"You were at the house the night Bryan Roarke died."

Nothing. Her eyes didn't even flicker.

"Dammit, I can't help you if you don't tell me what's happening."

"Why do you want to help me?" she whispered.

"I don't know," he snapped, his frustration over everything—her secrets, her cousin's murder, and his pent-up sexual frustration—all compounding at once. "Maybe because I haven't been able to get you out of my freakin' head for the past three months."

"That's a lie."

"Is it? Then you tell me why I can't decide if I should arrest you right now, just to keep you out of trouble, or tackle you to the mat and kiss you crazy all over again."

He saw it then. A flash of something he couldn't quite read in her eyes. Arousal? No, that wasn't it. Disbelief? Or was that fear?

What did she have to be afraid of? Unless . . .

She took two quick steps back, until her spine hit the punching bag she'd been taking her frustrations out on earlier, stopping her. "You need to go."

"Hailey—"

"No, Maxwell, you really need to go. Now. I've already said and done way more than I should have. I'm not answering any more of your questions. Go before I call security and have you thrown out."

"Just talk to me."

She shook her head slowly. "You can't help me. Don't even try."

The finality of her voice stiffened his spine. Something in her tone set his instincts on alert.

Before he could ask what she meant, she was gathering her sweatshirt and heading for the door. "Don't come back. Not unless you really do plan to arrest me."

Then she was gone.

# CHAPTER SEVEN

Somehow Hailey made it back to her room, closed and locked the door, then sank right to the floor. In the words of her ex . . . *holy hell.*

She pulled her knees up to her chest, dropped her head. Then just breathed. In and out. Until her heart rate slid back in the human range and her brain slowly came back online.

Okay, the whole sparring thing? Not her brightest idea. But when he'd walked into that gym, she'd been so frustrated with him and everything else, it'd seemed like the easiest way to get him gone. At the time, knocking him on his ass had felt like heaven. Until the tables had turned and he'd kissed her. Then she'd been reminded what true heaven was really like.

Her hand trembled as she brought it to her mouth and ran her fingers over her lips. Like she didn't have enough stupid fantasies swirling in her head where he was concerned? Thanks to the last two nights, she now knew what Shane tasted like, what he felt like pressed up against her, all hard and aroused, what it would be like to give in and take exactly what she wanted.

Dammit. *Dammit, Maxwell.*

She pushed up from the floor and started pacing. Around the couch, over to the cherry dining room table, across the room to the fireplace and back to the door. She wasn't going to think about Shane and that stupid—second—kiss. How either one had made her feel or the fact all she wanted was more. *Or* his admission he hadn't been able to stop thinking about her for the past three months. Nope. Nada. Not doing it. Going there would only get her in more trouble. And right now she had enough trouble to fill an entire freakin' Egyptian pyramid.

*So think, moron.*

Okay. He'd come for answers. But also, for some strange reason, to warn her. And for that she was thankful. If they could really ID her on that security camera, he'd have been here to arrest her. Not kiss her silly until she turned to gelatin.

*Don't go there.*

Right. She wasn't.

So that meant the video wasn't conclusive and they didn't have enough to take before a judge—at least not yet—which also meant they were probably going nuts searching for a murder weapon. And she knew they weren't going to find one. Not with her prints on it anyway. Not unless . . .

Her stomach rolled. And she thought of her missing Italian dagger. The one her father had left her in his will.

What if that warning in the elevator hadn't been a warning after all? What if it was simply a distraction? Everyone at RR knew the dagger was hers. If someone wanted to frame her for Bryan's murder, they couldn't have picked a better way to do it.

*Holy . . . hell.*

She was going to get charged for this. She could feel it coming, rolling in her blood like a wave on the Atlantic. There was a whole host of Roarkes who hated her and wanted a piece of the business. Though, yeah, just the thought a blood relative of hers could do something so horrible . . . her family was sick.

She needed to get the hell out of Lake Geneva. Before the cops found something else on her.

She reached for the phone. Though it was after midnight, she didn't care about the hour. Steve Gleason, her pilot, was staying just down the hall, in one of the only other habitable rooms in the resort's hotel. He answered on the second ring, sounding groggy as hell.

"Steve, it's Hailey. Change of plans. I need the jet fired up and ready to go tomorrow morning."

"Sure thing, Ms. Roarke." He yawned. "You tell me what time and we can be out of here in minutes."

Hailey thought through her schedule. She couldn't get out of the meeting in the morning, and if she disappeared before then, it'd be like slapping an I'M GUILTY sign right to her forehead. She could slink out afterward and no one would be the wiser for . . . at least a day. "The meeting with the city planning commission is at nine. Shouldn't take more than an hour or so. Have the plane ready and on standby at ten."

"No problem. I have to file a flight plan. We heading back to Miami?"

She wasn't sure. A lot depended on what happened in the next few hours. "Yes."

She hung up and immediately went into the bedroom to pack. Though she was sweaty and needed a shower, it could wait. She wasn't leaving a damn thing here because she wasn't sure when she'd be back.

If things escalated like she expected they would, the cops would come looking for her. Her timeline had just taken a drastic nosedive. No more playing CEO and taking her time while she looked for those damn statues in her father's ludicrous treasure hunt. The only way to clear her name now and find out who'd really killed Bryan was to get to the end first. She had no doubt when she had all six statues and figured out whatever this big secret was, the real killer would come after her.

He couldn't sleep for shit. Tylenol PM hadn't helped. Counting sheep in his head didn't do a damn bit of good. And there was no way he was touching the hooch in his kitchen cupboard. It hadn't worked in quite a while anyway.

Instead of staring at the ceiling until he felt like putting his fist through a wall, Shane dressed and headed for the office. As he parked it behind his desk, he figured if he couldn't sleep, he'd get caught up on some of that damn paperwork piling up. Maybe writing reports would take his mind off things he couldn't control.

Or didn't know what the hell to do about in the first place.

That's how Tony found him just after eight A.M. As office staff filtered into the Detective Division, the room went from the quiet din of the last few hours to the normal chaos Shane was used to hearing. He stopped typing as Tony eased a hip onto his desk. Tiny swirls of steam filtered up from the Starbucks cup in Tony's hand. "When was the last time you were here before me?"

Shane frowned, went back to typing. "I don't know. Never?"

"Yeah, that's what I was thinking." Tony took a sip, eyeing Shane over the lid. "You don't look so hot, my man."

He didn't feel so hot, either. But that little fact had nothing to do with his health.

"Tried to call you last night," Tony said.

"I was out."

"Yeah, I got that."

Tony's scrutinizing gaze told Shane he wasn't getting any more crap done until they had it out. He dropped his hands from the keyboard, swiveled and stared at his partner. "Spill it, goldilocks."

"I'm worried about you, wife."

"Don't be."

"You've got that look in your eye again," Tony said flatly.

"What look?"

"The one that says, fuck with me and you're gonna get it."

Shane rolled his eyes. "I always have that look."

"No." Tony shook his head. "Not like this. This one's been building for the last six months."

The reference to what had happened with Julie brought Shane's blood pressure up, but he clenched his jaw tight and didn't respond.

"The IA stuff didn't help," Tony added, not taking the hint. "But all this shit with the Roarke girl's making it worse."

Shane scoffed and went back to his computer.

"I'm not kidding," Tony said. His voice dropped so no one else could hear him. "If I get a call in the middle of the night that you ate your fucking gun—"

Shane inclined his head Tony's way. "That's not gonna happen."

"Is that a guarantee?"

Was it? Yeah, he realized, it was. Because he'd already discovered he didn't have a stomach for what that would take. While he didn't have a whole helluva lot of self-respect left, he wasn't about to hurt the ones he loved just because he was struggling with what he'd done.

Plus after running into Hailey Roarke again and finally getting a taste of those sweet and tempting lips, the only thing he could think about putting his mouth to right now was wet and warm and tasted a million times better than cold metal.

"Stop being such a nancy and quit worrying about me, would ya? If you want to stress about something, start with how the hell you're gonna afford three kids on your crappy salary."

At the reminder of his wife Robin's newest pregnancy, Tony sat back and grinned. "You should be so lucky to have my problem."

Shane snorted and started typing again. "Kids and I don't mix."

"Never know. Might cure that surly attitude of yours."

Shane flipped Tony the bird, then went back to typing.

Tony chuckled and took a sip from his Starbucks again. "Now that's the wife I know and love."

"Maxwell, Chen, quit your gossiping. My office. Now."

Shane looked over his shoulder toward Commander O'Conner's door and frowned. Tony slid off the desk and downed the rest of his coffee, then tossed the paper cup in the wastebasket in his crappy Jordan impersonation. "Five says the temple starts to throb before we even sit down."

Shane rose from his desk, feeling like a lamb being led to

slaughter as they both headed toward the commander's office. He felt like that a lot lately. "You're on. I need to win back the money you took from me yesterday."

"Hey, that train could've had three engines. It wasn't a lousy bet."

Shane snorted as they crossed the floor. The things they bet on to beat back the doldrums.

"Close the door behind you," O'Conner barked as the two stepped in the room.

No *Good morning. Hey, how ya doin'?* This couldn't be good.

Tony did the honors while Shane shoved his hands in his pockets and snapped open the lid of his Tic Tac box. O'Conner didn't gesture for them to sit, simply lifted a remote from his desk and pointed it at the TV on a shelf across the room. The vein on the left side of his temple pulsed visibly in time with the older man's heartbeat.

Tony jabbed Shane in the ribs and pointed. Frowning, Shane whipped a five-dollar bill from his wallet and handed it to his partner before the commander could turn around.

"Take a look, boys." On the TV screen, a local news reporter was standing with a crew in front of the Roarke murder scene.

"Shit," Tony muttered.

". . . *local police are still searching for clues to this gruesome murder in one of Chicago's premier neighborhoods. But those close to the Chicago Police Department confirm heiress Hailey Roarke, daughter of late hotelier Garrett Roarke and interim CEO of the elite Roarke Resorts, is being questioned by authorities in conjunction with her estranged cousin's death . . .*"

"Fuck," Shane mumbled.

". . . *All of this comes on the heels of Garrett Roarke's recent death. And sources within Roarke Resorts tell us the company is in an uproar as family members wrestle for control. What started out as a Chicago homicide looks to be quickly turning into murder, rich-and-famous style. This is Shelley Hanson reporting on-scene for channel . . .*"

O'Conner stopped the tape and turned toward his two detectives. That little vein at his temple vibrated against his pasty Irish white skin. "How the hell does Shelley Hanson know what the fuck's going on?"

When neither man answered, O'Conner's fiery eyes swung to Shane.

Shane lifted his hands, palms out. "Don't look at me. I dated her like twice. A year ago. She's not getting her shit from me."

"Well someone's leaking info to the press and I want it stopped. Crap like this makes us look like incompetent fools." His eyes shot to Chen. "You got enough to go before the judge?"

Tony shrugged. "Not yet. Nothing conclusive on that dagger."

"Dagger?" Shane asked, looking sharply at his partner.

Tony glanced at him. "Yeah. I was about to tell you before we came in here. Ruiz and Ogada found a dagger hidden in the basement. Had the initials LdM on one side of the handle, GR on the other. Forensics ran it but didn't come up with anything." He looked back at O'Conner. "Also got a call in to Garrett Roarke's lawyer in Florida. Thing looks like a collector's item. Piece like that had to be in a guy's will, don't you think? Looked ancient."

Shane's blood ran cold.

"Only if we're lucky." O'Conner dropped into the chair behind his desk and rubbed a hand down his face. "Okay, here's the deal. I've got press calling from all over the country on this one. *Enter*-fucking-*tainment Tonight* wants an exclusive, like they have a snowball's chance in hell at getting it. The Roarke sister, the one like Paris Hilton. What's her name? Nipples?"

Tony chortled. "Nicole."

"Yeah. Nicole. Media freakin' loves her. Speculation her sister might be up for murder's boosted all their ratings, which means my life's hell." He pinned Shane and Tony with a look. "I want that crime scene swept again. If that's the murder weapon, we have to make fucking sure before we go public. Chen, you get that link between the dagger and the Roarke woman confirmed, then you get in font of Judge Hamilton and get that warrant. I want this case wrapped up. Unsolved homicides where millionaires get hacked like sushi are not my idea of fun. Now get gone. Both of you."

The door snapped shut behind Shane, but he hardly heard it. He was in a daze as he walked toward his desk. LdM meant nothing to him. But GR was just too coincidental to be real. What were the chances Hailey's father had given her that dagger? Or left it to her in his will?

Considering everything else, pretty fucking good.

"Hey, Maxwell," Tony said, grabbing his coat from the back of his chair. "Got an art history prof over at Northwestern who said he could give us some background on that dagger." He lifted a print photo of the weapon. "Let's run down and check it out."

Motive, means and a murder weapon. All at the same time. It was too neat. Too convenient. The whole damn thing screamed stupid criminal.

If there was one thing Shane knew absolutely above all else, it was that Hailey Roarke was not stupid. She'd been a cop, after all. She knew how the system worked. And he couldn't get the fact he'd seen her leading with her left hand last night out of his head. Which meant only one thing. None of this was as it appeared to be.

"Yoo-hoo," Tony said, waving his hand in front of Shane's face. "Over here."

Shane glanced up sharply. "What?"

"Murder weapon. Research. You and me. Let's go, wife."

Sweat broke out on the back of Shane's neck. "Yeah. You go ahead without me. I gotta finish these reports."

Tony's brow dropped as Shane sat and reached for his keyboard. "Since when do you pass up being in the field for sitting behind a desk?"

Irritation edged Shane's voice. "Since I came in early to get this shit done. Now leave me alone so I can do it. They don't need two of us prowling around at the university. You can call me when you've got something."

Tony eyed him a long beat. Slid his coat on slowly. And though Shane didn't glance up, he knew his partner was looking at him like he'd sprouted horns and maybe wings to go with them. A meteor hitting the building right now would be less of a surprise than the fact Shane wasn't tagging along on this one.

Tension rippled between them as Shane's fingers raced over the keyboard and he typed words he didn't see. Screw it. He didn't care what Tony thought.

"Okay," Tony finally said in a wary voice. "Keep your phone on."

"I will."

Tony eyed him one more time like he knew Shane was lying through his pearly whites, but headed for the elevator anyway.

As soon as the double doors closed, Shane's pulse jumped. He killed the computer, grabbed his coat and hit the back stairwell.

Screw the no-more-questions. She was gonna tell him what the hell was going on even if it meant he had to string her up by her toes to get her to talk.

And dammit. That thought wasn't a turn-on. Not in the least.

# CHAPTER EIGHT

Billy Sullivan lifted his Rēvos to his forehead to get a clear view of the brunette in the slinky white string bikini across the pool at the South Beach Ritz. She was just coming up the steps, water running from her long dark hair, sluicing over her deeply tanned skin, sliding over her perfect little ass.

Now that girl was hot. Tiny little waist, nice rack, perfectly proportioned hips. And a mouth, ah hell, a mouth a guy would die to have wrapped around his—

"Something from the bar?"

Billy dropped his sunglasses back onto his nose and looked up at the redheaded waitress standing next to his poolside table, waiting to take his drink order. "Jack and Coke." He gestured with his shoulder across the pool where bikini-girl was stopped near a chaise, shaking her head to the side and blotting her face with a hot pink towel. "See the girl over there in the white suit?"

The waitress glanced up. The look on her face said, *I see her and know who she is, and you don't stand a chance in hell.* "Yes."

"Her next drink's on me."

The waitress glanced back at him, frowned, then headed for the bar with a shake of her head.

Billy leaned back in his chair, crossed his bare feet at the ankles and folded his hands over his waist as he sat in the shade of a big umbrella. The art-deco metal chair put a crink in his back, but he didn't plan on sitting here much longer anyway.

He watched as the waitress set his drink in front of him, then headed off around the pool with the froufrou pink concoction bikini-girl had been sucking back all morning. As the waitress delivered the drink, bikini-girl looked up with a startled expression, and when the waitress gestured across the pool, she shifted her sunglasses up to her hair and finally glanced his way.

He smiled, lifted his hand and waved, but didn't make any effort to sit up or join her across the pool.

Bikini-girl and the waitress shared a few words before the waitress headed back for the bar. Bikini-girl took a long swallow of her drink, eyes still locked on Billy.

If there was one thing he was sure of, it was that curiosity would finally get the better of her. After that it was all up to him.

Sure enough, ten minutes of watching him was all she could take. Martini glass in hand, she grabbed her white wrap, slid her perfectly manicured toes into her spendy, jewel-encrusted sandals and marched across the pool deck toward him.

Billy smiled as she drew close but still didn't bother to sit up.

"I haven't seen you around here," she said, stopping in front of him. She didn't put the wrap on to cover up her barely there bikini, not that he minded. She simply draped the sheer white fabric over her shoulder in a move he was sure she'd practiced a thousand times.

"I'm just visiting."

She took another sip of her drink, eyeing him over the rim. "Hmm. We haven't met. I'm—"

"We haven't officially met, but we're family. Or were."

Her dark eyes narrowed in obvious confusion. "I don't—"

"Name's Billy Sullivan."

He could practically see the wheels turning in that gorgeous but empty head of hers and fought from getting up and searching for a set of jumper cables to get the spark going and speed things along. "Why is that name so familiar?"

Okay, hot bod, but definitely not a Rhodes scholar.

"My brother's Rafe Sullivan. As in, the guy who married your sister."

Nicole Roarke's eyes narrowed. "Oh."

Bingo. Lightbulb just went on.

"And that makes you his . . ."

"Brother," he finished for her when she seemed at a loss for a connection. His impression of the Paris Hilton wannabe was seriously taking a hit.

Disgust brewed in her dark eyes. Obviously, she'd heard all about Hailey's thief of an ex-husband. That or just the mere mention of her older sister sent her mood spiraling. Interesting.

"What are you doing here?"

He shrugged. "Just hanging out. Taking a mini vaca. Saw you over there and thought I'd do the family thing and buy you a drink. Hailey's supposed to meet me here in an hour. Hey, you don't want to join us for lunch, do you?"

Her eyes widened slightly. "Hailey's coming here?"

"Shh." He sat up and grabbed her arm, forcing her into the chair next to him. For emphasis, he glanced around the poolside tables as if making sure no one had overheard their conversation. "Keep it on the down-low, would ya? She's been in some hot water lately. Our weekly meetings are private, and we want to keep them that way."

Interest flared in Nicole's eyes. She leaned forward on the table. "You meet her every week? Why?"

Billy sat back and grinned. "Why wouldn't I? Your sister's hot."

Nicole nearly choked on her drink. And he kept on grinning as he watched the green-eyed monster rear its ugly head. "Oh, my God. She's married to your brother."

"Was," he corrected. "They're not married anymore. And I think you have the wrong idea. It's not serious. Just . . . fun. Don't you do fun, Niki?"

"Of course I do," she said, looking disgusted by the question. "I'm twenty-one. Fun is my life."

She was actually closer to twenty-seven—little liar—but if she wanted to snow him, two could play at that game.

His grin widened. "I betcha we could have some real fun. The three of us. Wanna come up to our room?"

She pinned him with a look. "I'm not interested in a three-way with my sister."

"What are you interested in?"

Her eyes ran over him from the tips of his toes, up his swim trunks, across his bare chest and finally to his face. What she hadn't been interested in five minutes ago suddenly looked like prime grade-A beef in her eyes. God, he loved competitive sisters. "I don't know. What time did you say she's supposed to meet you?"

"Hold on." The cell in his pocket vibrated, and he pulled it out, reading the text message he'd sent to himself from another phone. "Speak of the devil." He held it out to her so she could read it.

*Srry, will b l8. drinks on me. call u l8er.*

Nicole handed him the phone. "That's too bad."

"Yeah," he said, faking disappointment. "Guess I have a little free time after all."

She bit the inside of her lip. And took all of two seconds to make up her mind. "You could come hang in my room for a while if you want. I need to get out of the sun anyway. And I'm sure I booked a much better view than she did."

His smile was slow and sure. Goddamn, but he loved sisters.

"I think that sounds like a fun idea, Niki."

"Not yet," she said, gaze sliding down his chest once more. "But it might be."

"Tell me something I want to hear." Hailey shifted the bag to her other shoulder as she walked briskly through the Lake Geneva municipal airport. A smattering of blue plastic chairs filled the only terminal in the building. A lunch counter and a couple small airline check-in stations occupied the open walls. She felt like she'd stepped into an old version of *Wings* without a young Tim Daly anywhere in sight.

"I have good news and bad news," Allie said through the phone at her ear. "Which do you want?"

"I could use some good news," Hailey said on a sigh. "Gimme whatever you've got." She pushed the glass door open and headed across the tarmac toward Roarke Resorts' Bombardier already waiting to taxi. The roar of the engines made it hard to hear, so she stuffed one finger in her free ear to block out the sound.

"Unfortunately you get both at the same time. Dad wrangled a copy of your father's autopsy report. He's looking through it now, and a few things stand out, but he doesn't have anything concrete yet. He's trying to get a copy of your father's medical records."

"Can he do that?"

"Unofficially, he can do anything he wants. Just depends if someone will give it to him. Where the hell are you, anyway? There's a ton of background noise."

"About to get on a plane. Tell me how this is good news."

"It's good if you're trying to find answers to unasked questions, H. You think his death wasn't from natural causes after all, don't you?"

Hailey didn't want Allie involved, but she'd never been able to keep a secret from her friend. "I'm not sure. It's a theory."

"Not a bad one in my opinion. It's a little coincidental that your father died only a month or so after stepping back because of stress. The question you should be asking yourself isn't really how he died but who wanted him dead and why?"

"That's a little obvious, isn't it?"

"Okay, maybe not the who so much as the why. Why now, H? If your father really was murdered, what triggered all this?"

"The fact he changed his will just over six weeks ago triggered it."

"And why did he do that?"

Frustrated, Hailey stopped in the middle of the tarmac. "I don't know. I don't know why he did any of the things he did. It's no secret we didn't have a good relationship. Hell, the last few years we haven't had *any* relationship at all. So I think it's safe to say he didn't confide in me about whatever started this whole nightmare in the first place."

"He did, though." At Hailey's exasperated huff, Allie added, "Look, don't get all worked up about this. Think of it like a case. One step at a time. One clue that leads to the next. It started with you, H. He called and asked you to step in for him at the resort. Why you?"

Why her indeed? She'd been asking herself that question for weeks and still didn't have an answer that made sense. At least not one that went with the whole died-of-natural-causes and I've-decided-to-send-my-loony-relatives-on-a-random-treasure-hunt scenario.

"I don't know, Allie. If I did I wouldn't be in this mess. Is that it?"

"No." It was Allie's turn to sigh. "I thought you might like to know. The prodigal daughter has returned. Flipped on the TV this morning and one of those rag shows had footage of her at the Ritz in Miami Beach yesterday."

"Lovely."

"Your face was also up there. Which is why she was on, answering questions about her reaction to Bryan's death and your possible involvement."

Well, Hailey had expected that, hadn't she? She just hoped Billy'd had enough time to get what she needed. "I can only imagine what she said."

"Trust me when I say, you don't want to know."

"Roarke!"

Phone in hand, Hailey turned at the loud voice and glanced over her shoulder toward the terminal's glass doors. Then cursed under her breath when she saw Shane striding toward her across the pavement, looking righteously ticked and seriously pissed off.

"Double shit," she muttered. "This just keeps getting better, doesn't it?"

"You can say that again," Allie said in her ear. "So now that your meeting's over, are you coming home?"

Shane pointed at her as he drew close, dark eyes blazing, hair ruffling in the wind created by her jet's engines. "I want a word with you."

"Allie, I gotta go. Talk to you later."

"Wait. H—"

Hailey flipped the phone closed quickly and stuffed it in the pocket of her slacks. "What are you doing here?" she yelled. The wind whipped her hair in her face, and she pushed it back with irritated hands.

He glanced at the plane, down to the bag that had slipped to her hand, then up to her eyes. "Don't tell me you're running."

Her frustration with everything was nearly at a breaking point. "Did you come here to arrest me or just push me over the edge?"

"Hailey—"

That answer was good enough for her. "Then I'm not running. See ya around, Maxwell."

His large hand wrapped around her upper arm and pulled her to a stop at the base of the plane's steps. "What did your father leave you in his will?"

"What?"

"Tick 'em off for me. Right now. And I don't care about the money. Anything specific or with sentimental value?"

She had no intention of telling him the truth, but at the moment all she wanted to do was get away from him, so cooperating seemed like her best idea. She glanced down at the brown leather jacket stretched across his broad shoulders. He was wearing only a thin navy henley underneath, the coat unzipped. He had to be freezing out here in the wind but either didn't care or hadn't noticed.

"Nothing much. Most of his holdings are still waiting to

be disbursed. The only things he left me were a safety-deposit-box key and the deed to his sailboat."

"What about a letter opener?"

Her stomach tightened. "I don't—"

"Small. Italian, looks like a dagger. Initials LdM carved into the handle. Think hard, Roarke."

*Oh, shit.* "Why are you asking me this?"

"A dagger just like that one was found at the scene. Forensics is running it now. No more games. I think it's time you tell me what the hell's really going on."

Her chest went cold. And suddenly all those what-ifs she'd been worrying about the last day became reality. "I have to go."

"Dammit, Hailey."

She jogged quickly up the steps and ducked into the cabin of the jet. "I'm ready, Steve."

A muttered response came back to her, but she barely heard it because Shane was there behind her again, grabbing her arm and whipping her back to face him. "This isn't a joke. If you run now you're going to wind up in deep shit. It's not going to take them long to figure out that dagger was in your possession only days ago. If you didn't really kill him or if it was an accident, tell me now so I can help you."

She pulled her arm from his grasp and stepped back. "Get off the plane, Maxwell."

"I'm not letting you do this."

"I don't need your help. And I'm leaving. With or without you. So either get off this plane now, or you're going to be in as much hot water as I am."

His jaw clenched and unclenched. The fiery indecision in his eyes said he was inches away from losing it. And for a fleeting moment she considered asking why her situation was so important to him, but then bit her tongue. There was something driving him, something deeper than the attraction that had flared between them from the first. Secrets she wasn't sure she wanted to know brewed in his dark eyes, as did the hint of danger she'd always sensed in him.

The heavy sounds of the cabin's door closing echoed through the room. Followed by Steve's voice telling her to take her seat as they were next in line for takeoff. As the plane started to rumble toward the runway, only one thing was clear.

Shane Maxwell had just sacrificed his career for her. Without knowing if she was innocent or guilty. When his department found out he'd not only let her go but had joined her, everything he'd worked for the last twenty years would be gone.

What kind of man did that for a woman he barely knew? And more importantly, what would he do next?

# CHAPTER NINE

As soon as they reached cruising altitude, Hailey flipped off her seat belt and headed for the back of the plane. Shane dug his fingers into the armrest of his chair as she brushed by him without a word. Since he'd been sitting here fuming for the last ten minutes, he figured enough was enough. His seat belt landed with a thump against leather as he followed her into the galley.

The Roarke company jet was impressive. A main cabin with a leather couch, four chairs that swiveled, grouped in twos with low tables between them. A door at the front of the plane led to the cockpit. At the rear, it opened to the galley and the lavatory, and behind that he didn't know what. Since Hailey wasn't in the galley he ignored the luxury and kept going, pushed the back door open and found her sitting on a large bed with her head cradled in her hands.

Ah, hell. For all her tough-girl attitude, she looked nearly ready to break.

She glared up at him when the bedroom door opened. "What do you want now?"

He held up both hands in surrender. "Just to talk. There's not enough room in here for you to kick my ass again, and I'm really not in the mood for it anyway."

Her heavy sigh said she agreed but didn't really want to. And he wished he knew what to say to get her to smile at him the way she had in Puerto Rico. Or a few days ago in his apartment.

"I didn't kill him," she said quietly.

His relief at hearing her admission was more than he expected. And it eased a space in his chest. "What were you doing at his house?"

"It's not his house. It's part of the Roarke holdings." She glanced warily up at him. Her blue eyes held his, and this time when his chest grew tight it wasn't because of stress or worry, but because of something else. Something that lit a tingling deep inside. Something he wasn't sure how to define, even if he wanted to. "I'm not sure you're going to like what you hear next. Or that you're even going to believe me."

"Try me." When she bit her lip, he added, "Like you said. I'm in this now, too, whether you want me here or not."

She looked back down at her hands. "It's complicated."

"Most things are."

Her silence sent his blood pressure up again, but then she surprised him by saying, "I already told you my father asked me to step in and help out with the company when his health went downhill. At first I said no, but he made the deal one I couldn't pass up."

"What deal?"

She pursed her lips, seemed on the verge of not answering, then said, "He promised if I helped him out with this, he wouldn't ask me for anything again. He'd stop pestering me to come back to Miami and join the business."

"You never wanted to?"

"Never."

He glanced around the fancy plane. Teak walls, plush carpeting, big mirror over the bed, down comforter and pillows on the thick mattress he could easily see himself tumbling over with her.

The Roarke Resorts up and down the East Coast were all five-star accommodations. Though not on the same scale as the Hilton empire, Garrett Roarke had made a lasting impression on the travel industry the past ten years. And it showed in this plane and the new resort being built in Lake Geneva.

"Why not?"

She shrugged. "No interest. When I was old enough, I walked away from it all. Working with them—my family—wasn't something that appealed to me."

"All of it?"

"I told you you wouldn't believe me."

He tipped his head and studied her. And thought back to the way she'd looked when he'd been in Florida. Someone he'd been able to talk to and laugh with for the first time in . . . hell, a long-ass time. A beat cop, he'd been dazzled by her from the first look. She was as far removed from all this wealth and prestige as he was. "I do believe you," he said slowly. "But if that's the case, why would he ask you to take over? You're a cop, not a CEO."

She rubbed her hands down her arms as if she were cold. "I have an MBA from Harvard." She quickly added, "I also grew up around the company. My father made sure I interned there every summer until I graduated from college. I know more about Roarke Resorts than most people who work there."

"Then why are you a police officer?"

She shrugged. "The job interested me."

What she didn't say, and what he was slowly picking up on, was that being a cop was also the exact opposite career her father had selected for her.

"I still don't understand why he asked you to step in and help out when he was sick. Why not one of the other officers of the company? There had to be a VP, someone with more experience or seniority. Was that the root of the problem with your cousin?"

"It probably didn't help. But no, Bryan and I always had a strained relationship. He's worked for the company for years, but he's never made it past regional VP. He's lazy, and my father knew that, which is why he kept him around but didn't promote him. My father was loyal to family without fault, no matter how they worked for him."

"So Bryan probably didn't like the fact you were in charge."

"Definitely not."

"And the board of directors didn't have any problem with you stepping in?"

She shook her head. "RR is a private company, not public. The board is composed of family members who all have equal interest. My mother, Bryan, me, my sister Nicole, and Bryan's father—my uncle Graham. There was one other member—my maternal grandfather, who invested a great deal of money years ago when my father started his first hotel—but he passed about eight months ago and his shares were divided between my mother, myself and my sister."

"Leaving Bryan and his father with less say."

"Right. My father could basically do whatever he wanted and the board had to go along with him. And my sister and I have been silent members for as long as I can remember."

"He didn't try to get your sister involved?"

She pinned him with a look. "You've seen my sister. She lives for the easy life. Parties, shopping and flashy magazine covers. She doesn't care who runs RR so long as it isn't her and her trust fund isn't impacted by any changes going on within the company."

Since you couldn't buy groceries without seeing Nicole Roarke's face on some tabloid, Shane figured that statement wasn't far off the mark. "So answer me this, now that your father's gone, why haven't you resigned? If you never wanted to be a part of his company in the first place, what's the point of sticking around?"

She took a deep breath and the ease with which she'd been talking to him seemed to fly right out the plane's small windows. "I was going to. After we got through the funeral and will reading. But then my father threw a wrench in the whole thing."

"How?"

She glanced up at him from her seat on the end of the bed. "Did Lisa tell you anything about my father's . . . eccentricity?"

He shook his head.

A humorless smirk curled one side of her lips. One that was so damn sexy, he had to resist the urge to cross to her and wipe it off her mouth with his own. "Let's just say he loved movies like *National Treasure*. Indiana Jones wasn't just a franchise, it was his idea of fun. When he heard about Lisa and Rafe finding the three Furies? He thought it was the coolest thing ever. And this from a man who hated Rafe Sullivan's guts the first time he laid eyes on him." She shook her head. "My father collected art and antiquities his whole life. Most of what he's collected isn't worth much, but he's got storage units full of ugly paintings and useless sculptures no one could care less about. Used to drive my mother nuts, but having them wasn't the issue. It was the *finding* that thrilled him."

She braced her hands on the mattress. "At the will reading last week, I expected him to hand the company over to my uncle Graham. Or to divide his shares equally among the rest of us and appoint Paul McIntosh as acting CEO."

"Who's Paul McIntosh?"

"Highest-ranking nonfamily officer. He's worked for the company since he interned there in college years ago. My father loved Paul. He was like the son my father never had. Paul . . . he's bright. And he'd probably be good for the company, but . . ."

"But what?"

She shrugged. "I don't know. There's something about him I'm not wild about. He's slick."

If there was one thing Shane always trusted, it was gut instinct. "He wasn't appointed, obviously."

She shook her head. "No. In fact, he wasn't even mentioned in the will, which was shocking to most of us there. But the biggest surprise was the terms of the will. My father left each of us a few trivial items—I told you what he left for me—but the bulk of his estate is still in limbo. As is the future of the company."

"How so?"

She shifted on the mattress. "At Christmas, he gave each

of us a copy of a famous sculpture, The Last Seduction. Are you familiar with it?"

He shook his head.

"It's a bronze. A man and woman, both nude, standing together, locked chest to knee. Her mouth at his throat, his head tipped back in, well, pleasure. It's been engulfed in controversy for years. Most historians believe it's one of the lost works of famous Italian sculptor Benvenuto Cellini, who was commissioned by the Medici family to create it. It depicts the last temptation of Alessandro de Medici—a Medici prince from the sixteenth century, the first Duke of Florence, and quite possibly the first black head of state in the modern Western world—who was murdered by an anti-Medici uprising headed by his cousin. Supposedly, Alessandro was seduced by his cousin's sister, then gutted with a dagger."

"Lovely way to go," Shane mumbled.

"Yeah, well, regardless of whether it actually went down that way or not, the sculpture was created shortly after his death, probably as an act of warning to any other factions considering a takeover attempt. There are records of it in Italian libraries and historical annals, but the original disappeared over two hundred years ago. Not before it was copied, though.

"Sometime in the late 1970s, replicas of The Last Seduction started popping up in auctions around the world. Each piece has had to be examined in depth because the foundry that created the copies was so good. My father got his hands on some of those copies and gave one to each of us. Bryan, in particular, was disgusted with the gift because it came in lieu of his normal Christmas bonus. I didn't much care, as I never wanted the money in the first place, but I hung on to my sculpture because I'd always liked the piece. My father'd had one years ago in his office. And when I used to go there, I don't know, something about it intrigued me."

She shrugged and looked down at her hands. "Anyway, no one thought much of it until the will reading. And then the odd gifts made sense. Five were given out. Each one is a piece of a puzzle. Put them all together and supposedly it leads you to the sixth. The person who finds the sixth inherits Roarke Resorts and his estate, minus the trust fund he's set aside for my mother, my sister and myself."

Shane's eyes narrowed. "A treasure hunt?"

Her eyes lifted to his. "Yeah. Pretty weird terms, huh?"

*Weird* was an understatement. "Why would he do that?"

She shrugged. "Maybe he figured it would prove who wanted the company more. Maybe he'd really lost it the last month of his life. None of us are sure."

"Lost it?"

A nervous look crossed her face. "Aside from all . . . this, I've heard some rumors in the company that he was getting paranoid in his old age. I'm sure the RR lawyers are looking into the legality of his will, but if there's one thing I know about my father, no matter how strange he may have been acting, he'd have made sure his will was sound. He had a head for business like nothing you've ever seen."

"And this . . . bizarre treasure hunt . . . it didn't make you want to step down?"

"It *did* make me want to step down. I had no interest in participating. Running the company, managing his money, none of that holds any appeal for me. But the morning before I came up here, my father's personal lawyer brought me a letter my father had left for me. In it he hinted this stupid quest was something I needed to be a part of, for reasons he didn't elaborate on but which made me wonder what was really going on. He also said if I participated, at the end I could truly walk away from everything Roarke related for the rest of my life without looking back. That I would finally be . . . free."

"And that convinced you?"

"No. What convinced me was being ambushed by the entire board that same day. All of them—even my mother—gathered to try to get me to resign. I don't like being challenged like that. And Bryan was in-your-face aggressive. He didn't care about the company. All he cared about was getting what he felt was due to him, even though he didn't deserve it. If Paul had talked to me privately and asked me to step aside, I may have, but not Bryan. Never Bryan. I wasn't about to hand over everything my father worked for so Bryan could drive it into the ground. My father and I may not have gotten along, but he taught me the value of loyalty. And I guess I felt I owed him this one small thing."

Loyalty was something Shane also understood. And admired. "So tell me what happened with your cousin."

She pointed to the bruises on her face. "He's responsible for this. Or, at least, someone he hired is. When I wouldn't sign the papers they'd prepared for me, Bryan made it pretty clear I'd be sorry. Minutes later some jerk in the elevator told me I hadn't taken the first hint, and this was the second."

Shane's spine stiffened.

"Obviously, the guy he hired didn't expect me to know how to defend myself, and I'm pretty sure he ended up looking worse than I did, but it pissed me off. That's when I decided to go along with this stupid treasure hunt, if for no other reason than to prove to these people they can't push me around."

"So that's why you were in the Chicago house."

"Each of the sculptures has a different number on the bottom. I needed to get a look at Bryan's."

"And you did."

She nodded.

"And what about the dagger?"

A worried look crossed her face. "I'm . . . not quite sure where it is."

"What do you mean 'not sure'?"

"I mean," she said, blowing out a frustrated breath, "I had it in the elevator after that meeting in Miami. After I got this"—she pointed at her face—"I was way more interested in getting out of there than picking up everything I'd dropped in the struggle. When I got home I realized it was gone."

"So you're saying you didn't take it with you into your cousin's house?"

She flicked him an irritated look. "I didn't have it with me in Chicago. Even if I'd had it, do you think I'm stupid?"

No, he thought this entire situation was stupid. And totally, completely over-the-top unbelievable. No one could come up with a story like this just to cover their ass. Who the hell would believe it? "So someone took it."

"I think that's the only possibility. Where did they find it?"

"Basement."

"I was never in the basement." At his silence she looked up. Crystal clear blue eyes that sent a tingling through his chest all over again. "Look, I know this looks bad, but I didn't kill him. I got what I needed and left. I wore gloves, just in case, so I know my prints aren't in that house. The only other thing they can use to tie me to the scene is . . ."

"Is what?"

She bit her lip again, almost as if she didn't want to tell him. Then finally mumbled in a low voice, "I cut my arm when I was there."

"You *what?*"

She closed her eyes. Opened them. "Okay, this part sounds bad, so don't freak out. But when I was in the house, Bryan showed up with his girlfriend. I ended up hiding under the bed and cut my arm on a spring that was sticking out."

"Christ Jake." He scrubbed his hand through his hair. "They pulled DNA from the house. Which they're going to try to link back to you."

"I know. Look, I didn't plan it, okay? And I cleaned it up." She looked back down at her hands. "I never suspected it would turn into what it has. I . . . I guess you can call it really bad luck."

She didn't know the half of it.

His eyes narrowed as he tried to piece together what she was telling him. "How'd you get out without being seen?"

"I waited until they fell asleep. Then I found his bronze."

"Where was it?"

"Freezer. He had it wrapped in tinfoil so no one would see it. It's where he used to hide things when we were kids."

"And you took it."

"No." She shook her head. "I only looked at what was carved into the bottom. I made sure I left it there."

He'd have to talk to Tony and have someone check the freezer, if they hadn't already. "Then what?"

"Then I left."

His eyes narrowed. "Then what were you doing in my bar?"

Maybe he imagined it, but as she twisted her hands in her lap, he thought he saw her cheeks turn the slightest shade of pink. "Well, I . . . I was a little wired when I got out of there, and I wanted to get a drink. And you, well . . . I knew it was your bar so . . ."

Now it was starting to make sense. "So you used me."

She glanced up sharply. "No, that wasn't my intention at all. It was so late, I didn't honestly think you'd be there. I only went because I was, well, curious. But I never intended to use you as an alibi because there was no reason I'd even need one."

A little of the pressure eased in his chest. *Curious* could mean a whole host of things, but the fact she couldn't look him in the eye meant she'd been curious about him. In the same way he'd been curious about her over the last three months.

He studied her resolute expression for any hint she was lying. Really looked hard, because, man, he couldn't afford to fall for something that wasn't real. But damn, if he could see it. All he saw was a woman who was being backed into a corner. "You mentioned the security system. How did you get into the house?"

A nervous expression crossed her face. "You're not going to like that part."

"Try me."

She let out a long breath. "Since Bryan changed the locks,

I had to get some help. I can pick an easy lock, but I'm not as adept at security systems as my ex."

Her ex, the thief. Reformed thief now, Shane figured, not that it mattered much to him. Considering how Rafe Sullivan seemed to have cleaned up his act since marrying Lisa, Shane was pretty sure he hadn't been the one to fly up to Chicago and help Hailey. Which left—

His jaw flexed. "Billy Sullivan."

Her eyes slid to his again, and this time they weren't wary, but very determined. "Whatever you do, don't mention it to Lisa. Or Rafe. I asked Billy for a favor and he helped because we're friends. But if Rafe gets wind of what Billy did, he'll skin him alive."

The fact she worried about either of the Sullivan men lit off a strange sort of jealousy. "So Billy was with you at the house."

She looked back down at her feet. "I know what you're thinking, Maxwell. And it's a no-go. I can't use Billy as an alibi. One more strike and he's looking at doing time. Even though the house is technically a Roarke holding, it was listed as Bryan's place of residence, and any way you look at it, we were trespassing. Billy would have to explain how he got us in and out, and he can't afford to do that."

Shane rubbed a hand down his face. "Jesus Christ, Hailey, B and E is nothing compared to a murder rap."

She pushed to her feet and faced him. "I know that. But I didn't kill him. Don't you think it's a little too convenient that everything's pointing at me? Someone wants me to take the fall for this so I back off. They stole my father's dagger to make sure of it. I just need some time. I guarantee as soon as I find that sixth sculpture, whoever killed Bryan will make themselves known."

"What part of that statement is supposed to put me at ease? The fact you're considering going along with this insane idea or that you're using yourself as bait for a killer?"

"That killer's most likely a family member of mine, Maxwell. I'm not afraid of him. But I'll tell you this much, if that person killed my father as well, I'll do whatever it takes to find them. Sitting in Lake Geneva, waiting for CPD to either arrest me or bring me in for formal questioning, isn't getting me any closer to figuring out who's behind all this."

"Wait." He held up his hand. "Who said your father was murdered? I thought he died of a heart attack."

Unease passed over her delicate features. "I'm not so convinced anymore. I think maybe he knew his failing health wasn't so natural. I think that's part of the reason he left me that letter."

If what she was saying was true, this went way beyond the death of her cousin. It dipped into money and greed and what people will do to get what they want. And for reasons he couldn't quite understand, he had a feeling she was at the center of it all. In ways she couldn't even comprehend.

He had an overwhelming urge to wrap her up tight and secure, to make sure she was locked away safe and sound from anything that could harm her. And even though he was the last person on the planet who probably could, he wanted to be the one to watch over her.

*You can't save her.*

That voice came out of nowhere to ping around in his head. What made him think this time would be any different? But she'd come to him when she'd needed help, whether she'd meant to or not. And that knowledge only made his need stronger. "So where are we headed?"

Her brows drew together to form a deep crease between her gorgeous eyes. "You're not going to insist we go back so you can hand me over to the police?"

"Would you consider it if I did?"

She shook her head.

"Then there's no point in trying, is there?"

"No." She crossed her arms over her chest, glanced around the room. "We have to land in Nashville to refuel. I'll make sure there's a car for you there—"

"Wherever you're going, Hailey, that's where I'm going, too."

Surprise registered in her glittering blue eyes. "What?"

"The way I see it, I'm stuck with you now. Chen's never going to believe any of this, not unless we can prove it, and I'm not about to let you go out on your own to lure in a killer. Even if he is family."

"Why do you even care?"

Why? Because even with her crazy story, he sensed she wasn't lying. And because where she was concerned, he couldn't turn his back on her. Not this time.

He shrugged. "Let's just say my instincts are telling me not to let you out of my sight. So I guess the decision's yours now. Either we do this together, or I haul you back to Chicago, kicking and screaming. What'll it be?"

Indecision brewed in her eyes, but her gaze never dropped from his. "I don't need your help, Maxwell."

"No, but you've got it just the same. Be smart and take the hand I'm offering."

# CHAPTER TEN

As Hailey sat beside Shane in the front of the rental sedan, heading into the Florida Everglades, she asked herself—for the thousandth time—how the heck she'd ended up here.

She glanced sideways at him, seated behind the wheel, studying the mangrove trees on both sides of the road that led west out of Homestead. Dark hair fell over his forehead. A day's worth of stubble covered his jaw. He'd tossed his leather jacket in the backseat when they'd climbed into the rental this afternoon, and the long-sleeved navy henley he wore stretched across wide, toned shoulders. He looked a little on edge, a lot dangerous and sexier than any man she'd ever seen.

She tamped down the zing of arousal rushing through her—the same one she got whenever she looked at him—and pointed toward a street sign a hundred yards ahead. "That's it."

He flipped on the blinker and slowed to make the turn. "Why in the hell would anyone live in the middle of this?"

"My uncle likes seclusion."

"This isn't seclusion. It's like my personal version of hell. Humidity, alligators, snakes and no Micky D's."

"Please don't tell me you eat that crap."

"Alligators?"

"Big Macs."

They bounced over a rather large pothole in the gravel road. "I'm a thirty-eight-year-old single guy who doesn't cook. What do you think I eat?"

"Didn't you ever see that movie about the guy who ate nothing but McDonald's for a month straight?"

"Heard about it. Definitely changed my thinking. These days I keep it to twenty-five meals a month minimum."

She couldn't help it. She smiled. With that toned body, there was no way he ate greasy burgers every day.

*Don't go there.* She looked back out the front windshield so she wouldn't. A car passed them in a blur of dust, going the other direction.

"How do you know he's even going to help us?" Shane asked.

The *us* in that question sent her stomach floating again, but she locked the feeling down and reminded herself he wasn't here for romance. If he wanted to tag along on this, she couldn't stop him, but that didn't mean they had to re-hash what had or hadn't happened. Lord knew, she didn't want to revisit the rejection if she didn't have to.

"Graham's the only person in the family I've ever gotten along with. He's not money hungry like the rest of them. When I joined the force in Key West, he was the only one who congratulated me."

"You said he's on the Roarke board?"

"Yeah. When my grandparents passed, they left a small inheritance to both their sons. My father convinced Graham to invest his portion in my father's new hotel chain. Graham never had a head for business, and my father knew that. He's always been more interested in nature. If he hadn't invested the money, he'd have squandered it away."

"He never worked for the company?"

"Not officially. But over the years he's been a sounding board for my father. He might not know the ins and outs of the business world, but he's got good ideas. And my father used those ideas to expand into markets he otherwise might not have touched."

"Does he live out here year-round?"

"No. He's got a place in the Bahamas, too. And he likes

to travel. When I saw him last week, though, he mentioned he was staying here for a few weeks. Reconnecting with nature, I guess you'd call it."

"That's not what I'd call it," Shane mumbled as they crossed a rickety bridge over a narrow slough and followed the road through the dense thicket of trees.

"C'mon, Maxwell," she teased, enjoying the way he was loosening up the farther they got from Chicago. "You're not afraid of a few mosquitoes are you?"

"It's not the mosquitoes I'm worried about. It's everything else that's hiding in that water."

A clump of cypress trees covered in climbing ivy rose on the right side of the gravel road, interspersed with hardwoods like ash and maple. Saw palmettos grew in clumps around their bases. Tall reeds and bushes emerged from the slough on the left, and every once in a while—if you looked closely—you could see the movement of small birds, turtles and the alligators her uncle loved slinking through the grasses.

The winding road curved to the left another mile or two; then the trees opened to reveal a two-story log home with a wide porch, well kept and surrounded by lush green lawns. As Shane killed the engine and glanced around, it was obvious this wasn't what he'd expected.

"Not a shack," she said as she popped her door and climbed from the car.

He pushed the sunglasses he'd picked up at the airport into his thick, dark hair to get a better look at the house. "Likes to be secluded, huh?" He tucked his hands into the pockets of his loose jeans and fell into step beside her across the lawn. "Does he maintain the grounds all by himself?"

"Are you kidding? He's in his sixties. That's too much work for a man in his thirties. The Everglades have a way of taking over if you're not careful. He has a crew that takes care of the property for him."

"What does he do with his time?"

"He tinkers, mostly with his garden." At his puzzled expression she added, "He's a man who knows a ton about everything and is an expert at nothing. He's never been focused on any one thing for as long as I've known him."

"Great. A handyman millionaire. That explains this place."

She smiled. "That's why I like him."

She knocked. And waited. When several minutes went by without so much as a sound from inside, she cupped her hand at the glass and peered into the living room window.

"The swamp's bringing out all kinds today. First that guy from the company with all those papers for me to sign, now you."

She turned at the gravelly voice and looked to the end of the porch where her uncle Graham was standing with a bucket in one weathered hand and a fishing pole in the other. He wore frayed denim shorts and a dirty white Key Largo T-shirt, but he looked just as familiar as he always did. Smiling, she walked toward him, returning the hug he gave her and shifting toward Shane. "Uncle Graham, this is Shane Maxwell. A friend of mine."

Graham came up onto the porch and shook Shane's hand. "Nice to meet you. Any friend of Hailey's is a friend of mine." He looked her way again. "Long drive. What are you doing here? And good God, girl, what happened to your face?"

Dammit. She'd forgotten to add extra makeup to her yellowing bruises. "Walked into a wall. Nothing big." In an attempt to change the subject, she glanced at the bucket in his hand. "What do you have there?"

He lifted the yellow plastic pail. "Crawdads. Hungry? I could cook us up some lunch."

"No, thanks." Hailey put a hand on his arm. Out of the corner of her eye she saw Shane grimace. "We didn't come to eat. But if you've got any of that famous tea of yours, I'd love a glass. There's something I want to talk to you about."

A smile slinked across his wrinkled face, and he gestured for them to follow as he opened the screen door. "Miss Carmine made some this morning before she left. Come on back."

Graham moved through the long hallway that split the house in two. At Shane's curious glance, Hailey whispered, "Carmine's his housekeeper. She's worked for him for years. They tend to be more than employer and employee, if you get the drift."

Shane nodded, and a clicking sound came from his pocket as he followed her. "Crawdads?"

"A delicacy in the South. Don't tell me you've never had them."

"No, and I don't plan to, either."

The hall opened to a large central kitchen with white Formica counters, an oversize island and appliances Hailey had always figured had come with the house. They looked to be forty years old. She moved to the cupboard while Shane settled at one of the bar stools surrounding the island.

Graham opened the refrigerator and pulled out a pitcher of tea. "So what do you do, Mr. Maxwell?"

"Shane. Thanks." He took the glass Hailey handed him. "Detective."

Graham's eyes lit. "Oh. So you work with Hailey in Key West."

"Not exactly—"

"Maxwell's sister is the one who recently married Rafe," Hailey cut in.

"Sullivan," Graham said with just a hint of disgust. "I didn't know there were two women out there dumb enough to make the same mistake."

A smirk came from Shane. Hailey ignored it and frowned at her uncle. "Very funny."

"Oh, come on now," Graham said as Hailey added ice to each glass and he poured tea. "He was never good enough for you, and we both know it."

"Good enough wasn't the issue. But that's not why we came out here."

Graham nodded and, because he knew it was a topic she didn't like to discuss, moved on to what he probably suspected was her reason for being here. "You just get back from Wisconsin?"

Hailey took a drink of tea, set the glass down. "Yes. I did. We're two months behind schedule, but I think we've found a way to shave off some time. Should put us closer to the grand opening we scheduled for Memorial Day."

Graham shook his head. "That son of mine knows how to screw up a wet dream, doesn't he?" He sighed as he swirled the ice in his glass. "I'm afraid he's got no focus. Just like me."

Shane lifted the glass to his lips and proceeded to spew iced tea all over the counter in front of him.

Hailey grabbed a napkin and came around the counter to pat his back. "Are you all right?"

When he could speak, he looked from the glass to her face. "Tastes like straight sugar."

"Yankee," Graham muttered.

"That's because it's sweet tea," she told him.

"Where you from, son?" Graham asked.

"Chicago."

Graham clucked his tongue. "They definitely don't know tea in Chicago. Pizza maybe, but not tea."

Hailey handed Shane the napkin and turned back to her uncle. Okay, enough chitchat. They needed to get to the root of why they were here. "Have you watched the news at all lately, Uncle Graham?"

He shook his head. "When I'm out here you know I don't do anything but garden and fish."

She walked around the counter so she was standing at his side. "I'm afraid I have some bad news."

His eyes narrowed on her face. "What kind of bad news?"

"Maybe you should sit down. You know your heart—"

"Goddamn, girl, my heart's just fine. Stop beating around the bush and tell me what you came to tell me."

She stared at him, then finally said, "Bryan's dead."

"What?"

She explained what Shane had told her—as much as she knew—and waited while he processed it all. He didn't sit, even when she suggested—again—that he move to the table, just stood in the same place staring at his untouched tea.

"You're sure?" he asked.

"Yes. I'm so sorry." She tightened her grip on his hand.

"Does the family know?"

"Yes."

"No one told me."

Another strike against her family. "I'm sure Madeline's been busy with arrangements. And it's possible they tried to call you out here. You're not always reliable about listening to your messages. I tried to call you after I found out."

"I . . ." He put a hand up to his mouth, rubbed his lips. "I always knew he was going to go before me." When he glanced up, his eyes were filled with grief. "That's a terrible thing for a father to say, isn't it?"

Her heart broke for him. "No. It's not your fault. Bryan wasn't the easiest person to get along with. He did things his way, and in this case, someone didn't like it."

"Do they . . . do they know who killed him?"

"No," Shane said, speaking up for the first time. When Graham's clouded eyes turned his way, he added, "Someone's trying to make it look like Hailey's responsible, though."

Graham's gaze shot back to her. "Why would anyone think that? You don't even like to kill spiders when you find them in the house. Anyone who knows you knows you couldn't intentionally hurt someone. Especially Bryan."

Though this was just about the worst conversation she could conceive of having, warmth bubbled through her. Graham was probably the only person in the world who believed in her innocence. Her family certainly didn't. Shane hadn't until he'd heard all the details, and even now she wasn't completely convinced he believed her 100 percent. But Graham was on her side. He always had been.

"It's complicated, Uncle Graham. You know Bryan and I never got along. Anyone who wants me gone from RR could play on that fact. But this goes beyond that. I think it has to do with Daddy's will."

At the mention of her father's will, Graham frowned in disgust. "Your father should have had his head examined, instead of his heart."

"I know."

"Why do you think that's what this is about?"

"Because," Shane said, "CPD found your brother's dagger in the house. Hailey said she had it with her at the board meeting in Miami, but hasn't seen it since."

"You're investigating my son's death?"

Shane's dark gaze slid to Hailey. And just like it had in the car, awareness pulsed in her veins under that heated stare. "In a roundabout way, yeah, I am."

She pulled her gaze from Shane and refocused on her uncle. "The only way I'm going to clear my name and figure out who really did kill Bryan is to find the sixth sculpture first."

"How will that help?"

"If my hunch is right, whoever killed Bryan wants Roarke Resorts, and thanks to my father, the only way to get it is to go along with this stupid treasure hunt."

"You think the person who did this did it to get his sculpture? A botched robbery?"

"Maybe," Shane said. "And maybe there's more to it than that. But that's what we're going on now."

Graham rubbed a hand over his face. Fatigue and grief radiated from his lean frame. Hailey reached for his hand when he lowered it. "Uncle Graham. I need your help."

He let out a long breath. "It's in my study. You're welcome to it. But, Hailey." He wrapped his knobby fingers around hers. "Is it worth this? You never wanted this damn company. Certainly there's a way to prove you didn't have anything to do with Bryan's . . . death. You're a good girl. The police will figure that out."

A sad smile pulled at her mouth. Same old Uncle Graham. Always seeing the best in people. Even in his no-good son who'd caused him more grief over the years than any parent deserved. Sure, Graham hadn't been the best father, but he'd tried. And that was a lot more than Hailey could say for her own dad.

She could see in Shane's eyes that he agreed with her uncle. She turned back to Graham. "I have to do this. There's more to it than Bryan's death. When I can, I'll tell you the rest."

He gave her a fierce hug. "I'm proud of you. Your father would be proud, too, you know."

Hailey closed her eyes and hung on tight. "I doubt that. And save your praise until I figure this out. Daddy was right about one thing. I wasn't a very good cop to begin with."

"That's not true. Your heart's just always been somewhere else." Graham eased back. "My bronze is locked in the cabinet in my study. You know where the key is, and you're welcome to it. But you still need Nicole's. And your mother's."

"I'll get them."

He ran his hand down her cheek. "Such confidence. I wish Bryan could have had some of your resolve." Sadness crept over his face again, and he turned to look across the counter at Shane. "I appreciate anything you can do to help my niece in this. It's nice to know she's got one ally out there." He looked around the kitchen as if he'd never seen it before. "If you don't mind, I think I'm going to go lie down for a bit."

"Can I help you upstairs?" Hailey asked.

"No." He waved a hand. "No. I just need some time alone." He paused at the kitchen door and turned to look back. "Thirty-eight. The number on my bronze is thirty-eight."

"Thank you, Uncle Graham." Her heart pinched. "Do you mind if we take a look at it anyway?"

"No. You two . . . you take what you need."

His sad smile stayed with her even after he left the kitchen. Hailey reached for her tea again. "Bryan was a real jerk, but that . . . that was heartbreaking. No child should die before their parent."

"Happens more often than you think," Shane said, rising and taking his full glass of tea to the sink while she sipped hers. He carefully avoided the bucket of crawdads and dumped his glass in the other sink well. "From what I gathered, your cousin had a long list of enemies. You weren't the only one who benefited from his death."

"I'm just the most obvious."

He turned and looked at her with those dark eyes. "Yeah."

There was a lot he wasn't saying, and she didn't have the energy to try to figure him out. And as much as she loved her uncle, she needed to get what she'd come for and find out if Billy had gotten her the next piece on her list.

She drained her glass and took it to the sink; then she turned and headed for the hall. "His study's through here. Let's see if his sculpture answers any questions."

They made their way down the hall and into his cluttered study. Hailey walked around behind his dusty desk and pulled open the top drawer. "He keeps it locked in his liquor cabinet." She fished around until she found the keys, then turned to the mahogany cabinet against the far wall. The key slipped in the lock and turned with a click. She pulled open the double doors and stared inside.

"What's wrong?" Shane asked, coming to stand behind her.

Hailey could hardly believe it. "It's gone."

# CHAPTER ELEVEN

He was good at puzzles. After all, that's what he did every day of his damn life. Pieced together clues, looked for hidden meanings, motives and possibilities. Put them all together until he had a complete picture. But, this one . . . Shane had to admit, this one stumped him.

Sure, he had a laundry list of possible suspects running through his head, but those sculptures? They were a mystery.

"Is it possible Graham gave his sculpture to someone and forgot?"

"No," Hailey said, staring out the window as they bounced down the same dirt road they'd come in on.

"Then someone took it. But who?"

"That's the sixty-four-thousand-dollar question, isn't it?" Hailey sighed. "I can think of a couple of people who might be interested."

Shane frowned. Yeah, he could, too. But after Hailey had told him about the numbers on the other sculptures, he didn't have a clue how they all fit together or what the hell they meant. Maybe her father really had been wacko there at the end like everyone was insinuating.

"I guess it doesn't much matter," Hailey said. "Graham gave us his number and that's all we really need." She chewed on her lip for a second. "It could be a phone number."

"Maybe." Shane rolled the numbers around in his head again. "Thirty-eight, twenty-five, zero five. What about a combination? Didn't you say he left you a safety-deposit-box key? Have you looked at what's in the box yet?"

"No. I didn't have time before I went up to Chicago. That's definitely a possibility. I should check it out when I get back."

"We," he said flatly.

Her gaze flicked his way. And out of the corner of his eye he saw the hesitation as she struggled not to tell him she could do it on her own.

Her eyes shifted forward again to gaze out at the setting sun. "You know, Maxwell, I really appreciate your help so far—"

"If you're considering telling me to take a hike, save your breath."

"It'd be easy for you to go back to Chicago and tell them you tried to stop me but couldn't and don't know where I went. You're not past the point of no return."

Wasn't he? He felt like it. "Your uncle wasn't what I expected."

She frowned at the change of subject. "What did you expect?"

"I don't know. Not that. Not . . . normal."

She glanced his way. "Am I that bad?"

One side of his mouth curled. "You have your moments. But no, that's not what I meant. I was thinking more about your sister. And your cousin. And the wealthy in general."

"Part of his charm. Money doesn't mean anything to him."

He glanced sideways at her. Dusk was starting to settle over the Everglades, and a warm glow on the horizon reflected off her face, making her blonde hair look darker, her skin softer, her eyes somehow bluer. "Did you miss it? The money. Now that you're back, it's gotta be nice. That jet alone costs more than I'll make in my lifetime."

"I never missed it. It all came with conditions."

"Still—"

"Look, Maxwell, what you don't understand is that it was never mine. The money, the houses, the education. My father controlled all of it. He still does with my sister. It's his money paying for her condo, her vacations, her fun. Up until his death, he'd say jump and she'd ask 'how high?' All her crazy antics and gallivanting around? That's just her way of rebelling. I couldn't live that way. Even before I graduated I knew I couldn't let him control me like that."

They drove in silence a bit, bouncing on the dirt road. And though he kept trying to put her in a nice, neat box—sexy cop, spoiled heiress, reluctant CEO, damn irritating suspect—she kept changing things on him. There were layers to Hailey Roarke he hadn't known existed, and every one of them intrigued and excited him in a way that left his blood warm and his head jumbled.

"What's wrong with your uncle's heart?" he asked.

"It's weak. Heart disease runs in the family. He's been on medication for years. I just hope this doesn't push him over the edge."

He nodded. "So what now?"

She glanced at her watch as they approached the same slough they'd crossed earlier. "It's probably too late to hit my father's bank and check that safety-deposit box. I need to see Billy anyway."

"Sullivan? What for?"

"He has something I need."

"Don't tell me you—"

A popping sound cut off his words a split second before the tire blew.

"Fuck." Shane gripped the wheel tight and tried to keep the rental on a straight path over the creaky old bridge.

"What the—"

The second tire blew before Hailey got the words out, and suddenly they were sliding sideways, heading for the edge of the bridge, which lacked any kind of modern safety railings.

"Hold on!" Shane tried to correct, but it was too late. The tires went over, the car went nose down before either could reach for the door. They hit the murky slough ten feet below with a whoosh and rush of water that began filling the interior of the car the instant metal met water.

Hailey's head hit the window with a crack. Shane's neck

snapped forward and back. Even as he was shaking the haze from his mind, Hailey was unstrapping her seat belt and working his free. "We have to get out of this water. Now."

He smelled the stench of stagnant water. Didn't waste time arguing, not when she was so obviously making perfect sense. He tried the door, but it wouldn't open.

The engine was now waterlogged, and as the car sank, water spilled in until it was waist deep. He kicked at the automatic window that wouldn't open, then pulled his gun from his shoulder holster. "Watch your eyes."

Water gurgled around them as he turned away and fired once, breaking the glass and kicking out the rest with his foot. Warm liquid rushed in on a gush. He managed one deep breath and grabbed Hailey's hand before the water was over their heads.

They swam up—at least he hoped it was up. The slough was deeper than he'd thought, and so damn cloudy from silt and debris he couldn't see two inches in front of his face. Just when he was sure they were going the wrong way, they broke the surface.

He gasped in a breath as Hailey let go of his hand and moved toward the shore. And that's when he felt something brush his leg.

"Get out of the water!" Hailey yelled.

But it was already too late. Whatever had touched his leg clamped on tight and pulled.

"Shane!"

He was under the water before the pain in his lower left leg even registered. But when it did—shot up his leg like a firestorm—and he realized what had a hold of him, he let instinct rule. He kicked with his free leg, and when that didn't do shit to free him, he aimed the gun still in his hand at the SOB he couldn't see. Then said one quick prayer he wasn't about to shoot his own foot off and fired.

His lungs burned. He felt pressure and release on his leg. The instant he was free he swam with everything he had left as he fought the panic rising in his chest.

Hailey was running back into the water as he reached the shore. "Shane!"

Water splashed around him as she skidded to a halt. "Oh God, Shane." She wrapped her arms under his and pulled him far enough onto the shore so they were out of reach of any lazy gators hiding in the tall reeds. A feeding frenzy erupted in the center of the slough, splashing and snapping and the sounds of jaws clamping shut tight.

He fell back against the ground and worked to get air into his blazing lungs. Hailey tore the denim on his left leg up to his knee. "You're bleeding."

He still had a death grip on his gun, and he lifted his head just enough to get a good look at the damage. His shoe was gone. His jeans were ripped and frayed. Crimson blood ran down his calf all the way to his toes, which he couldn't feel. But at least they were still there.

Okay, no way that shit just happened.

Hailey whipped off the light sweater she'd changed into on the plane and dabbed at his leg until they both saw the four evenly spaced puncture wounds where the fucker's teeth had sunk in.

"Oh, my God," she whispered. Then louder, "Okay. The skin's not torn badly. That's good. It's not that bad. You're okay. See? You're okay," she said again as if saying it enough would help convince her of that fact.

His leg hurt like a son of a bitch, but to keep from freaking out about the fact he'd just been attacked by a frickin' gator, he pushed the pain aside and focused on her. Wet hair hung around her face. Water slid down her cheek to drip over her shoulders and the white cami she'd worn beneath her sweater. A small cut oozed blood where she'd cracked her head against the glass of the car.

He gripped her hand to stop her frantic search for more wounds. Then held on tight until she looked up at him. "Hailey. I'm fine. Stop."

Fear reflected deeply in her blue eyes. Fear for him, he realized.

"I'm okay," he said again.

She stared at him just long enough to make his heart rate kick up, and not from nearly being the evening snack.

"Jesus, Shane." Her eyes slid closed.

Oh, man, but he really loved how she said his name. Wanted to hear her say it again. In his bed. Naked beneath him. Over and over again.

"I never liked those shoes much anyway."

Her eyes popped open, and she stared at him like he'd lost his ever-lovin' mind. Then she laughed. A nervous, relieved sound that vibrated through every cell in his body.

Addendum. He wanted her *screaming* his name.

He was seriously screwed if after very nearly being eaten alive, all he could think about was how sexy she looked and how badly he wanted to touch her.

To keep from doing just that, he refocused on what had just happened. "Hailey, somebody shot—"

"Do you see it?" They both froze at the voice yelling from across the slough.

Hailey hit him in the chest with the full force of her weight before he saw her move. One minute he was sitting on the ground, the next they were rolling down a slight embankment into tall reeds and bushes that scraped against this legs and arms.

He hit the dirt with a thud. Rocks and twigs stabbed into his back and shoulders. Hailey landed flat on top of him, then whispered, "Shh" in his ear.

He didn't dare move. One, because he could barely think, let alone breathe, and two, because as soon as his head stopped spinning he had a sudden flash of being very nearly eaten alive moments before and realized he had no idea what else was hiding in these reeds besides them.

He'd lost his gun as they'd rolled, not that it would be much use now after being thoroughly waterlogged. While a Glock could be fired underwater, a whole host of bad things could have happened, like the damn thing exploding in his hand or the blast leaving him deaf as a door since underwater firings were four times louder than those on land. He'd seriously lucked out, but he wasn't testing fate one more time. As it was, his ears were slightly ringing, making it hard to hear the voices yelling around them, but one thing got through: there were two people out there looking for them, most likely the same ones who'd shot out their tires and now hoped he and Hailey were gator bait.

"I don't see anything," one voice yelled from across the slough. Male. Deep. "It went in here, didn't it?"

"Yeah," the other answered. This one female. "Look. The gators have something down there."

Shane thought he heard water splashing but couldn't be sure. But when he looked up, he couldn't have cared less. Hailey was frozen above him, head tipped slightly to the side so she could hear better, eyes intent on peering through the reeds. She was beautiful, even soaking wet and dripping things he didn't want to think about. Calm and collected. Thinking when his brain seemed to be shorting out.

His blood warmed as he stared up at her, and suddenly he was keenly aware of the way she was lying full on top of him, locked tight from knee to shoulder. How full and lush her breasts were, pushing into his chest with just the right pressure. How flat her stomach was, how her hips seemed the perfect size to fit with his. And every time she breathed, his pulse quickened, his skin tingled and blood shot straight to his groin.

*Do you really think she needs you to save her? Look at her.*

Okay, he'd obviously lost some serious blood in that gator attack. That or he was in shock. Because no matter what he did, he couldn't get his brain to focus on anything besides her. Not the pain in his leg or the two dipshits out in the brush searching for them or the fact he was growing hard beneath her and really should think about something else to kill his erection before she realized what was happening and freaked a little herself.

Footsteps came closer to their hiding place. Hailey sucked in a breath and held it. He tried like hell not to move, even though—shit, she had to feel that thing now.

"What do you think you're doing?" the male voice asked.

"I thought I heard something."

Silence.

Against him, Hailey's heartbeat picked up and pounded like wildfire in her chest.

He looked to the side without moving his head, and saw female boots not five feet from where they lay hidden. Screw the whole gun-possibly-exploding-in-your-hand scenario. He'd give his left nut for his Glock right now.

"Well?" the man asked.

"I don't know. Must have been gators. Or a snake."

Lovely. Snakes. If that didn't kill the mood, nothing did.

"There's no way she survived that crash. Those gators are going nuts over there."

The woman pivoted around and began walking away. "I told you not to shoot out the tires. If the bronze was in that car—"

"It wasn't," the man snapped. "Just relax."

"Relax? How do you expect me to relax? If she's dead we won't ever get that damn statue."

"I already have it."

"What?" the woman asked. "How?"

"Did you really think I was going to leave it there?"

Silence. Then, "Okay, but don't you think three dead Roarkes in the same month are going to draw suspicion?"

"Not for us." Irritation coated the man's words. "The fewer Roarkes around to get in our way, the better. Now quit stressing. As far as I'm concerned, the dumb bitch got what she deserved."

Shane's chest grew cold. Just that fast.

He grasped Hailey's arms and pushed. Startled, her gaze shot to his, and as if she could read his mind, her hand clamped over his mouth with stunning force and she locked her legs around his hips to keep him still. His blood was a roar in his head, his only thought the need to extract some long-awaited vengeance on the POS mere feet from them. But then he focused on her wide, cobalt blue eyes, and like an antidote to his rage, the pleading he saw there got through. Brought him down. Made him remember where he was and with whom.

She held on to him as the footsteps disappeared. An engine turned over somewhere in the trees, roared to life, then faded in the Everglades.

When nothing but the sounds of splashing water and cicadas chirping nearby met their ears, she finally pushed off him and moved back to sit on her feet. "Are you okay? Did I hurt you? How's your leg?"

He pushed up slowly, his emotions a tumble of things he didn't want to think about or remember or, shit, even acknowledge. "Fine. Who the hell was that?"

She recoiled at his harsh tone, but he didn't flinch. Dammit, this was why he shouldn't be here. The past and the present were intermixing for him.

"I'm not sure," she said.

He pushed aside his fucked-up emotions and focused on her. On the fact she'd gone still as stone when that woman had nearly been on top of them. And the fact right this minute she was staring straight into his eyes.

She was lying. In Wisconsin, anytime she'd evaded his questions she'd looked at him head-on, but when she'd finally told him the truth on the flight down here, she hadn't been able to make eye contact. Which meant one thing: she'd recognized one of those two voices. Or maybe both. And she wasn't about to tell him because she'd known he was ready to tear the guy's throat out with his bare hands.

She didn't trust him. Not to protect her. And that royally pissed him off.

"We can't go back to Graham's," she said. "I don't want him in the middle of this."

"And what if he's already in the middle of it?"

"He wasn't," she responded as if it were fact. "He cares less about RR than I do."

Shane wasn't so sure of that. And it was just a little too coincidental that they'd been ambushed right after leaving her uncle's place.

"Either way," she went on, "we need to get out of here so you can have that bite looked at."

"No hospitals." He refused to let those sexy blue eyes pull him under when she looked up. His brain was working now, and he wasn't about to get distracted again. Couldn't protect her? Like hell he couldn't. "An animal bite will get reported. Last thing we want is my name in the system because it'll lead CPD right back to you."

"Right. Yeah. I hadn't thought of that." She glanced down at her knees as if contemplating her options. "I think I know someone who can help us. It'll be a bit of a drive, though."

"How long?"

"An hour and a half?"

"I can make it."

She nodded, pulled her waterlogged cell from her pocket. "Damn. It's dead. Can you walk?"

"Gonna have to, aren't I?"

He ignored the regret in her eyes. Ignored the little stab in his chest when she looked at him like that or the way it made him wish he'd met her a year ago, before his world had turned to shit. "There's another house about a quarter mile away. We can get a ride there."

"Fine, let's go. I've had enough of the fucking Everglades to last me the rest of my life."

He pushed to his feet—one bare, one in a soaking wet Nike—and focused on the pain in his leg as he picked his way across the ground behind her. That, at least, was real. And just what he deserved. Not some fantasy he didn't have any right daydreaming about.

# CHAPTER TWELVE

He was working up a good case of ticked off. And she wasn't exactly sure why.

Though Shane's surly attitude irritated her to no end, Hailey cut the guy some slack. If she'd been bitten by an alligator, then pushed down a hill and pinned beneath someone while rocks and branches and bugs and other things she didn't want to think about stabbed into her back, she'd be in a pretty foul mood right now, too. Not to mention the fact he had no idea where they were heading, or that he had to be in a bit of pain.

They'd been driving south on Highway 1 for the last hour. Her uncle's backwater neighbors had been happy to help them out, no questions asked, as if alligator bites were a common occurrence to them. They'd given Shane a pair of flip-flops and some bandages, then driven them as far as Homestead so they could get another rental. She'd figured it'd be faster to drive, so she'd called Steve and left the plane on standby, then phoned Graham and told him what had happened. Though still in a daze from the news about Bryan, he'd assured her he was fine and that he knew how to defend himself, should anyone come poking around. That didn't exactly put Hailey at ease, but she'd learned long ago Graham did what he wanted when he wanted.

She flipped on the air conditioner as she drove down the Overseas Highway. Shane sat in the passenger seat, arms crossed over his chest, head back against the headrest, eyes closed. He hadn't said much since they'd climbed into the car, but that was fine with her. After everything that had happened today, she wasn't in the mood to chat, either.

Her mind spun as she thought about the male voice in the swamp. The same one she'd heard in the elevator just before the lights had gone out and she'd been given a black eye as a "warning" to step away from Roarke Resorts. There was no doubt in her mind the two voices were one and the same. Which meant someone was following her. But how?

She wiped her brow. It was muggy tonight. Darkness had already set in, and her headlights reflected off the road, making the pavement hard to see. When she realized the air conditioner wasn't working, she turned the knob to high and wiped her forehead again. Her hand was shaking when she set it back on the steering wheel.

Okay, that was weird.

Shane tilted his head sideways at her. "Are you trying to freeze me out now?"

She might have found the comment funny, but as she gripped the steering wheel and blinked several times, looked out at the water on both sides of the car and remembered what had happened back in that slough, she realized nothing about this was funny. "Um. No, I . . ."

His brow dropped as he took a good look at her. "What's wrong?"

She gave her head a swift shake. Tightened her fingers. "I'm not sure."

"Hailey." He sat up. "You're sweating."

"I know. I—"

It hit her then. A wave of nausea that rolled through her stomach like a hurricane on the gulf. "Oh . . . I don't feel so good."

"Pull over."

Somehow she did. And Shane was around the car in a flash, bad leg and all, helping her out of the driver seat and walking her to the passenger door.

"Jesus, you're cold. Do you feel like you're going to get sick?"

"I don't . . . know." She wrapped her arms around her stomach as he opened the door and helped her inside.

He looked up and down the road, while she worked simply on breathing and not losing her lunch. A few cars passed by, but traffic was relatively light this time of night. "How much farther?" he asked.

She took deep breaths, leaned back in her seat much the way he had earlier and closed her eyes. "Um, another half hour. Maybe. I don't know."

"Do you always get carsick?"

She shook her head. "Never."

She didn't hear him climb back in the car or the door close behind him, only registered the vehicle was moving. But she caught the curse that slipped from his mouth, just before another wave hit her gut and this time sent blinding pain right into her skull.

For a fleeting moment it registered that this wasn't car sickness. But before she could figure out what else it could be, she was too wrapped up in the pain to think of anything else.

Billy felt like he'd just competed in the Ironman. And the Tour de France. And the Boston Marathon, all rolled into one. Holy hell, did he have any fluids left in his body? Even his eyes were bone-dry.

The bathroom door opened, the light flipped off, and Nicole came skipping across the room, draped in some sheer nightie thing Billy didn't remember seeing her in before. She took one flying leap and bounced on the bed on her knees. "I'm starving. Aren't you hungry?"

Billy groaned from the mattress jostling his aching body. Four rounds? Five? He'd never thought it was possible to be completely limp from sex, but then he'd never met Nicole Roarke. Jesus, maybe she was a serial killer and this was her MO: screwing guys until they were so weak she could pick them up and toss their bodies to the sharks.

Considering she came from a family of bottom-feeders, that idea probably wasn't too out there.

That lovely thought got pushed out of his head as she leaned across his chest and reached for the phone on the bedside table. "I need protein. Scrambled eggs and bacon. What do you want?"

"Ice water," he croaked. "A great big pitcher. And ooh, cinnamon rolls." He lifted his head slightly from the pillow. "You think they have any of those in the kitchen this time of night?"

"They have everything. With cream cheese frosting?"

His stomach rumbled. A good sign he wasn't on death's doorstep after all. "Yeah. And a steak. A nice big juicy one."

She laughed and relayed his order into the phone, adding juice and toast and a big plate of pasta as she twirled her finger around his naked chest. When she hung up, she laid her palms on his chest, looking up at him with big, dark-as-night eyes that weren't nearly as satisfied as he'd thought earlier.

If he hadn't known this girl was Hailey's sister, he'd never have picked her out. The two looked nothing alike. Unless you counted that mischievous glint in both their eyes.

"So, Billy," she said all innocent. "Not that this hasn't been fun, but don't you think it's about time you tell me what's really going on here?"

He probably should have been surprised by the question, but over the past few hours, he'd discovered Nicole Roarke wasn't at all what he'd expected. Though she'd done a good job at keeping him busy with her hands and mouth, even before this little Q&A he'd had a feeling she was working hard to keep him distracted. And not just because she had a competitive streak where her sister was concerned.

His eyes narrowed on the mole that was a little too perfect just under her left eye. "What do you mean?"

One manicured index finger circled his right nipple. "You're not sleeping with my sister."

"How do you know?"

That mischievous glint flared. "My sister couldn't handle you."

He barked out a laugh and ran his hands down her barely there top. "So confident."

"I am. I also know my sister. And she's not the kind of woman to have a fling with just any guy. Especially not with a guy who goes around banging women he meets at a beach bar."

"Is that what you are? A girl who hangs out at beach bars waiting for guys to bang you?"

"Not unless they have something I want."

That got his attention. His hand stopped on the small of her back as he peered down at her. She blinked twice, looking completely innocent. But as he'd learned the last few hours, Nicole Roarke was anything but childlike. "I think my head's a little fuzzy from the last few hours. Just what are we talking about here?"

She eased back to sit cross-legged next to him on the bed. "My sister's not so dumb. And neither am I. I know she sent you here to get my bronze. Interesting tactic, by the way. I wouldn't have guessed she'd be so underhanded as to pay a guy to seduce it out from under me."

He pushed up slowly and leaned back against the headboard. "What makes you think she paid me?"

"Why else would you be here?"

Why else? Good question. He hadn't planned to sleep with her. Didn't really think she'd go that far, but as soon as they'd gotten back to her suite, he'd forgotten what he'd come for and instead focused on her. A couple drinks on her terrace had turned into lunch, which had quickly turned into a whole lot more. She was smart. And quick on the uptake. And he'd enjoyed talking with her and watching her eat. She had the sexiest way of chewing, and when she smiled at him, his insides turned to Jell-O.

He'd made up some lame excuse about Hailey texting him and canceling their rendezvous, and though he hadn't expected Nicole to buy the lie, she had. When she'd taken a bathroom break after their meal, he'd given the suite a thorough check and found no bronze. He should have left then—before she'd come out—but he hadn't been able to get his feet to the door in time. And when she'd walked back toward him, wearing nothing but a sheer black robe that had done zip to hide her curves underneath, he'd forgotten everything but his own name.

"I'm not sure," he said, "but just so you know, she didn't pay me." His eyes narrowed on her perfect face. "Why did you sleep with me if you knew what I was after?"

She shrugged, wrapped her arms around her updrawn knees and fingered her pink-polished toes. "Why wouldn't I? It's what you expected, isn't it?"

He couldn't quite gauge her mood, but she didn't seem angry. If anything, she looked just the slightest bit . . . hurt.

Why the hell would she be hurt? Unless—

His brain skipped back over the last few hours. And a couple of things they'd done he'd have thought a girl like her would have already been a pro at. In retrospect, though, it was actually more like he'd had to *teach* her what a guy liked. And how.

A strange feeling settled over him. "Niki, you've done this before, right?"

"What?" she asked without looking up. "Sex? Of course."

"No," he said cautiously. "This afternoon-pick-up-a-guy-in-a-beach-bar thing."

She didn't answer, just picked at her toenail polish.

"Niki." He reached out and lifted her chin with his index finger. And saw, without her even uttering a sound, her answer.

Exasperation settled in her eyes. "Oh, don't look so shocked. I know I have a reputation. But I happen to be very particular about who I sleep with."

"How particular? How many times have you done this?"

She pursed her lips and looked up at the ceiling.

"Nicole, answer the damn question."

"The beach bar thing? Never."

"No, the sex thing in general. How many guys have you slept with?"

"That's none of your damn business."

"Right now it's all about my business."

She huffed. "Fine. One. Well, two now."

"Oh, shit." His stomach dropped.

She climbed quickly off the bed and pointed at him. "That's not the point."

He rose, forgetting the ache in his bones. "Why the hell did you sleep with me then?" Too late he realized he was naked and quickly grabbed the sheet from the bed to wrap around his hips. Good God, could he screw this up any more than he already had? He didn't have the statue, and now he'd slept with Hailey's virgin sister.

"Oh, don't go getting all moral on me. I was attracted to you, you were attracted to me. You didn't have any problem fucking me before. So don't go looking all shocked now."

He cringed. "Don't say it like that. And before I didn't know you were a virgin!"

"I wasn't a virgin."

"Okay, pretty damn close to a virgin."

When she didn't respond, only crossed her arms over her chest and glared at a spot on the carpet in front of him, he knew he was close to the truth. And staring at her with the rumpled bed between them, he realized why she'd looked so damn innocent before. Because she was.

*Holy shit.*

He threw his arm out to the side. "Why do you go gallivanting around the globe like some two-bit hussy if you're really not?"

She leveled him with a look that could have turned flesh to stone. "That's none of your business, either. Now do you want my sculpture or not?"

He could barely follow her words. Now she was back on the stupid bronze?

"The Last Seduction, Billy," she said again. "I know Hailey sent you here to get it. I want to know what it's worth to her. And to you."

He stared at her. And made a decision without even thinking. "It's not worth anything to me."

"Then why are you helping her?"

"Because she asked me. And because we're friends."

"That's it?"

"Yeah, that's it. There's nothing going on between us. She doesn't even know I'm here."

She studied him a long beat, then asked, "Then what did she ask you to do?"

"She wanted me to see if the bronze was at your place."

"How would you do that? It's not like . . ." Understanding dawned in her eyes. His brother, the thief. Certain skills ran in the family. "Oh. I see. So you broke into my place."

He shook his head. And not for the first time, a shiver of guilt over something he'd done slinked through him. "I came here instead."

"Why?"

This time it was his turn to shrug. "I guess I wanted to see if you were like the tabloids say you are."

"And you found out I am."

"I found out you're not at all."

They stared at each other. Neither said anything. And in the silence he sensed she was trying to decide if he was being honest or completely full of shit.

"I don't have it anymore," she finally said.

"Where is it?"

She shrugged, purposely evading his question, but added, "I have an idea who has it."

His eyes narrowed. "What do you want, Nicole?"

That mischievous glint returned to her dark eyes. "I want in on the action."

He'd have been less surprised if she'd hauled off and sucker punched him in the gut. "Why?"

"Let's just say I have a score to settle with someone who underestimated me."

"Hailey won't go along with this."

"Hailey," she said with just a hint of disgust, "doesn't have a choice. If she wants to know what's on the bottom of my bronze, she'll go along with it." When he only stared at her, she added, "Don't believe me? Call her and find out."

If he were smart, he'd run long and hard in the opposite direction. Instead, he saw himself wavering. Partly because— even after their marathon sex session—he was still wildly attracted to her. And partly because he owed her for what he'd just done.

And wasn't that just a kick in the pants? All of a sudden he'd developed a conscience.

A knock sounded at the door. Nicole flicked him a look just before turning. "Make up your mind, Billy. But do it quick. If Hailey's not interested, I'll move on to the next person on my list. And I'm already bored with this conversation."

Shane drove ninety down Highway 1 toward Crawl Key. Hailey was on her side, facing away from him, head back, eyes closed tightly, just trying to breathe. He'd known as soon as he'd taken one good look at her when she'd slowed the car that something was wrong.

"Hold on," he said. "We're almost there." He reached over and placed a hand on her arm to reassure her. Her skin was cold and clammy. When she didn't respond, he moved his hand around to her shoulder, then chest, only to realize her heart rate was slow and irregular.

"Hailey? Are you with me?"

Nothing.

"Shit."

He whipped the car into the Monroe County Medical Examiner's Office, where she'd planned to take him to get his leg patched up by a friend of hers, and killed the engine. A green Acura and a beat-up Dodge pickup were the only other two vehicles in the parking lot.

Hailey didn't move when he jerked the passenger door open or when he lifted her into his arms. And when her head fell against his chest like dead weight, his anxiety went through the roof.

The door to the building pulled open just as he reached it, and a woman Shane faintly noticed had dark hair said, "Oh . . . shit. What happened?"

The friend. Allie-something. Hailey had mentioned her in the car before she'd gotten sick. "I don't know." The door snapped shut behind him as he moved Hailey quickly into the lobby. "She was fine forty minutes ago."

Allie placed a hand on Hailey's forehead. She turned quickly. "Dad!"

A gray-haired man who had to be James Hargrove, the Monroe County ME, pushed open the door at the end of the room. He was wiping his hands with a towel when he stepped into the room. "What's all the ruckus abo—"

His words died when he saw Hailey in Shane's arms. "What happened?"

"I don't know. She was driving. Started complaining about not being able to see. Then said she didn't feel well."

James pulled her eyelids open. "Has she been sick?"

"No. I thought she was just carsick. She was sweating. Then her hands were like ice and her heart felt slow."

James felt for a heartbeat. And his expression changed from concerned to frantic in an instant. "Bring her in back quickly. Allie?"

"I'm here," Allie said from behind Shane as they all headed down a dim hallway.

"Grab the bag from my office."

James led them into a room Shane knew instinctively was a morgue. He laid Hailey on the metal table James directed him to. Her head lolled to the side, her shoes clanked against the cold steel. She moaned and tried to roll to her side.

Allie came rushing back in with the bag. "I've got it. Here."

"Hold still, Hailey." James ripped open Hailey's dirty T-shirt, revealing her pale skin and red bra. He took the stethoscope Allie handed him and listened to her heart. "What did she last eat?"

"Ah." Why wasn't she talking? Shane ran a hand through

his hair. "A sandwich on the plane. But that was five hours ago."

"Nothing since? Did you eat the same thing?"

"No. And yeah. Turkey. Both of us. What's wrong with her?"

"What else?" James asked with a clip. "Anything to drink?"

Hailey's head moved on the table. One of her legs came up. She groaned.

"Water. A diet soda, I think. I'm not quite sure."

"When?"

Crap, how long ago had that been? "At least three to four hours."

"Her heart rate's dangerously low." James dropped the stethoscope and turned. "I need ten cc's of atropine. Right now."

Allie's face paled, but she turned away and did what her father asked without question, like she'd assisted him before. James went quickly to a cabinet on the wall and rummaged around until he found something he wanted, then hustled back to Hailey's side. She moaned, her face taking on a strange color as she tried to move. James's hand on her arm stopped her from twisting to her side.

"What's going on?" Shane asked. "What's wrong with her?"

"I don't know. But I think she's having an allergic reaction to something. You sure she didn't have anything else to eat or drink?" James asked, readying a syringe after Allie handed him the vial.

"Yeah. Nothing. Nothing but . . ." He looked up sharply. "Tea. She drank a whole glass of sweet tea when we were at her uncle's place in the Everglades."

Both their heads came up.

"Graham's house?" Allie asked.

Shane nodded.

James and Allie exchanged glances. Then James stuck the needle in Hailey's arm, depressed the syringe and helped Hailey roll to her side. "Get me that pan," he said to Shane.

"Allie, I want the charcoal pills from my bag, and then brew some strong tea. She's gonna get sick before this is over."

The two moved like a blur. Shane did what James told him, held Hailey's hair back when she got sick and kept her lying down when she tried to get up. But every time she emptied her stomach or James gave her another injection of atropine to bring her heart rate back to normal, Shane's own stomach and chest reacted with a jolt.

It wasn't until well over an hour later, when James had forced her to drink the tea and take the charcoal pills, that the sickness finally passed and things quieted down.

Allie had brought in a pillow and a couple of blankets and was sitting at Hailey's side, talking softly. The room smelled like herbal tea and industrial cleaners.

"Let me take a look at that leg."

Shane tore his gaze from where he'd been watching Hailey. The older man was only about five-ten, built lean but muscular, and according to Hailey, the best damn ME in the state of Florida. Originally, Shane hadn't been too keen on getting his leg patched up in a morgue, but after he'd seen the way James worked, he was damn thankful this one had been here tonight.

"It's fine." Shane went back to looking at Hailey.

James let out a long sigh. "Son, you're gonna be no help to her if your leg falls off from infection. Sit down over here and let me have a look."

It was hard to argue with rationale like that. Making sure he still had a good view of Hailey, Shane sat in a plastic chair, slid off his borrowed flip-flops and lifted his leg so James could take a look.

"Puncture wounds aren't deep," James said as he examined Shane's leg. "I don't even think you need stitches. You got lucky. Antibiotics aren't generally given with animal bites if stitches aren't needed, but considering this happened, what, three hours ago?"

"Yeah. Maybe closer to four."

James nodded. "That and the fact it hasn't been cleaned yet, I'm going to give you a course just to be safe."

As he went to work cleaning and dressing Shane's leg, Shane lifted his chin but made sure to keep his voice low. "Is she going to be okay?"

James glanced over his shoulder where the girls were still quietly talking. "Yeah. Should be fine after a good night's sleep. We got it all out of her system."

"What was it?"

James stuck the last bandage in place and gently placed Shane's foot on the ground. "I don't know for sure, but my guess is some kind of poison in liquid form. This wasn't just food poisoning, not the way her heart reacted. Did you drink any of that tea when you were at her uncle's place?"

"No. Too sweet. I spit it out."

James handed him the first course of antibiotics and a bottle of water, then sat in the chair to Shane's left. "Take this one now. Dosage instructions for the rest are here. You have to take the whole course for the antibiotic to work." He handed him a box of pills. "I'm giving you some for Hailey, too, but I don't want her to start taking them until tomorrow when her stomach's back to normal. That cut on her arm should have had stitches. It's looking a little red. I don't want it getting infected."

Shane nodded and downed the pill.

James looked back at Hailey. "I bet the sugar in the tea masked any bitter taste."

"You think her uncle poisoned her?"

James turned his way, and his voice lowered so much Shane could barely hear what the older man said. "Hailey asked me to look into her father's autopsy report. Did she mention it to you?"

"Briefly."

James nodded. "I was able to get a copy. Garrett Roarke officially died of a heart attack. I called his physician. Six weeks ago Garrett went in complaining of chest pains. He was diagnosed with congestive heart failure. A few weeks later he's dead. No one thought much of it because of the earlier diagnosis and the family history. But the kicker? When I spoke with his physician, he told me he'd prescribed an ACE inhibitor, which expands blood vessels and decreases resistance."

"Why is that bad?" Shane asked.

"It's not," James clarified. "Actually, it's pretty routine. Only in Garrett's case, his autopsy showed elevated levels of cardiac glycosides. Or the drug digoxin. Better known as digitalis."

Shane's brow lowered. "I've heard of that before. Isn't that a poison?"

"Yes. But it's also commonly used in heart-failure patients to increase the pumping action of the heart. Only in Garrett's case it was never prescribed."

Shane studied James's weathered face. "So you're telling me he was taking a heart medication that wasn't prescribed to him. Why would he do that?"

"I'm not so sure he knew he was taking it," James said softly. "In fact, I'm not entirely sure his original diagnosis was completely accurate." At Shane's wrinkled brow, James said, "It's not as hard as one would think to mimic a heart attack, Detective. You slip a relatively healthy man a little digoxin, or oleander or lily of the valley and wait for it to take effect. He's going to feel like something's wrong. He goes to his doctor, has a full workup. They won't be testing for any drugs, but looking at his heart. They give him a diagnosis, put him on medications. Now he's got a history. Someone slips him a little more digoxin over the next few weeks, not enough to cause a problem but to keep his symptoms going. Then bam, a high enough dose to trigger a heart attack. Local ME doesn't suspect anything because, hey, guy's already got a history, and after all, it runs in his family. Toxicology report comes back showing elevated levels of digoxin, no big deal. It's a heart-failure drug, after all. Only in this case, no one asked what he'd actually been prescribed."

Shane looked over at Hailey as a weird sort of under-standing dawned. He thought back to being in Graham's house and how worried she was that the news of his son's death would be bad on the older man's heart.

She'd said she wasn't so sure her father's death was natural after all. If what James had just told him was true, her father really had been murdered. And every person in her family who had any ties to Roarke Resorts—Graham included—was a suspect.

"Can you prove it?"

James sighed. "Wish I could. But according to Hailey, Garrett's already been cremated."

*Damn.*

"Do you think she was given digoxin?"

James shook his head. "I'm not sure. Oleander, lily of the valley, digitalis, they all work the same, though. Any one of them could have been the culprit here. But when you said you'd been out to see Graham Roarke . . . that's when I had a feeling something wasn't right. You know he's a hermit, that he lives out in the boondocks. Man's also a horticulturist by hobby. He'd know which plants are poisonous and which aren't."

Yeah, of course he would. The question was, why Hailey? And why now? And why the heck would her uncle have a batch of poison ready and waiting in his fridge if he hadn't known Hailey was coming to see him?

"I'm not sure about your connection to Hailey," James said as he shifted around and reached for something from his pocket, "but my gut's telling me you're someone Hailey can trust, and right now she needs that." He pulled out a key, handed it to Shane. "I have a condo here in Marathon. It's not being used and I'd like you two to have it for the night. Hailey needs a chance to recharge her batteries. The place isn't fancy, but it's clean and no one will bother you."

"We'll be—"

"No arguing." James held up his hand. "I have to head

back to Key West, and as much as I love Hailey, I don't want Allie wrapped up in this. That might be selfish—"

"It's not," Shane said, taking the key. Hailey trusted this man, and every instinct inside Shane said he'd be smart to trust him, too. At least for tonight.

James nodded slowly. "You know, when Hailey called and told me who she was bringing down here, I was skeptical. Especially considering everything that's been all over the news about her up there in Chicago. But you're all right, Maxwell."

It was odd for Shane to be flattered, but he was. James Hargrove was a man Shane didn't mind being complimented by.

James looked over to where Allie was still quietly talking to Hailey. "My daughter the cop won't be so thrilled with that decision. Those two are thick as thieves."

"She'll get over it," he said, watching Hailey and feeling an odd sort of tenderness in his chest. "I'm not going to let anything happen to that thief."

A slow smile spread across James's face as he pushed to stand. "Good to hear. She needs someone watching out for her, whether she thinks so or not."

"One question," Shane asked when James reached for his bag from the floor.

"Yes?"

"How does a coroner manage to have so many medical supplies on hand?"

"He volunteers," Allie said from across the room.

At Shane's raised brow, James lifted his bag slightly. "It's something I've done for a number of years. I help out at a low-income clinic, make house calls for some of the elderly down here who can't make it to their regular appointments. I don't mind working on the dead, just so long as I get to practice on the living now and then." He winked at Shane. "You're about Matt's height and size, one of the guys on staff here. He usually leaves some extra clothes in his locker. Let me go see what I can find."

*Practice on the living.*

Shane watched James walk away, then looked over at Hailey, her blonde hair spilling over the pillow Allie had brought for her, her eyes sliding closed as she listened to her friend talk. In this case, James hadn't just practiced. He'd saved a life.

A life Shane was even more resolute about saving himself.

# CHAPTER THIRTEEN

Eleanor turned off the engine of her Mercedes and glowered toward the house. Why Graham insisted on living like a backwater redneck when he had millions in the bank, she'd never understand.

She pushed the door open, then frowned as she slid her Christian Lacroix pumps onto the gravel drive thick with weeds. Morning dew coated the wisps of grass and flowers she didn't have any clue how to name and couldn't care less about. Graham, of course, would know each and every bloody thorn on the property.

She stumbled twice on the uneven rocks and was nearly ready to turn around and head back to civilization when she heard a voice from the shadows of the front porch that stopped her cold.

"Been a while since you've been all the way out here."

Her pulse jumped, even though she'd prepared herself. It *had* been a long time. An even longer time since she'd been alone with her brother-in-law.

She lifted her chin. "Hello, Graham."

He didn't rise from the red metal chair, only eyed her over his mug of coffee. Or whiskey. Or whatever it was he drank at nine A.M. these days. "Eleanor."

There'd been a time he'd called her Ellie. But that had been before. When she'd been young. And not nearly as smart as she was now.

Ignoring the memories, she headed up the three wooden steps to stand before him. "We need to talk."

"Figured you'd come out here. Also figured there's nothin'

talking can do to solve any of this." He looked down into his mug. "Won't bring back my boy. Definitely won't bring back your husband."

She sensed his deep-seated regret, and was almost suckered in before she remembered whom she was talking to. "I'm sorry for your loss."

"Are you?" he asked with narrowed eyes.

"Yes. I came to tell you Madeline's scheduled the funeral for Friday."

"Friday. Well, that's not a surprise, now is it? But that's not the real reason you're here."

Her stomach lurched, but she worked to look calm. He may appear to be a country bumpkin, but Graham was sharp as a spear. And just as dangerous. She'd learned that long ago.

She chose her words carefully. "We have a deal, and I expect you to live up to it, no matter what's happened."

He set his cup on the aged wicker table to his left with a loud clank and pushed his lanky frame from the chair. Even at sixty-four, worn and wrinkled and weathered from his years of fun in the sun, he still intimidated her as much as he had when he'd been wild and reckless and in his prime in his thirties. Maybe more, because he was the only person left who knew the secret that could ruin her. "My son is dead, Eleanor."

"I didn't kill him."

"Who did?" When she didn't answer, his slate gray eyes grew cold. "You and I both know Hailey didn't kill Bryan. That girl could no more murder someone than . . ."

"You?"

His eyes flashed, and that strong, square jaw flexed, just as it had back then. "Yeah. Me." He tipped his head to the side. "But then, you know all about that, don't you?"

Silence fell like heavy smoke between them.

Though her heart was racing and she sensed her blood pressure inching up, she broke the stare-down by walking across the porch and leaning one hip against the railing as if she didn't have a care in the world. "If Hailey had stayed in Chicago, she wouldn't be involved now. The police there would have figured out she didn't have anything to do with Bryan's death."

"You say that like you know it for a fact."

She pursed her lips. She'd underestimated Hailey one too many times, and she wasn't about to do so again. She leveled Graham with a look. "If she comes here looking for your bronze—"

"She already did," he said smugly. "I gave it to her yesterday."

Her eyes widened, and she eased away from the railing. "You . . . what did you tell her?"

"Nothing she didn't already know. But I was tempted. Oh, was I tempted, Eleanor. Especially after she informed me of Bryan's death before you or my dear daughter-in-law could find the time to bother."

Betrayal welled in her chest, but she tamped it down and remembered the only way to keep everything in line was to remain calm. This would not blow up in her face. "You're difficult to get hold of out here."

"Not that difficult. You're here now, aren't you?"

She bit the inside of her lip. Arguing with him had never been productive. "You realize all you did was send her on a wild-goose chase, don't you? This little treasure hunt of Garrett's won't pan out. The company's lawyers are already looking into a glitch in the will should those stupid statues even be found. It's only a matter of time before it's overturned."

"But you know they won't all be found, don't you?" he asked smugly. "Tell me, Eleanor, did you send those morons to run her off the road? Jesus, you could have killed her."

Run her off the road? What was he . . . ?

When he only stared at her, she drew in a breath. In the end she didn't really care. "I don't know what you're rambling about. You're getting as senile as your brother. But no, all the sculptures won't be found. Hailey will not get this company. And you'd be wise to talk her into turning herself in if you see her again. She's only making more trouble by running."

"Such the devoted mother. Tell me, Eleanor, who's she making more trouble for, her or you?"

She ignored the taunt. "I want your word you won't say anything."

"I gave you my word once before."

"Before was a long time ago."

He pursed his lips in disgust. "My word's the same now as it was then. That hasn't changed. You know that more than anyone."

That tightness returned to her chest. There'd been a time when she'd actually thought she'd loved him. What a fool she'd been. "I'm not the only one who stands to lose here, Graham. Remember that."

His eyes softened. Just a touch. "Why don't you just tell her the truth? Your father's dead. Your husband's dead. No one can control you anymore. No one can hurt you. End this game now."

"Do you think that's what this is?" she asked in shock. "A game?"

"I know that's what it is to you, Eleanor. That's all Garrett ever was. All I was. You're not happy unless you're fighting for something you don't really want. And when you get it, you throw it away. Look where you've ended up. Look where all three of us ended up."

A knot formed in her stomach. Graham didn't know what he was talking about. All she'd ever wanted was for her husband to want her back. Everything she'd done had been with that one goal in mind. Everything that had happened from the first stemmed from the fact Garrett had wanted something else.

No, this wasn't a game. This was her life. And it was all she had left. She wasn't about to let Hailey ruin it for her now.

She turned before he could stop her, hardened her voice before it could break and headed back to her Mercedes.

"Ten o'clock, Friday. It'll look bad if you're not there, so do try to be on time." She pulled the car door open and shot him a withering look just before climbing inside. "And find a tie. It's the least you can do for your only child."

He hadn't slept. Not that he'd expected to.

Shane sat on the side of the bed in James Hargrove's small Marathon condo and watched Hailey, asleep on her back, her head tipped to the side, one delicate hand up by her face. Lying there like that, her golden blonde hair spilling over the pillow, her dark lashes forming spiky crescent shapes on her creamy skin, she looked more like Cinderella than the hard-as-nails woman he knew could kick him into the next county if she wanted to.

She'd pushed off the sheet sometime in the night, and thanks to the T-shirt now twisted around her belly, he knew her red lace panties matched the bra he'd seen yesterday in the morgue. Red that was going to haunt him the next time he closed his eyes.

Since Hailey had been half out of it with exhaustion when they'd arrived at the apartment last night, he'd tucked her into the master bed, then settled on the couch. Several times he'd gotten up in the middle of the night to make sure she was breathing, and each time he'd come into the room to check on her and she'd made those sexy little mewing sounds in her sleep, a little bit of his self-control slipped away.

Probably shouldn't have driven up to Lake Geneva yesterday morning, he thought as he watched her. Definitely shouldn't have gotten on that plane. Absolutely, *positively* shouldn't be drooling over her in her underwear right now like a peeping-frickin'-Tom. Especially after everything she'd been through yesterday. But hell if he'd change any of it if he could.

He waved the takeout coffee under her nose, the one he'd picked up this morning when he'd gone out to get a new cell and call Tony. Watched as her eyelids fluttered. Her chest rose and fell with her shallow breathing and her lilac scent wrapped around him like a gentle caress. "Coffee time. Wake up, Sleeping Beauty."

She stirred. Grunted and waved a hand through the air. Then flipped to her side away from him. And try as he might, his eyes ventured down. To skimpy red lace that didn't cover nearly enough of one gorgeous ass. What was left of his gray matter turned to gelatin, and he grew hard. Just that fast.

He jostled her shoulder. "Wake up, Hailey. I brought you a present."

It was like rousing the dead. When she finally rolled back after several repeated attempts and pried one eyelid open to peer at him, it was all he could do not to laugh. Her hair now stuck out at odd angles from her thrashing about, and disorientation twisted her features. Her one open eye slid from his face down to the coffee. Then she groaned and rolled away again. "No more coffee. I had enough last night to last me a year."

"James said the caffeine was good for your heart. And considering what you went through yesterday, a little more won't hurt. Sit up, now."

She finally acquiesced only because he wouldn't let her fall back to sleep. Slowly, she reached for the paper cup and took two big sips. "Stop looking at me like that. It's bad enough you watched me puke my guts out yesterday. I don't need you studying me like a science experiment."

"You didn't go on a bender, Hailey. You were poisoned. Big difference." When she rolled her eyes, he touched her arm to get her attention. "You scared the hell out of me last night."

Her cheeks turned the slightest shade of pink before she glanced back down at her hands. And oh, man. She looked so damn sexy in the morning. All groggy and rumpled. He had an insane urge to find out if this was how she always woke. Tomorrow morning. And the morning after that. And the one after that.

"I heard what you and James were discussing. It still doesn't make any sense to me."

"It makes a lot of sense. Your uncle wants you gone. If I wasn't so damn worried about you now, I'd head over there and beat the truth out of the SOB."

Her eyes shot to his. "Graham did not have anything to do with this."

"How do you figure? We ate the same damn things yesterday except for that tea, which he gave you. Minutes later some crackpot takes a shot at us as we're driving away. I'd say that's two for two that he wants you gone."

She shook her head in defiance. "I don't know what was in that tea, but he didn't purposely set out to poison me. He couldn't."

"How do you know?"

"I just do. As for those two, he didn't have anything to do with them, either. They had to be following me."

"How in the hell do you figure that?"

"Because one of them gave me this." She pointed at the fading bruise on her face. "I recognized his voice. The other one . . ."

Almost as if she'd said too much, her mouth snapped shut. And there it was. What he'd suspected back in the slough. She'd known her attacker and purposely kept quiet.

*She doesn't think you can save her.*

Considering the way he'd reacted yesterday, that was probably pretty accurate. She'd been the one to hold him down so he hadn't revealed their hiding place. She'd been the one to get them most of the way to Marathon. She'd been the one to deal with his bad mood until she'd fallen ill.

"Hailey—"

"No, Maxwell. It wasn't Graham. So get that out of your head. We're not dragging him into this. His son just died."

"How do you know he didn't kill Bryan?"

Her eyes narrowed. "That's a terrible thing to say. You saw him yesterday—"

"I saw a man who's a pretty good actor."

"—he was a wreck," she said louder, rolling over him. "For

all his flaws, Graham loved Bryan. He didn't have anything to do with what happened in Chicago. End of story."

They stared at each other, tension filling the air like a helium balloon, until she finally gave up and went back to her coffee. As she looked down, a blush crept up her face. She snagged the sheet to pull it back up around her waist.

So much for that gorgeous view. Not that he couldn't call it up in his mind now whenever he wanted. And so much for her thinking rationally where her family was concerned. Not that that was going to stop Shane from pushing Graham Roarke to the top of his suspect list.

Hoping to ease some of the strain between them, he lifted the bag at his feet and set it on her lap. "I got you something."

Cautiously, she set her coffee on the table next to him and peered into the bag. Then, though she fought it, a wry smile spread across her face as she lifted the blue cotton tee and read the words printed across the front:

*I worked with Tommy on the docks*
*'til the union went on strike.*
*It's been tough.*
*I'm just sayin'.*

"Where did you get this?" she asked.

"Store down the road. You'd be amazed what's open this early."

"Not really." She stared at the words, ran her fingers over the letters. "Tourist area. People are up early here to avoid the heat." Her smile widened. "I love Bon Jovi."

He had a feeling. "Guy's gone country."

Her brilliant blue eyes slid to his, then back to the shirt. "Travesty. I still have hope he'll see the light, though." She looked into the bag again. "What else is in here?"

He *wasn't* thrilled they liked the same kind of music—classic '80s rock. "I figured you needed something clean to wear. I got you a pair of those short pants, too. Had to guess on size, though."

"Capris?"

"Is that what they're called?"

She pulled out the khaki pants the girl at the store had helped him pick out and looked at the tag in the back. "Pretty close. Thank you."

Yeah, and his chest *wasn't* swelling from her gratitude, especially when he'd been such a jerk after that whole scene in the slough. "Look, Hailey, about what happened yesterday—"

"I really don't want to talk about my father yet. I need more coffee first." She folded the clothes neatly and put them back in the bag. "What did you tell Chen?"

He clenched his jaw at her change of subject. "What little we know."

"Did you tell him where we are?"

"Do I look stupid to you?" When she flicked a look at him, he blew out a breath and added gentler, "Much as I trust Tony, the less he knows right now, the better off he'll be. I don't want him lying for me." Not again, at least.

He thought about telling her Jim Hill with the DA's office had already figured out Shane and Hailey knew each other and that he was jumping to conclusions about Shane's involvement in her cousin's murder. Tony also had told him her father's dagger had somehow gotten lost in evidence. But Shane decided to keep both pieces of info to himself for now. Though her coloring was better, Hailey still looked tired. And he didn't want to overwhelm her if he didn't have to. Besides, he still felt the need to clear the air. "So about what happened at the slough."

She reached for her coffee again. "Don't worry about it. It was no big deal."

"Yeah, it was," he said. "It shouldn't have happened and I was a jerk about it. So . . . I apologize."

She sipped her coffee like a woman parched. "Seriously, Maxwell, no biggie. I'm used to moody men." She pulled her

T-shirt down, then pushed the covers off and rose quickly from the bed.

He was momentarily distracted as he watched her long, bare legs move across the bedroom. Then her comment registered. "I'm not moody."

"You're not quite as bad as Rafe, but you have your moments. I need to take a shower."

"Hailey, wait. I'm trying to say I'm sorry here."

"You did."

She made it halfway across the room before he realized they had to be talking about two very different things. "Hold on. I think maybe you misunderstood."

"No, I got it. Physical reaction, nothing more. I know you don't want to be attracted to me, so stop stressing." She flipped on the bathroom light and started to close the door.

And that's when he stopped thinking.

He was across the room in two strides, slapping a hand on the door and pushing it open before she could close him out. "Wait a minute. You think I'm not attracted to you?"

Her huff was part exasperation, part embarrassment. "Look, I already said it's no big deal, okay? I know you're only helping me as a friend and because of some loyalty to Lisa and Rafe. And though I was a little resistant to it at first, I do appreciate it, whatever your reasons. So let's not hash this to death, okay? You're a guy. You have reactions to . . . things. We've got other situations to deal with, like—"

Reactions? Oh, shit. She thought he was talking about his hard-on.

"Stop." He held up a hand. "In the first place, my sister has a ton of friends I wouldn't help cross the street, let alone fly around the country for. And in the second, the jury's still out on Sullivan, so don't for a second assume I'm here out of some misplaced loyalty to him. You are right about one thing, though, I am a guy, and I do have *reactions* to things, but if that's all this is, then you tell me how normal it is for a guy who's not attracted to a woman to get turned on in the middle of a swamp when he's just been shot at and pretty damn near eaten for lunch? And you tell me why my heart was in my throat the whole time we were at the morgue last night and you were lying on that table barely moving."

She stared at him. Blinked once. "How much caffeine did you have this morning?"

"Obviously not enough because you're still not following anything I'm saying."

Her eyes narrowed. "No, I heard you. You're attracted to me. So what? I know you don't like it." She jabbed a finger into his chest. "It's pissing you off right now, admit it!"

Before he thought better of it, he grabbed her by the elbows and pushed her back against the bathroom counter. "Does this feel like I'm pissed at you right now?"

"Maxwell—"

She didn't get a chance to finish her protest. His mouth was on hers before the second word was even out. Before his brain clicked in to the fact she'd been through the wringer last night and didn't deserve to be handled so roughly just because he had a temper.

A muffled grunt came out of her as she opened to obviously tear him a new one, but he cut her off by dipping inside for a lick before it was too late.

He tasted the coffee he'd brought her this morning and the sweetness he remembered from their kiss in his apartment. As he changed the angle, he wrapped his arms around her to lock hers tight against his chest so she couldn't haul off and punch him. And when he figured he'd made his point crystal clear, loosed his grasp and eased back a fraction of an inch.

She was breathing heavily as she stared up at him, but her eyes never left his. "Was that supposed to convince me of something?"

"Yeah," he said cautiously, watching for any sign he'd hurt her. He couldn't see it. What he saw was the same feisty woman he'd met in Key Biscayne. The same one who'd knocked him to the ground in her resort's gym in Lake Geneva. The same one who hadn't backed down from him on her plane when he'd gone to stop her from leaving.

Her ice blue eyes narrowed as her fingernails curled into his chest. "Word to the wise, Maxwell. You can't push me around like that and get away with it."

A lick of pain shot up his pecs—one that felt way too good. "Too bad you liked it so much."

"I don't like arrogant, controlling men," she said with eyes that told him just how much she did like him.

"And I don't like women telling me how I feel. You're not in my head so—"

He didn't get to finish his statement. Because her hands were suddenly in his hair and her mouth was slanting under his all over again. And then she was pulling him back into her and kissing him. Hard.

So much for not being in his head. Somewhere in his gray matter it registered that confrontation turned her on and that he should avoid it at all costs where she was concerned, but that was part of her charm. He liked that she wasn't afraid of him, that she didn't back down from a fight, that she knew what she wanted and went after it. And oh, man, as she pressed up against him now, all warm and soft and curvy in just the right places, he realized he didn't care about what he *should* do and instead focused on what he could.

Whatever measly brain cells were still firing shorted out with a pop that echoed through his entire body. She was like a drug, one he couldn't get enough of.

The phone in the living room rang. He ignored it, nipped her bottom lip between his teeth until she moaned, then stroked his tongue against hers while her fingers tightened in his hair and her body pressed full against his. Their kiss was a power struggle that he loved—her taking charge, his grappling for control—over and around until both of them were breathless and neither won.

His hands slid to her waist, and he lifted her easily to sit on the counter, then pushed his way between her legs to get closer still. She opened for him, licked into his mouth until his blood roared in his ears. Her kiss turned frantic, her fingers sliding down his shoulders, his arms, to the base of his T-shirt, up under to scrape along his skin. When her fingertips brushed the edge of the scar on his side, he pushed it from his mind and gently guided her hand somewhere else. And though something in the back of his head screamed, *Hello, moron. Do you really think this is a good idea?*, he ignored it. Ignored everything but the driving urge to get inside her. To let her take him wherever she wanted to go. For as long as she wanted to go there.

The phone shrilled again. He kissed her deeper. Shifted closer, tried to push away the sound. Heat from her body burned every inch of his skin, luring him in with the promise of ecstasy. Her fingers wove back into his hair, and she pulled just hard enough so he groaned from the shot of pain in his scalp. Then she arched against him, into him, until all his blood went due south.

*Brrrriiiiiing*

"Goddammit." He broke free of her mouth, stalked into the living room and jerked the phone off its cradle. "What?"

Silence. Then, "Who is this?"

"Don-fucking-Juan. What the hell do you want?"

More silence, and then a chuckle came through the line. One he'd heard before. "I want to talk to Hailey, Don. Is she there?"

*Billy.* Scowling, Shane looked across the room to where Hailey was standing in the doorway to the bathroom, breathing heavy and looking so damn sexy with her blonde hair all wild and her lips swollen from his mouth, he had only one instinct—to toss her over his shoulder and cart her off to bed like the caveman he'd become.

She crossed the floor quickly and took the phone from his hand before he could do just that. "Hello? Billy? You got my message. Yeah. I'm fine. What happened?"

Shane didn't follow her end of the conversation because his brain took that opportunity to jolt back into gear. As he watched her, all calm and collected as if the last few minutes hadn't completely thrown her for a loop like it had him, he realized she wasn't just any feel-good drug to him. She was the worst kind. Like meth. Overpowering. Blocking everything that mattered. One hit and he was a goner.

His heart rate kicked up. And he knew, right then, why he'd really come down here after all. It hadn't been just to protect her or to prove to himself that he could. He'd been talking himself up one side and down the other about being noble and doing the right thing, but that wasn't what this was about. This was about her. And him. And what he'd wanted to do to her from the first second he'd laid eyes on her.

"Okay, Billy, thanks." Hailey clicked off the phone and turned his way. "He's got news for me about Nicole's bronze. We're going to meet him in Miami in a couple of hours. I need to call Steve and have him fly down and pick us up. It'll be faster than driving." Her brow wrinkled as she looked at him. "What?"

He stared at her. Swallowed hard. Tried like hell to get his heart to stop hammering in his chest, but nothing worked. "Who was the guy in the swamp yesterday?"

"What?"

"Who was it?"

She pursed her lips. He could see she was contemplating not telling him. And damn if that didn't piss him off. "I'm not sure."

"But you have an idea."

She hesitated. Finally nodded. Let out a long breath. "I think it might have been Paul McIntosh. But I can't be sure."

"The guy with your father's company?"

She nodded.

Good God, this family was like the Mansons and the Hiltons and the Rockefellers all rolled into one. He ran a hand through his hair. "Okay, here's the deal. I wasn't ticked last night because I got a hard-on from being pinned beneath you. I was pissed because I knew you were holding out on me. If we're going to work together on this, you have to be honest with me. Even if you're not sure how I'm going to react."

"Maxwell, I—"

It irked him that even now she wouldn't use his first name when she used Billy's so damn easily. "Let's get one thing clear here. I do want you. I've wanted you since we met, and that doesn't piss me off, it jacks me up. But trust me when I say, all that's gonna do is cause problems between us, especially when you can't tell me the truth. So be careful what you ask and how you answer right now."

Her eyes widened. "Is that a threat?"

Was it? Yeah, he realized, it was. There was only so much of her he could take before he broke. Then took her down with him. And sexy power struggle aside, he knew she didn't want him like that.

"That's up to you." He refocused on what was really important. "If that guy is the same one from the elevator, it means he wasn't working for your cousin like you thought he was."

She bit her lip. Stared at him. Then finally said, "No. I already thought of that."

"Which means—"

"He wanted me out of the picture even before Bryan was killed." She hesitated, then added, "The woman was Lucy Walthers. She's a secretary at RR, the one who was with Bryan the night he was killed."

The one he'd interviewed. "So she set your cousin up."

"Possibly. But Paul isn't a family member, so even if he found the sixth statue on his own, the company wouldn't be awarded to him."

"Unless he's working for someone else."

"Yeah," she said quietly.

At her frown, he added, "The only way to figure out who that is, is to find the next bronze."

She stared at him. And the look of frustration in her cobalt eyes made his chest tingle. "I should go take that shower so we can leave."

He nodded slowly, even as a frisson of guilt he didn't want slithered in. "Hailey?"

She turned to look back from the bathroom doorway. "What?"

"Just so we're clear on one more thing. I'm hotheaded sometimes. It gets me into trouble. And I'm not always good about apologizing when I've been a real ass, so—"

"If you even try to apologize for what happened in the bathroom, Maxwell, I promise I'll go back to the Everglades and find your gun so I can shoot you with it myself."

The mischief sparkling in her eyes eased the pressure in his chest. "You wouldn't dare."

"Watch me."

He did. With eyes he couldn't tear from her if he tried. She disappeared into the bathroom with all the grace and regality of the heiress she was, head lifted high, blonde hair flying behind her, but the only thing he saw was that red lace now branded into his brain, peeking out from beneath the hem of her oversize tee, calling to him like a drug to an addict for one more hit.

# CHAPTER FOURTEEN

Nicole took her seat next to Billy in the grandstand of the Calder Race Course and fingered the ticket in her hand. "Why are we here again?" she asked, looking around the sparsely populated stands as she pulled her jacket tighter to her shoulders.

"Because it's fun. And because I'm pretty damn sure this is the one place no one will recognize you." He tugged the Miami Heat bucket cap lower to shield her face more, then looked down to the track with eyes that lit up like fireworks. "Here they come."

He rose and clapped like an idiot with the other few desperate souls braving the crappy January weather for the chance to win a couple measly bucks. Even stuck two fingers in his mouth and let out an ear-piercing whistle. Frowning, Nicole rose, too, so she'd blend in, then wished she hadn't passed up his offer for popcorn when they'd walked through the building. She was starving. And she didn't even *like* popcorn.

She breathed out a sigh. Glanced at her watch. Looked up and around. No sign of her sister. No sign she'd be out of here anytime soon.

"They're getting ready," Billy said with a grin at her side. "Which horse did you pick?"

She had no idea. Working up a good scowl, she lifted the paper and held it out to him with a flick of her fingers. "Sunbolt."

"Sun*down*," he corrected, leveling her with a look. "Babe, you gotta know your horse."

She stared at him. Then nearly laughed. She'd never seen a guy get so worked up over something as silly as betting on an animal that could break its leg and have to be put down in the first ten feet.

A horse whinnied below. The gates snapped shut. Just before the bell sounded, he leaned over and put his mouth on hers.

"For luck," he said as he pulled back. Then his attention was off her and focused solely on the massive animals tearing up the track far below them as if the moment had never happened.

Warmth slid through her veins, and before she could stop it, her chest bumped.

Okay, stupid to get worked up over one little kiss, especially when they'd screwed each other senseless the whole night and day before and when neither obviously trusted the other, but she felt butterflies in her stomach just the same. She chanced a look sideways at him, standing there, cheering like a loon for a horse he had no attachment to aside from the fact he'd slapped a twenty on it to win, and found herself grinning right along with him.

Billy Sullivan wasn't like any guy she'd met before. Immature, cocky, a real James Dean, *Rebel Without a Cause*–in-the-twenty-first-century kind of guy. But smart. Way more fun than any of the stuffy and arrogant playboys she'd dated before. And, oh, yeah, sexy as hell with those hazel eyes and all that thick light brown hair. Maybe that last part was why she'd done what she had with him, but even before the thought hit she knew it was a lie.

True, she'd gone to bed with him because she'd been attracted to him. Even knowing what he was really after. But mostly she'd slept with him because there was something about him that appealed to her on a much more basic level. Something a little bit lost, a tiny bit wild, and a whole lot misunderstood. Something . . . a lot like her.

She pushed that thought out of her head and turned back to watch the race. Then grinned all over again when Billy started jumping up and down, grabbing her arm and yanking her with him as the horses sped down the stretch and GoldenEye, his pick, came in first.

He lifted her up and twirled her around. Then planted a big sloppy kiss on her lips before pulling back and grinning down at her. "You are my new good-luck charm."

"Sunburst didn't win."

"*Sundown* came in second."

She did her best to glare at him, though she knew she did a half-assed job. "Whatever. Does that mean we can leave now?"

His smile widened. "No way." He grabbed the race schedule from his back pocket and flipped it open. "Let's double down."

She groaned for effect, then felt those butterflies take flight when he slanted a cheesy smile her way and sat to fill out his race form.

Oh, trouble. This guy could end up being a serious problem if her sister didn't show up soon.

Footsteps echoed from somewhere above. And as if summoned from the cauldron of hell, a pair of cheap sandals stopped on the opposite side of Billy's chair, next to the end aisle where they sat. "Don't tell me you're betting."

Billy looked up to the left, and a slow smile spread across his tanned face. Without tipping her head up so her face was still shielded, Nicole's gaze followed until she was staring right at her sister.

"Not just betting. Winning." He rose and gave Hailey a quick hug, then frowned when he eased back. "What the hell happened to you?"

"What the hell hasn't happened to me?" Hailey said with what could have been humor but sounded more like whining to Nicole.

"Let's not attract attention." The man standing at Hailey's back grasped her hand and pulled her into the row directly behind Nicole and Billy's seats.

Though Nicole hadn't gotten a good look, her thoughts

echoed Billy's sentiments. Hailey's face was bruised, her eyes looked tired, her hair was covered by a Florida Marlins cap and she was wearing some plain-Jane capris and a shapeless T-shirt under a very boring Windbreaker Nicole would never be caught dead in. But the guy she was with? Okay, now *he* was interesting.

Nicole shifted slightly to get a better view. Though he was sitting kitty-corner behind her and she had to really look, she wouldn't be a woman if she didn't notice those midnight eyes, that brown hair so dark it seemed black, and at least two days' worth of stubble on his square jaw that gave him the whole dark-and-mysterious look. Of course, he had a real don't-mess-with-me air about him, but that toned body flexing beneath his sweatshirt? Um, yeah. Okay. *That* was interesting, too.

Who the heck was he? And what was he doing with her sister, now, when Hailey was obviously in so much trouble?

It was clear Billy and the mystery guy knew each other. No real introductions were made as he and Hailey sat. And for some reason, Nicole got the impression neither liked each other all that much. Another interesting piece of info.

"Who's your friend?" the guy asked Billy.

Billy turned to face her, hooked one arm over the back of his seat and shrugged. And Nicole knew she was on her own.

Slowly, she turned and lifted her face so the brim of her stupid bucket cap was out of her eyes. Then she smiled. "Hello, Sis."

To Hailey's credit, she didn't show any surprise. Unless of course you noticed the little tic above her left eye. The one that only came out when she was really peeved. "What are you doing here?"

"Racing. Wait, betting." When Billy coughed, she glanced his way. "What? Is that wrong?"

"Billy?" Hailey said from between what Nicole knew were clenched teeth. "I suddenly feel the need to place a bet. I think I need your help."

"I don't think that's such a—"

"Back off, Maxwell." Hailey stood before her hunky dark bodyguard could stop her.

On a long sigh, Billy handed Nicole his race schedule. "Hold on to this for me." Then he was gone. He and Hailey moved to the top of the grandstand where they couldn't be overheard, away from the few stragglers who'd stuck around to watch the track below being groomed for the next race. And though Nicole couldn't hear what they were saying, she could only imagine the conversation.

She chuckled to herself and looked back at her unexpected companion. "So . . . Maxwell. Is that your first name, last name or some kinky nickname my sister gave you?"

"Last."

"You got a first name, sexy?"

He didn't seem interested in having a conversation, was too busy twisting in his seat to look up where Hailey was reading Billy the riot act. Nicole knew Billy could handle himself, but it irked her beyond words that this guy's eyes had skipped right over her like she wasn't even there. To focus on Hailey, who looked like she'd just gone ten rounds and picked up a new wardrobe at K-Mart on the way here just for shits and giggles. Nicole decided to try another tactic.

She moved up one row and sat next to him. He obviously hadn't heard her move, because when she touched his arm with her fingers, his eyes shot to hers and he looked at her like she'd shocked him with a cattle prod.

"Sorry," she said with a grin, then a quick nibble on her bottom lip she'd perfected over the past few years to draw attention to her mouth, which she knew was one of her best assets. "My neck was getting sore there. You don't mind, do you? They'll probably be a while."

He looked down at her hand, still resting on his arm, then back up to her eyes. "Do you really think this is a smart move on your part?"

Her smile faded, but she didn't move her hand. Dark and mysterious just became dark and irritating. "Who are you?"

"A friend."

"Hailey doesn't have any friends."

"How would you know?"

"Because you have to have a heart to have a friend, and she clearly doesn't."

His eyes narrowed.

"Don't believe me?" she asked, pointing up the grandstand to where Hailey and Billy were still arguing. "That's how she treats her friends. And anyone who doesn't do what she wants."

He leaned close to her, so close she barely heard his words. "If that's true, then why do you care?"

"Because she owes me."

"For what?"

"That's none of your business."

"From here on out, girlie, anything that has to do with her *is* my business. Don't mess with me."

"Nicole."

Billy was striding toward her, looking righteously ticked off and sexier than she'd ever seen him. Oh, yeah. Serious trouble. Her blood warmed all over again. "Come on, we're going."

She rose slowly when he reached for her arm and caught a glimpse of Hailey, three steps up at his back, looking pretty ticked herself. Oh, now wasn't this just fun? Good times. Just like the old days. "Where are we headed?"

"Someplace a little more private." Billy's fiery eyes shot between her and Hailey's mystery man, and judging from the flash Nicole saw there, it was clear he'd witnessed at least part of her conversation.

Well, that was a good thing, right? About time she stopped having fantasies of lovebirds and put this guy in his place. Besides, as fun as he was, that's not why she was really here.

Of course, why that thought suddenly left a hole the size of a grapefruit in her chest was a mystery she didn't want to go examining now.

She followed Billy up the steps and tugged her hat lower

as she neared her sister. When she reached the same step, she stopped briefly and leaned in close. "I'm sure I'll be hearing from you. In the meantime, though, a bit of advice." She lowered her voice to a whisper and added a shot of sass she knew would hit its mark. "Find a mall."

By the time they reached the parking lot, Hailey was fuming. Billy and Nicole must have parked on the opposite side of the building because they were nowhere to be seen.

"Hold up, Roarke. My leg's still sore from being yesterday's snack."

She slowed as she reached the first tier of parking spaces and turned toward Shane, hobbling behind her. "Sorry. I'm just . . ."

"Pissed. Yeah, I got it. If you decide to turn that temper on me, all I ask is you give me fair warning. I'm not up for having my ass handed to me today."

She glared at him. And like water rushing through her veins, all that anger slid away. She had to look to her left to keep from chuckling. If there was one thing she could say for Shane, when he wasn't being a moody SOB, he had a way of reminding her things weren't as bad as they seemed.

*Yeah, right.*

She heaved out a sigh. "I could seriously kill her."

"Shh." He moved closer with a half grin that did strange things to her insides. "I wouldn't let anyone hear you say that if I were you. We're still trying to prove you didn't do that the last time someone ticked you off."

"You're a real comedian." She frowned. "The difference here is this time I mean it."

He tipped his dark head. "I'm getting the impression you and Paris Hilton in there aren't close."

"What was your first clue? The sparks flying or the fact the entire track was about to spontaneously combust?"

"What's she doing here?"

"Beats me. She doesn't care a single thing about RR. She couldn't even bother to be present at the will reading. But she's not stupid. She's obviously figured out the will's solid. And now she's worried about making sure she keeps her meal ticket."

"So she recruited Sullivan?"

"Probably. He's only human, and she's . . . well . . ." She waved her hand. "You saw her. She's every guy's fantasy."

He scoffed. "Not mine."

She leveled him with a look. "I saw you with her."

"Saw me what?"

"Saw her working you."

His brow wrinkled. "I like my women a little bit smarter and lot less pushy."

"Don't get all bent out of shape," she said as she started walking again. "She was only coming on to you to piss me off. Odds are good that's why she hustled Billy, too, because she *knew* that would get to me." Her temper bubbled up all over again at just the thought.

"Hold up." His hand on her arm pulled her back to face him. "Are you jealous?"

"Of Nicole?"

"Of your sister and Sullivan."

"Why would I be jealous of Nicole and Billy?"

"I don't know. You tell me."

The clip to his voice told her the idea got under his skin, and just the thought had a memory flash of their heated kiss this morning skipping through her mind. Her skin tingled as she remembered his hands on her body, what he'd felt like all hard and hot pressing up against her, how good he'd tasted. And what they would have both done if the phone hadn't stopped them.

Then she heard his gruff admission: *I do want you. I've wanted you since we met, and that doesn't piss me off, it jacks me up.* Followed by his numbing revelation that the heat between them would only cause problems, ones she didn't want.

She was sick to death of people telling her what she was supposed to do, how she was supposed to feel, what was best for her. Her father had done it for years. Her ex-husband was still doing it under the guise of friendship whenever he saw her. Now Shane was trying to do it, too.

Her eyes narrowed. "If you have something to ask, Maxwell, just spit it out."

He slipped his hands into the pockets of his jeans and flicked something that made a clicking sound.

"You know, that's really starting to annoy me. What is it?"

He pulled out the square plastic box and gave it a little shake before repocketing it. "Tic Tacs."

"Nervous habit?"

"You could say that. Safer than Jameson." His eyes grew serious before she could ask what that meant. "Why would Sullivan go along with your sister? I thought you said he was helping you. Looks to me like he's working against you."

She turned and resumed walking again, because, yeah, that's how it looked to her, too, and she didn't like it. "He may be a genius, but he's still a guy. And Nicole knows men."

"Sullivan's a genius?" he said with disgusted disbelief from close behind. "Now who's being the comedian?"

"His IQ's in the Nobel Prize–winning-genius category. Not that you'd ever know by looking."

"No way."

"Way."

His footsteps echoed behind her. "Then what the hell's he doing with you?"

Oh, that did it. She stopped. Pivoted. Leveled him with a look.

He read her reaction and quickly held up his hands. "That's not what I meant. I should have said with any of you. Rafe, Kauffman, my sister." When her glare narrowed, he raked a hand through his already disheveled hair. "Shit, this is coming out wrong. I'm just gonna shut up now."

"Smart man." Temper back to bubbling, she resumed walking and mentally ran over what Billy had told her. Nicole wanted in. And she wanted part of the prize at the end or she wouldn't give up her bronze.

Yeah, right. Like Hailey believed that one.

But what did Nicole *really* want? Money, sure. Security, of course. A way to get out from underneath their mother's thumb.

Hell, that last one was the same damn thing Hailey wanted.

If she was ever going to prove she hadn't killed Bryan and find out what her father had been up to, she needed those numbers on the bottom of Nicole's statue. But enough to partner up with the viper? Oh, that was almost asking too much.

"If you're thinking through something, Roarke, just say it right now."

How the heck did he know what was going on in her head before she did?

"Don't read my mind," she said without looking his way. "It's irritating."

He slipped his hands in the pockets of his jeans. That click-click-click came from his pocket again. "I wasn't. I could practically see the little mouse on the wheel in there."

"You're a regular Jay Leno today. What got into you?"

"Don't know. Coulda been loss of blood from yesterday. Mighta been that caffeine I was pumping you with earlier. More than likely, though, it was you. This morning."

Three words: *You, this morning.* That's all it took to make her completely forget whatever she'd been thinking before.

She glanced over her shoulder only to catch a deep scowl on his face, not the humorous expression she'd hoped to see. The man was a complete mystery. One minute he was kissing her with a rabid passion she hadn't experienced in, yeah, forever, the next he was looking like just the idea ticked him off.

No, that wasn't it, she realized as she studied him. The next he was looking like a man who *did* want her but didn't like the idea of her wanting him back.

And what the hell kind of sense did that make?

She was just about to ask that very question when glass in the passenger window of the car to her left shattered, raining tiny bits and pieces all over the concrete at her feet.

"Get down!"

The air left her lungs in a rush as Shane slammed into her from behind. He took her to the ground hard, rolling so his back took the brunt of the impact. Then he was on top of her, his arms and head and chest shielding her face and torso from the flying glass.

A second and third gunshot slammed into the car above them. Before she even got her bearings, Shane rolled off, grabbed her hand and jerked her around the other side of the vehicle to push her down near the wheel well, using it to block their sniper.

He pulled her Beretta from his shoulder harness, where he'd put it this morning after she'd given it to him on the plane. "Goddammit. I miss my fucking gun."

So did she. Why had she given him hers? Good thing she'd thought to grab her backup pistol before leaving the plane.

She draped her bag over her head so the strap ran across her chest, chanced a glance around the car they were hiding behind, then pulled out the semiautomatic when she saw movement.

"What do you think you're doing?" Shane asked as she checked the magazine.

"He's by the gray van over there." She snapped the magazine back in place. "Cover me so I can get around behind him."

His hand snaked out so fast, she didn't track it until he had a death grip on her Windbreaker. "Like hell."

"Maxwell, we're both trained—"

"Last I checked, you're a wanted suspect. A paper-pushing wanted suspect. You plug somebody and you really are going to go to jail. And if you think I'm letting you get close to this son of a bitch, you're higher than a kite."

Glass shattered above them. He grabbed her head and pushed her down so the debris didn't hit her.

She swatted at his arms with her free hands. "I'm not going to keep running from this guy—"

"Guys," he corrected. "There were two in the swamp, remember?"

"Shh," she said, looking to the side. "Listen."

Shane loosened his grasp, went still. "He's reloading."

That was enough for her. As soon as he let go, she was off. Ducking behind cars and moving quietly and quickly so as not to be seen.

"Goddamn it, Roarke."

She ignored Shane's muttering and inched her way up until she was only one row from where she'd seen their sniper hiding between a minivan and a beat-up Camry.

Her heart pounded in her chest. She thought back to the way her attacker had cornered her in the elevator. Sending her a message, he'd said. Well, he was about to get one right back. She was done playing the helpless female. She wanted to know if it was indeed Paul and what was really going on.

Bracing her back against a dirt-covered Suburban, she wrapped both hands around the 9mm and slowly peered around the corner of the vehicle. Nothing moved within a twenty-foot radius. Security obviously hadn't heard the shots because no one came running. Cars honked on the street a quarter mile across the massive parking lot. Shouts and cheers echoed from inside the track where the next race had already started. Above, palms swooshed and swayed in the growing breeze. But all Hailey heard was her pulse. Strong and hot and heavy in her ears.

Her eyes zeroed in on the van. She counted to three. Took one step and was jerked to a stop by a hand around her mouth that came out of nowhere.

"Don't you fucking move."

# CHAPTER FIFTEEN

"I thought *I* had a death wish," Shane whispered in Hailey's ear. He jerked her back tight against his chest and didn't loosen his hand around her mouth or the one with a death grip on her wrist. "But, lady, you take the cake. Are you *trying* to get yourself killed?"

She stiffened, but he didn't let go, not even when she ground that cute ass of hers into him, briefly sending his brain spinning to thoughts other than the fact some moron on the other side of this SUV wanted to blow holes in their heads.

They had a real communication problem going on here. That and a power struggle he liked way too much.

"If we're going to do this," he whispered so quietly only she could hear, "we do it together. On three?"

She froze, then nodded once. She still had the 9mm clamped between both hands. Adrenaline pumping, he moved in stealth mode toward the other side of the SUV. When he was in position, gun drawn, crouched low near the front tire, smelling rubber and asphalt, he gave her the signal.

She disappeared around the back of the Suburban as he crept past the hood. Though his first instinct was to pull her the hell out of here where she couldn't get hurt, he was starting to realize Hailey Roarke did things her own way. No matter the consequences.

And damn if that didn't light him up more and piss him off all at the same time.

He peeked around the side of the SUV, careful not to be

seen or get caught in the crossfire if Hailey started shooting. But he found nothing but air between this vehicle and the next one.

"Goddammit," Hailey muttered, gun lowered as she came around the other side herself.

Shane pushed up on his legs, and they both took a careful sweep of the cars directly around them in case their sniper was hiding close by.

Nothing.

He was holstering his gun when Hailey came back into sight, a frown across her mouth, one gorgeous crease between her bonny blue eyes. "Spineless bastard ran off. I'm sick to death of this cat-and-mouse game."

So was he, but mostly because she was as unpredictable as their would-be assassin.

As soon as she slipped the safety on her 9mm, he grasped her by the arm, swung her around and pushed up so her back was against the silver Suburban and he was all she felt at her front. His mouth was hard, hot and aggressive against hers, and if he left a bruise on her soft and supple lips, right now he didn't care.

He pulled back but didn't let her go. "Don't ever do that again."

The shock in her eyes was replaced with a fiery passion he was all too willing to see flare up. "Don't turn into the all-macho male, Maxwell. I'm not a rookie."

"No, you're stupid."

Her eyes flashed. "Watch it."

He ignored her temper and zoned in on the one thing that still had his pulse in the triple digits. "What if there'd been more than one, Hailey? Did you stop to think about that? If this person knows you, like we think, then they know you aren't going to sit back and do nothing. Which gives them the advantage because they're *expecting* you to go on the offensive like this."

"So you're saying I should play the victim? I don't think so."

Oh, man. He *wasn't* getting turned on by her aggression. Definitely not.

"I'm not saying be the victim. I'm saying be smart. I don't particularly want to get my head blown off because you're frustrated."

She leveled him with a look. "Is that all you're worried about?"

"No, goddammit," he snapped. "I'm worried about you, but you're too bullheaded to see that. You might have a fancy-ass degree from some yuppie school up north, but they sure the hell didn't teach you a thing about compromise. If you're not going to let me be the one to take the risks, then at least don't go all half-cocked on your own. You don't have to do everything alone. What's it going to take to get that through your thick skull?"

She stared at him without blinking, and didn't move, not even when he lifted his brows and said, "Well?"

Her muscles relaxed beneath his hands, one at a time, and finally she said, "I'm not sure what you want me to say."

He let go and stepped back, knowing his emotions were close to a breaking point. She didn't get it. But then why would she? Even he didn't understand what it was about her that set him off and lit him up all at the same time. Half the time he wanted to toss her over his shoulder and lock her up in a closet where she couldn't get into any trouble and the other half he wanted to strip her naked and keep her quiet with his hands and mouth and other parts of his body he seriously didn't need to be thinking with right now.

And that was a bad combination—really bad, considering his history.

He ground his teeth together because it was safer than putting his fist through a car window. "Try, 'Okay, Shane. I won't do that again.'"

"Okay, Maxwell," she said with just a hint of sass, "I'll try not to do anything to get your head blown off again."

She pushed past him and sauntered back toward their rental, looking every bit as enticing as she had the first night he'd met her in Key Biscayne when she'd knocked his ass to the ground and pinned him on that cold stone patio. She'd called him Maxwell back then, too. And holy shit, figuring out a way to get her to say his first name was turning into an obsession.

She suddenly stopped and glanced his direction. "If we hustle, we can hit the bank and maybe figure out what's in that safety-deposit box before the place closes."

*We.*

She was tossing him an olive branch. A smart man would take it.

"What about your sister?"

A muscle in her temple pulsed, but she resumed walking before he got a good read on her emotions. "If we're lucky, Billy will find a way to get rid of her. For good."

Shane doubted that. Frustrated, he took one more look around the parking lot before following. He'd seen the dopey look on Billy's face when the kid had been talking to Nicole before either of them had realized he and Hailey were there. No way Billy was going to be able to get rid of Nicole, not unless she wanted to go.

He supposed in that respect, he and Nicole had something in common.

He popped a handful of Tic Tacs in his mouth, his temper slowly sliding back to even. By the time he reached the rental, Hailey was already behind the wheel. She flashed him a superior grin as he slid into the passenger seat.

She waited until he clicked his seat belt, then batted her long eyelashes at him. "All set, Rambo?"

"Now who's being Jay Leno?"

She shifted into gear. "I'm just trying to work on that whole compromise thing." She pulled out of the parking lot and onto the street. "You know, sharing the driving, being in control, grouchy attitude and all that. I can do it, too. See? I can compromise right along with you." Her glittery eyes rolled his direction. "You want compromise? You haven't seen nothing yet, honey."

Olive branch? Forget it. She was waving a big ol' red flag, taunting him until the steam was blowing out his nostrils and he was pawing at the ground to get at her.

And hot damn, he was loving every minute of it.

He smiled then, a slow curve of his lips as he took her in from head to toe. "By all means, show me. I can't wait to see what happens next."

Billy knew when to bite his tongue. This was one of those times.

Dark clouds rolled in off the Atlantic, ones that fit his badass mood like a glove as he drove eighty down the Florida Turnpike toward his apartment in Miami. Yeah, the address sounded nice, but it wasn't on the beach, wasn't posh and luxurious like Nicole was used to, wasn't even fully furnished since he could barely afford the frickin' rent. Sure, it was several steps up from his last place in Bunche Park, but still . . . little miss high-and-mighty was about to get a shock to her system. And he couldn't wait.

He whipped off the freeway a little too fast and gritted his teeth to keep from snarling when she had to reach up and grasp the safety handle above.

"Slow down, would you?" she snapped. "You're going to give me whiplash."

"Was that a request from you? Wow, you need something from me? Really? Besides sex?" His jaw tightened. "There's a news flash."

"You don't have to be such a smart-ass."

He glared her way. "Deal with it. I'm already bored with this conversation."

She pressed her lips together and stared out the windshield, but she didn't let go of the safety handle, and he noticed the way she inched closer to the door when she thought he wasn't looking.

Had he scared her? Man, he hoped so.

He jerked the car into his parking spot, slammed on the brakes and shoved the car in park. "Get out."

Her eyes flicked from one side to the other as she took in his two-story apartment complex, the cracked sidewalks and the covered portico that was badly in need of repair. "It's pink," she muttered as she climbed out and closed the door.

"You wanted in, princess?" he said with just enough bite to make her wince. "You're gonna have to slum it with the rest of us peons."

"Billy—"

He pointed toward the stairs. "Second floor. Number 242. Go now."

Like a good girl, she went. But as she passed, he saw the flash of temper in her dark eyes. No, little miss high-and-mighty did not like this at all.

He clenched and unclenched his jaw as he followed her up the stairs, tried like hell not to look at her ass and failed. Just like all the other times, last night he'd proved to be the fuckup everyone thought he was. When was he going to learn?

She was waiting at the door when he rounded the corner, arms crossed over her ample chest, fire flashing in her eyes. He stuck the key in the lock, pushed the door open and waited while she marched by him with her head held high and her pride wrapped around her like a shield.

His own temper nearly at the breaking point, he slammed the door and dropped his keys on the small half-moon entry table his mother'd had in their house when he was growing up.

The air-conditioning was the only thing that marginally cooled him out. He went straight to the refrigerator, grabbed a beer and popped the top. Then guzzled half the thing before turning and looking over the kitchen counter toward Nicole, standing in the middle of the living room turning her nose up at his measly furnishings.

Was his ego hurt that she thought he lived in a ghetto? It shouldn't be. She didn't mean anything to him, not really. Hot sex and a hot bod. That's all she was. Instead of being everyone's fuckup, it was time he started using that million-dollar brain God had given him. "You lied to me."

She turned slowly to face him as he came around the corner into the living room, blocking her path to the door. "I did not."

"Then you conveniently omitted the truth."

She huffed and rolled her eyes.

"Yeah, you know. That doesn't work on me." He brought the bottle to his lips and took a long swallow.

"If you're trying to intimidate me, it's not working. I've seen you naked, remember?"

"Yeah, I remember. Your little distract-and-dismay technique worked. For about a day. Gotta admit. You were good. And that whole, you're-only-the-second-guy-I've-been-with and I've-never-had-a-one-night-stand thing? Had me going."

She dropped her arms. "I never had a one-night stand before you."

"Tell it to somebody who cares. You're a lying little piece of—"

She stomped her foot and curled her fingers into her fists. "Don't you dare even say it. You don't believe me? Fine. But it's the truth. One guy. Three years ago. It wasn't all that memorable and I didn't particularly enjoy it. So I never had the urge to try again until—" She closed her mouth tight. Glared at him, hard. "And I don't know what my sister told you, but I didn't lie to you. I just didn't tell you everything." She tipped her head and shot his anger right back his way. "But then why would I? You're just some hustler I picked up at a beach bar."

He moved in close and leaned down so she got the full effect of his temper. "Don't fuck with me. You told me your bronze was gone, but it's not, is it? You've got it. You've always had it."

"Do you think I'm stupid enough to just give it away?" she scoffed. "Security, Billy. That's all I've got. But the bronze isn't the real issue here, is it? It's the numbers on the bottom that matter. And I know mine by heart. I always have. Just like I know what's on the bottom of my mother's sculpture. If Hailey thinks she can go around me to get what she needs, she's going to be sorely mistaken. Our mother isn't going to let Daddy's little treasure hunt be finished. She's got her own reasons for that, and if Hailey knew what they were, she wouldn't believe them. I guarantee our mother won't help Hailey. Which means I'm the only one who can."

As he listened to her words, Billy saw a little bit of himself in Nicole. All the years he'd resented Rafe for being older, wiser, the son who could do no wrong. Is this how he looked? Vengeful? Bitter? Empty?

"Why do you hate her so much?" he asked, seeing her, and himself, in a whole new light.

"Who? Hailey?" Nicole's eyes widened. "I don't hate her."

"What do you call it?"

She looked around the room as if searching for an answer. "Competition," she finally said.

"Not everything in life's about winning."

"It's not?"

Slowly, he shook his head.

"Then why are you here, Billy? Are you telling me you aren't trying to prove something to someone by helping my sister? That you're just doing it out of the goodness of your heart?" She rolled her eyes. "I don't buy that for a second. You and I are way too much alike for that to be true."

Surprise rippled through him as her words registered. In the silence his chest tightened and a whole lot of *aha!* pinged around in his brain. For a guy with an above-average IQ, he was a class-A dumbass.

All this time he'd been telling himself he'd been helping Hailey out of friendship, that doing this would prove to Rafe and Pete and everyone else that he wasn't the fuckup they all thought he was. But that wasn't the truth, not really. His mother was in a hospital in Puerto Rico, probably dying right this very minute, and he was in Miami looking for a piece of metal that, in the grand scheme of things, meant very little to his life. Every time Rafe had called over the last month to ask him to come back, he'd given some lame-ass excuse why he couldn't. The reality was he was hiding. Pretending nothing bad was happening. That life was just fine and dandy. Proving to himself that when all was said and done, he didn't need family. Didn't need anyone for that matter. Not his aunts and uncles in Puerto Rico. Not his brother or his brother's new wife. Not even his mother, the only person who'd ever really believed in him.

He swallowed hard as his stomach dropped. Then nearly came out of his skin when the phone rang. He reached for it with a hand he hoped like hell didn't shake. "Yeah."

"Jesus, Billy. I've been trying to call you all afternoon. Turn your fucking cell on."

*Rafe.* Wonderful. Just what he needed right now.

He reached a hand up to rub his suddenly throbbing forehead. "I was busy. What do you want?"

Rafe, the ever-confident, always-in-control rock of the family, heaved out a sigh that sounded like he held the weight of the world on his shoulders. "I need you to come home. Now. And this time no excuses. The doctor just left." He paused. And over the line, Billy heard Rafe's voice crack. "They don't expect her to make it to morning. Billy, this is it."

# CHAPTER SIXTEEN

She was as nervous as a virgin on prom night.

Madeline Roarke stared out at the rush of people wandering up and down the Hollywood Beach Boardwalk. *Boardwalk* was a silly term in her mind. There were no "boards" here, not like the boardwalks in New Jersey and Delaware. Just a long stretch of grimy pavement that ran up and down the never-ending beach.

Behind her, music played from the open door of an ice-cream parlor. The sun was starting to set, and a warm glow she didn't feel reflected off the water and sand and the faces of each person passing by her hiding place.

She shouldn't have come. But when she'd gotten the note . . . she'd had no choice.

Her hand slid around the strap of her purse, her eyes darted from side to side behind her oversize Ralph Lauren sunglasses. Her stomach tightened as she looked for anyone waiting for her. But no one had paid her one ounce of attention since she'd stepped foot on the boardwalk. No one recognized her. No one even cared who she was.

That was a good thing, right? Maybe the note was nothing but a prank.

Shoring up her courage, she took one step away from the building where she'd been hiding in the shadows, and made it as far as the Hollywood Grill before a boy, no more than eight, came barreling out of nowhere and slammed into her from the side.

She shrieked and whipped around just as ketchup and

mustard splattered her white slacks and ran down to drip onto her Ferragamo flats.

"Sorry," the kid mumbled, holding a hot dog in his hand, then tore off around her and hollered, "Wait up!" to his buddies.

Disgusted with the child, the location, at the world in general, Madeline shook the red and yellow goo from her fingers and grimaced. Nothing was worth this. She didn't care who had sent her that blasted note. Someone was toying with her. Had probably paid that kid to run into her. No one knew about what she'd done.

"Look at that," a voice whispered in her ear. "Déjà vu, Maddie?"

Madeline froze. Swallowed. And turned slowly to look into the face of a woman she despised.

Lucy Walthers smiled like the innocent girl she wasn't, tucked her short blonde hair behind her ears and nodded at Madeline's dripping fingers. "If I were you, I'd find a napkin. Wouldn't want anyone remembering this image. Strikes a little too close to home, doesn't it?"

Madeline's throat closed, and her heart fired rapid beats. Without a word to Lucy, she ducked into the café and found napkins on a nearby table.

Could she run? She thought about it as she cleaned her hands and wiped at her shoes. But how far would she get? The fact the little tramp was standing out there right now instead of the police meant she wanted something. Did she think Madeline had that stupid bronze? What else could this be about?

The look of victory in the younger woman's eyes grated Madeline's last nerve when she stepped back into the cool January air. "Let's walk, Maddie. What do you say?"

Madeline clutched the strap of her bag as she turned and Lucy fell in step next to her. Her eyes flicked over each face they passed, her brain thinking through her options. But when Lucy started talking, the only things Madeline focused on were the other woman's words.

"The way I see it, Madeline, you've gotten yourself into a bit of trouble. One word from me and the police will be breaking down your door."

Here it came. The threat. Madeline held her breath. She'd thought Bryan had been alone that night. She'd gone there to confront him. To tell him she'd had enough of his lies and cheating and his obsession with the Roarkes. She'd wanted a divorce. And freedom. And she'd wanted him to pay.

That freedom now looked a million miles away.

"Nothing to say to that?" Lucy asked.

Words lodged in Madeline's throat. "What do you want from me?"

"Nothing much. Just your help in one very small matter."

She stopped walking to turn toward her enemy. "Why should I do anything for you?"

"Because if you don't, I'll go right back to those Chicago detectives and tell them I suddenly remembered something important."

"They won't believe you."

"Won't they? Don't you think it's only a matter of time before they realize Hailey wasn't even there that night? What about your alibi, Madeline? Where were *you*?"

Madeline's voice dropped to a whisper so the people passing couldn't hear her. "I should have gone upstairs and gutted you while I was at it."

Lucy grinned. "Lucky for us, you didn't." Her smile dropped. "Now here's what you're going to do, Madeline. You're going to get me Eleanor's bronze."

"I would rather—"

"I know you would. But you'll get it just the same. You and Eleanor are thick as thieves at that stupid country club. You'll get it, and you'll bring it to me. And if you don't . . ." She shrugged. "I think the police would love to know how you were waiting in the shadows for your dear beloved husband to come downstairs, then murdered him in cold blood and framed Hailey for the whole thing."

Madeline's skin chilled. Sickness welled in her stomach.

But she lifted her chin, determined not to give this woman an inch. "You live in a fantasy world." She turned to leave. "Get your own damn bronze."

Lucy chuckled at her back. "Don't be so sure, Maddie," she called. "Do me a favor. When you get home, check your earrings. I'm pretty sure you're missing a pearl. A South Sea pearl, hanging from a little silver catch. White, I believe, isn't it? Or was."

Madeline's feet stilled. And in the bustle of the boardwalk, her heart all but stopped.

Lucy circled around to stand in front of Madeline. And in her soulless black eyes, Madeline knew she was cornered.

Lucy tipped her head to the side. "Now let's go through this one more time. Eleanor hasn't been cooperating. That's where you come in. You're going to get us Eleanor's bronze. And you're going to do it tomorrow."


"Well, that was productive."

Hailey ignored Shane's snarky comment and stared at the key in her hand as they exited her father's bank in downtown Miami. Ever since the incident in the parking lot of the Calder Race Course, Shane had been in another of his moods, though this one was way more sarcastic and just a little suggestive.

Okay, not touching that one. She'd decided—when she was standing in a dressing room at some no-name mall, slipping into clean clothes that weren't covered in parking-lot grime—that his enjoyment of the push-pull power struggle between them was a really bad sign. Because she liked it, too. And she had a strange feeling one of them was going to get seriously burned when it bubbled to a head.

"It looked like a safety-deposit-box key," she said, pushing the thoughts aside. "I just assumed that's what it was."

"I'm getting the impression we can't assume anything where your father's concerned." He walked next to her, his hands shoved into the front pockets of new low-slung denim that fit him like a glove. The long-sleeved black Under Armour shirt with the white stripes down the sleeves looked damn sexier on him than any hunky sports model she'd seen in *Sports Illustrated*.

She averted her gaze because, yeah, just looking at him in those new duds did things to her blood she didn't like. "True. But why would he give it to me without some kind of explanation as to what it goes to?"

He tugged the baseball cap lower over her face and frowned. "Couldn't you have found a Cubs hat on that rack? Shit, I'd even settle for a Red Sox cap at this point."

"You don't like the Yankees? They're like America's team."

He stopped in the middle of the sidewalk and stared at her like she had three eyeballs. "You're sick, you know that?"

She couldn't help it. She laughed. "It's only baseball, Maxwell."

He slapped a hand against his heart. "Only baseball? *Only* baseball? That's *only* my heart you're ripping to shreds and throwing on the sidewalk."

She rolled her eyes and kept walking. "Please tell me you aren't one of those guys."

"What guys?" he said, catching up.

"*Those* guys. The ones who don't have a life from March to October because they're either at the ball field or glued to their TVs. The ones who base their year on whether their team wins the pennant, then plot ways to murder their Yankee neighbors when the Yankees take the World Series. Again."

"You say that like it's a bad thing."

She shook her head and bit her lip to keep from laughing. Dammit, she liked him. More with every passing hour.

"And if I don't have a life," he added, that clicking coming from his pocket again, "it's not because of baseball."

"What's it from then?"

"Work, I guess. These days my job is my life."

She stopped and looked at him. "A job is what you do. Not who you are."

"You don't really know who I am, Hailey."

She studied him. Tried to read his mood but couldn't.

No, he was right. There were facets to Shane Maxwell she definitely didn't know. And suddenly wasn't entirely sure she wanted to know. Yes, he intrigued her. And yes, she was attracted to him—wildly attracted to him. But the distance he kept between them, the way he seemed to need to be here helping but didn't appear to like it a lot of the time was a contradiction she just didn't understand.

She kept walking as thoughts of what he'd said ran through her mind. The things he must have seen working homicide. She'd seen her fair share of death and cruelty in the Keys, but she knew instinctively it was nothing compared to what he witnessed every day in Chicago. No wonder he kept to himself and was impossible to read.

A thought occurred to her as they turned the corner and headed for their rental two blocks down, one she'd had numerous times over the past three months but hadn't thought of the last few days until right now. "Why aren't you married?"

"How did we go from your dad's wacko mind to my marital status?"

Good question. "If you don't want to answer, that's fine."

"It's not that I don't want to answer. It's just not exciting." When he didn't elaborate, she was sure he was letting the subject drop. But then he surprised her when he said, "I thought about it once. Briefly."

"What happened?"

"Nothing. It just wasn't meant to be."

There was more, though. A whole lot more he wasn't saying. She could sense it in his suddenly tense shoulders and the fact he was looking down at the pavement and not at her.

Oh, yeah. He had facets.

They walked another half block in silence, darting around other pedestrians before he said, "What about you?"

"I think you already know my marital status."

"Not that. Why did you marry Sullivan in the first place? You two don't have a thing in common."

"Of course we do."

He shot her a *yeah, right* look. "He's a thief, you're a cop. He's into art, you couldn't care less—"

"I like art."

"Not like he does. Thing is, I can't figure why any woman would marry him, let alone you."

"I'm not married to the man anymore. You'd get further if you asked your sister."

He frowned. "She already told me why. Hell, she's told everyone. Something about him speaking Spanish and . . ." He stopped himself, almost as if he'd said too much.

And Hailey smiled, because this facet of Shane Maxwell, at least, she knew how to handle. "Sex. Yeah. There was that."

He grimaced. "Christ Jake. I don't need that image in my head."

At his repulsed expression, Hailey stopped. Could it be . . . ? "Are you jealous?"

His brows drew together. "Of what?"

"Of Rafe."

A look of dismay crossed his face, masked quickly by contempt. "Not on your life."

She let the topic drop but her mind was spinning. In the gym at the Lake Geneva resort Shane had wanted to know if she was seeing Billy, and when she'd said no, he'd kissed her. Hard. He *was* jealous. The realization sent her heart skipping. Being attracted to her was one thing. Kissing was really just a physical connection. But jealousy? That came from the gut. And the heart.

Her pulse kicked up. And in the silence between them, she asked herself, could she handle a man like Shane Maxwell? Not just sexually, but long-term? Down the line? When she figured out what was happening with her father's will and life was back to normal? He was moody and dark and married to his job—even if that job was responsible for the perpetual scowl on his face. No, life with him would never be easy. But it also wouldn't be dull.

Shane stopped at the rental and pulled the passenger

door open for her. "I didn't get the impression your sister was going to work with us."

His nearness sent goose bumps over her skin. His words pulled her from her musings and reminded her she had other, more important, things to think about. "I didn't, either." As she climbed in and he walked around the vehicle, she tried not to think of all the little things he did that made her pulse skip, things like opening doors for her, adjusting her hat so no one would recognize her, buying her a Bon Jovi T-shirt she was probably going to save forever. His overprotective personality was irritating as hell, but if he was jealous of her relationship with Rafe, it meant this thing going on between them was more than him having to always be in control or take over a situation. It meant he felt something for her. That what kept him here wasn't a mystery, but her.

And *that* thought sent her heart rate into the triple digits as he slid behind the wheel and turned on the ignition. "She's probably at Billy's," he said. "You want to go talk to her?"

Hailey looked down at her hands. "I'd really rather slit my wrists."

He glanced at her fingers. "Be a shame to put scars on those pretty arms."

Okay, that kind of talk wasn't helping. She looked up and out the passenger window toward a homeless man pushing a shopping cart. "That pretty much leaves my mother."

"You don't think we need all five sculptures after all?"

"If we can get my mother's, I think we can probably figure it out without Nicole's piece."

He frowned. "Because you've been so successful so far? Thirty-eight, twenty-five, oh-five. You already said those numbers don't mean anything to you."

"Yet," she said quickly. "But they will. We just have to get my mother's bronze to decode the damn thing."

He eyed her warily. "Why do I get the feeling this might not be as easy as it sounds."

Because it wasn't. She ignored the little trip in her heart whenever she looked at him. "What's your mother like?"

"The glue that holds our family together."

She sighed and glanced back at the homeless man, now rifling through a garbage can. "I bet she cooks."

"She does. Not so much anymore that we're all out of the house, but at least once a month she does a big family Sunday dinner with all the trimmings."

Hailey remembered meeting Colleen Maxwell at Rafe and Lisa's wedding. The woman had hugged Hailey, right off the bat. With a big cheesy grin that didn't match her husband Darren's scowl at all. Hailey imagined Colleen Maxwell was the kind of woman who would listen to you when you had a problem, hold you when you longed for support and tell you the way it was when you needed advice.

"How does she feel about your career?"

"Hates it."

Yeah, Colleen Maxwell was the kind of mother Hailey had always wanted.

She rubbed a hand over her forehead and tried not to let the memory sting. But it did. "My mother's not like that. In fact, we don't get along all that well. Not that that's a surprise. But I'm hoping she'll help me out. She was never wild about Bryan, though that doesn't really make a difference. What does matter is that she doesn't want to see my father's company fall into incapable hands."

"Does she want it?"

"God, no. She has no interest in working."

He tapped his finger against the steering wheel, deep in thought. "What about McIntosh? Does she have any connection to him?"

"To Paul? No way. She thinks he's an arrogant SOB. Which he is." Was he adding her mother to his list of suspects? He was really stretching now.

He didn't look so convinced, but didn't push the topic. "So you want to go see her?"

About as much as she wanted a hole in her head. But what choice did they have left? It was down to Nicole or her mother, the lesser of two evils. Neither option looked all that appealing from where she was sitting.

"I guess that's our only—"

Her cell rang, and she flipped it open, a burst of relief rushing through her when she saw Billy's number. "You couldn't have picked a better time to call."

"I need a favor, H."

The seriousness of Billy's tone killed the smile on Hailey's face. "What happened?"

"I just got off the phone with Rafe." His voice wavered. "It's bad, Hailey. I need to get to Puerto Rico. Like, yesterday."

Suddenly her father's will was the last thing on her mind. "Of course. I'll call Steve and have him get the jet ready. Can you get to Opa-locka?"

"Yeah," he said at the mention of the executive airport. "I'm heading there now."

"Okay." She rubbed her throbbing temples. "Okay, I'll meet you there. Just . . . stay positive, Billy."

"Positive isn't going to do it this time."

The line went dead, and even though she'd been mentally preparing herself for this moment for months, she hadn't expected to feel like a piece of her was dying, too.

"What happened?" Shane asked.

She closed the phone quickly and slipped it into her pocket. Think positive. That's what she'd do. That's what she always did. "Change in plans. We're going to Puerto Rico."

"What?"

Too late she realized a piece of her *was* dying. And it had been for a very long time. She'd just been ignoring it, hoping it wouldn't ever come to pass.

"Drive, Maxwell." She leaned back in the seat and closed her eyes to keep from bawling like a baby. "Just . . . drive."

# CHAPTER SEVENTEEN

Shane didn't mind hospitals. He spent a fair of time in them, interviewing victims and witnesses, checking up on suspects. He'd gotten to know the trauma docs at Cook County Hospital pretty well, even played softball with one of the PAs who worked the ER. But he'd never had anyone he cared about die. The closest he'd come was when his ex-partner, Jack Taylor, had taken a bullet to the cheek during a random burglary call.

Funny how things worked out. Today all that was left of that rainy night was a thin scar down the left side of Jack's face. But the experience had been enough for Jack to say sayonara to CPD. In the last three years, Jack, a self-proclaimed lazy-ass bachelor, had started his own PI firm, which was growing by leaps and bounds, gotten himself hitched, and, last Shane had heard, was expecting a kid.

A kid? Shit. Jack as a father? The apocalypse had to be in sight.

He waited while Hailey and Billy checked in at the information desk. Both were strung tight as a trapeze wire. He knew Hailey and Teresa Sullivan were close. As he watched Hailey wipe a hand over her brow and take a deep breath when she thought no one was looking, he realized just how rough this was for her.

He paid for his Tic Tacs at the gift shop and glanced through the glass wall toward the main lobby. Nicole had flopped down on a couch and was flipping through a magazine. She was wearing the same outfit she'd sported at the racetrack—tight white capris, a V-neck blouse that dipped way too low, and a pair of yellow three-inch sandals. If she was trying to draw attention to herself, she was doing one helluva good job. The hat she'd had on at the track had done shit to conceal her identity.

Why the hell Billy had brought her, Shane didn't know. Hailey'd been more than peeved when Billy had shown up with the girl at the airport, but she hadn't said a word about it. Considering no one on the flight had said much of anything, he figured that was probably a good thing.

He looked toward the information desk and pocketed his Tic Tacs. Billy and Hailey exchanged a few words, then Billy headed for the elevators while Hailey walked in Shane's direction.

He met her at the doorway and tried not to think about how tired she was, how the yellow bruises on her cheek and around her eye were finally fading to showcase her creamy skin, how soft her hair looked down around her shoulders or the fact ever since Billy had called today, she'd had a perpetual shine to her eyes that made him want to drag her close and protect her from the world.

"She's on the fourth floor. Billy already went up."

*You can't save her.* Shane crumpled the receipt in his hand and tossed it in a wastebasket, wishing that little voice in his head would take a hike for good. "Bad?"

"Not good." She crossed to her sister before Shane could ask what that meant. "We're going upstairs, Nicole. Just stay here and don't get into any trouble."

Nicole rose quickly from the couch and dropped her magazine on the coffee table. "I'll go with you."

"No," Hailey said with a quick shake of her head, turning for the elevators. "You won't."

"Hailey—"

She whipped back so fast, Nicole's eyes flared. "This isn't open for negotiation. So sit your ass back down and be quiet. A woman's dying, Nicole. For once in your life think about someone other than yourself."

It was a family dynamic Shane would never understand.

Sure, his three sisters bugged the hell out of him at times—Keira with her constant blind-date attempts that usually required a gallon of alcohol on Shane's part just to get through the evening, Catrine the drama queen with her bored-out-of-her-mind-housewife phone calls in the middle of the afternoon when he was working, and Lisa, his twin, the only person in the world who could read him better than himself—but he loved them just the same. This thing between Hailey and Nicole, though? There didn't seem to be any love lost between the two, and not for the first time, Shane wondered why.

Thinking about his own family dynamics brought him around to the fact his mind-reading twin was upstairs right this minute with her new husband. And realizing that reminded him why he'd kept his distance from Lisa the last six months. Parking it on the couch with Nicole and hanging until Hailey and Billy came back down seemed like the safest alternative all around.

"You know," he said when Hailey pressed the elevator call button, "maybe I should stay down here as well. Keep an eye on Nicole."

"She's not going anywhere."

"Never know. Seems to me she's pretty damn unpredictable." A lot like someone else he knew.

Hailey finally looked his way, and he saw then what she'd been hiding on the flight out here. Pain. Raw and undiluted. The kind you hoped no one else ever had to go through. The kind he dealt with every day of his damn life.

She crossed her arms over her chest. "It's fine if you don't want to go up."

The elevator door opened, and she stepped inside. When he followed without a word, she glanced at him with a startled expression.

The doors slid closed. He tucked his hands into the front pockets of his jeans and shrugged. "Girl in the gift shop said there's a kick-ass coffeepot up on the fourth floor."

Okay, that spark of relief in her shiny eyes made all this

just a little too deep. So he pulled his gaze away before those stormy Caribbean blue pools of hers could suck him under and he did something really stupid. Like dug himself in deeper than he already was and reached for her. Gave her the comfort he sensed she was needing. Took some right back for himself.

They rode in silence to the fourth floor. The doors opened with a ping, and he followed her down the hall toward Teresa's room and what Shane immediately recognized as Rafe's deep voice coming from inside.

He'd met Teresa Sullivan at his sister's wedding. But the lithe woman lying in the hospital bed beneath a thin layer of blankets, with wires and tubes trailing to machines behind her, looked nothing like the smiling mother he'd chatted with nearly three months before.

Rafe sat in a chair to her left, holding her hand in his big palm. Lisa was perched farther down on the edge of her bed, one hand on Teresa's blanket-covered leg, the other holding Rafe's other hand. On Teresa's right was Billy, who'd obviously just come into the room. The two exchanged some sort of words in Spanish. Then Teresa glanced past Billy to where Hailey and Shane were standing in the doorway.

Her dark eyes, so much like Rafe's, brightened ever so slightly.

"There's my girl," Teresa said in a raspy voice. She dropped both her boys' hands and reached for Hailey.

Hailey went to the older woman without restraint, easing down to hug Teresa. And Shane stood rooted where he was, knowing he needed to back out of the room but unable to get his legs to work.

More quiet words were exchanged between the women. Hailey sniffled. And faintly Shane heard Teresa say, "Don't cry." But it wasn't until he felt something at his elbow that he realized others were in the room and that someone was touching him.

His sister Lisa had a big ol' *What the hell are you doing here?* look on her face that dragged him out from under the tidal wave pulling him down. And he was just about to guide her into the hall to try to explain before she jumped to her own conclusions when Teresa looked around Hailey and said, "I was hoping I was going to get to see you again, Detective. Come closer so I can get a better look at you. These old eyes don't work so well anymore."

Ah, yeah. Now if this wasn't awkward, nothing was. Shane didn't move. Only stumbled forward when Lisa nudged him. But he knew better than to reject a dying old woman when she reached for his hand.

"I'm very happy to see you with my girl," Teresa said.

"It's not what you think," Hailey said quickly.

A knowing smile spread across Teresa's pale face. "Yes, it is. And I'm glad." Her smile faded. "Rafe and I were watching CNN earlier. I heard what happened to your cousin. I'm very sorry, *m'ija*."

Hailey glanced sideways at Shane, still holding Teresa's other hand, flicked a look at Rafe on Shane's other side, then back at Teresa. "Thanks. I want you to know I didn't—"

"I know. You couldn't." Teresa closed her eyes, took a deep, labored breath, then opened them again to focus on Hailey. "M'*ija*, I have something for you. In my jewelry box. At the house. When you and Rafe got married, your father sent me a letter to hold for you. He didn't want me to give it to you unless something happened to him. I wanted you to have it weeks ago, when I heard about your father, but—"

"It's okay," Hailey said, her grip tightening on Teresa's hand.

"Yes," Teresa said, her eyes sliding shut once more. "It is. Your father loved you, *m'ija*. I know he didn't always show it, but he had his reasons. Don't forget that."

Shane could tell from the look on Hailey's face she didn't believe that for a second, but she masked it well and smiled for Teresa's benefit.

"Now." Teresa's eyes popped open, and for the first time since Shane had stepped in the room, they were clear. Crystal clear and dark as night. She pulled Hailey's and Shane's hands together, placed hers over the top, then focused on Shane. "Hailey is the daughter I always wanted but never had. One of the happiest days of my life was when she came into our family. Doesn't matter what happened between her and my son, she's still family. I know she doesn't think she needs anyone to take care of her—"

"Mamá—" Rafe warned from the other side of the bed.

"—but she does. I'm counting on you to make sure nothing happens to her and that those police officers you work with in Chicago figure out she had nothing to do with what went on there."

Shane's eyes shifted from Teresa to Hailey, who was looking up at him with a wary expression and eyes so blue he knew if he let himself he could easily dive in and never come up for air again. Beneath his hand, he felt Hailey's skin, warm and soft and alive. So different from how he felt 90 percent of the time. And that hum in his blood, the one he was discovering wasn't just a sexual reaction, ratcheted up another notch until every cell in his body was aware of only one thing: her.

*You can't save her. But maybe . . . she can save you.*

"I will," he said softly, never once looking away.

Teresa let out a long breath. Then she released both of their hands. "Good. That's . . . good."

Their eyes held even as Teresa closed her own. In the soft skin of Hailey's hand, he felt her pulse pound in time with his. It wasn't until Teresa sighed that Shane and Hailey both managed to tear their gazes from each other.

Teresa reached for Hailey one more time with weak arms. "Come here, m'ija."

The two hugged. More quiet words were spoken. Then Teresa dropped her arms and turned her head to the side to look where Rafe and Billy and Lisa were standing quietly watching the whole scene. Rafe's and Lisa's eyes were both red-rimmed and bloodshot. Billy just looked lost.

Quietly, Shane eased out of the room to give the family privacy. And as he leaned against the wall in the middle of the corridor, his heart thumping hard against his ribs, he tried to make sense of what had just happened. For some reason he had the strangest sense the ice he'd built up inside was slowly starting to thaw and break.

The elevator door opened down the hall, and Peter Kauffman, flanked by a woman with short dark hair, headed his direction. Both were holding small paper coffee cups with steam wafting from the lids.

"Maxwell." Surprise was evident on Kauffman's face when he reached Shane. He didn't ask the obvious question, but instead introduced Shane to his fiancée, Kat Meyer, and made small talk about Teresa.

It wasn't a shocker Kauffman was here. He and Rafe were tight as brothers. What was a shocker, though, was the fact all that resentment Shane had built up for Kauffman over what had happened to Hailey no longer seemed important.

Moments later, Hailey stepped out of the room, and though there were tear tracks on her cheeks, she didn't break down, didn't reach for him. Didn't even look his way. She said a quick hello to Pete and Kat, then announced she needed some fresh air before turning and striding away from Shane down the hall.

If he'd been thinking, he'd have given her space. But that connection they'd shared in Teresa's hospital room had done something to him. And he followed without a second thought.

She made it as far as the wide, tall windows that looked down to the parking lot before breaking down. He caught her just as her knees crumpled and pulled her tight against his chest. "Let it out."

Her hands clenched into fists against his chest, and her face dropped to his shoulder. He wrapped his arms around her and held her close while she cried. And wasn't it strange that normally a hysterical woman made him want to run for the hills, but this one? This one he couldn't seem to get enough of no matter the situation.

He didn't talk, just rubbed her back and held her while

she worked through her emotions. And he knew when she finally had because she went still in his arms.

"I hate that you've seen me like this."

*There* was the feisty woman he remembered. Her voice was muffled. And so damn sexy, all rough and spent from the past few days, it made him think of holding her like this in his bed. Naked. Just the two of them.

"Like what?

"Like *this*. A blubbering mess." When she pushed back, wiped her cheeks and waved her hands, he realized she'd pulled up her temper. But that was okay. If this was what she needed to do to work through losing Teresa, he'd argue with her all she wanted. "I'm so not *that* woman. The kind who cries and gets sick and needs someone to take care of her. Teresa was just plain wrong. You know that's not me."

"I know exactly who you are, Hailey." Her mouth snapped shut when he stepped close and ran his thumb over her cheek to wipe back a tear.

Yeah, he realized as he caressed her soft skin. Over the last few days she'd definitely thawed him out. To the point where he was actually starting to feel again. To think about the future. About what it could be like. With her in it. But would it be enough to make up for what he'd done?

He dropped his hand and fought the urge to kiss her. "Do you want to stay here?"

Slowly, she shook her head. "I want to go find my father's letter."

So did he. So they could wrap this up. And maybe then he could figure out what he was going to do about Hailey Roarke.

Nicole tossed her magazine on the coffee table in the lobby of the hospital. Pursed her lips and tapped her toe against the carpet. What was taking so long? She glanced at her watch. She'd been sitting here for nearly two hours. Were they just going to leave her down here all night?

Frustration growing, she headed for the Coke machine

she'd seen down one of these corridors earlier. The elevator opened and Billy walked out.

She stilled. Caught her breath. Then wished she'd been ten seconds earlier and nowhere to be seen. He looked like hell, eyes all red, hand shaking as he rubbed his forehead. Though he was alone, one look told her everything she needed to know about what had happened upstairs.

"We're going," he barked without looking at her face.

She fell in line next to him not because he'd ordered, but because . . . hell, she wasn't even sure why anymore. "What about Shane and Hailey?"

"They left an hour ago."

They had? She hadn't seen them. But then there had to be numerous entrances and exits in this place.

"Get in," he said when they reached the car. He didn't hold her door for her like he had earlier in the day, didn't give any indication he even wanted her there. Just snarled at her and turned over the engine, then glared off into space.

And she knew she had a choice, right then. Walk away from him and all this for good or . . . not. Quietly, she climbed in, closed the door and clicked her seat belt.

He drove faster than she liked, weaving through the streets of San Juan while "Maria, Maria" blared out of the radio. She didn't bother asking him where they were headed, but she wondered. Especially when the early evening lights of the city turned to darkness and a sea of green.

Forty minutes later he pulled to a stop in front of a run-down shack. The jungle was thick here, large palm fronds and trees she didn't know how to identify hiding parts of the dilapidated building. Without a word, he got out of the car and disappeared behind the cabin.

She stayed, taking in the unwelcoming environment. Then figured enough was enough and went to look for him. She heard water running, like from a river or stream, and smelled damp earth and moss. As she pushed her way through vines that snared her arms and legs, she cursed under her breath at the fact it was humid as hell and she was sweating—not to mention ruining her good shoes—then stumbled when the foliage opened up and she found herself standing on the edge of a cliff that seemed to drop at least a quarter mile straight down.

Her breath caught. The wind danced lazily across her skin, birds screeched far below, and the sky was so close she thought she could touch it. In the distance, a mountain range rose, the peaks covered with clouds.

But the view didn't capture her attention. The man standing dangerously close to the edge with his hands shoved deep into the pockets of his jeans, his eyes staring straight down, was all she could see.

He wasn't planning to jump, was he? Her mind spun as she searched for something she could say to talk him back from the ledge. And came up with only one thing she knew he'd be interested in.

"Three." When Billy didn't bother to look her way, she added, "That's the number on the bottom of my mother's bronze. Well, oh-three."

He still didn't turn to face her, which she figured couldn't be a good sign. She glanced from him to the ledge he'd inched closer to as her anxiety shot up a notch.

"I saw it last spring, hidden in the back of her closet. I'd gone in there to pilfer a pair of shoes because . . . well, I knew it would tick her off." She waved her hand even though he still hadn't looked at her. "That part's not important. What is important is the fact it's gone now. I went looking for it when I was home a few days ago. And when I asked Matilda where she'd put it, the housekeeper said my mother had gotten rid of it. We had a little 'tiff' as my mother calls it, because I wouldn't give her mine. I haven't talked to her since."

When even that didn't get a response, she eased down to sit on a large boulder, but her muscles were tensed and ready in case she had to lunge and pull him back.

Her heart beat like wildfire when she said, "She doesn't think too highly of me, my mother. The only consolation is she doesn't think highly of Hailey, either."

And boy, didn't that make her sound like a bitter Jan Brady? *Way to go, Nicole.*

She blew out a breath. Wished he'd look at her or say something, and when he did neither, figured she'd just keep on going. "You asked me why I hate Hailey? I don't. Not really. I mean, not in the way you think. It's just . . ." She shrugged. "Nothing breaks her. I was the one my mother favored. I was the one who got away with everything. Daddy . . . he tried. Early on I remember him stepping in and intervening on our behalf with our mother, but she never backed down. And after a while, he just kinda stopped. But Hailey . . ."

Her voice trailed off as she thought about the numerous battles Hailey and Eleanor had had over the years. About Garrett's repeated attempts to draw Hailey into RR and their mother sloughing the idea off. Hailey had never wanted to work for Roarke Resorts on principle. No one had bothered to ask Nicole.

"If anything," Nicole said quietly, "it made her tougher. She doesn't need anybody. Not like me."

"Why are you telling me all this?" His harsh voice brought her eyes up from the ledge she'd been studying as memories ran through her mind. But he didn't look at her. He was still staring off into the ravine below.

"I don't know. I guess maybe because halfway up this mountain I realized if you were planning to kill me and bury my body in the rain forest somewhere, there aren't many people who'd miss me."

He finally turned and focused on her, his hands shoved deep into his pockets, his foot mere centimeters from the edge of the cliff. That strong jaw of his flexed beneath a day's worth of stubble, and though there was still anger and pain in his eyes from losing his mother, there was something else, too. A hint of something soft that shored up her courage and made her go on, even though part of her knew it was a really dumb idea. "Sisters should miss each other, don't you think?"

"You have a long way to go to convince Hailey of that."

She sure did, didn't she? "I can help by giving her the numbers."

"You don't want them for yourself?"

Did she? She looked out across the valley and thought about her family, Hailey, everything Billy had just lost. Was her need to prove her worth to Eleanor Roarke really that important in the grand scheme of life? She shook her head. "I wouldn't know what to do with them. I'm not Hailey."

He glanced across the rolling hills to the blue-green mountains beyond. "The native Taíno people believed the good spirit Yuquiyu reigned from the mountaintop throne of El Yunque over there." Her gaze drifted to the mountain off in the distance. "Do you believe in spirits, Nicole?"

She knew he was talking about his mother, and the tender spot in her chest that had started as a pinprick the night they'd spent in her hotel suite grew by leaps and bounds. She'd felt it expand at the racetrack, even when he'd been so mad at her he couldn't seem to see straight. Felt it even more now as a lost look crept into his eyes.

"I believe there's a lot I don't know," she said softly. "And after everything that's happened today, I'm not ruling anything out."

He looked down. Toed the soil near the ledge of the cliff. Rocks and dirt broke free and bounced down the embankment, picking up speed until nothing was left but a soft thud echoing up from far below.

She tensed. And just when she was sure he was going to tell her he did believe in spirits, then step off that ledge, he eased back, turned and walked toward her. The relief that pulsed through her entire body was as sweet as wine.

He stopped when they were toe to toe. "Stand up."

She did, slowly, as her eyes ran over his square jaw, up to his hazel eyes and light brown hair so different from his brother's.

"I don't like lies," he said. "And I won't put up with half-truths."

"I . . . I can do honest."

"I'm not so sure. You've been scheming so long, I don't even know if you can handle honest."

"I can try."

He stared at her until her skin tingled. And just when she was sure he wasn't going to say anything else, he said, "This is my uncle's land. I come up here when I need to be alone."

"You stay here? By yourself?"

"Sometimes." He tipped his head. "Do you like being alone, Nicole?"

Her heart pounded against her ribs. He didn't touch her, didn't take his hands out of his pockets or move any closer. But there was something in his eyes. Something sad and broken and lost and yearning. Something a lot like what she'd been feeling most of her adult life. Something . . . that told her the answer she gave right now would change everything between them.

"No," she said softly as she pulled up her courage. "I don't want to be alone anymore."

"Neither do I," he whispered.

He leaned down to brush his mouth over hers. Then wrapped his arms around her and finally, *finally* kissed her with the sweetest mouth she'd ever tasted.

# CHAPTER EIGHTEEN

Hailey couldn't sleep.

She threw back the covers on the guest bed in Rafe and Lisa's monster house and pulled on her clothes. The letter she and Shane had found in Teresa's jewelry box hadn't answered any of her questions. It was just more garbled clues about keys and locked treasures, and at the moment she was so frustrated with her father and everything else, she couldn't stay still.

She pulled open the door as quietly as she could and tip-toed down the old hardwood floors until she reached the stairs. The top step creaked, and she paused, hoping she wasn't waking the entire house.

The old plantation-style colonial was way bigger than either Rafe or Lisa needed, but since they were still in the process of getting the San Juan branch of Odyssey up and running, they were using some rooms for storage. They'd also moved Teresa here from the small bungalow Rafe had bought for her in the city, and the fact she wasn't here left a giant void in the house that Hailey could feel all the way into her bones.

Tears pushed at her eyes again at the thought of Teresa, but she forced them back and continued down the stairs. She'd mourn later. After she figured out her father's blasted riddle and cleared her name. Until then, she couldn't let herself get sucked down into the pain. Teresa would never have wanted that for her anyway.

The oversize kitchen was dark when she stepped into the room. She felt for the light switch.

"*Carajo*," Rafe exclaimed as the fluorescent bulb above popped on. "Have some mercy here."

Hailey jumped, looked toward the old butcher-block table where he was sitting with a coffee cup in front of him, rubbing his eyes. "I'm sorry. I didn't know anyone was in here. I'll turn the light off."

"Don't bother now. You already blinded me."

Though his snarky comeback shouldn't have made her smile, it did. Because this, at least, was normal.

"There's coffee if you want it," he mumbled, still rubbing his eyes.

Since it was two A.M., and she knew she wasn't getting any more sleep, she figured *Why not?* "Thanks."

She found a mug in the cupboard and poured herself a cup, then came back to the table to sit beside him. He looked like death warmed over, and he'd lost weight since she'd seen him a few weeks ago. "Is Lisa sleeping?"

"Yeah." He eased back in his chair. "We've been at the hospital pretty much every day this week."

That ache filled her chest again, along with the feeling she should have been here rather than off in Chicago chasing treasure. "I'm so sorry, Rafe."

"Yeah. Well . . ."

He stared at his mug. Then finally those dark eyes of his lifted to her face, and she realized, in that moment, marrying him had not been a mistake. She'd loved him—still loved him—just not in the way either of them needed. Teresa was right: they were family. In one of those twisted ways most people wouldn't understand. In a way that meant more to her than any of her Roarke blood relatives, save Graham.

"So that cop," Rafe said. "You gonna tell me what the deal is there?"

She almost laughed. Yep, this was the man she knew so well. Always sticking his nose where it didn't belong, looking out for her more like a big brother than an ex-husband. "There is no deal. He's just helping me."

"Looks to me like he's doing more than just helping. How the heck did you run into him anyway?"

"He came to question me about Bryan's murder." He nodded in a way that made her flick him a look. "It's not what you think."

"What do I think?"

"That there's something going on between us. There isn't. I mean . . ." She looked into her coffee because even she knew her protest sounded stupid. What the hell *was* going on between her and Shane? She rose to get more java. "I don't know what to tell you."

Rafe snickered as he lifted his mug to his lips.

"I thought I heard a party going on in here," Lisa said from the doorway. Her short red hair was tousled, and she wore cotton capri sleep pants and a baggy T-shirt. She kissed Rafe on the top of his head as she walked by, then reached for a mug from the cupboard.

Hailey made room at the counter. "Hope we didn't wake you."

"No." Lisa poured coffee into her mug. "Couldn't sleep."

"She can't sleep without me," Rafe said. "Isn't that right, *querida*?"

Lisa frowned and took her mug to the chair on Rafe's other side. "Damn irritating is what I call it," she mumbled.

A smile spread across Rafe's face as he reached for Lisa's hand on the table. One that told Hailey, yeah, he was hurting now, and it would take a long time for him to heal, but he'd be okay.

Lisa set her mug down. "So Shane told me what happened at your uncle's place in the Everglades."

"What happened in the Everglades?" Rafe asked, suddenly serious.

Oh, man, now there was a story she didn't want to repeat to this man. She already had one overprotective alpha male watching her every move. She did not need two.

When Hailey avoided the question by picking up her coffee and taking a long drink, Lisa dove into the story. Starting with their car going into the slough and ending with her little poisoning scare.

That tired look was gone from Rafe's dark eyes when his attention focused on Hailey. "Okay. You're not leaving this house."

Hailey rolled her eyes and headed for the refrigerator, looking for something to keep her hands busy. "As if that's gonna stop me. Lisa, do you guys have eggs?"

"Yeah, all the way in the back." Lisa pushed back from the table and joined Hailey at the fridge. "I think there's even some bacon in the freezer."

Rafe turned in his chair. "Stop avoiding the topic."

"What topic?" Pete asked from the doorway, his messy blond hair matted on one side.

"I'll make more coffee," Lisa announced, turning for the pot.

"Did we wake you?" Hailey asked as she set breakfast makings on the counter.

Beside Pete, Kat yawned. "No. The mix-master in my bed woke me."

Pete grinned in that lazy way of his and wrapped an arm around Kat's shoulder. "Usually you like it when I wake you in the middle of the night."

Kat rolled her eyes. Hailey and Lisa chuckled.

"So what topic are we avoiding?" Pete asked, finding an open chair at the table and dropping into it.

"Hailey and Shane," Lisa said.

"Poisonings, murder and car chases," Rafe huffed.

"'Kay, wait." Pete held up a hand. "The heiress and the cop are finally getting it on. I picked up on that. But you're going to have to repeat that last part."

Kat's brows lifted. "Wow. No one around here does anything normal, do they?"

Hailey rubbed her suddenly throbbing head and turned toward Lisa. "I think I need alcohol."

Lisa grinned. "I'm pretty sure we have all the makings for screwdrivers in here somewhere."

Oh, now wasn't that appropriate?

While Lisa and Rafe filled Pete and Kat in on the drama surrounding Hailey and her father's will, Hailey played bartender. Rafe took his mug to the sink and started in on breakfast, cracking eggs into a bowl and whipping them up for his famous omelets. The kitchen was a buzz of activity, voices chattering, plates and glasses clinking. It was like every other get-together they'd had over the years, so long as you overlooked the fact it was two A.M. and the reason they were all here was because they'd lost someone they loved.

The kitchen door opened with a clank, and Billy came in, dressed in the same clothes he'd worn that day. Though the rest of them had all gotten some kind of sleep, the dark circles under his eyes and his sallow skin confirmed he hadn't slowed down since leaving the hospital. Conversation quieted as he stepped into the room. Especially when he pulled an exhausted Nicole in after him.

Hailey's gaze flicked from Billy to Nicole, then over to Rafe. And she didn't miss the flash of temper in Rafe's eyes.

Rafe's attention returned to the stove, where he flipped an omelet. But his jaw clenched and unclenched in that controlled way of his that said he was good and truly ticked. "Wondered when we'd see you again."

The brothers' tumultuous relationship was nothing new, but Hailey had thought the two had turned a corner when they'd brought Teresa to Puerto Rico several months ago. They'd seemed to be getting along and working together, until the last month or so when Billy had lit back to Miami to pick up his old life, working for Pete at Odyssey now and then and doing freelance security work that was 10,000 levels beneath that Nobel Prize brain of his.

Billy closed the kitchen door with one hand but kept the other wrapped tightly around Nicole's. "We've been at Marc and Michaela's house."

Rafe glanced over at the mention of his aunt and uncle, Teresa's younger brother and wife who lived in San Juan. "What were you doing there?"

Billy shrugged. "Planning. Mamá wanted to have a wake, just like we did for Dad when he died. I want to make sure we do it right."

Rafe flipped off the fire. His brows drew together in a way that said this obviously wasn't where he'd expected Billy to run off for after leaving the hospital. "I would have gone with you. If you'd waited—"

"Rafe," Billy cut in. "You got a houseful of people here. And besides. I want to do this. You've been handling everything up until now. I think it's way past time I stepped in and did my share." When Rafe's mouth dropped open in protest, he added, "Let me take care of this. For Mamá. It doesn't make up for any of the other crap I've done, but it's a start."

You could have knocked Rafe over with a fingertip, that's how shocked he looked. The room was silent as everyone listened. Luckily, Lisa had the faculties to break the silence and step forward to hug Billy. "I think that is the best gift you can give her, Billy. She'd love that."

"Thanks, Lisa."

That seemed to break the spell Rafe was under, and without hesitation, he moved forward to hug Billy as well. Conversation picked back up in the kitchen, the tense weight of Billy's arrival lifting like a cloud being swept away. And as tears burned Hailey's eyes again, she knew yep, these guys were family. And she wouldn't change it if she could.

Realizing Rafe had left the eggs cooking on the stove, Hailey moved to transfer them to a plate.

"What's going on in here?"

She turned quickly at the sound of Shane's deep voice and looked up to find him standing closer than she'd expected. His hair was rumpled, his jaw stubbled, his feet bare. In a light blue T-shirt and faded jeans, he looked sexy and dangerous and way too much like the comfort she needed right this minute.

She squeezed between Pete and Kat, set the first omelet on the table along with a handful of forks, then returned to the counter to grab a rag to wipe her hands. "Well, let's see.

Billy and Rafe just had a moment. We're eating breakfast because no one can sleep. Screwdrivers are in the pitcher over there, and I don't have a clue what's going on with Nicole. What are you up to?"

"Tony left a message on my cell. Said he had some info for us."

Okay, well, if that wasn't a buzzkill, nothing was. Not for the first time, Hailey wished he hadn't picked up a replacement phone in Marathon, though part of her was dying to know what was happening in Chicago. "Did he elaborate?"

"Not yet. Said he'd call back."

Since there was no sense stressing over what she couldn't foretell, Hailey reached for a glass. "Do you want—"

A piece of paper was shoved in her face. Hailey turned, only to see Nicole handing her a note. "Here. This is both of them. Mine and Mother's."

Glass forgotten, Hailey hesitantly took the slip of paper from her sister. She was aware of Shane's rapt attention at her side as she opened the paper to peer at the numbers inside. "You're giving them to me, just like that?"

Nicole shrugged. "They're just numbers."

Conversation in the kitchen died down once again, only this time she and Nicole were the center of attention. "Why now? I don't under—"

"Look, it's no big deal, okay? I mean, if you don't want them—"

For whatever reason, Hailey realized her sister was offering her a gift. And when she saw the way Nicole shot a nervous look at Billy, and the sappy, stupid expression on Billy's face while he watched Nicole from across the room, Hailey knew something monumental had happened here tonight. "I didn't say that. I just . . ."

"Yeah, well," Nicole said, crossing her arms over her chest, looking increasingly uncomfortable with the conversation. "I only physically have the one statue. I put mine in my safety-deposit box after Bryan was killed, just in case."

"I don't need the actual statues," Hailey said. "Just the numbers."

"That's good because I'm petty sure Mother destroyed hers. You know she never liked that thing. She only hung on to it because Daddy gave it to her and wouldn't let her get rid of it. She was more than interested in getting mine, though, after the will reading." Nicole glanced at the note. "Oh, and that third number is from Graham's bronze."

Hailey's brows drew together. "How did you get Graham's?"

"I went to see him."

"When?" Shane asked at Hailey's side.

"A couple of days ago. The day before Billy and I saw you at the racetrack."

"Did you call him ahead of time?" Shane asked. "Did he know you were coming?"

Nicole's brow wrinkled. "Yeah, I called him from Mother's. I wasn't just gonna surprise him. He's got a heart condition, you know."

Shane's gaze flicked to Hailey. "The tea could have been targeted for her. If he knew she was looking for the bronzes on her own—"

"That's quite a stretch, Maxwell," Hailey started, even as her stomach tightened. She still didn't believe Graham could do such a thing. To family, no less.

Nicole's confused gaze flicked between them. "Look, I don't know what you two are talking about but as far as the numbers go, I only have three. I still don't have Bryan's—"

"I do," Hailey said, turning back to her sister. And with Bryan's number that made five out of six. They were so close she could almost taste it.

She didn't miss the flare of excitement in Shane's voice as he realized the same thing. "Lis, you got paper and pens? We've got a little puzzle we could use some help decoding."

Madeline's stomach was a coil of nerves as she stood in the middle of Eleanor's study staring at a Jackson Pollock on the wall. Probably worth a fortune, she figured, but to her it looked like random chaos and a great big headache. Garrett had always hated the painting, which is why it hung on the wall. There were several throughout the massive house, all in much more prominant locations. A sign of the many battles Eleanor had won over the years.

"I thought Friday's funeral arrangements were all decided," Eleanor said at her back.

Slowly, Madeline turned and looked toward Bryan's aunt, dressed in crisp peach-colored slacks and a cream silk blouse. It was no secret she and Eleanor had never gotten along. Eleanor was a Schmidt through and through—refined, from old money, as polished as the fancy boarding school she'd attended. She was as far removed from Madeline's middle-class upbringing as were the pearls around the older woman's slim neck. But they had one thing in common—both their husbands had lived up to the Roarke reputation to the full extent of the name. And that was something Madeline would never forget.

"I lied to your housekeeper. I'm not here about the funeral."

Eleanor's eyes narrowed, and she turned and pulled the parlor door closed with a snap. "Perhaps you'd better tell me what this is about, then." She sat behind her desk, lacing her elegant fingers together on the surface as she looked up with raised brow and waited.

Intimidation. Eleanor was good at it. But this time, Madeline was in control.

"I want the bronze."

Eleanor didn't even blink. "You have no interest in RR."

"I don't want it for that."

"For what, then?"

"Peace of mind. You could turn on me anytime. That doesn't seem like a partnership. Not the one you proposed."

Eleanor leaned back in her chair. And in the silence, Madeline's pulse picked up. "No."

"What?"

"I said no." She leaned forward to reach for a pen on the

smooth desk surface. "Now if you'll excuse me, I have work to do. You can show yourself out."

Madeline stood slack-jawed. Though part of her had expected this, there was still an element of disbelief to Eleanor's smug attitude. "All I have to do is tell one person—"

"Tell them what, Madeline?" Eleanor said with ice in her words. "No one will believe you. Because you and I both know it *never* happened."

"But you—"

"This conversation is over. If you were smart you'd think long and hard about ever bringing it up to me again. The door is behind you."

The finality to Eleanor's words stung like a slap in the face. As Madeline slowly made her way out of the mansion and stopped on the front steps to peer up at the bright sky, all the worry and fear she'd been dragging with her the last few days became reality. If she didn't produce the bronze, Lucy was going to turn her in. She had no doubt the bitch would do it without a second thought. Life as she knew it would end, unless she came up with a way out.

She glanced back at the heavy doors, now closed, and felt her stomach roll with a wave of disgust and hatred for a family she'd never understood, but tried so hard to be a part of. There was only one way out of this mess now, one way to be free, and it involved destroying the social ladder she'd spent so many years climbing.

She reached for her cell phone and dialed her father-in-law. As it rang, a strange sense of victory washed over her. People would talk. They'd say her backwater upbringing had caught up with her. But that was okay; she could deal with the gossip. Because she knew when the secret Bryan had discovered finally came out, Eleanor would be the one really suffering.

"Look at them. You'd think world peace hinged on the outcome of those numbers the way they're enraptured by them."

Hailey turned from where she'd been refilling her coffee

mug for the umpteenth time to glance toward the kitchen table where Lisa was watching the four men hunched together, trying to decipher her puzzle. Rafe, with his golden skin and dark hair standing up straight where he'd obviously pulled at it; Pete, all blond and buff, methodically calculating something in his head; while Billy, the Irish white boy of the group, tore a paper into six parts, wrote one number on each and started reorganizing them so they could look at different patterns. Then there was Shane, Mr. Dark and Skeptical, leaning back in his chair with his arms crossed over his chest, a coffee cup at his elbow and a scowl on his sexy face.

Yeah, they were a group all right. She'd seen them put their heads together like this once before, when they'd been plotting to get Tisiphone back, the Greek Fury relief that had brought Rafe and Lisa together in the first place. But she'd never predicted all four would ever be working together again. Especially knowing what Shane thought of the others.

"They're definitely something," Hailey said as she took a sip of fresh coffee. "Though what that is, I'm still not sure." She'd given up on the screwdrivers, knowing alcohol was the last thing she needed tonight. After they'd eaten Rafe's omelets, the men had decided to get busy on her numbers while Nicole and Kat volunteered to clean up, and Hailey and Lisa had tried to keep the peace among the four. It had worked for a while, except now frustration levels were growing.

Lisa crossed her arms over her chest and leaned back against the counter. "He keeps glancing over here to check on you."

Hailey had seen the way Shane was watching her all night, and it only increased her anxiety. "He's uncomfortable."

"Oh, please," Lisa scoffed. "My overprotective twin knows how to handle my domineering husband. He's worried *you're* uncomfortable."

"Why would he worry about that?"

"Because that's what he does. He worries about everyone but himself. Always has. Growing up, it was about me and my sisters and our mother. About making sure we were all taken care of long before he was. It's part of the reason I finally moved to San Francisco. I love him to death, but man, he can be stifling."

Hailey understood that. As she watched Shane lean forward to reach for her father's cryptic letter to explain something to Billy, she thought about all the ways he'd been stifling her over the last few days. True, it was irritating as hell to have someone watching out for you like that, but at the same time, like nothing she'd ever known. No one had ever been so concerned about her before. Not her ex-lovers or her ex-husband. Not even her father.

"I knew it," Lisa said quietly at her side.

Hailey turned to look at the woman who'd become a close friend over the last few months. "What?"

"You're in love with him."

"What? No, I'm not."

Lisa's smile was all-knowing as she reached out to touch Hailey's arm. "It's okay. I'm not going to tell anyone. Especially him."

"Good, because I'm not—"

"Hailey," Lisa said with a look. "You're talking to the most stubborn woman on the planet, here. No one knows about denial more than I do."

Hailey's heart thumped against her ribs as she turned back to watch Shane move Billy's papers around in front of him. His deep voice drifted to her ears, and though she couldn't hear the exact words he used, just the sound sent electricity flowing through her veins.

Was she in love with him? Is that what was happening here? She was crazy about him, in a way she'd never been about anyone—even Rafe—but was that love?

"Look," Lisa said even softer. "I love the idiot because he's my brother, and well, he's a lot like me. I think you'd be . . . no, I think you *are* good for him. But there's something you need to know about Shane."

Hailey tore her gaze from the men to look at her friend again. "What?"

Lisa glanced at her brother, then turned her back so the men couldn't see her face. Quietly she said, "Something happened to him about six months ago. I'm not sure exactly what. He never talked about it, but it was some situation one night when he'd gone after a suspect. They fought. The other guy had a knife. Shane got cut and ended up in the hospital for over a week—punctured lung and some serious internal injuries."

Hailey thought back to the scar on Shane's side. The one she'd run her fingers over when they'd kissed in his apartment.

"I was on a dig when it happened," Lisa went on, "and he wouldn't let our mother tell me. I only found out after I got home when he showed up at my apartment in San Francisco, unannounced, a week after getting out of the hospital. He stayed with me for two weeks before going back to Chicago, but he never once talked about it. Ever since then, he's been different. Quieter. More withdrawn. At our wedding, here in San Juan? When he was with you? That was the first time I'd seen him smile in months. But since being back in Chicago he seems to have fallen back into that same funk as before."

Hailey's mind ran to the way Shane had reacted when she'd touched that scar, how he'd immediately pulled back and seemed disoriented. She looked at him across the room. *I'm me and you're . . .*

"I didn't tell you this to change how you feel about him," Lisa said quietly. "I just thought you should know. He won't talk to anyone about it. I've tried to get him to see a counselor, but he shuts down when I bring it up. The man's got a real distaste for anyone in the head business. I just . . . I wanted to help you understand why he can be so frustrating. At least lately. And yeah, to warn you. Relationships are hard enough. When you add in some of the stuff Shane's been through, it makes them a lot harder."

Hailey watched as he scratched his stubbly jaw, then glanced in her direction. Their eyes met, held, and he shot her that sexy half smile before refocusing on something Rafe was saying.

Oh, man. Lisa was right. And Hailey had sensed it long before this conversation. She knew the statistics better than anyone: cops had lower life expectancies, higher divorce rates, higher instances of alcohol and drug abuse and, for some, suicidal tendencies. Considering everything she knew about Shane, none of that was a surprise. But now that she'd left law enforcement, and had—admittedly, if only to herself—begun to enjoy working in the private sector, could she handle all of Shane's issues on top of her own? And if she could, would what she felt for him be strong enough to weather whatever his job threw at him next?

She didn't know. And that, coupled with not knowing how he felt about her deep down, only made her heart pump faster as Nicole walked past Shane and around the table to peer over Billy's shoulder at the numbers laid out in front of the men.

Nicole tossed the towel in her hands on the far counter and leaned over Billy to slide her arms around his neck and down his chest. "You guys have been arguing for an hour. No luck?"

Billy frowned. But he ran his hand down Nicole's arm in a move that was so unconsciously tender, it made Hailey smile. She never in a thousand years would have guessed those two would hook up, but as her father's unexpected death had taught her, she needed to let go of expectations. "No. Got any bright ideas?"

"Hmm." Nicole bit her lip and reached past Billy to rearrange the numbers. "Let me see."

Shane pushed back from the table and stopped at the counter near Hailey and Lisa to refill his coffee. "No way he's Nobel Prize smart." When both women smiled, he added, "Though if he ends up an ambulance chaser, it won't surprise me. He argues like a damn lawyer."

Hailey chuckled. And just as she was about to answer him, she heard Billy exclaim, "Say that again."

They all turned to look toward the table.

"Florida Keys," Nicole said, pushing up to stand. When she

realized everyone in the room was staring at her, a sheepish expression crossed her face. "I mean. That's what it looks like to me. Longitude and latitude."

Hailey moved next to Nicole to look down at the numbers.

"See?" Nicole said as Shane moved closer to look as well. "Twenty-five degrees, three minutes, five seconds. Eighty degrees, thirty-eight minutes, forty-two seconds. The Florida Keys are north longitude, west latitude. The numbers are a location."

"How do you know the coordinates of the Keys?" Rafe asked from across the table.

Nicole shrugged. "When I was in high school we had to pick a location and do a report on it. Numbers are something I never forget. And those are the coordinates of—"

Hailey placed a hand on her sister's arm. "Daddy's island."

"His what?" Shane asked.

"My father bought an island in the Keys just after I was born," Hailey said. "He used to take his sailboat there now and then. There aren't any buildings on it, just grass and trees and—"

"Sand," Nicole added, frowning.

Hailey nodded. "Yeah. I haven't been there since I was a kid. I completely forgot about it."

Suddenly, Nicole's eyes widened. "What were the clues again in that letter from Daddy?"

Shane handed Hailey her father's letter from the table. "The answer lies with me. The key is set in steel."

"He was cremated," Nicole said, thinking. "What does it mean, the answer lies with him?"

Shane's eyes met Hailey's. "You got a number for your father's lawyer?" he asked. "I've got a strange hunch."

"Yeah." Hailey nodded, already reaching for the phone. So did she.

"What hunch?" Kat asked as Hailey reached for the phone.

It was well after three A.M., but Ron Arnold answered on

the second ring. And the answers he gave to Hailey's questions were a punch to the gut.

A lump formed in her throat as she thanked him and pushed end on the cordless phone, then turned to look at the expectant faces peering back at her. "Dad wasn't cremated," she told Nicole. "Mother ordered it, but Ron stepped in at the last second and intervened. Per the terms of his will, he wanted to be buried on his island."

"No way," Pete muttered from across the kitchen. "You think the sixth sculpture's buried with him?"

It was beginning to look like the only answer.

"We need to have that body exhumed," Shane said. "Dr. Hargrove thought your father had been cremated. If he wasn't, they can run a tox screen and prove he was murdered."

Hailey nodded slowly. Right. But if they left it up to the authorities to exhume the body, she wouldn't get that sixth statue. And she needed it to lure out her father and Bryan's killer before the cops tracked her down and carted her off to jail.

Even though it turned her stomach, she knew she only had one option. She also knew Shane wasn't going to like it one bit. "Yeah, you're right. But we have to do it first."

She watched that lazy, relaxed mood Shane had been in crash and burn as he raked a hand through his hair. "You're certifiable. You're not digging up a grave to look for treasure. This is your father you're talking about."

"I know that—"

"She's right," Lisa said.

Shane glared his sister's way. "You stay out of this."

"Watch it," Rafe said.

Lisa placed a hand on her husband's chest. "Chill out, Rambo. We're all sleep deprived here." She glanced back at Shane. "You know as well as I do if the authorities dig up her father first, whatever's in his coffin gets added into evidence. And if that happens, according to what you both told us about her father's will and Bryan's murder, Hailey won't find out what this is all about or who set her up."

"What about the second part?" Nicole asked quietly in the tense silence. "'The key is set in steel.' What does that mean?"

Hailey bit her lip and tried to think as Shane paced around the kitchen. "It could just mean the key he left for me. We never found out what it went to."

"That's not steel," Shane said in a clipped tone. "It's brass."

Hailey blew out a breath. Yeah, he was definitely not happy.

"What else did he leave you?" Pete asked.

"Um. The key, the deed to his sailboat and—"

"The dagger," Billy finished for her.

Shane stopped pacing.

"What dagger?" Rafe asked as Hailey looked toward Billy.

"It's more like a letter opener," Hailey told him, very conscious of the way Shane walked out of the room without a word. Okay, so he was pissed. What did he expect her to do? "Small, Italian. Daddy picked it up at auction several years ago. Supposedly it was used to kill Alessandro de Medici. The same person The Last Seduction depicts."

"Maybe that's the key," Kat said.

Yeah, it could be. Hailey nodded. Her father's dagger was definitely made of aged steel.

"Too bad it's gone," Billy mumbled.

Rafe glanced at his brother, and like a lightbulb going on, his eyes narrowed. "How the hell do you know that? And while I'm thinking of it, what were you doing with Hailey and Nicole in the middle of all this in the first place?"

Okay, that was one part of this whole fiasco Hailey definitely did not want to have to explain to her ex-husband. "I told him about it," she said quickly, shooting Billy a warning as she sat in the nearest chair. "But he's right. It is gone. The last time I saw it was at the Roarke offices in Miami when I was attacked in the elevator. And if that's the key to something my father designed, we're screwed because according to Maxwell, they found it at the murder scene in Chicago. Whoever set me up did it well."

Silence settled over the room. And a sense of defeat washed over Hailey. It couldn't end like this. Not after everything that had happened. She closed her eyes and rubbed a hand over her brow.

A soft clank came from the table in front of her. And when she opened her eyes, she was staring at her father's dagger. Almost as if she'd willed it into appearance. Only instead of gleaming under the kitchen lights like she'd envisioned, it was wrapped in a clear plastic evidence bag, labeled by CPD.

"Oh, shit," Lisa muttered.

Hailey's eyes shot to Shane, who had backed up to stand alone in the doorway.

Her mind flashed to their confrontation on the tarmac just before she'd gotten on her plane to come down here. He'd been pissed. And now she knew why.

He'd taken evidence. From a murder investigation. Long before he'd known whether she was truly innocent of killing her cousin. And he'd done it all for her.

Words lodged in her throat. She pushed up slowly from her chair.

He'd screwed his career. For her.

The phone on his hip rang before she could put her thoughts into words. He flipped it open, pressed it to his ear and said, "Maxwell." A heartbeat later he added, "Yeah, Tony. I can talk." Then with one last lingering look her way, he walked out of the kitchen.

# CHAPTER NINETEEN

Shane rubbed a hand over his hair as he came back into the kitchen twenty minutes later. The news from Tony was good but not great. And he needed to talk Hailey out of this crazy grave-robbing idea before it was too late.

The kitchen was quiet and dark, a dim light shining above the stove. Lisa was the only person in the room, sitting at the table with her arms crossed over her chest.

Oh, yeah. He knew that look.

"Where'd everyone go?"

"To get some sleep," she said. "Big day tomorrow."

Oh, lovely. He definitely didn't need this. "You're not all going."

She lifted one brow. "And you have me to thank for that. Rafe and Pete were more than happy to dump everything here and take off for a few days to help Hailey. As it is, I talked them in to letting Billy and Nicole go instead."

"I don't need Billy Sullivan tagging along."

"Too bad. I hate to point this out, little brother, but this isn't about you. It's about Hailey. And Nicole. And where Nicole goes, Billy seems to want to go. So I think you're stuck with them."

Shane rolled his eyes. Just what he wanted—to have Sullivan and the Paris Hilton wannabe dogging them. Neither would talk a lick of sense into Hailey.

"I'm gonna try to get a few hours' sleep." He turned for the back stairs that ran from the kitchen to the second level.

"Hold on." When he looked back, she pushed away from the table and came to stand in front of him.

She was almost a foot shorter than he was, and they didn't share any physical characteristics other than the shape of their eyes. But personality-wise they were the most alike of any of his siblings—bullheaded, persistent, bordering on OCD, and overly perceptive, especially when it came to each other. He'd like to think those were twin traits, but something in his gut said even if they hadn't been twins, Lisa would still be able to read him like an open book.

His lips thinned because he already had an idea what was coming. "What?"

"I hope you know what you're doing."

"Lisa—"

"No." She held up a hand. "Don't give me that. If what Hailey said is true, someone doesn't just want her father's company, they want to see her gone for good."

"That's why I'm here."

"Is it?" Shadows played over her face and that fire red hair of hers as she stared at him. "Because I have a feeling you're here for something else. And judging from the way you've been the last few months, I'm worried you might not be able to handle it."

His jaw clenched. "I can handle it just fine. Don't worry about me."

"I do, though," she said quietly as he turned for the stairs. "A lot."

"Well, don't. I'm fine."

He made it two steps before her voice stopped him. "One more thing."

He heaved out a breath and gripped the banister. "What now?"

"Whatever it is you can't seem to let go of, be sure you've got it under control before things go any further with Hailey. Don't play loose and easy with her, Shane. Because no matter how tough she looks, that girl's been through a lot. And I'm not so sure she'll be able to handle it when you finally crash and burn."

He should have reassured her he was keeping his distance

from Hailey, that he was only here to help solve this puzzle, that he wasn't interested in anything but making sure justice got served and that nothing happened to Hailey in the process. But there were too many contradicting thoughts running through his head for him to formulate a coherent sentence. And that little voice whispering *See? Even Lisa doesn't think you can save her* was so damn irritating, all he wanted was his box of Tic Tacs and about three hours of peace. Instead, he said nothing and continued up the stairs.

The second level was quiet and dark when he reached it. Floorboards creaked as he moved down the hall. When he pushed open the door to his room, he did a double take.

Filtered moonlight through the window highlighted a trail of white specks along the taupe carpeting. He knelt to pick one up, only to realize they were Tic Tacs. *His* Tic Tacs.

What the . . . ?

He closed the door and followed the trail around a corner, only to pull up short when he saw Hailey sitting on his bed, wearing nothing but that Bon Jovi T-shirt he'd bought for her in the Keys. Her curly blonde hair fell around her shoulders in a gentle sweep, her legs were long and bare, one sexy thigh crossed over the other, her eyes luminescent in the dim light.

He swallowed. Tried to kick-start his brain so he could come up with one logical reason for her to be in his room, dressed like that. But no matter what he tried, all he could come up with was how damn sexy she looked and what he'd wanted to do with her from the moment they'd first met.

"Did Chen have info about the investigation?"

He nodded slowly.

Their eyes held. She bit her lip. Swung her top foot slightly. His gaze went down the long, shapely line of her leg to her purple-painted toenails. "Good or bad news?"

His blood warmed. *Don't play loose and easy with her.* "A little of both."

She sat where she was a few seconds, then pushed up and crossed the floor to stand in front of him. The lilac scent he associated with her drifted around him, heightening his senses, reminding him exactly what she felt like, tasted like and what he would have done in the Keys if Billy's phone call hadn't interrupted them.

*She won't be able to handle it when you crash and burn.*

"If you don't mind," she said, her blonde curls falling over her shoulder as she tipped her head to the side, "I think I'd rather wait and discuss Chen's news later. Right now I'm way more interested in how you got my father's dagger."

Her eyes were the bluest he'd ever seen. Her skin, like porcelain in the low light. At that moment, even exhausted from everything that had happened the last few days, she looked like she could handle just about anything life threw at her. She was a thousand times stronger than he was on a good day, and they both knew it. Not physically, but mentally, emotionally, and God, he wanted to be part of that. To remember what it felt like. If only for a minute.

"If your department finds out—"

"They won't. Evidence gets misplaced all the time."

Her eyes held his. And quietly she said, "You took it before I even explained what was going on with my father's will. Before you'd even made up your mind whether I was guilty or not. Why?"

He could give her a dozen logical reasons why he'd done what he had, starting with using it to lure out the real killer, to prove to the pompous Jim Hill at the DA's office that he hadn't been in on it with her from the start, to prove to himself his gut reaction was still right. But none of those were the real answer. And tonight at least, he was tired of pretending what was happening between them wasn't personal. He reached for her left hand. Lifted it. Ran his fingers down her smooth palm. "You're left-handed."

"I am."

"I didn't figure that out until I saw you boxing. But by then I already knew you hadn't killed your cousin."

"How?"

*Don't say it.*

"Because the woman who came to my apartment the night her cousin was killed couldn't possibly have kissed me like she did if she'd just committed murder."

*Too late.*

Heat flared in the depths of her eyes, and in the silence between them he heard her heart beating just as fast and erratically as his. Slowly, she lifted her hand. One lone Tic Tac clattered against the inside of the plastic case as she tipped it from side to side. "I think you're down to your last one. Do you want it?"

No, he wanted her.

She shook the mint into her hand, placed it between her thumb and forefinger and lifted it to his mouth. Her skin was silky smooth as it ran across his lips, then pressed inside to slide across his tongue. He tasted mint and her. Eyes locked on his, she slipped her fingers out of his mouth, brought them to her own succulent lips and licked first her thumb, then her forefinger before closing her lips around the digit and sucking.

Oh, man. She was playing him. It didn't take a rocket scientist to see the games in her eyes. He drew in a breath as he watched, felt all the blood in his head rush straight into his cock. And when she moved closer until her scent was a roar in his head and heat encircled his entire body, he knew his last thread of restraint had snapped.

"Do you feel like sharing?" she whispered.

"Yes."

"Good." A ghost of a smile flitted across her face. "Because wintergreen is my favorite flavor."

He opened at the first touch, cupped her face in his hands as he slid his tongue deep into her mouth and reveled in the groan that came from her chest. The mint slid from his tongue to hers. Her hands trailed up his chest, around to the nape of his neck, her fingertips sending sparks of desire through every inch of his body. She moaned as he pulled her tighter to him and his erection pressed into her belly. Her hands tightened in his hair as his mouth slid across her jaw to find her earlobe and the soft skin of her neck.

"Hailey?"

"Hmm?"

"You're my favorite flavor."

"Oh . . ."

He'd been hesitant. These last few days he'd tried to keep his distance. But she'd made the first move tonight, broken through every one of his walls until all he could see and feel was her. And now there was absolutely no turning back.

"I want you," he whispered, walking her backward toward the bed as he licked and nipped at her neck.

"Mm . . ."

"I want you in every position I've imagined. On your back, on your knees, on that damn airplane of yours."

She shuddered when his lips found an especially sensitive spot. "On my plane? I like the sound of that . . ."

He bit her earlobe gently until she moaned. "I want you calling my name."

The back of her legs hit the mattress. "Oh, yes, Max—"

"No." When she tried to cut off his words with her mouth, he pulled her arms from around his neck, pinned them to her back to get her attention and said, "My first name, Hailey. Like you did in the Bahamas when I got shot. Like you did when that damn alligator bit me in the Everglades."

Even before she opened her mouth, he knew what was going to come out. "I thought you might be dying both of those times. You look pretty healthy to me right now, Maxwell."

He felt like he might just die. If she didn't give him what he needed.

"Shane," he corrected.

Her blue eyes sharpened, and she smiled a slow and sexy little grin full of sass and challenge that supercharged his blood, and told him, oh, yeah, their little power struggle was alive and kicking. "Maxwell."

He flipped her around so fast she gasped. Her back was pressed tight to his chest and her cute little ass was grinding into his hips. Then he locked her arms around her front with one of his so she couldn't move, used his other hand to tip her head to the side and ran his tongue down the column of her neck until she quivered. "In a matter of minutes you'll be screaming my first name."

"Don't be so cocky," she said in a breathy tone he absolutely loved.

He rubbed against her backside. "I can't help it. It's what you do to me."

"Oh . . . do that again."

He nipped the juncture of her neck and shoulder, ran his tongue over the spot and sucked until she groaned. Then pushed her to her stomach on the mattress.

She went down easily, no fight, no resistance. Kneeling on the bed, he wrapped one arm around her waist and lifted, repositioning her higher into the pillow and using the opportunity to peek at the color she wore beneath her Bon Jovi tee.

Black. Satin and lace. His mouth watered at the thought of ripping the flimsy panties off with his teeth. He flipped her T-shirt up her back as he lifted her hips and pressed his lips along the base of her spine.

"Maxwell—" She came up to her hands, peered back at him over her shoulder.

As he trailed kisses along her back, he pushed his hand inside her shirt, around her torso and underneath to grasp one full, luscious, bare breast in his big palm.

Whatever protest she'd been about to make died on her lips. She moaned, pushing into him and arching her back.

His blood pounded. His cock strained to be set free. He trailed his lips up her spine until the T-shirt was around her shoulders and he could pull it free from her body. He dropped it on the floor, leaned over and kissed her shoulders, her neck, the mole just under her right shoulder blade. Then reached around to caress her breasts and draw her nipples into tight, stiff peaks against his fingers.

"Maxwell . . ." She pushed back into his hips, her body making him harder, her words that much more determined.

"Do you want more?"

"Yes . . ."

He brushed her hair over her shoulder and kissed her jaw. "Say, 'Yes, Shane, I want more.'"

She smiled, arched into him again. "Mmm . . . Yes, I want more."

God, she was stubborn. And he couldn't help it. He smiled. Because for the life of him, he couldn't remember another woman who left him more frustrated, more needy, more challenged and turned on than she did. "Officer Roarke, you are really asking for it."

Her squeal when he threw her onto her back was half laugh, half shock, but her moan when he pressed her into the mattress and kissed her hard was pure approval. Her hands ran to the hem of his shirt, up under until it was yanked from his body and they were skin to skin, her mouth taking him on a journey of a thousand senses.

He pulled back before she could seduce him into forgetting his goal, kissed his way down her neck to her succulent breasts. They were perfect in his hands, soft and silky, the tips like little pink erasers when he brushed his fingertips over them. And in his mouth? Heaven.

She groaned, arched up, dug her fingernails into his scalp until a lick of pain shot though his skin. But he didn't stop. He drew her deep into his mouth, first one breast, then the other, traced her nipples with his tongue as his hand slid south and her legs opened to make room for him.

"Oh, God, Maxwell . . ."

He worked his way down, over her toned abs, across the flat expanse of her belly, to the edge of her silky black panties. His tongue traced the edge. She shuddered. He lifted his head to peer up her body to her arousal-flushed face. "Are you ready to give in yet?"

A wan smile flitted across her features. She didn't open her eyes, though, not even when she reached for his hand on her belly and pulled it back to her breast. "Not even close."

"I thought you'd say that."

He gripped her panties with his teeth and stripped them

from her luscious legs. And when her eyes flew open and she gasped, pushing up on her elbows to look down at him, he smiled.

He had a raging hard-on. And seeing her there like that, naked and laid out for him like an offering, all he wanted to do was strip off his jeans and bury himself inside her.

Instead he dropped to his knees, grabbed her thighs and pulled until her calves were hanging off the bed and his mouth was brushing dangerous kisses against her inner thigh.

She drew in a breath. Swallowed—hard—while he drew closer to her sweetest spot. And watched him with lust-glazed eyes.

He licked the juncture of her hip. Her head fell back and her eyes slid closed. He breathed hot over her mound—careful never to make contact—until she groaned, opened wider and lifted her hips, searching.

"Ready?"

"Please . . ." She thrust up again.

"Please, Shane," he corrected, running one hand up her neglected leg, while the other found her breast and squeezed.

"Oh . . ."

Her back arched. He licked the opposite hip juncture. Trailed his tongue lower. Bit just hard enough to make her tremble.

"Dammit, stop teasing me, Shane. I need you right now."

He didn't hesitate, dove in with one long, lingering lick, split her thighs with his hands and circled and swirled until she came in his mouth.

He might have been able to hold off, could have slowed things down now that he'd gotten what he'd wanted, but when he heard her screaming his first name as her climax peaked, every rational plan about being a slow and easy lover went sailing out the window.

His mouth found her belly, her breasts, her neck, her mouth. She didn't hesitate, pushed her tongue inside and kissed him crazy while her hands wrestled with his pants and finally set him free. Somehow he found the presence of mind to pull a condom from his wallet—condoms he'd bought that morning in the Keys, just in case—eased back on his knees and nearly lost it when she sat up, ripped the foil open and rolled it down his length.

Her hand squeezed, stroked, drove him wild. Her eyes held his until he was afraid he'd come just from that minor touch. But it was her words that did him in. "Yes, Shane," she whispered. "I want more."

He hooked one arm around her thigh and lifted, shifting his knee under her slightly so he could thrust inside her on a long groan. The angle arched her back, pushed the tips of her breasts higher. He leaned forward and drew one deep into his mouth and felt her whole body shudder.

"Oh, Shane . . ."

That did it. Feeling her tighten around him with her release as she called his name was all he could take. He shifted, captured her mouth with his and finally let go.

Hailey came awake with a start. She'd been dozing, snuggled next to Shane in his bed, warm and sated and . . . safe.

She eased up on her elbow, looked down at him. He was really something. Her sex clenched at just the thought of what he'd done to her earlier, and a smile played across her face. Making love with him had been so much hotter and exciting than she'd expected. She'd loved what he'd done to her. Loved their wrangling and the fact he knew what he wanted and didn't back down. Loved even more that, though it was obvious he'd been fighting his attraction for her all this time, when it came down to it, he wanted her just as much as she wanted him. The fact he'd taken her father's dagger proved that tenfold. Honestly, she just loved . . . him.

Her heartbeat quickened as the knowledge set in. She loved him. Even with his frustrating moods and confusing angles and dark secrets she wasn't sure she wanted to know about. She just . . . loved him. The thought created a sweet ache she didn't want to get rid of.

She ran her hand over his skin, needing to touch him. He

moaned in his sleep, tilted his head her way, and she smiled at the approval as her finger circled his belly button, then up to the edge of his ribs. And that's when she saw the scar. Up high on the left side. A three-inch jagged pucker of skin she hadn't noticed during their earlier power struggle. She gently brushed the uneven ridge.

His eyes flew open, and his hand clasped around her wrist with such force, she gasped. She didn't have time to get one word out before he flipped her to her back and wrapped his other hand around her neck so tight it closed her windpipe.

She choked, gasped, kicked as her hands flew to her neck to pry his fingers loose. His eyes were black as night and glazed over, but even through the blur of tears and darkness circling in, she saw the malevolence.

"Shane . . ." she rasped.

A microsecond passed, though it felt like a year. His eyes cleared, focused on her face, ran down to his hand, clamped around her neck. Then he instantly let go.

"Oh, God, Hailey. Oh, shit. Are you okay? Oh . . . fuck."

She rolled to her side, coughed, drew ragged breaths to ease the burn. The mattress dipped. Seconds later he was back with a glass of water and a cold, damp rag, which he laid gently across her neck. "Jesus, Hailey. I'm sorry. I'm so sorry. Sit up and drink some water. The cold will help so it doesn't bruise. Just let me massage it—"

She pushed his hand away. "Stop."

He let go immediately. Stepped back until his legs hit the plush chair near the wall and seemed to go out beneath him.

She wasn't hurt. Not really. He'd scared her more than anything, and as she lay on her side and watched him lean forward on his knees and rest his head in his hands, she knew he was suffering way more than she was.

What had happened to him? She remembered the way he'd reacted that night in his apartment when he'd been kissing her. He'd pulled back then, fallen against the arm of the couch much like he had just now. And then it had happened just after she'd touched that scar on his side, too.

She'd always sensed a dangerous element in him, something lurking right beneath the surface, but she hadn't seen it until tonight. She only knew one thing for certain. What had just happened had been a reflex. He would never do anything to harm her intentionally.

He didn't hear her climb off the bed or cross the floor. He was obviously too wrapped up in his own guilt. It wasn't until she rested her hands on his knees and lowered to the floor in front of him that his head lifted and surprised, sad eyes locked on hers.

Oh, she was right. Not in a million years would he ever hurt her.

"I'm sorry. God, Hailey, I—"

She pushed against his shoulder. He fell back easily, no resistance, no worry that she was going to retaliate. Her eyes ran over his naked body, to the scar on his side, to the one on his shoulder where he'd taken a bullet only a few months before. Without a word she leaned forward and pressed her lips to the scar on his shoulder.

"No, don't. Ah, God . . ."

His fingers dug into the padded armrest. His entire body stiffened. But he didn't push her away. Didn't stop her from doing whatever she wanted to him.

She kissed. Licked. Laved her tongue over the scar until his breathing went ragged. Then trailed her lips down his chest. To his nipples, now hard and standing at attention, lower still to trace his pecs and the tiny indentation of his sternum.

His teeth ground together as her mouth moved to his left side, across his ribs. She felt his legs tense against her, but he didn't squeeze, didn't do anything to stop her from reaching the spot he knew she was heading to.

She kissed all around the puckered scar on his side, knew from his rigid muscles and rapid breaths he was digging his toes into the carpet and his fingers into the chair's plush fabric. Chancing one look up, she saw his eyes tightly shut and his jaw so hard she knew this was the root of everything between them. Why he continually pulled back, why he had the overwhelming need to protect her, why his job was his life and why he wouldn't walk away from a career that was making him miserable.

Her lips brushed the scar gently, just a whisper. Once. Twice. Just until he got used to it and his muscles relaxed slightly. Then again. And again. She ran her tongue down the line. Licked and kissed. And when he finally gave in and relaxed, she moved away, back across his abs and lower still.

"No, don't do that. I—"

She didn't listen. Took him deep in her mouth until his words were cut off on a groan. He swelled beneath her tongue, and while she loved him, she ran her fingers back up to the scar on his side, felt him shudder at the touch and grow even harder in her mouth.

She wanted him to remember this. To take whatever bad memory touching that scar brought out and replace it with this. With her.

"Hailey. Ah, God . . . stop . . ."

She finally let go. Climbed over him. Straddled his hips and lowered to take him in before his eyes even opened.

His hands slid to her hips, but he didn't move. The guilt etched deeply into the lines of his face nearly broke her heart.

She gripped the back of the chair and tightened around him. His breath caught, and slowly his eyes drifted to hers. "Make love with me, Shane. Right here. Right now. No more ghosts in the room with us." She lowered her mouth to his and felt her heart expand in her chest when he lifted his lips to hers. "I just want you."

"Hailey—"

"I know," she whispered. "Just let it go and love me."

# CHAPTER TWENTY

Hailey stood under the shower spray until her skin wrinkled. As she thought about the night before, her heart bumped and a slow ache for what Shane had been through filled her chest.

She'd climbed out of bed as quietly as she could just after eight A.M., leaving him sleeping like a rock on his side. She was tired, but he'd looked emotionally wrung out, so she'd wanted to give him as much rest as possible. They'd made it back to bed sometime just before dawn, where he'd loved her so thoroughly every cell in her body was still supercharged, even hours later.

A smile pulled at one side of her mouth as she thought about the varied sides of him. Controlling one minute, playful the next, challenging, then serious and so damn sexy, he took her breath away.

She sighed, rinsed the rest of the soap away. Knowing she needed to quit daydreaming if they were ever going to get out of here, she flipped off the shower and jerked the curtain back. Only to scream when she saw the body standing on the other side of the tub.

She pressed a hand against her heart and covered her horror-movie-heroine fright with a nervous chuckle. "Shane. God. You scared me."

"Sorry." He held up the towel in his hands as she stepped out, then wrapped it around her dripping body.

"Did the shower wake you?" She eased in to kiss him, then took the hand towel he offered for her hair.

"No."

Leaning to the side to wring the water from her locks, she studied him. He was wearing nothing but the same worn jeans he'd had on yesterday. His chest was bare, that stubble on his jaw thicker, darker, his eyes as intense as she'd ever seen them. But the hard set of his mouth told her he was still upset over what had happened last night.

Okay, she wouldn't push him. She reached for the moisturizer she'd left sitting on the counter by the sink, determined to make this light and normal. They hadn't had any normal in their relationship yet, and they could both use it. "Good. I want to get going as early as we can. Hopefully Billy and Nicole are already up. I called Steve. He's on his way to the airport now to get the jet ready."

"Listen, Hailey. About last night. I . . ."

She caught his guilt-ridden expression in the mirror over the sink and longed to see that cocky smile of his instead. "If this is where you thank me for the best sex of your life, I'll save you the trouble and just say simply, you're welcome."

He frowned instead of smiled. "That's not what I was talking about. I meant, the second time we . . . I . . ." He ran a hand through his hair. "Shit. I didn't use a condom."

Okay, of all the things she'd expected him to be concerned about, that wasn't it. She turned slowly to face him.

"I take full responsibility, and I should have been way more careful with you. But I didn't expect . . ." He rubbed a hand down his face, looked everywhere but at her. "You surprised me, and I should have stopped but . . . yeah. You know, I'm just making this worse." He blew out a breath. "I don't want kids."

Her mouth fell open, then snapped closed. "Ever?"

His eyes finally met hers. "Never."

Something inside her heart pinched. Though she wasn't ready for kids now by any means, she always envisioned herself with one or two down the line. She'd even gone so far as to consider the possibility of doing it on her own if she never got married again, although she hoped it didn't come to that. The knowledge that he didn't want kids . . . ever? For some reason that made her feel nothing but . . . loss.

"Why not?" she asked. "You're so protective of the people around you, you'd make a great father."

He shook his head, rested his hands on his hips and looked down at the floor. "No. I wouldn't. And I won't, ever. I'm always careful. Last night I wasn't. Yeah, last night . . . that just reinforced my decision to be done with it and get a vasectomy to guarantee nothing like this happens again."

Whoa. Now that was drastic. He was really serious.

"If there's a chance you could get pregnant from last night—"

Um, yeah. This was soooo not a conversation she wanted to be having with him right now. Talk about ruining the romantic mood she'd been in all morning long. "I'm on the pill, Shane."

"You are?"

She nodded, hating the spark of relief she saw in his eyes. Okay, it was dumb, considering they'd only been together a couple of days and he'd made no promises to her regarding anything long-term, but why did he have to regard the idea of a baby with her as so goddamn depressing? "Yes. Better to be safe than sorry in my view. It's highly unlikely you'll end up a daddy from what happened last night."

He blew out a long, relieved breath. One that grated on her nerves. She reached for her brush from the sink and brushed out her hair before she could react. *Ignore it. You're thinking twelve steps ahead of where he's at. Just let it go and enjoy being with him right now.*

She forced a smile. Dropped the brush, then tightened her towel around her breasts and moved in to kiss him on his cheek. "If you want to worry about something, worry about how the heck you're going to top last night. You raised my expectations."

Her grin did little to ease his mood. If anything, it seemed to etch those lines deeper into his face.

He followed her out into the bedroom and watched as she

peeled off her towel and slid into fresh clothes from her bag, which she'd set near the dresser last night when she'd come in to wait for him. "Hailey, we need to talk about the rest of it."

Oh, man, he was seriously trying to ruin her good mood. She pulled the T-shirt over her head. "The rest of what?"

"What happened. What I did to you."

Now this was what she'd expected him to start with. She tugged on jeans, buttoned them. "You didn't hurt me, Shane. I'm fine."

"You're not fine. Your neck's all red."

"That's from the hot water in the shower," she lied.

"We both know that's not true."

She glanced his way. Okay, yeah. He was definitely still feeling guilty. "I startled you. You surprised me. I'm not made of glass, though, so stop treating me like I am. Now I know not to startle you awake again." She glanced around the floor for her shoes.

"There won't be a next time," he mumbled.

"What?"

"Shit." His jaw clenched. But he didn't once look away from her face. "I tried to keep my distance from you. I really did. Because I didn't want what happened last night to happen in the first place. But now that it has . . . now you know why I won't let it happen again."

"Hold on a minute. What are you saying?"

"I'm saying, while we figure out who set you up, I'll be staying somewhere else."

Her eyes narrowed as his words sank in. "Wait. Let me get this straight. I know this doesn't have to do with you wanting me, because I was there last night. I know you do. So you're telling me now you're not going to sleep with me again, all because I startled you awake?" She rolled her eyes. "That's the dumbest thing I've ever heard."

"Hailey—"

"I already told you there's no chance I could have gotten pregnant. If you're worried about that I'll make sure we—"

"Jesus, Roarke, I killed a man!"

Her mouth snapped shut, and silence fell like a dark shroud between them. In the stillness, he rubbed a hand down his face. "Fuck, I didn't want to tell you this."

Yeah. She could see that in the tension etched into his face. "You're a cop. And . . . things happen in the line of duty. So . . . I'm not sure what that has to do with you and me."

He looked up at the ceiling, seemed to gather his thoughts. And suddenly she wasn't sure she wanted to know what he was about to tell her. "You asked me if I ever thought about marriage. I did. Once. About a year ago. Tony and I got called out on a homicide. In the projects. A twenty-two-year-old hooker had been sliced and diced. We knew it was her pimp who did it. He'd cut her in places to make sure if she lived she'd never work again."

Hailey's stomach rolled. "That's sick."

"I got the job of knocking on doors, looking for witnesses. This one apartment, two doors down . . . a girl answered. She was young. Early twenties. Skin and bones. And scared out of her mind. But what I noticed most were the bruises all over her face. Someone had beaten her good. She wouldn't talk to me, but I had a hunch she knew more than she was letting on. So I went back a few days later and tracked her down.

"She was wary at first. But after a while I got her to open up. Her name was Julie. She and the victim were friends. They worked for the same SOB."

"She was a hooker, too."

"She didn't tell me much, and I knew the same POS who'd killed the other girl had beaten Julie black and blue to keep her from talking. But I went back anyway. Several times. Until she agreed to have coffee with me in a café several miles away."

Hailey sensed immediately something bad was coming, and her stomach tightened. "What happened?"

He looked toward the windows, somewhat lost in memories. "She'd been in Chicago less than six months, followed her boyfriend there from North Dakota, and then he'd ditched her. She hadn't known anyone, didn't have any money. There was no one she could call back home for help. She'd met Dee Dee—the girl who was killed—at the bus station. Dee Dee'd given her a place to stay, had told her how she could make some cash, had introduced her to Malcolm."

The pimp. The way Shane said the man's name sent ice to Hailey's veins.

"Julie was . . . pretty. Like the girl next door. And so damn sweet, even after all the crappy luck she'd been served. She'd gotten in with the wrong people. And she was stuck."

"You helped her," Hailey said, as understanding dawned. Of course he would have. He was a protector. Remembering the way Shane had reacted to her bruised face in Lake Geneva, she knew without a doubt he'd helped this girl.

He nodded, swallowed. "She didn't want me to. Took a couple of months before she'd let me. Going back and seeing her, talking her out of staying. But eventually . . . yeah, I helped her get away from Malcolm. I got her hooked up with a new apartment on the other side of the city, in a good neighborhood. Got her a job with my ex-partner, Jack, doing secretarial stuff at his PI firm. Made sure Malcolm didn't know where she'd gone. Since no one would talk about his involvement in Dee Dee's murder, we didn't have crap on him, but I knew he did it."

Hailey's stomach tightened. "Then what?"

"I kept my distance from her for a while. If Malcolm thought I'd been the one to get her out of there, I didn't want him following me to find her. After about three months, I figured things were safe, you know? So I went to see her at Jack's office. And the change in her . . . it was like night and day. She was a different woman. Her hair was short, her eyes sparkled. She'd gained at least ten pounds that made all the difference. And she smiled. All the time. It was like . . . the way I think she might have been before she'd come to Chicago."

A tiny piece of Hailey's heart pinched. "You loved her."

His eyes finally met hers, only they weren't soft like his words, they were very hard, and very dark. "No. But I could have. I think . . . I wanted to. I took her to dinner. And the whole time she was grinning at me and talking nonstop about Jack and her job and how happy she was, all I could think about was what it would be like to be with her. Not just for sex, but long-term. With someone who had that much energy and love of life."

This was the woman he'd considered marrying. Hailey almost didn't want to hear the rest. Knew she had to.

"I walked her back to her apartment," Shane went on, not waiting for a reaction. "I wanted to go inside with her, but I didn't want her to feel like she owed me or that I was only interested in sex. When she invited me in, I said no, even though I was already thinking about when I was going to see her again. I kissed her good night instead, then left."

She didn't know how, but Hailey instinctively knew that was the last time he'd seen her. "Then what?"

Shane's eyes hardened. "He'd been waiting for her in the apartment. All those months he'd been watching me, waiting for me to lead him right to her. As I was walking back to my car he . . ." Shane's eyes slammed shut, and he swallowed, hard. "The things he did to Dee Dee were nothing compared to what he did to Julie."

Hailey pressed a hand against her mouth. "Oh, Shane. That's horrible. But it wasn't your fault. He—"

Shane's eyes popped open, and her words died when she saw the danger flare in their depths. "If it hadn't been for me, she'd still be alive. I couldn't bring her back, but I sure as hell could do something about him."

Now it all made sense. "You went to arrest him," Hailey said quietly.

"No," Shane corrected in a tone that held nothing but ice. "We didn't have enough evidence to bring him in for questioning, let alone arrest the piece of shit. I went to kill him. I waited and I planned, and I made sure enough time had passed so it wouldn't look like a retaliation hit. But I had absolutely no intention of bringing him in or letting him see even a thread of justice."

A lump formed in Hailey's throat. And she thought about the scar on his side. "You found him."

"Yeah," Shane said coldly. "I did. We fought. I took a knife to the side, which is how I got the scar, but in the end, he's the one who left that warehouse in a body bag."

He didn't elaborate, but she could almost envision the scene. The run-down slum, the empty warehouse. The sounds of fists cracking bone and bullets echoing in the vast space.

"There was an Internal Affairs investigation. They knew about Dee Dee. They knew about Julie and that I'd gotten her a job with Jack. They knew I was up to my eyeballs in shit. The only reason I didn't go down is because Tony lied for me."

Hailey's heart went out to him. The man had a clear dividing line between right and wrong, and in his mind he'd stepped over that line. Way over. She thought about what Lisa had told her in the kitchen last night, about how much Shane had changed in the last few months, how he never smiled and had pulled back from those he cared about. The memory of what he'd done and that law he was forced to uphold because of his job were obviously eating away at him.

She took two steps toward him, cautious not to touch him yet, because his eyes were still blazing and he looked ready to pound something, but she was determined to get him to listen to her. "What Malcolm did to Julie and Dee Dee was wrong, Shane."

"I killed a man, Hailey. In cold blood. Premeditated and all that shit."

She wasn't so sure of that. She knew him way better than he thought she did. For whatever reason, he was trying to get her to think badly of him right now. Only it wasn't working. She remembered how he'd been adamant Lisa and Rafe go to the police when things had turned during their search for the Furies and he'd been shot. How he'd pressured her to come clean with him in Lake Geneva about Bryan's murder. No matter what he thought he'd gone there to do, his moral compass would have kicked in at the last minute.

The scar on his side confirmed that. If he'd gone there just to kill Malcolm, he could have done it without the struggle, without the injury that had left him in the hospital for over a week, without the scar that told her he'd more than likely killed Malcolm in self-defense.

"When did Chen arrive?" she asked.

"Right after it happened."

"And what was IA's final finding?"

His jaw clenched. And he hesitated, then finally said, "Exonerated."

There it was. By definition that meant the incident had never happened, or his actions were found lawful and didn't violate any written policies. His partner would never have been in the area unless Shane had called and told him where he was. And if Chen had known, then Shane hadn't wanted to go through with his plan in the first place. "Self-defense is not murder, Shane," she said quietly.

"Doesn't matter," he snapped. "I went with the intention of killing him, and I did."

She took a step closer. "You stopped him from killing any other young girls. No one in their right mind would blame you for that. I certainly don't. And if you expect me to be shocked, you're talking to the wrong person. I worked the streets, remember? I know bad things happen to good people and that justice isn't always served. If you'd have taken him in, there's no telling how long it would have been before he was out again."

"You don't get it, Hailey. What I did to him doesn't matter right now." He took a giant step back before she could touch him. "I killed someone for a hooker I barely knew. I didn't love her. Didn't even really know her. What I feel for you is a thousand times stronger and a million times hotter, and that makes me dangerous. To you, to anyone who crosses you, to the SOB who's setting you up for your cousin's murder.

When I said what happened last night between us won't happen again, it's not because I don't want to be with you. It's because I don't trust myself around you. And I can't—won't—let anything happen to you because of me."

A thousand thoughts and feelings rushed through her. He hadn't said he loved her, not in so many words, but it was there, hanging in the silence between them. Her heart soared, and a joy the likes of which she'd never really known swept over her.

But just as quickly it dropped like a stone into her stomach.

Because the tone of his voice and the look in his eyes finally registered.

What he felt for her wasn't enough to convince him she was good for him. Not enough to get him to see that she'd made him laugh and smile the last few days when no one else had in almost a year. Not enough to break through the barrier of guilt he'd built around himself. Somehow, she had to get him to see he wasn't responsible for what Malcolm had done.

"You can't blame yourself because you weren't there when it happened, Shane. You did everything you could to help her, to get her a better life." She moved toward him. "You can't stop living because of it, either."

He stepped out of her reach before she could touch him, and the searing look in his eyes warned her not to try. "You can't just say that and expect me to feel it. You weren't there. You didn't see what he did to her. You don't have to live with the knowledge if you hadn't gotten involved, she'd be alive now."

"Who's to say Malcolm wouldn't have killed her anyway?" she countered. She wanted to pull him close, tell him it would be okay, but she knew it wouldn't be. Not until he was able to let this go. "Shane—"

"Look," he said quickly, "I'm not trying to hurt you. I'm just telling you the way it is. I'm not relationship material. I thought last night . . . maybe there was a way . . ." He lifted one hand. Dropped it. "But I know now there isn't. This ends here."

He sounded so final. Like he'd made up his mind and she had no say in it whatsoever. But instead of being hurt, she was suddenly angry. Frustrated beyond belief because he couldn't see what he was about to throw away. "So that's it. All because you say so. End of story. Thanks for the fuck, and see ya."

"Don't say it like that."

She glanced around the room that only a few hours ago had been cozy and warm and the only place she'd wanted to be. Now just seeing the rumpled bed and remembering what they'd done there left a hollow ache in her chest. "Why not? That's all it was, wasn't it?"

"No, it wasn't. It was—"

She finally spotted her shoes under the chair on the far side of the room. To distract herself she dropped into the same chair they'd made love in last night and stooped to tie the laces. "You're going back to Chicago as soon as we find that sixth sculpture, aren't you?"

His mouth snapped shut. Then quietly he said, "Yes."

She nodded. Didn't bother to look at him. Hated that the ache was spreading. Hated even more that she wouldn't tell him to leave now and save her some angst. Because if she did, there'd be no way for him to change his mind. And how desperate did that make her? God, was she ever going to learn with men? "Then I guess we'd better get busy finding that bronze so you can get home sooner rather than later."

"Hailey—"

A knock at the door cut off his words.

He glanced at the door, then back at her. "I don't want it to end like this."

The regret in his voice was too much, and she stood quickly, pinned her eyes on his and pulled up the one trait that had saved her every other time life had thrown her a curveball. "I think you do. I think this makes it easy on you."

A fist pounded against the door, followed by Rafe's muffled voice. "Maxwell?"

Irritation creased Shane's features as he jerked his head to the side. "What?"

"Open the damn door, cop. I'm not gonna keep yelling in my own house!"

"Fuck," Shane muttered, stalking to the door. He disappeared around the corner. "What?"

"Good morning to you, too, sunshine," Rafe grumbled. "Glad to see you slept so well. Your sister sent me up here to tell you breakfast is ready. And to find out if Hailey said anything to you last night. No one seems to know where she is."

"I don't—"

She'd had it with all the men in this house. Hailey grabbed her bag from the floor, headed for the door and pushed her way past Shane. Rafe's surprised eyes darted to her. "I'm here," she said. "Are Billy and Nicole ready to go?"

"Uh, yeah." Rafe shot a curious look between Hailey and Shane.

"Good. I want to get out of here as quick as we can." She brushed past Rafe and headed for the stairs.

"Hailey, hold up," Shane called.

She didn't dare stop. Did not want to get between her ex-husband and the man she'd just spent an amazing night and maddening morning with. And there was no way she wanted to know what kind of male posturing was going on behind her. "I'm leaving in twenty minutes, with or without you, Maxwell. So if you're still planning on tagging along, you'd better get your ass in gear."

# CHAPTER TWENTY-ONE

A January storm was rolling in off the Caribbean as they set out across the Keys. Hailey glanced up at the swirling sky and couldn't help noticing it fit her mood to the letter. After landing the Roarke Bombardier on the short flight strip in Marathon, they'd rented a power boat and set off for her father's private island. Shane and Billy were above, driving the boat, while Nicole held her head over the side, green as grass. Hailey had retreated belowdecks to get some peace and quiet. And to get away from Shane's scrutinizing gaze.

She hadn't been in the mood to talk with him, but he'd needed to fill her in on Chen's phone call last night. Bryan's autopsy results had come back, and they weren't what anyone had expected. Technically, his heart had stopped. He hadn't actually died from the neck wound after all. Though that was good news for her, it didn't clear her name completely. And though the toxicology report hadn't come in yet, Hailey couldn't help focusing on what it would say when all was said and done.

Would it be the same thing that had killed her father? Digoxin? Or the poison she'd been given that had made her so sick? One thing was eerily clear to her now, though: only one person in her family had a heart condition and also was a horticulture hobbyist. And Hailey had been at his house just before she'd gotten sick.

"How much farther?" Nicole asked as she slinked down the steps from the deck, looking pale. She flopped onto the couch next to Hailey in the tiny cabin of the boat and placed a hand on her stomach with a groan.

"Do you *still* get seasick?" Hailey asked with a frown, secretly happy for the interruption. She didn't like where her thoughts were going. And she didn't want Shane to be right. "I thought you'd outgrown that. Remember the time we sailed up Lake Worth and you puked all over the settee in Daddy's new boat?"

"Yeah, I do," Nicole tossed back, trying to get comfortable and looking miserable. "And thanks for reminding me of that fun memory. Though it does explain why you got the deed to Daddy's boat, and I didn't."

"I'm sure if he thought you'd wanted the boat, he'd have left it for you."

"Yeah, right," Nicole muttered.

Hailey glanced up the steps. "You'd do better up there where you can see the horizon, rather than down here."

"No, thank you. Your boyfriend's biting everyone's head off. I didn't particularly want to watch Billy deck him."

Twisted as it was, the thought of that warmed a cold space in Hailey's chest. Right about now she'd pay money to see Billy take a swing at Shane.

"What happened between the two of you, anyway?" Nicole asked.

Hailey's smile faded. "Nothing." Nothing she was going to get into with Nicole, anyway. Nothing she was going to remember herself, either. If he didn't want her, well . . . she wasn't going to force herself on him. She had more self-respect than that.

Nicole obviously knew a dead end when she saw one, because they sat in silence, the water lapping the hull and the distant muffled conversation from above the only sounds in the small salon. Having Nicole here was more than a little odd. And the fact her sister had suddenly decided to work with Hailey instead of against her was the biggest shocker of them all. Had Nicole finally matured? Or was that Billy's influence?

"Nicole," Hailey said hesitantly, not sure if she should delve into this topic but needing to regardless, "about Billy—"

"What about him?"

How could she put this delicately? "He matters to me. Even though Rafe and I aren't married anymore, he's family, and because of that, I know he puts on a front, but he's got a big heart underneath. I don't want to see him get hurt. If you're just toying with him—"

"For your information, he *used* me. And just so you know, I'm the one who'll probably get hurt in this when it's over, so there's nothing for you to worry about."

The defensiveness in Nicole's tone told Hailey her sister was being serious. But it was the worry on her face that suggested Hailey had misread the entire situation. "You've . . . fallen for him."

Nicole flicked her a look. "Yeah, right." Then focused on her hands. Shrugged. "Maybe."

"Not maybe. Definitely."

"And you don't like that, do you?"

Hailey thought about Nicole giving her the numbers last night and figuring out the coordinates of the island and the way Billy had stepped in without being asked and arranged all of Teresa's funeral plans so Rafe didn't have to. She also remembered the way Billy had been torn between coming with them today and staying in San Juan and how he'd only agreed to tag along once Rafe had made him go. If Nicole was the reason Billy and Rafe were finally going to get their relationship back on even ground, then maybe her hanging around with Billy wasn't such a bad thing after all. "I didn't before. Now . . . I'm undecided."

"I'm so excited," Nicole muttered, sounding put out, but looking like she was greatly relieved.

"Why weren't you at the will reading?"

Nicole didn't seem surprised by the question, and she shrugged, focusing on a spot halfway across the floor. "Wasn't invited."

"What do you mean, not invited?"

"I mean, *our mother* didn't bother to tell me when it was. She didn't want me involved in this little race. Though she was more than happy to take my sculpture when I came back."

"She's collecting them, too?"

"Not for the same reason you are. She's destroying the ones she gets her hands on."

Hailey's eyes narrowed. "How do you know this?"

Nicole pinned her sister with a look, the same one she'd given as a teenager whenever Hailey had come home from college and tried to make nice between the two of them. "I'm not as brainless as everyone thinks."

"I don't think you're brainless, Nicole. Flighty, maybe, but not brainless."

Nicole rolled her eyes. "Did it ever occur to you that a lot of it was an act? Yeah, I like to have a good time, but I graduated college with a 4.0 GPA. I know as much about Roarke Resorts as you do, but not from working there, from studying and paying attention. Did you know that all those years you were trying to get away from Daddy and the hotels, I was just trying to get him to give me a chance? I finally quit because it was obvious he wasn't interested and I was sick of hearing 'No, Nicole, you're not ready.' Sheesh, getting into Harvard's MBA program first try didn't even impress him. So I didn't go. Instead I did what they seemed to expect of me. I left and I partied and I had a good time."

Hailey stared at Nicole, for the first time seeing her as something other than the spoiled younger sister. Suddenly, Nicole's outlandish behavior made sense. All these years, while Hailey thought she'd been taking advantage of their father, Nicole had been doing exactly what a five-year-old did when she couldn't get someone to notice her. She pushed and prodded and got into all kinds of trouble because even negative attention was better than nothing at all.

"I didn't know any of that," Hailey said softly.

"There's a lot you don't know, Hailey. About me and Mother and Daddy and everyone who works at RR."

Hailey was beginning to think that was true. And it was time those things changed. Especially now, when she was seriously contemplating staying on at RR when all of this was said and done. "So tell me."

Nicole's eyes held hers so long, Hailey wasn't sure Nicole would confide in her. Then Nicole surprised her and said, "You know Mother wasn't with Daddy the night he died."

"I know. She was at her country club at some fund-raiser for cancer research."

Nicole shook her head. "She wasn't at any country club. She was with Paul McIntosh. They've been having an affair."

"What? How do you know this?"

"Because I saw them together. And because I overheard a conversation they had about it." When Hailey only stared at her, Nicole added, "There's that whole brainless bimbo thing. People tend to forget I'm around."

Holy . . . Paul McIntosh was a good twenty years younger than Eleanor Roarke. And for the last year, Hailey's father had been trying to get Hailey to go out with Paul in the hopes they'd one day get married. He was the only non-Roarke executive officer of the company, and it was no secret Garrett had thought of Paul as the son he'd never had.

There was only one reason Hailey could see for the two of them to be together. And it all circled back around to her father's will. She looked at her sister. "Did you give her the number from your statue?"

Nicole's lips thinned. "Of course not. I know it's a horrible thing to say considering she's our mother and all, but I didn't trust her. I still don't. She purposely kept me from Daddy's will reading so I couldn't participate."

Hailey stood and paced the small salon as thoughts of her mother and Paul swirled. Were they working together? If so, that explained why she was destroying statues after she found them.

"Something else you should know," Nicole said. "Remember your little run-in in the elevator at RR?"

Hailey stopped and looked at her sister. "What about it?"

"It was Paul."

Hailey had been right. She'd recognized that voice but hadn't wanted it to be true.

"That means Lucy Walthers is the one who planted your dagger," Shane said from the steps.

Hailey looked up sharply. He was standing with one foot on the salon floor, one on the step behind him, both hands braced against the narrow walls, his midnight eyes focused right on her. She hadn't heard him come down the steps, but she didn't miss the bump in her heart or the way the reaction pissed her off.

She turned her attention to Nicole. "How do you know that?"

"I eavesdropped on a phone conversation when I was home a few days ago. I don't think Mother intended for you to get arrested, just detained."

"So I'd be out of the picture while she and Paul looked for the sixth sculpture. But how does Lucy figure in? And does Mother know about her?"

"I don't know," Nicole said.

"Did Lucy kill Bryan?" Shane asked

"Now that," Nicole said, glancing at Shane, "I don't know." She looked back at Hailey. "But it's safe to say none of them have been sitting back doing nothing like you thought all this time. Mother doesn't have your number or mine, but odds are good she got Graham's and Bryan's. And she knows where Daddy's island's located. If she happened to recognize the longitude and latitude coordinates—"

"Then she's already either been here," Hailey cut in, "or will be shortly."

"Yeah," Nicole said, looking between Hailey and Shane again in a way that told Hailey Shane was watching her with that heated look and Nicole was more than a little curious what was going on between them. "But here's the thing I don't get. Why does she care who runs RR? It won't affect her."

"Some people like power," Shane said.

"No." Hailey looked around the salon as she remembered

arguments she'd overheard her parents having when she was a child. Eleanor screaming about the hours her father worked at the resort and how she wasn't his true love. About how much Eleanor hated that company. Every single person who worked there.

Slowly, wheels began clicking into place in Hailey's mind. "She just wants to make sure a Roarke doesn't end up running it. Especially one of her children."

"Murder's a drastic way to go about it," Shane said.

A sick feeling settled in Hailey's stomach. Yeah, it was. But no one in her family ever did anything that seemed to make a lot of sense.

"Not when you've never liked your kids in the first place," Nicole muttered from the couch. "I never understood why they even had kids. You," she looked at Hailey, "yeah. I get that. You only have to do the math to know she was pregnant when they got married. But me? Seven years later? When it was obvious neither of them enjoyed being a parent? Why bother?"

"I don't know," Hailey said. "But lucky for you. Otherwise you wouldn't be here."

"No," Nicole said. "Unlucky for her. Because we're going to find that sixth statue before she does. And then she'll be the one answering the questions."

"Arnold said the plot your father picked for his burial is located on the top of that hill," Shane said, pointing across the no-name island that belonged to the Roarke family.

The key was fairly flat, about a mile square, if that, with a small rise covered by a scattering of trees and shrubs, right in the middle of the landmass. They'd anchored the boat off the east side and had split up to hike around and take a look at anything out of the ordinary. Billy and Nicole had gone to the western shore, and Shane and Hailey were taking the east. They planned to meet up somewhere in the middle.

Hailey held out her cell phone to see if she could catch a signal. The clouds were really piling up and the sky had taken on a gray color that didn't look promising. Though the temperatures this far south didn't drop drastically, there was a chill to the air.

"Lucky for you I called him back and found out my mother had her lawyers interfere and put a stop to Daddy being buried here."

Damn lucky, as far as Shane could see. He'd already contacted Tony and had him phone the Dade County ME to have Garrett Roarke's tox screen run again, and he was more than a little thrilled at the knowledge they weren't going to have to dig up a dead body after all.

He was also more than a little curious about the reason Eleanor Roarke was so adamant about having her husband cremated when that obviously wasn't his dying wish.

He followed Hailey through the beach grass. Though she wasn't ignoring him outright, she'd definitely cooled considerably, and that little spark they'd shared since meeting up again in Chicago was long gone.

His gaze swept the landscape in an attempt to ignore the sway of her hips or the fit of her jeans or the way she'd left her hair down this morning to spill blonde, sexy curls around her shoulders. When she stopped abruptly at the edge of the rise, he nearly ran into her before slamming on his own brakes.

"I've been here before," she said, glancing around.

"Nicole mentioned your father used to bring you here when you were kids, right?"

"But only a handful of times when he needed space from our mother and brought us sailing. Nicole used to get seasick, so it didn't happen often. And on the rare instance he took us, I was left in charge of Nicole on the beach while he hiked inland for whatever reason." She glanced toward the hill. "I don't ever remember walking in with him, but I'd bet a hundred bucks I've stood right here before."

The look in her eyes told him not to bet against her.

They picked their way around flowering shrubs and vines until they came to a rock mass on the opposite side of the hill. Shane would have kept walking, but Hailey stopped him with a touch to his arm. "Wait."

Electricity zinged along his nerve endings, just as it had last night whenever and wherever she'd touched him. A sense of loss coursed through him and he contemplated pulling her close and telling her he'd changed his mind. But what would that do? Only prolong the inevitable. Build her up for his eventual crash and burn like Lisa had predicted. Distract him and ultimately put her in danger.

No, he wasn't willing to risk her safety. He pushed the reaction down and eyed the eight-foot-tall rocks she was now walking around. Following, he noticed what had caught her attention, a separation in the rock that looked like it led to a cave of some kind.

"Did you grab the flashlight from the boat?" she asked.

He tugged the flashlight from his belt and handed it to her. She flicked it on, then moved toward the rocks, turning sideways to get between the two biggest ones and the gap that seemed to lead inside. Cloth rasped against rock, but the cave must have turned abruptly, because from Shane's position, he couldn't even see her light anymore. "Anything?" he called.

Silence met his ears, and he was just about to go in looking for her when she appeared from between the rocks with wide and excited eyes. "Call Billy and Nicole. I think I found it."

# CHAPTER TWENTY-TWO

"It's steel," Billy said, running his hand down the large metal door built into the rock wall in front of him. "Rusted steel, but still steel."

They were all inside the narrow cave opening, their flashlights illuminating the darkness. Behind and around them, rock walls loomed, while the musty scent of earth clung to the air.

Shane shined his light over the door again, zooming in on the handle. "Doesn't take a key like any I've seen before." He glanced at Hailey. "Guess that means the one your father left you wasn't to this, either."

Hailey bit her lip and moved forward to trace her finger along the edge of the door. To the left, also in steel and embedded in the rock, was a circle with a rectangular hole cut out of the middle. On the top and bottom of the circle, small indentations could also be seen, like two little balls had been pressed into the steel.

"'The answer lies with me. The key is set in steel.' This is definitely steel but . . ." Hailey pushed against the circle, then the small indentations, hoping there was some kind of release somewhere. Nothing happened. "Not a key. This is a lock."

"Let me take a look." Hailey moved out of the way to give Nicole better access. "Do you remember what Daddy used to say about The Last Seduction?"

Hailey glanced at her sister's shadowed face. "That it was priceless."

"Yeah." Nicole ran her hand over the lock. "I did some

research recently. At auction, the bronze would probably go for a cool million—that is, if you had the original. That's a good chunk of change, but definitely not priceless. I got the impression, though, that Daddy never cared about the original. He was more interested in the copies. And to him, those were what were priceless."

Hailey looked back at the door where Nicole's fingers were covering the lock.

"If this is where his puzzle led us," Nicole went on, "then it makes sense he's got the last copy stored in here somewhere. And the key—"

"Would be related to them as well," Hailey finished. She reached for the backpack slung over her shoulder and pulled out the dagger her father had given her. The one still encased in the evidence bag Shane had set in front of her last night.

The guard on both sides of the blade curved up and outward to swirl around and form two small metal balls. She opened the plastic bag.

"Hold on, Roarke," Shane said, placing a hand on her arm to stop her.

She heaved out a sigh of frustration and looked up. "You said Bryan died of a heart attack. That means this isn't the murder weapon. So my handling it now isn't going to make a difference."

"True, but I don't think it's a smart idea to—"

"Are you planning to give it back to your partner or turn it back in to evidence?"

Their eyes held, and in the darkness she saw the answer in his obsidian eyes long before he answered. "No."

Of course he wouldn't. Because doing so would put her in jeopardy. And he wouldn't ever do anything to hurt her. Intentionally or otherwise. Why couldn't he see what had happened last night was a reaction to her touch, not a reflection of him? When was he going to figure out she wasn't some fragile, breakable woman who needed protecting?

He dropped his hand, and because she knew the answer

to both of those questions already, she turned away and refocused on her task.

She pulled the dagger that had killed Alessandro de Medici out of the plastic bag. The metal was cool, the blade sharp enough to cause trouble if used properly. "Here goes nothing," she said on a breath as she lifted the tip of the blade to the center of the steel circle and pushed.

Metal scraped metal as the blade slid into the rectangular hole, until all that was left was the handle sticking out. Both metal balls on the ends of the guard pushed perfectly into the twin indentations above and below the circle.

She let go of the hilt and wiped her sweaty hands down the thighs of her jeans. "Now what?"

"You turn keys," Billy said. "See if it'll move one way or the other."

They all seemed to hold their breath as Hailey turned the hilt to the right and met only resistance, then repositioned her grip and turned the handle to the left.

Her heart rate picked up as the dagger began to turn. The steel door in front of them made a clicking sound and pushed inward with a heavy groan.

"Christ Jake," Shane muttered at her back. "I don't believe this."

Neither did Hailey. Almost. "I told you my father was eccentric. Just like *National Treasure*."

The flashlights illuminated a long corridor that seemed to run into the center of the hillside. The floor was dirt, the ceiling some kind of concrete mix. As they moved inside, Hailey couldn't help wondering just how long ago her father had built this bunker. And why so far from civilization.

They came to a stop halfway down the corridor, where three steel doors were lined up in a row, each set roughly twenty feet apart. Billy's light shifted from one door to the next as he clucked his tongue. "Okay, Monty Hall, let's make a deal. Will it be door number one, door number two, or door number three?"

Nicole chuckled.

Shane ran his hand up the edge of the closest door and shifted his flashlight to get a better look. "Hinges on this one are all rusted out. It hasn't been opened in a long time."

A strange sense of déjà vu settled over Hailey as she stood there staring at the middle door. A feeling that she'd been here before, with her father. A lifetime ago.

"It's this one." When Shane glanced at her with a *how do you know?* look in his dark eyes, she said, "He . . . I'm pretty sure he brought me here."

"When?" Nicole asked. "Not with me. I've never seen this place before."

Hailey shook her head. "It was before you were born. Just before." Memories spilled into her mind, memories of the way her father used to be—doting, caring, smiling—memories she'd forgotten all about because he hadn't been that way in a long time. "It was dark. I was only seven, and he woke me up in the middle of the night, put me on the boat. I don't remember much about the trip, just that he said we were going to have an adventure. He brought me here. I was inside this room." She turned toward Nicole. "He told me things were about to change. I thought he meant change at home with a new baby in the house—you. But that's not what he meant. I didn't realize until years later that he'd meant he was changing. And he did. That's when he pulled back and turned into the father we both knew."

Nicole glanced warily at the steel door. "So what's in the room?"

Hailey's gaze followed. "I don't remember."

In the silence, Billy scratched the back of his head, and in typical Billy fashion, tried to lighten the mood. "C'mon, you two. It's not like the boogeyman's in there or his dead body's gonna pop out when you open the door." Three sets of eyes shifted his way, and his expression grew nervous. "Okay, maybe that was a bad analogy."

Hailey took a deep breath and reached for the key her

father had left her—the one she and Shane had thought went to a safety-deposit box—the one she instinctively knew now unlocked this door.

"Hold on." Shane's hand on her wrist stopped her from sliding the key into its lock. "Are you sure about this? Tony can prove your cousin died of heart failure, not by your hand. And we've got enough evidence with what happened to you and your father's autopsy report to make a strong case you weren't involved with any of it. With what we know about your mother and McIntosh and your uncle, the authorities can figure out the rest. If you don't want your father's company after all, you don't have to go in there."

He was right. And a small part of her recognized that. But an even bigger part knew if she didn't go in, she'd always wonder what her father had been trying to tell her. Why he'd so badly wanted her to find his statues. And how it related to their rocky relationship and every question she'd always been too afraid to ask about her family.

"It's not just about Bryan," she said, looking into Shane's dark eyes. "Or about what I want. There are a thousand reasons for me to leave and only one reason to stay. And all I know right now is that one reason to stay is the most important reason of all."

"And what's that?" he asked quietly.

"Trust." Her heart pinched. "Even with everything bad that happened between us and all the arguments, in the end he trusted me with whatever secret he's been hiding all these years. Until just now, I'd forgotten the man he'd been before. I'd forgotten how much he really did love me. Something changed him. Something I know in my heart he wants forgiveness for." She shook her head. "I can't leave until I know what that is. I won't. And it hurts me, more than you will ever know, that he couldn't tell me the truth when he was alive."

His eyes held hers, and her heart squeezed tight under his heated gaze. Did he hear what she was telling him? Would he see the similarities between what her father had done to her and what he was doing now? Why couldn't he understand that more than his protection she just needed him?

His eyes ran over her face. And just when she thought he was going to reach for her, he dropped his hand. Then stepped back and nodded once. "Try the key then."

She tried not to let his reaction hurt her. But it did. Like a sharp slice right to her heart. Taking another deep breath, she turned the key in the lock and pushed the heavy door open with her shoulder.

A hissing sound echoed, as if a seal was being broken, and as Hailey moved into the room and shined her light inside, she drew in a deep breath. This wasn't a dirt-floor cave. The room was concrete from floor to wall to ceiling. A panel on the wall blinked multicolored lights, and she stepped toward it, noting the readings that indicated the high-tech ventilation and climate-control systems. Behind her, the others filed in, their flashlight beams jumping over wooden crates and boxes piled nearly to the ceiling.

"My God," Nicole said. "Look at this place. I knew Daddy had storage units full of crappy art, but this . . . this is unbelievable."

Hailey's pulse beat as she moved to look at a long rectangular crate to her right. The heavy ink on the outside said *Renoir*.

Behind her, light flared, illuminating the room, and she turned to look over her shoulder where Shane had found an old lantern. She glanced back at the crate in front of her. "No way that can be real."

"Here." Shane handed her a crowbar.

"Where did you get this?" She took it. Set her backpack on the floor.

"It was by the lantern."

"You guys are *not* gonna believe this," Billy said from across the room. "These boxes are labeled van Gogh, Picasso, Monet, Adams, O'Keeffe, Rubens, Manet."

Hailey's heart rate picked up as she slid the crowbar between the wood. Shane braced his hands on the box to hold it steady. "Go for it," he said.

She pulled, and the front of the box popped open. Shredded paper and stuffing spilled out. She reached in, pulled the cover off the painting and simply stared at the famous image of a black pitcher full of multicolored flowers.

"*Anemones,*" Billy said behind her. "1898. Holy shit."

"How do you know the name—" Hailey began.

He reached over her shoulder for a sheet of paper that had been stuck between the wrapping and the painting. "This used to be in Pete's collection. I remember seeing it at Odyssey." He snapped open the envelope with the words *Odyssey Gallery* stamped on the outside and extracted the papers. "It's the provenance." He looked up with wide eyes. "It's real. This painting alone is worth a small fortune."

Hailey turned to look over the hundreds of boxes stacked in the room. They couldn't all be real, could they? Sure, her father had been an avid art collector, but most of his stuff wasn't worth much and meant little to anyone but him.

A strange pounding started in her stomach, worked its way up her chest until it felt like her heart was going to come out of her skin. She moved around the room, her eyes running over names she recognized but could barely believe, until she came to one marked Cellini.

"I think I found it," she called to the others who had taken up searching as well.

Shane was at her side in a flash, crowbar in hand. He knelt next to her on the pristine floor and ran his hand over the two-foot-square wooden crate at the bottom of the stack. He handed her the crowbar. "Here. Take this."

Her pulse pounded as he and Billy worked to move the boxes stacked on top. Then she simply watched as he took the crowbar from her again and pried the lid off the crate.

Shredded paper and stuffing filled the inside of the crate. A white envelope with her name written in her father's handwriting stared up at her.

Her fingers shook as she lifted it, slid open the flap and extracted a folded slip of paper. Shane rummaged around in the crate and seconds later pulled out the bronze sculpture that matched the one Hailey had secured safely at home.

A man and woman, both nude, standing together, locked chest to knee. Her mouth at his throat, his head tipped back in pleasure. It was roughly eighteen inches tall, six inches round at the base. Solid and real. The immortalized image of ultimate seduction and the last moment of one man's life.

She reached out a hand, ran it over the cold metal. Felt her skin tingle as her thumb brushed Shane's skin.

When Shane turned it, she saw Cellini's name branded into the base.

"Shit," Billy muttered. "Nicole, gimme that fancy phone of yours. Hold it up, cop." He snapped a picture of both the underside and the sculpture upright. "I'm sending this to Pete. He'll know if it's real or not."

"It can't be real," Nicole said in awe. "He had the original the whole time?"

Slowly Hailey opened the letter and stared down at her father's slanted handwriting.

*My Dearest Hailey,*

*If you're reading this now, it means I'm truly gone. I know you have questions. About this letter. This place. About the bronze in this box. I can only answer the most obvious ones. Stated simply, this sculpture is yours. It has always been yours. Your mother gave it to me just before you were born, and I've saved it all these years for the time when I could give it to you and you would finally understand. Know that I loved her dearly. Still love her, even now, where I am. And that you were never a mistake. I've made errors, the greatest of which was letting time and circumstances control all of us. And I've carried the weight of those errors with me most of my life. I thought I was doing what was right for you. I know now I wasn't.*

*I can't change the past. I can only hope one day you'll find it in your heart to forgive me. You and Nicole. Everything in this room, I've saved for both of you. It doesn't make up for not being there for you, but maybe someday you'll understand. The greatest treasures I ever found are in this room, save two.*

*The bronze is yours, Hailey. Roarke Resorts belongs to you and your sister. What you do with it is up to you.*

*There's one last thing I want you to do for me. You figured out the code on the replicas. There's one last place you need to visit. All your remaining questions will be answered there.*

*I love you.*

—GR

Hailey stared at the numbers on the bottom of the letter. The ones that were very clearly another longitude and latitude reading.

"Fuck me," Billy muttered as Hailey handed the letter to Shane with shaking fingers. He was staring at a text message on Nicole's high-tech satellite phone. "Pete says it could be real. The marking—Cellini's name branded into the base—that was his trademark. He's going to send the picture to Maria Gotsi at the art institute in Athens and have her take a look at it."

"There's something else in here," Nicole announced, pawing though the box. Carefully, she pulled out a rectangular piece of wood, brushed the shavings off and flipped it in her hand. "It's a picture of Daddy and some woman. It's . . . oh, my God."

"What?" Hailey asked, shifting to get a look at the frame her sister was holding. The photo was at least thirty years old, a younger version of their father, standing on a beach flanked with palms. But the woman in his arms wasn't Eleanor Roarke. She was young and blonde, with sky blue eyes and a face Hailey knew by heart. Because it was a face Hailey looked at in the mirror every single day.

"Oh, my—"

"It's you," Nicole said. "That's . . . you."

"No," Hailey said, staring at the photo. "Not me."

In a moment of clarity she remembered every unkind word Eleanor Roarke had said to her over the years, the way she'd belittled Hailey from the time she was a child, the cold shoulder, the disgusted looks Hailey had never understood. The way she'd coddled Nicole. She saw Eleanor's face in her mind—her perfect Italian complexion and dark looks. And heard her cultured voice screaming at her father in the middle of the night that she'd never been the love of his life.

All this time she'd thought Eleanor had been jealous of the company. Now she knew . . .

"That's . . . my mother." She looked from the framed photo to the image of seduction cast in bronze. "He had an affair."

"Details," a voice echoed from behind. They all turned and looked toward the door, where Paul McIntosh stood with a superior expression on his face and a 9mm in his hand. The barrel of which was pointed right at Hailey. "None of which matters much to me. Now be a good girl and hand over the bronze before someone gets hurt."

# CHAPTER TWENTY-THREE

The cell phone on the edge of Eleanor's desk in the study of her Palm Beach home vibrated, dragging her attention away from the computer screen she'd been studying. She glanced down only to realize Nicole was sending a picture.

She lifted the phone—the one with the special software her assistant Melvin had loaded for her that hacked into Nicole's phone—and narrowed her eyes as the picture slowly loaded. It had been easy enough to get Nicole's phone when she'd been here, to make the switch so she didn't notice. It's how Eleanor had been tracking her daughter; how she knew Nicole had been in Puerto Rico; how she knew now Nicole was somewhere in the Keys.

The fact Nicole was with Hailey sent Eleanor's blood pressure skyrocketing, and she breathed deep to keep it in check. She didn't know Hailey's exact location, but the Roarke jet had a GPS tracking device, and right now it was parked in Marathon. The signal from Nicole's phone was coming from a small island in the Keys. What on earth were those two doing together? And why did she get the feeling nothing from this could possibly be good for her?

Her eyes slid back to the computer screen as she focused on the small aerial photo of the island. A beep indicated the picture on the phone had downloaded and she glanced over, only to feel the muscles in her chest squeeze so tight it was hard to get air.

She pushed back from her antique desk quickly. Stood with the phone in hand. And stared down at a photo of The Last Seduction. The text message accompanying the picture read simply, *Pete—we found #6. Real or fake?* The second picture was of the artist's imprint in the bottom of the base.

The pressure beneath her breastbone was so great, Eleanor's hands shook and the phone fell from her hands to land against the carpet with a thud. It couldn't be. They'd found it? After everything she'd done to make sure neither one of them ever learned the truth?

Slowly, as the panic mounted, she moved through the elaborate house she'd decorated all on her own. She reached her bedroom—a place Garrett hadn't stepped into for a year before his death—and opened the safe she kept hidden behind the Warhol painting. Her fingers shook as she turned the combination and pulled the door open. The private investigator's report was hidden in the back, secured in a folder a quarter inch thick. Every year he updated it, because knowing Stella Adams's location was the only way Eleanor had been able to sleep at night.

God, how she hated Jamaica. The heat. The people. The smell. The pressure in her chest eased and she stared down at the most recent report with a mixture of revile and disgust. Thirty-five years she'd kept her secret safe. Now it was about to come out. There was only one thing left to do.

"Give it to him, Hailey."

Hailey's eyes snapped Shane's in direction, and he didn't miss the shock that flared in their blue depths. "Are you crazy?"

"Listen to the man, whoever he is," Paul said. "He's obviously smarter than you are."

Shane's gaze ran from the gun in McIntosh's hand to the slim blonde hanging in the shadows behind Roarke Resorts' chief financial officer. Lucy Walthers. He recognized her from the night he'd questioned her at the Roarke house in Chicago.

His blood ran hot, but he played it cool. His hands were at his side, his eyes watching everything. The gun in the holster at his side had never felt so heavy before.

"What do you think you're doing, Paul?" Hailey asked.

"Taking what's mine." Paul's beady eyes shifted from Shane to Billy, then finally to Hailey. And in them? Nothing but contempt.

"Stealing from us won't get you anything," Hailey said, taking a step around Shane that royally pissed him off. Was she brain-dead? "You're not a Roarke. You still won't get the company."

"Eleanor will get it for me."

"You think that," Nicole piped in. "But you're not so sure. She could be using you."

Fire flashed in Paul's eyes as they darted to Nicole and back to Hailey. "She'll come to her senses." He laughed, but the sound held absolutely no humor. "I've earned this."

The way he was suddenly looking around, waving the gun and taking steps farther into the room set Shane's nerves on instant alert. He stepped in front of Hailey slightly, saw Billy do the same with Nicole. Out in the hall, Walthers was pacing, like the entire scene had her nervous as a whore in church.

"Stay behind me," Shane mumbled so only Hailey could hear him.

"Funny thing is," McIntosh said. "If you had just married me like your loony father wanted, none of this would have happened. We wouldn't be here, and he'd still be alive."

Hailey's fingers dug into Shane's upper arm, and then she was in front of him, moving so fast he barely had time to grab her around the waist and pull her back before she launched herself at McIntosh. "You son of a bitch! You killed him?"

"Hailey!"

A smug expression crossed McIntosh's face.

"Did you kill Bryan, too? Did he find out what a bastard you are!"

Shane's grip tightened around Hailey so hard, he knew he was leaving bruises, but goddamn she was strong, and so fired up he knew if he let go she'd sail across the room and claw the man's eyes out without a second thought. "Don't do anything stupid," he hissed in her ear.

McIntosh chuckled, watching Hailey struggle as if it amused him. Out of the corner of Shane's eye he saw Billy take two steps to the man's left. Nicole inched toward a stack of crates. "Bryan was dumb as a post and so pussy-whipped he didn't even see what hit him. You have Lucy to thank for that."

In the hallway, Lucy stopped pacing and shot a worried look their way.

"I'll see you rot in prison for this." Hailey's tone turned to ice, and she stopped struggling, but the venom Shane felt pumping through her was worse than the way she'd lashed out. Because it meant she was unpredictable. And if there was one thing he needed her to do right now, it was stay calm. "You and my mother for what you've done."

"Your mother? She's as stupid as you are. So worried about her own secrets she didn't even realize what was going on around her. But she was a good fuck. I will give her that. Even at her age." His eyes ran down the length of Hailey's body in a way that sent the blood roaring to Shane's head. "Not as good as you, though, right? I mean, look at you. You've got to be one spicy little slut in bed."

He glanced over her shoulder at Shane. "Is she? I bet she is. C'mon, man to man, you can tell me. Miss Ball-buster here never gave it up for me, but I bet she did for you." His licentious gaze ran back to Hailey. "Yeah, I bet for him you're a regular Jenna Jameson."

Shane heard the click in his brain, the one that told him he was going from stable to dangerous; the one he'd heard in Chicago just before he'd ended up with a knife in his side.

"Too bad I won't get to compare," McIntosh went on. "But you and you friends here are going to have a nice long time to get to know one another when we're gone. You can bone your brains out then." He looked up and around. "How long you think the oxygen will last in here, Lucy?" he asked over his shoulder. "Think they'll make it three days?"

Mumbling came from the hallway, but McIntosh only smiled. "In three days I'll be sitting pretty at RR. And hiring the worst private investigator in the city to look for the missing Roarke sisters."

His smile faded. And the gun in his hand gleamed under the lantern's bright light. "Now give me the bronze. Lucy and I are really fucking tired of chasing you two around, and I've had it with her complaining."

Billy had reached the far side of the room, and because McIntosh was intent on Hailey and the bronze she'd picked up, he didn't notice Shane take one step forward or Billy move in from the side.

"You want it?" Hailey asked. "This? This piece of metal?"

"Yes, I do. Bring it here."

"Hailey," Shane warned under his breath. "Don't you dare move."

Her jaw clenched. And slowly she lifted the sculpture until it was chest high. "Then you can have it, you bastard."

She heaved the statue hard, a chest pass the NBA would be proud of. But McIntosh saw it coming, and his hand holding the 9mm lifted.

"Goddammit!" That roar erupted in Shane's brain. He threw himself in front of the gun, tackled McIntosh before he could get a shot off. The bronze hit the ground. The gun slid from McIntosh's grip with a thud against the floor. As they grappled, Shane faintly heard screaming, feet pounding and the sound of a gunshot out in the hall. He had enough time to lift his head and see Hailey heading for the door, just before McIntosh's fist slammed into his jaw. "Prick!"

They wrestled, but it didn't take long for Shane to get the upper hand. He shoved his knee hard into McIntosh's spine and yanked up on his arm until the man cried out in pain. He glanced up and around for something to secure the man's wrists. Nicole was crouched behind a stack of boxes, eyes wide. Shane hollered for her to bring him some wire from the crates.

When McIntosh tried to get up, Shane shoved him face-first into the concrete. "Stay down, asshole." He wiped his mouth, glanced down at the blood on his hand as Nicole cautiously brought over the wire. The man grunted as Shane wrapped the wire tight around his wrists. "Where's your goddamn sister?" he barked at Nicole.

"I . . . I don't know."

"Fuck this." He shoved off McIntosh. Reached for the gun on the ground and checked the safety. Then he handed the firearm to Nicole. "Stand here. Keep this pointed at the son of a bitch. If he so much as moves, shoot his ass."

McIntosh whimpered. Nicole's eyes grew so big, the whites could be seen all around her dark irises. The gun trembled in her hand. "Wh-where are you going?"

"To kick your sister's ass."

Hailey and Billy were dragging a dirty and sobbing Lucy Walthers back toward the storage room when Shane reached the hallway. He should have been relieved, happy Hailey wasn't hurt, but at the moment all he saw was red. She hadn't listened to him. Again. Was she trying to get herself killed?

He jerked Walthers out of their grasp and dumped her on the ground next to McIntosh.

Hailey looked at Billy. "Do you have that phone?"

He tossed it to her, went to Nicole and gently took the gun from her hand, wrapping one arm around her and cradling her against him.

Hailey immediately dialed. "Allie? Yeah, it's me. Listen, I've got some trash that needs to be picked up." As she disappeared out into the hall to talk to Alice Hargrove, Shane was left with nothing to do but watch her go.

He walked across the floor while Billy spoke quietly to Nicole. Shane's adrenaline was still pumping as he picked up the bronze and looked at the two entwined lovers.

Last Seduction? He didn't see that. All he saw was greed. And revenge. And a woman who was so goddamn independent, the only way to get through to her was by force.

Hailey's voice drifted into the room. He heard her giving Allie their location on the island. He looked over at Billy and Nicole. "Police are on their way. Hailey and I have to make tracks. They'll ask questions, we'll get pulled in—"

"And you two will never figure out the rest of this," Billy said, arm still around Nicole. "We'll wait for the cops. You two just get lost before they get here."

Shane nodded. Took one more look at Walthers and McIntosh on the ground, then turned for the door with the bronze tucked under his arm. And told himself not to lose his temper with Hailey. Not yet, at least.

Shane hadn't spoken a word to her on the boat ride back to Marathon. Hadn't asked if she was okay or even looked her way. And Hailey tried not to read anything into that. Tried to tell herself she didn't care whether he was worried about her mental health.

But it was hard. Especially when they climbed on the Roarke Bombardier and she gave the pilot the coordinates from her father's letter, found out they were heading to Jamaica, told Shane, and he *still* didn't say a single word in response. Just strapped in and waited for takeoff with clenched jaw and eyes that seemed to look off into space.

Okay, he was ticked. Didn't take a brainiac to figure that one out. She twiddled her thumbs while the plane gained momentum and they shot into the air. The second they were high enough, she flipped off her seat belt and hit the galley for something to drink to settle her nerves.

She was pouring her second shot when Shane picked her up by the elbows and turned her around to face him. The bottle of bourbon slipped from her fingers and hit the counter with a crack. "What the hell are you—"

His mouth was over hers before the words were even past her lips, but she knew instinctively this wasn't a gentle kiss. Wasn't a loving kiss. Wasn't even an *I'm sorry for everything you've been through* kiss. It was hard and wet and a little bit mean as his teeth sank into her bottom lip hard enough for a lick of pain to shoot though her skin. He didn't give her a chance to say yes or no or anything in between, because he was yanking her off the floor and pushing her through the door into the private cabin and shoving her down to the mattress before she even realized they were moving.

He was pissed. She could feel the anger pumping off him in hot, rolling waves. Knew he was replaying what she'd done in that bunker and using it to punish her. And while her brain told her rough, angry sex was a really bad idea, especially after the way things had gone last night and this morning, her own adrenaline was still so high, she didn't care.

She thrust her tongue into his mouth, found the edge of his shirt and scored her nails up underneath and across his bare back until he roared. He answered by biting her lip again, then ripping her T-shirt open right down the center to expose her bra and stomach.

She gasped. Barely had time to react before he was pulling her breasts free without even unlatching her bra and devouring them with his mouth. His arousal rubbed against her hip. Electricity rushed over her skin.

Oh, God . . .

Bad, awful, really dangerous idea. So how come with him it felt so right?

His teeth scraped her nipple as his hands found the snap on her jeans, ripped them open and stripped her bare. "Goddamn, you're going to listen to me," he growled. "Even if I have to force you to."

She moaned as his mouth ran low, lower, until he was pushing her legs wide and dragging his tongue up her cleft.

"Shane . . ."

Her back arched. Her fingers slid into his hair. Light flashed behind her eyes as he worked his tongue over and around, taking her places she'd never been. And when he pushed two fingers inside her, thrust deep in time with his tongue, all that adrenaline and anger and pent-up rage tipped the scales into a mind-blowing orgasm that rocketed through her entire body.

He flicked his tongue over her as she came down the other

side, then sank his teeth into the pressure point between her thigh and torso until she groaned.

It didn't hurt. If anything, it superheated her blood all over again. She pushed her hips up against him as he licked and sucked the spot, and reached for him, desperate to have him inside her like he'd been last night.

But before she could wrap her hands about his shoulders, he was off the bed, wiping his mouth with the back of his hand and pacing the small room like a caged tiger ready to strike.

Her brain was still nothing but sex-fuzz as she pushed up on her elbows to look for him. Why wasn't he inside her right this second? She glanced down the length of his body and discovered—to her surprise—he wasn't hard anymore.

A chill spread through her veins, forcing out all that sultry heat. And in that moment she became achingly aware of the sound of the jet's engines, the air hissing through the vent above, the heave and draw of his breath across the room. He was completely clothed, and her breasts were hanging out of her bra, her panties were ripped and her jeans were dangling from one leg.

That wasn't sex. That wasn't pleasure. That was a point, which he'd made crystal clear. He didn't need her. He didn't want her. But he was in charge.

A sick feeling settled in her stomach. She fixed her bra, pulled on her jeans and looked around for her bag so she could find a shirt not shredded by his hands.

"When I tell you to do something," he said in a low voice from across the room, "that means do it. It doesn't mean lose your fucking common sense."

"Go to hell," she snapped.

She jerked on a shirt, managed to get the collar over her head before he grabbed her by the arm and whipped her back to face him. "I can't keep you safe if you don't listen to me!"

She shoved his chest, enough to get him to stumble back a few steps so she could yank her shirt down. "I don't need you to protect me. I've been doing it all on my own my whole life. Who the hell do you think you are anyway?"

He took a step toward her. "Goddamn it, Hailey—"

"I'm not Julie, Shane!"

He stopped midstep. And something unreadable crossed his face.

And that's when it hit her, like a blast to the sternum that stole her breath. "Oh, my God. You're not here because of me."

"*What?*"

Her eyes grew wide. "Why didn't I see it before? All this time I thought you came down here with me because of how you felt about me. Because you wanted to help me." She shook her head as she thought about how he'd walked away from his department without a second thought, taken her dagger from evidence, lied to his partner on the phone. "But that's not why, is it?"

"Yes, it is."

"No." She shook her head, his actions and words and the way he'd tried to keep personal distance between them all finally making sense in her head. "You're here because of her. So you can prove you can save the girl and still get the bad guy in the end. And that's why you're so angry with me now. Because you can't do that if I don't play the helpless female who needs you to protect her."

She knew she was right when guilt crept into his eyes. "Hailey—"

"Oh, God." The room spun, and her stomach rolled. And when he moved toward her, she flinched out of his reach so his heat couldn't brand her skin. "I can't believe I was a complete fool."

"That's not what this is—"

"Don't lie to me!" She held up her hands to block him, clenched them into fists as her stupidity registered. And felt her heart crack, right there in the silence between them. She closed her eyes and took a calming breath. "Just . . . do me the courtesy of at least not lying about it now."

He didn't answer. And as she stood there gathering herself, she tried to figure out what it was about her and men. Why did she keep falling for guys who didn't really want her?

Slowly, she opened her eyes, only to find him watching her cautiously. The anger that had driven him before was gone, replaced with a guilt-ridden look that said, yep, she'd been right.

Her chest tightened, so much so she thought it might just implode. And then in a rush, all that betrayal and rage slid out on a wave and was replaced with a numb feeling that seemed to grow from her core and radiate outward until all she felt was . . . nothing. Nothing but empty and utterly alone.

She made a decision then, the only one she had left to make.

"When we land, I want you to leave. I want you off my plane and out of my life for good."

"I'm not leaving you when—"

"Don't." She held up a hand to keep him from touching her. But she didn't yell. Didn't snap. Didn't have enough left in her to lash out at him. "Don't take away what little dignity I have left. Just . . . don't."

She left him standing in the bedroom alone, made her way through the cabin and up to the cockpit where she sank into the copilot's seat and stared out at the clouds like a sea of white ahead of her.

White and vast and empty. A lot like her life.

Steve glanced sideways at her, and she knew without even asking he'd heard at least part of what had transpired. "You okay?"

She should be embarrassed. Humiliated. Seething over what Shane had done. But she couldn't muster up enough emotion to feel anything but numb. "Yeah, I'm fine. Just get me to Jamaica, Steve. From there . . . I'll figure things out on my own. Just like I always do."

# CHAPTER TWENTY-FOUR

Hailey pushed her sunglasses into her hair as the Jeep she'd rented at Ken Jones Airport outside Port Antonio, Jamaica, passed through a shaded section of the twisting two-lane road that ran up a steep hill. The air was thick and hot, and sweat slid down her spine as she glanced from the trees to the road, then to the family she passed dragging a cart filled with vegetables.

Steve had offered to come with her, but she needed to do this on her own. She lifted the map from the passenger seat, glanced at the circle she'd made on the other side of Port Antonio that matched the coordinates from her father's letter. She'd left Steve at the airport with directions to wait for a call from her. And she'd walked away from Shane without a second look.

Her hands tightened on the wheel as she thought about Shane. What had her last evaluation with the Key West PD said? *Competent but impulsive.* And her captain had made a point of adding that she was especially impetuous when a situation became personal.

She glanced at the passenger seat, where The Last Seduction sat in a bag along with the photo of her father, his letter and her Beretta, just in case. Okay, so she might be a tad bit rash, and Shane was right about one thing—she was independent—but after everything that had already happened, she wasn't stupid.

At the top of the hill, the road curved to the left and disappeared around the bend. To the left, a small drive was marked with a small sign that read, THE GATE HOUSE. She made the turn and slowed the Jeep as it bounced over holes in the road, then down a steep slope covered in flowering vines and palms. It weaved around until finally opening and coming to a stop in front of a stately three-story plantation-style building perched on a cliff that overlooked the bay on one side and the Caribbean on the other.

Hailey killed the engine and climbed from the Jeep, slinging her bag over her shoulder as she took in her surroundings. Salt permeated the air, and the crash of waves could be heard somewhere below. A small Jamaican boy, who couldn't be more than three, appeared from the bushes and came running up to her car.

Startled, Hailey looked down. A woman in a long red skirt hollered from the bushes and came rushing after him, speaking in a language Hailey didn't understand. The woman looked her up and down a few times before scolding the boy and ushering him back off into the trees.

Hands on hips, she inclined her head and said, "You be lookin' for Miss Stella, I'm a guessin'."

Stella? For the first time since she'd decided to come here, nerves bubbled in Hailey's stomach. She tucked her hair behind her ear and nodded. "Yes. I am. She lives here?"

"Aye, and works here." The woman turned for the house, waved her hand for Hailey to follow. "She not be expectin' ya. She woulda told us had ya been a comin'."

Expecting her. That meant this woman, Stella, knew all about Hailey. She followed down a long path that led up to the stately white house with its wide porch and wood shutters. But they didn't go in. At the last second the woman veered away and followed a gravel path that ran around the side of the house.

"Miss Stella be finishin' up a class."

Voices echoed from inside the house. Laughter, the sounds of children's feet running.

"What is this place?" Hailey asked, adjusting the strap of her bag.

"Hmmm . . ." The woman seemed to mull over the question. "The Gate House is like a safe place for women. Where dey can be creative. An artists' school for dose who have the talent and nowhere else to go."

An artistic women's shelter? Hailey had never heard of such a thing.

They passed out of the shade of the house and came around the back. A wide yard ran from the back porch, down sloping grass to a view that looked out over the blue-green Caribbean.

"Oh, my," Hailey said, taking it in.

"Miss Stella be in da rose garden." The woman stopped. Pointed toward a flowering arbor to the left. "Through that arch there. Follow the path 'til you find her." Her attention shifted, and she began yelling in that language Hailey didn't understand, then was gone.

Hailey headed toward the garden. The path wove through more trees and flowering bushes until she found herself standing on the edge of another lawn, this one surrounded by roses of all shapes and sizes and colors. A few chairs were set up in a half circle, and a slim woman with long blonde hair stood with her back to Hailey at the far side, folding an easel.

Hailey cleared her throat and the woman stopped, turned with a smile and froze. "Oh . . . my God."

She'd seen the picture, so Hailey shouldn't have been surprised by the face, but she was. Because the woman standing in front of her now looked like an older, prettier version of herself.

Neither moved. Or spoke. Finally Hailey stepped forward until they were no more than three feet apart. "You seem surprised to see me here now, but not surprised in general."

The easel forgotten, Stella lifted her hand to her mouth with wide eyes. "I . . . how did you find me?"

Hailey slid the bag from her shoulder and pulled out the picture and letter her father had left her. She handed them to Stella and waited.

Stella's eyes softened as she looked at the picture. Then,

with hands Hailey noticed were shaking, she opened the letter and began to read. Emotions passed over the woman's face. Emotions Hailey couldn't quite read but that a tiny part of her hoped were sadness and regret.

When Stella finished reading, she folded the note, looked one more time at the photo and handed both back to Hailey. And when her eyes lifted, they were damp. "How did he die?"

The details of her father's death were not points Hailey wanted to talk about right now, so she said simply, "A heart attack."

Stella nodded. "I didn't know. I'm so sorry."

Hailey reached into the bag and pulled out the sculpture. "He left me this."

Stella's eyes widened, and she took the bronze with a shake of her head and wry smile. "I gave it to him. He had such a love of art. It was our connection, you know. We used to talk about it all the time. This"—she ran her fingers over the statue—"had been my mother's. It was the only thing she left for me when she died. It seemed right to give it to Garrett."

"It's worth a great deal of money, you know."

Stella looked at the entwined lovers wistfully. "I didn't know that at the time, but I do now. It wouldn't have mattered, though. I never cared about the money. Neither did your father."

"How did you meet?"

On a sigh, Stella looked at Hailey. "I was working as a maid at your father's first hotel. It had just opened in Florida. He . . ." A smile slid across her face. "He nearly ran me over in the hall one morning when I was delivering coffee. It ended up all over him, all over me. I was so afraid he was going to fire me. I was only twenty-one. My mother had died recently in a car accident and my father's health wasn't very good. And we needed the money." She glanced down at the bronze. Smiled so sweetly it touched a spot in the center of Hailey's heart. Maybe it wasn't so numb after all. "He didn't, though. Your father laughed so hard he nearly cried. And then he whisked me off to find clean clothes and apologize until he was blue in the face."

"You loved him," Hailey said, even before she realized her thought had been put into words.

"I did," Stella said, nodding, cradling the bronze against her chest. "Very much. The few months we were together were . . . some of the best of my life."

"What happened?"

Stella sighed before handing the statue back to Hailey. "Your father was already engaged at the time. To Eleanor Schmidt. I didn't know it when we met. He didn't tell me until after . . . after I found out I was pregnant with you. I never would have been with him if I'd known, and . . ." She looked down at her hands. "He told me he didn't love her. That he didn't want to marry her. But that he was trapped because Eleanor's father had invested a huge amount in his hotel endeavor. The success of his company hinged on his marrying Eleanor. He told me he was going to try to get out of it, though. And I, well . . ." She lifted her shoulders. Dropped them. "I believed him."

"But he didn't."

Stella shook her head. "They wouldn't let him. When your father told them I was pregnant, Eleanor's father came to see me. He tried to buy me off so I'd disappear with you. No one would know about your father's affair, he could marry Eleanor like had already been planned and things would be the way they were supposed to be. But I wouldn't agree. My father got involved then. He was appalled at the things Phillip Schmidt demanded. Irate that they thought they could throw their money around and get what they wanted. And when Garrett told the Schmidts he wasn't going to turn his back on me and his child, things got ugly."

Hailey remembered how domineering her maternal grandfather had been. And the tension that had always existed between Phillip and his son-in-law. "Then what happened?"

"Garrett was convinced we could make things work. Privately, he called off his engagement to Eleanor, but I don't think the family ever announced it. Things cooled down for about a month. When your father and I were together, he didn't talk much about the situation, and I was young and so in love, I was afraid to bring it up and ruin our time together. Then my father died unexpectedly and . . . I found myself all alone.

"I was scared. And anxious about the pregnancy. Garrett was working more and more, stressed about the hotel. We argued. About nothing. About everything. It became clear if the Schmidts pulled their support, he was going to lose all he'd worked so hard for. Every cent he'd had was in that hotel. Every cent his brother'd had. I couldn't let him do that. I loved him too much."

"So you left him? Left me?"

She shook her head sadly. "No, Hailey. I loved you. But I loved your father, too. Oh, it seems so silly to say it now, but back then, I was torn. Alone. Young. Confused. Afraid the way things were going, I was going to be raising you by myself with no money, no place to live. Nothing. And so when Eleanor came to me and said she had a solution that worked for all of us, I listened.

"She knew Garrett was never going to ignore you. His sense of loyalty ran too deep. And she knew he wouldn't turn his back on me, either. But she was hurting, I could tell that, and I sensed a part of her loved him, too. She suggested I be the one to walk away from him. That she would go on an extended trip so no one knew the truth, and when the baby was born—you—she would come back and raise you as her own."

"And you agreed to this? Just like that?"

"No. Not at first. But I thought about it a lot after she was gone. You have to remember I had nothing, Hailey. No education. No family. I'd lost my parents' home to medical bills. Garrett was preoccupied with keeping the hotel afloat, and I felt like a burden. A mistake he'd made that he was now paying for. I had to make a decision about what was best for him and for you and for all of us. And I made the only one I felt I could at the time."

She took a breath, and the slight action looked like it pained her. "I let you go. I let you both go."

Hailey thought about Eleanor Roarke and all the years she'd spent feeling like an outsider in her own family. Now she knew why. "But you never thought to contact me? Not once in thirty-four years?"

"I couldn't. It was part of our agreement. As long as I stayed out of your life, your father, his hotel, you . . . all of it was safe. The only way Eleanor would agree to still marry your father after his infidelity was if his secret never came out." Her eyes softened. "But I watched, Hailey. I knew where you were, what you were doing. I was so proud of you when you went to Harvard. When you became a police officer. I have the newspaper clipping of your wedding in a frame in my bedroom."

"I'm not married anymore."

A sad smile crept across her face. "I know that, too." She took a hesitant step forward. "It's not that I didn't want you. I did. Very much. I . . . I need you to know that there hasn't been a day that's gone by that I haven't questioned my decision."

Hailey looked at the bronze in her hands. "Did you ever see him again?"

Stella glanced down at the statue. Opened her mouth. Closed it.

"Don't hold out on me now," Hailey said.

"He came here to see me. Just over a month ago. After thirty-four years, he wanted a second chance." Sorrow filled her eyes. "Hailey, I'm remarried now. Happy. I met a man who loves me and puts me first. A part of me will always love your father, but he . . ."

"Is part of your past," Hailey finished when Stella's words trailed off.

Sadly, Stella nodded. "I thought maybe that meant things had changed. I told him I wanted to see you. But he warned me not to. Not until he had a chance to tell you the truth on his own. I had no idea he would die before that happened."

Hailey's heart pinched. If her father had loved this woman as much as Hailey was beginning to believe, she couldn't help wondering why he'd waited so long to go after the one thing he'd still so obviously wanted. And what had happened to make him change his mind?

A fleeting thought of Shane passed through her mind, but she pushed it away. "Where did you go? After you left?"

Stella walked across the garden and reached for a bloom from a nearby rosebush. "I traveled for a while. Worked odd jobs to pay my way. Sold some paintings on the side for extra cash. In Louisiana I met a woman who fell in love with my work and took me in. She was what you'd call an art connoisseur. She helped me get my paintings into a few key galleries."

All of the sudden, the name registered in Hailey's brain. "Stella? Stella Adams?" When Stella nodded, Hailey's mouth dropped open. Several boxes in the bunker she'd just come from that morning were labeled *Adams*. And Pete had a whole room set aside at Odyssey devoted to the famous landscape painter. "Oh, my God."

A smile crept across Stella's face. "I'll take that as a compliment." She nodded back toward the house. "The woman I mentioned in Louisiana? This was her mother's home. I used to come here to paint when I needed some space. When she died, her daughter suggested we set it up as an artists' community. One especially for women with talent or interest who had nowhere else to go. I thought it was a wonderful idea. If there'd been a place like this when I'd been pregnant with you . . . well, things might have been very different."

"Why didn't he ever tell me?" Hailey asked. "I mean, as an adult. I understand why he kept quiet when I was a child, but what would the harm have been in telling me now? Why the secrecy and this stupid treasure hunt if all he really wanted to do was lead me to you?"

"I don't know," Stella said quietly. "I wish I did, but—"

"Because he couldn't."

Hailey turned at the sound of a voice she knew all too well.

Graham was standing just on the edge of the grass. "He couldn't, Hailey. It was part of the prenuptial agreement Eleanor and her father made him sign."

"Graham, don't."

Hailey flinched at the sound of Eleanor's voice, and all three of them looked toward the shadow of a large magnolia tree.

What the . . . ?

"Why not, Eleanor?" Graham's voice hardened. "Garrett's dead. It's time all of it came out. Once and for all. She already knows about Stella."

"All of what?" Hailey asked, looking between the two, a strange feeling brewing in her chest.

Eleanor never looked away from Graham. "Don't do this."

He stared at her, then finally said, "Eleanor doesn't care who runs Roarke Resorts, Hailey. Not really. McIntosh was a good choice because she thought she could control him. But she couldn't. Could you, Eleanor? He went off on his own, tried to find Garrett's bronzes without you. Recruited his girlfriend, Lucy, to get the ones he couldn't get on his own. Like Bryan's. And Nicole's. And mine."

"That's enough."

"You're right, it is. I should have spoken up when Garrett died."

"I didn't kill my husband."

"No, you didn't," Graham said, still watching her. "But you caused it. Just like I did. It ate at him. All these years. The documents you and your father made him sign, the ones that prohibited Hailey from ever getting a piece of a company that was rightfully hers if he ever told her the truth about Stella. The way you belittled Nicole so she'd never be interested in RR. You made them miserable. All of them. Fractured what little happiness they could have had because of your need to control. Because of your need to make sure no one knew what you'd done—what we'd done. Garrett put up with it for a long time until it broke him. Until he was convinced there was no other way. When he found out he had that heart condition—"

"I didn't kill him!"

A chill spread down Hailey's spine.

"No," Graham said, his tone rising. "But you didn't do anything to stop it, either. You knew he'd gone to see Stella. That she'd turned him away. And even then, when he came to you and told you he wanted out, you laughed in his face. Called him crazy. You're still controlling everything, after all this time, aren't you? No one would have cared how his affair impacted you thirty-five years later."

"I cared!"

Graham shook his head sadly. "That was the problem. You did, so much you wouldn't let him go, even now. I found him, Eleanor. In his office. The night you were with your boyfriend. I found him with the heart medication he'd swiped from my kitchen even though he knew an overdose would do exactly what his doctors were trying to prevent."

Hailey gasped. Her father had killed himself?

"He did that to spite me!" Eleanor yelled. "Even in death he couldn't be the husband I always needed. He had to get the last word in."

"He died because you and I ruined his life! Don't you see? You and all your poisonous weeds were choking everything he'd created. He didn't want that for Hailey and Nicole. It might not be the way any of us would have done it, but this treasure hunt of his made sense to him. And in the end it did exactly what your precious prenuptial agreement was supposed to prevent. It set the truth free."

"His will means nothing!"

Graham shook his head, a mixture of rage and heartache brewing in his eyes. "Madeline called me. I know what you did to my son."

He turned quickly to face Stella before Eleanor could answer. "Thirty-five years ago your father died of a heart attack—"

"Graham, don't!" Eleanor screamed.

"—it wasn't a heart attack. It was murder. Calculated so no one would know. So you would be left alone with no choice but to take Eleanor's offer and walk away from Garrett for good."

"No . . ." Stella's hand flew to her mouth.

"I helped her," Graham said with gut-wrenching sorrow. "God, I shouldn't have. But I loved her. My wife had just left me with Bryan, and Eleanor had been the one person I could confide in, because she'd gone through the same thing with Garrett. I . . . I was blinded by her. And when Eleanor came to me with the idea, I thought just the attempt would be enough to prove my loyalty to her. To get her to see I was the man for her and not Garrett. Your father wasn't supposed to die, Stella. I swear that to you now. I calculated a low dosage. I didn't know his heart was so weak, but then he—"

The sound of a gunshot ripped through the stillness of the early evening air.

*No!*

The bullet hit Graham dead center in the back. His eyes flew wide. He gasped in a breath. Then he was falling forward, toward Stella. Falling down . . .

Stella screamed. Hailey ran forward to catch him. "Graham!"

She got to him before he could take Stella down with him. He was heavy, slamming into Hailey with all his weight. They both went to the ground hard, and Hailey rolled him, unable to believe what had just happened. Her eyes flashed to Eleanor, holding the gun in her rock-steady hand. Hailey's training kicked in, and she quickly assessed the situation. Realizing her bag with the Beretta was ten feet away and Eleanor's barrel was trained on them, she knew there was nothing she could do until she got Graham stable.

Blood poured out the exit wound in Graham's chest. She scrambled to her knees and pressed against the wound to stop the bleeding. Tears sprang to her eyes when she realized it was useless. "Graham, no, no, no . . ."

"Hailey . . ." His hand closing over hers on his chest stopped her frantic movements. She focused on his kind slate gray eyes, even as her vision blurred and a sob caught in her throat. "I told . . . Madeline . . . to go to the police. She said . . . it was an accident. You believe her . . . don't you?"

"Yes," she whispered, not understanding his words but hoping to comfort him. "Yes. Of course it was."

That seemed to calm him. He closed his eyes, his hand tightening around hers. "Tell Nicole how sorry I am. I love her. I . . . love you . . . like my own. I'm sorry. So sorry . . . for all of it."

"No. Don't go," Hailey said, squeezing his hand. "Not like this. Graham . . ."

"I warned him," Eleanor said from across the yard. "If he had just listened to me, this would not have happened."

Graham took a stuttering breath. His grip relaxed, and his eyes lost focus. As Hailey felt him dying, she didn't care about what he'd done. All that mattered was that he'd come here to try to make amends.

"Graham . . . no, please . . ."

"We need to call an ambulance." Stella made a move at Hailey's side.

Her scream brought Hailey's head around until she was staring at the woman she'd thought was her mother, pulling Stella backward by the hair with a gun aimed at the other woman's temple.

Oh, God. She was going to kill them, too.

"There will be no ambulance," Eleanor said coldly. "No one to rescue you. This is your fault. Don't you see that? If it weren't for you, none of this would ever have happened."

The pain in Hailey's chest was fresh and raw, but the voice ringing in her ears pushed it down with a wave of rage.

Eleanor's eyes were wild and black as night. "I tried to make things right. I worked so hard so that no one ever knew what you'd done. I even raised your miserable daughter for you, but you *still* managed to come back to ruin my life. This is my life!" she screamed. "I'm not going to let you ruin it anymore!"

"Eleanor," Hailey said calmly, pushing slowly to her feet, "put the gun down. Enough people have already been hurt."

"You." Eleanor's frantic eyes swung Hailey's direction. "If you had stayed out of it, Graham would still be alive. You did this!"

Hailey held up her hands. Her eyes shifted to her bag, where she'd left her gun, then back to Eleanor. How long until someone from the house came running? They had to have heard the shot. They knew Stella was down here. The woman who'd given Hailey directions knew Stella wasn't alone.

Eleanor kicked Hailey's bag away, looking smug. "No one's coming to save you." The gun in her hand shook. "They'll call it a murder-suicide. You came down here looking for Stella, and Graham followed. He knew you were going to turn him in for what he'd done. He killed both of you, then shot himself. I'll make sure the police link Andrew Adams's death back to your father's. Both of them died by the same poison. They'll know Graham was the mastermind behind it all."

As Eleanor rationalized it all out loud, Hailey sensed she had minutes, seconds before Eleanor started firing. Eleanor's eyes were barely tracking. She knew she was trapped.

"I know what it's like to love someone who doesn't want you," Hailey said quickly. Eleanor's surprised eyes darted her way. Seemed to focus. *Yes, keep looking at me.* "To give your heart to someone and have them trample it. I've been there. Not once, but twice."

"Men are pigs."

"They are," Hailey agreed. Inched forward. Hoped she could lull Eleanor enough to make a move for the gun.

"I could have told you that thief you married was a loser. But, no, you didn't listen to me, either. You never did."

"He was," Hailey lied, willing to say anything to keep Eleanor distracted. "The other one . . ." She thought of Shane. "He didn't want me, either. So you and I, we're not all that different. I know what you're feeling."

"You don't know," Eleanor said. "Not unless he left you for a slut like this. Do you know what I gave up for your father?

Do you know how hard I worked to make him love me? But he wouldn't. Not after her."

Eleanor's eyes flicked to Stella, then back to Hailey and suddenly widened as she realized Hailey had moved close. And whatever calm she'd slowly been sliding into imploded. "Oh, I don't think so." She took a big step back, tightened her hand in Stella's hair and pulled until Stella yelped. "I see what you're doing, and it won't work. You're not getting away this time."

Hailey's adrenaline pulsed. If it weren't for the gun pressed against Stella's temple, Hailey could take the woman. She was stronger than Eleanor, and she had youth on her side. But she was too afraid Stella would get caught in the cross fire. She'd already lost her father and Graham. She wasn't about to lose the mother she'd just found.

And that's when she noticed a shadow shift ever so slightly in the trees behind Eleanor.

*Shane.*

She could just make out his eyes, peering back at her in the dense foliage as Stella and Eleanor argued.

Her heart jumped as their eyes locked. A silent communication where she knew impetuousness and doing things on her own wasn't going to save her or Stella. She had to rely on him. He was here. He'd come for her. Even after she'd told him she never wanted to see him again.

"Enough arguing!" Eleanor bellowed. "Say good-bye to your daughter." She pulled the gun from Stella's temple, pointed it at Hailey.

"No!" Stella screamed.

The gun bobbled, started to move back to Stella, and Hailey didn't hesitate. She dropped low and lunged for Stella.

Two shots rang out, almost simultaneously. Followed quickly by another. And another.

Hailey's right side hit the ground. A searing burn suddenly erupted like fire in her shoulder. Stella grunted as she landed with a thud.

"Hailey!"

Footsteps pounded across the ground.

"Hailey!" Stella rolled out from under Hailey and scrambled to her knees. "She's bleeding! Help me, she's bleeding!"

Hailey gasped as Shane skidded to his knees at her side. "Christ Jake, hold on, Hailey. We need an ambulance."

Stella leaped to her feet, then was gone.

Shane's gun hit the ground near her head. She looked up at the hazy clouds rushing by overhead as he pulled her shirt out of the way. "Eleanor . . ."

"She's gone. Don't worry about her." He ripped off his T-shirt and pressed it against her shoulder. "Jesus, are you trying for matching scars? Because this isn't the way to go about getting one."

The panic in his voice belied his snarky words, and she closed her eyes. Rescuing her was one thing. Being worried about her . . . that was something she couldn't let herself think about. Not now. "What are you doing here, Maxwell? I thought I told you to"—she grimaced as he pushed down—"get lost."

"Yeah, well," he said as he worked, making her feel like a rag doll in the process, "I figure you don't listen to me, no reason I should listen to you." She ground her teeth against the pain as he wrapped his shirt up and around her shoulder.

"I need an ambulance!" he hollered.

Voices and yelling could be heard from way off. The pounding of feet getting closer. Shane's labored breathing.

Hailey closed her eyes and tried to focus on nothing.

"Come on, Roarke," he said. "Tell me what a jerk I am. Tell me how you want to kick my ass. We both know I deserve it."

"I don't have the energy." She was suddenly dog tired. More exhausted than she'd been her whole life. And ready to be done with everything. Him, her family, all the lies and hurt. Especially the ache in her chest that was growing by leaps and bounds after everything she'd seen and learned today. "You saved the girl, Maxwell. Got the bad guy—"

"Yeah, that's why you're lying here bleeding. Where's that goddamn ambulance!"

"But I'm not dead. Which . . . is where I'd be if it weren't for you. You can go home a hero now."

"I'm not going anywhere without you," he whispered close to her ear. "Hailey, do you hear me? I said I'm not leaving you, and I'm not."

She took a long breath. Let it out slowly. Voices echoed around her. She felt hands on her body. Heard someone with a thick Jamaican accent tell Shane to move out of the way so they could treat her, but she didn't open her eyes. Couldn't.

"Blood pressure's dropping . . ."

"We need to move her . . ."

"Get that stretcher over here!"

"I'll be right here when you wake up," Shane whispered in her other ear, even after she thought he'd gone. "Don't you dare give up on me. Do you hear me, Roarke? Don't you dare give up . . ."

# CHAPTER TWENTY-FIVE

"Shane."

Shane's eyes popped open at the sound of his name. He was sitting in a small corner room at Port Antonio General Hospital, where he'd been holding vigil the last twenty-four hours.

"Shit, man, you don't look much better than her."

*Tony.*

Shane pushed out of the chair by the side of Hailey's bed and looked toward the door where his partner was standing with a scowl on his face. He didn't have to ask to know what Tony was seeing: three days' worth of stubble, hair that was probably sticking out all over, matted and wrinkled clothes.

He was groggy as hell, stiff and sore, but he met Tony halfway across the room with a fierce handshake. "I didn't expect you to get here so soon."

"O'Conner wants this wrapped up." He nodded toward the bed. "She gonna be okay?"

Shane's gaze followed, and just like it had every time he'd looked at Hailey in that bed, his stomach clenched. "Yeah. It was touch and go for a while. Bullet did some damage inside. But it looks like she's gonna pull through just fine."

Tony nodded, looked around the run-down room. Shane knew what else his partner was thinking. The place was clean, and the level of medical care here so far seemed pretty good. But it was Jamaica. Shane couldn't wait to get Hailey back to a facility in the States. "How'd you get her a private room?"

"Stella Adams set it up." Shane scrubbed a hand through his hair. "She's got some clout with the people down here."

Tony nodded again. "Still can't believe that's her mother."

"Yeah, you and me both," Shane said quietly.

"We reran Bryan Roarke's tox screen based on the info you gave me. Came up positive for cardiac glycosides. Chemical found in plants like digitalis, lily of the valley and—"

"Oleander," Shane finished, rubbing his shoulder. "Yeah, I know."

"Not a common method of murder if you want to do it on the sly, because you have to know the dosages, but it's effective." He looked toward Shane. "Madeline Roarke turned herself in. She's pleading out. Saying Eleanor told her what to do. Apparently, good ol' Bryan found out about Eleanor's involvement with Andrew Adams's death. Not sure if Graham Roarke told him or what, but either way, Bryan was blackmailing her for control of the company. To get back at him, she told Madeline about his affair with Lucy and suggested a way to teach him a lesson. Madeline's claiming she thought the poison would just make him sick, not really kill him."

Shane huffed, stuffed his hands into his pockets. "You believe her?"

"No. But she's also been pretty adamant that she didn't cut him."

Shane shook his head. Any way you sliced it, Madeline Roarke was looking at doing some serious time.

"One thing's for certain," Tony said. "She didn't set Hailey up. Lucy Walthers is also talking. She's the one who planted the dagger to frame Hailey. Wounds came after Bryan had already died. DA's pretty convinced she did the cutting."

God, these people were sick.

"What about what happened to Hailey at her uncle's place? Who mixed the poison with the tea?"

"We're not quite sure. But when we went through McIntosh's apartment we found Graham's bronze. You said he was the one who ran you off the road at Graham's property, right?"

"Yeah. Hailey recognized his voice."

Tony nodded. "There were two different factions at work here. Eleanor and what she was trying to do to keep her secrets from coming out, and McIntosh and his quest for control of Roarke Resorts. As for that poison in Graham's tea—"

"Yeah?"

"Graham Roarke was taking digoxin for his heart condition. We found the medication in his kitchen. Wouldn't have been hard to mix some of that in a fresh batch of tea if you popped in to commit a theft. And if you happen to kill off a Roarke or two in the process? Makes it a lot easier to get control of the company you want so bad."

"Jesus." Shane ran a hand over his hair. "So it wasn't mixed for Hailey. But for Graham."

"Looks that way. McIntosh and Lucy Walthers won't see freedom for a long time, don't worry."

"And Hailey's father? You think it really was suicide?"

"It's looking that way." Tony let out a breath. "That woman . . . Eleanor? Man, sounds like she was a real piece of work. Real puppet-master pulling all the strings. I have a sinking suspicion neither of us would be right in the head after living with her for five years, let alone thirty plus."

Shane only nodded.

"Speaking of that dagger," Tony said. "Funniest thing. Still hasn't turned up in evidence. Doubt it'll ever show up. What do you think?"

Shane glanced at his partner. There was a good chance they were never going to figure out what Lucy had used to cut Bryan, but Tony was making sure Shane's ass was in the clear no matter what. "I owe you, man."

"Yeah, you do. Again," Tony said with a half grin. "Which is why I don't feel guilty about dragging your ass back to Chicago when I'm done questioning everyone here. The sooner we get this cleared up with O'Conner, the better it'll be for you. And her."

Shane nodded and looked back at Hailey. And realized in that moment he hadn't had a single Tic Tac in the last two days. "I'll go back with you. But I'm not staying."

Tony stared at him a beat, then said, "You've got a little over ten years until your pension kicks in. What are you—"

Shane turned his eyes on his friend. Maybe his only true friend, because he knew every one of Shane's darkest secrets. "Tony, you and I both know I won't make it to retirement. Not the way I'm going now. I'll be lucky to last another three years without getting myself killed, or worse, getting you killed. You're always telling me to get a life. Well . . ." He looked back at the bed. "Maybe it's about time I listened."

In the silence, he knew Tony was considering whether he was serious. "What are you gonna do?"

Shane shrugged. "I don't know. Jack's always trying to get me to switch over to PI work. I've got a few possibilities."

"You gotta have people skills for that, wife."

Shane chuckled. "I've got people skills, Goldilocks."

"Oh, yeah," Tony said, rolling his eyes. "You rank right up there with Commander O'Conner." He nodded toward Hailey's bed. "What about her?"

Shane's chest tingled. What about her? That was the million-dollar question, wasn't it?

"I don't know," he said. "But this isn't about her. It's about me. And finally letting go of things I should have let go of a long time ago."

"Well, I'll be damned. I never thought I'd see the day."

Shane frowned, because this conversation was suddenly way more real than he needed right now. "Don't get all excited. I'm not there yet. I said *maybe*."

A slow smile inched across Tony's face. And his light eyes sparkled when he nudged Shane in the shoulder. "It's a start. Hot damn, but it's a start, wife. I'm gonna go do those interviews so we can make tracks. Something tells me you won't be staying long in Chicago."

When he was alone, Shane sat in the chair by Hailey's bed and took her hand in both of his. Her fingers were long, her skin soft, her nails—he hadn't noticed them before—neat and trimmed, perfect. Just like her. There was so much about her he hadn't noticed, like the faint freckles across the bridge of her nose or the way her hair formed a swirl, right at her temple.

One thing he had noticed, though, was how calm she'd been in that scene with Eleanor. And how she'd trusted him to be there for her. Even after admitting to Eleanor that she loved him. That hadn't been an act. And every time he thought of it, he felt this sharp stab right beneath his breastbone.

Her head moved slightly on the pillow. Her fingers tightened against his. He tensed when he saw her eyelids flutter and finally open to stare up at him. She blinked several times before she rasped, "You don't look like Prince Charming."

The relief at hearing her voice was swift and consuming. "I'm not. But now that I know you're okay, a razor and a shower should take care of the ugly old troll look."

She didn't laugh at his stupid joke, but he cut her some slack, seeing as how she'd just come to after surgery.

"What are you doing here, Maxwell?"

Not *Shane*. But he'd cut her some slack on that as well. He squeezed her hand. "I told you I wasn't leaving until I knew you were okay."

She rolled her head to look up at the ceiling. "Well . . . now you know I'm fine, so you can go."

She was giving him an out. All he had to do was take it. He'd told himself from the start this was where it ended. Not with her in this bed, but with her alive and safe, the person who was setting her up in custody or dead. There wasn't any logical reason for him to stay, and yet, he wasn't moving.

*She loved him.*

"I do actually have to leave," he said cautiously, because something strange was happening in his chest. Something that felt a lot like all that regret he'd heaped on himself being slowly replaced with warmth. "Ah, Tony's here. O'Conner needs me to go back to Chicago to clear up a few things."

"Then you should go."

Her words were cold. Her attention anywhere but on him. The hurt in her voice stabbed at him, but he dealt with the pain because somehow he knew he was going to make this and everything else up to her. He just wasn't sure how yet. "I . . . I have a few things I need to take care of in Chicago, but I want you to know I'll be back."

"Don't bother."

"I will. That's a promise, Hailey."

She rolled away from him, and he knew the movement had to cause excruciating pain, but she didn't make a sound.

He rubbed a hand over that ache in his chest. "Stella's been waiting to see you. I'll send her in on my way out."

When even that didn't garner a response, he rose slowly and headed for the door. And in the silence, knew exactly what he needed to do. Maybe knew, for the first time in his life.

*Florida*
*Four weeks later*

"Man, that's a big crowd." Nicole's voice echoed through the room as the office door snapped shut behind her. "The place is packed."

The coffeepot bobbled in Hailey's hand, and she took a deep breath to settle the nerves bouncing around in her stomach. Slowly, as conversation picked up behind her, she lowered the carafe so no one would see her hand shake, reached for a packet of sugar and winced at the dull throb in her shoulder.

She was still working through physical therapy, but her doctor had assured her the bullet hadn't done any lasting damage. At least not to her shoulder. The fallout from the scene in Jamaica, though, was another matter entirely.

"Jeez," Nicole said, brushing past Hailey to reach for a

bottle of water on the counter. "I've never seen you this nervous. I didn't realize public speaking freaked you out so much."

"It doesn't," Billy piped up from his spot on the couch, where he'd been munching on trail mix from a bowl at his elbow. "At least it never did before." He grasped Nicole's hand when she got close and tugged her onto his lap. Nicole giggled as Billy planted a kiss near her ear. "So what gives, H?"

"This is a big day," Stella interjected before Hailey had to answer. "The press isn't nearly as interested by the changes you both have planned for Roarke Resorts as they are in getting info about what happened with Eleanor."

Hailey glanced at her mother—her *real* mother—standing near the big oak desk in the middle of the room. It'd taken a couple of weeks, but that's how she was starting to think of Stella. Like the mother she'd wished she'd always had. Stella was a lot like Teresa Sullivan—strong, opinionated, but with a heart as big as Hailey had ever known. And for that reason, it hadn't seemed strange at all when Stella had introduced Hailey to her husband—Mark Walker—a rancher from Texas Stella had met at a gallery opening in Dallas eight years before.

The woman had every reason to despise everything Roarke related after what had been done to her and her father, but here she was, welcoming Hailey *and* Nicole into her family, taking a break from her own work so she and Hailey could get to know each other better, supporting Hailey and her decision to stay on as CEO of RR even though it had to stir painful memories inside her.

Painful memories had to swell in Nicole, too, but you'd never know it by looking at her with Billy now. Hailey glanced at her sister and the silly smile on her face. For all the years they'd spent being resentful of each other, it was odd to have Nicole here now, though Hailey was thankful for her company. And completely blown away by the fact Nicole had put her personal feelings aside and seemed to understand their father hadn't pulled back just from her but from both of them, and only because of Eleanor.

It was both Stella and Nicole's strength Hailey was cling-
ing to now as she faced her own insecurities. She'd half expected Nicole or Billy, or even Allie, to try to talk her out of
leaving the Key West PD for good. But none of them had.
She and Nicole were working together to run Roarke Resorts. She as CEO and Nicole as president of Operations.
And when Hailey had announced she wanted Billy heading
security, no one had seemed surprised. But the kicker had
come later, when not a single one of them—Stella included—
had protested Hailey's suggestion to convert RR from a private company to a public one and open it to shareholders,
even though that had never been part of her father's vision.

Graham had told her once the reason she hadn't excelled
in law enforcement was because deep down, it wasn't her
passion. Maybe he was right. Maybe this was what she was
meant to be doing. It felt right, just as donating all the art-
work in her father's storage bunker to Stella's Gate House
had felt right, but she wished the ache she'd been carrying
around in her chest the last month would ease up and cut
her a break.

"They already have enough details about Eleanor," Allie
said from the conference table, where she was studying Hailey's notes for the press conference. "And Bryan. And Paul."
She looked up. "The only thing you might want to mention
is Madeline's role in all this. If she hadn't called Graham to
warn him about Eleanor, things might have gone down very
differently."

Yeah, Hailey already knew that. If Graham hadn't shown
up in Jamaica to try to stop Eleanor, she and Stella might
be dead now. Pain stabbed at her, like it did whenever
she thought of Graham, but she breathed through it. And
thanks to Stella—even though she'd been the one wronged
in all of this from the start—no one knew a thing about
what Graham had done to earn Eleanor's loyalty all those
years before.

Another reason Hailey was falling for her mother.

"Why don't you all give Hailey and me a moment alone

before the press conference," Stella said, eyeing Hailey at the counter across the room.

"Good lucks" were tossed Hailey's way as everyone filed out of the administrative offices at the Roarke Royal Floridian. It had been her father's first hotel, where he'd met and fallen in love with Stella. For some reason it seemed fitting to hold this press conference here, now.

When they were alone, Stella crossed to the minibar and pulled out a can of ginger ale. "Drink this. It'll help settle your stomach."

Hailey took the offered can. "Thanks. It's just nerves."

Stella eased her hip against the counter. "For the record, I had horrible morning sickness with you. Granted, mine didn't start this early, but it used to wipe me out for the entire day. I'm afraid genetics are not your friend on this one."

Hailey's hand halted in the act of setting the can on the counter. "I . . . don't know what you're—"

A sad smile slid across Stella's face. "You can't keep dodging him, you know. You're going to have to face up to this and tell him."

That ache she'd been fighting flittered across Hailey's chest. Now she could add mind reader to her mother's list of skills. Not only was the woman a world-class painter, charitable philanthropist and amazing wife, she also didn't miss a thing.

"I'm not dodging him."

"Hailey, he's called every day for the last two weeks. And security at the RR building downtown said you have a standing order not to let him past the elevators. I'd say that's dodging him." Her voice softened. "I haven't pushed you on this because you've been dealing with a lot, but you're miserable. And this has nothing to do with your father's company or what happened in Jamaica. It has to do with him, doesn't it?"

Tears Hailey hated with a passion burned the backs of her eyes. Dammit, she'd only just found out she was pregnant and the hormones were already doing a number on her. "He's only persisting because he feels guilty over what happened. It'll pass."

"Honey, that's not guilt. That's a man who wants a second chance. Trust me, I've seen him."

Hailey's eyes slid sideways to glance at Stella, and in the silence between them, she asked the question she'd been grappling with for the last month. "What if he doesn't deserve one?"

Stella rested a hand on Hailey's arm. "Everyone deserves a second chance. Don't harden your heart so much you miss the good parts in life that are right in front of you. That's what Eleanor did. It's what I was doing before I met Mark. It's what your father did for way too long." She ran her fingers down Hailey's cheek and smiled. "There's way too much passion inside you to let life pass by like that. Don't waste the precious gift you were given."

Stella's words echoed through Hailey's head as she made her way to the ballroom in the east wing of the resort. Nicole had been right, the room was packed, but there were familiar faces as well. Billy and Nicole stood off to the side. From the corner of her eye, she caught Stella's proud smile and the way Mark slipped his arm around her waist in a protective move. She spotted Pete and Kat, Rafe and Lisa, Allie and both her parents in the crowd, all there in support of her and this new chapter in her life.

Okay, so it wasn't the traditional family she'd always dreamed of, but it was hers, and Stella had been right about one thing: she wasn't about to waste any of the gifts she'd been given.

When she was done with her statement outlining the changes to the company, she opened the floor to questions. Most were, like she'd expected, centered on the scandal with Eleanor, but Hailey dodged as many as she could, just like she'd practiced. And finally, realizing the crowd was getting antsy for something juicy, she decided it was time to pack it in.

"I'll take one last question." She glanced around as hands

shot into the air and voices shouted out, then stopped cold when she heard a voice she knew all too well.

The reporters in the front of the room must have noticed her strange expression, because they turned to look, and like the sea parting, they split down the center of the room to where Shane was standing in the back wearing jeans and a long-sleeved blue T-shirt stretched across his chest that read:

*Sometimes a prayer is really all you need.*
*Just ask Tommy & Gina.*

Her heart kicked up against her ribs. Her stomach fluttered. The stubble she'd gotten used to seeing on his jaw was gone, his hair was shorter than she remembered, and he looked tan from this distance. But no matter how sexy he was, the only thing she could think about was how she'd felt on that plane just before landing in Jamaica.

"I just have one question," he said. "The Cubs don't hold spring training down here. Are you sure you still love this town?"

She caught the reference to her favorite Bon Jovi song, the one she had programmed into her phone, and his teasing tone. And knew she was seconds away from a complete meltdown. *Damn hormones.*

She leaned into the microphone and sent him a withering look. "Thank you, everyone, for coming out. But I'm afraid I don't have time for any more questions after all. This press conference is now over."

Shane figured he'd broken at least three laws getting into this damn place. And thanks to that fence Billy hadn't warned him about, which he'd had to scale to avoid Joe Six-Pack the security guard, his right knee was now lit up like a Christmas tree. All that, coupled with the fact Hailey had been giving him the slip for two weeks, was enough to get him good and pissed. So there was no way she was slinking away now.

He watched which door she headed for, and as the press was swarming, trying to get the rest of their questions answered, he hit the back exit, looped around the property and used the key card he'd swiped from the security office—thanks to Billy—to get into the main building.

It took about ten minutes, but just like he'd expected, the stairwell door opened and closed with a snap, followed by Hailey's deep intake of breath and slow release. Her shoes clicked as she moved up the steps, then stopped abruptly when she turned and found him sitting on the second flight, waiting for her.

The scent of lilacs surrounded him. And okay, yeah, that wasn't happiness to see him, but he was going to change that.

He rose slowly. "I'm really hoping that quick exit meant you just didn't hear the question."

Irritation coated her features. "How did you know I'd be here?"

"A little bird told me you haven't been too hot on elevators lately."

Her jaw clenched. "Nicole needs to keep her mouth shut." She moved around him and reached for the railing on the far side of the wide steps. "Excuse me, I'm busy."

"Hold up, Hailey." He turned to look after her. "I just want to talk. You can slow down for a couple of minutes, can't you?"

He thought he heard her mumble *not for you*, but ignored it when he saw her moving up the stairs without even pausing. "I left CPD."

That did it. She stopped. And a flicker of hope went off like a firework in his chest.

"Turned in my resignation and got a job doing investigative work for . . . this place I know. A lot less stress. Better hours. And people aren't dying to meet me." When she didn't laugh at his joke, he scrubbed a hand through his newly cut hair and added, "You were right. About the job. It was eating away at me. I didn't realize how much until I left."

"I'm glad I could help," she said, not turning to look at him. "But I really have work to get back to." She started climbing again.

"How's your shoulder?"

"Fine."

He skipped steps quickly to get in front of her. She stopped and glared at him. "You're in my way."

"Look, I know you're ticked at me, and you have every right to be. I was a jackass, and I don't deserve a second chance, but . . ." It was now or never. "That's what I want. It's why I'm here. For a chance to make things up to you."

"Don't, Maxwell." She pushed past him.

He ignored her words, gently grabbed her good arm and turned her to face him, one step up at eye level. "I know you love me," he teased. "I heard you. And if you didn't, you wouldn't still be so damn pissed. Just to show you how serious I am, I'll let you kick my ass. Right here. I won't even try to fight back."

Her expression didn't change, not even when he smiled and moved a fraction of an inch closer. "Come on, Roarke," he whispered. "We both know that's an offer you can't refuse."

"I'm pregnant."

His smile wobbled. "What?"

"I'm pregnant. I found out a few days ago." When his mouth fell open, she added, "I didn't plan it, if that's what you're thinking. Apparently antibiotics mess with birth control pills. I knew that . . . know that . . . but I think it's safe to say I was under a little bit of stress when James gave them to you for me, and everyone knows stress also screws with birth control so, yeah . . . surprise."

She didn't look happy about this little surprise, and he couldn't quite read her mood to tell if she was serious or just trying to make him suffer, so he asked, "You're pregnant? Really? When—"

She huffed and moved up two steps to put distance between them. "I was going to tell you when I figured out what to say. I mean, it's not like this isn't a big shock to me, too, you know. I wasn't planning on having a kid right now, at least not until I found someone who really wanted to have one with me. But I've already decided I'm keeping this baby, so don't even think about trying to talk me out of it. And I don't need your help in this. I'm only telling you because you deserve to know and . . ." Her brows snapped together. "Why are you smiling?"

He was, wasn't he? Hot damn. Who would have ever predicted that?

Holy crap, he was going to be a father. And it didn't scare the shit out of him. Not one bit.

His grin widened. "Because you're pregnant. That's just . . . wow." He glanced at her flat belly, hidden behind tailored slacks and a red blouse that showcased her curves and lean figure. "You do realize twins run in my family, don't you?"

"*What?*" She gave her head a shake, held up a finger and pointed at him with a fire in her eyes he'd missed the last few weeks. "That's not funny. And besides, I already looked it up. Genetics only matter if it runs on the mother's side. Which it doesn't, thank God."

"Tell that to my father. And his uncle. And his father, too, while you're at it."

The color drained from her face. "That's just . . . mean."

He moved up the stairs toward her, knowing he was grinning like a fool, but not even caring. "You're going to have to marry me, you know. I was planning on letting you get used to the whole dating thing before I brought it up, but we don't have enough time for that now."

She scrambled backward up the steps to get away from him. "I'm not marrying you."

"Sure you are. I'm Irish Catholic. My mother will freak if we have these babies without a wedding."

Her kiss-me lips parted in a sexy little "oh." She hit the top step, stumbled and caught herself before he could. "You're not even a practicing Catholic. And stop saying *babies*. There's only *one* baby."

"Sex, babies, marriage. That's the way the Maxwells have been doing it for years."

"You don't even want kids," she sputtered as her back hit the stairwell wall.

"I didn't before." He braced a hand on the wall near her head, trapping her. "But you changed things." His other hand landed gently on her belly, and he looked down where he touched her as warmth spread up his arm and into his chest. "You changed everything, Hailey. I love—"

"Shane, don't." The pleading in her voice and the use of his first name cut through his playful banter, and he focused on eyes so blue, he felt like he could see forever. "Don't say things you can't take back."

His smile faded. "I'm not. I lo—"

"No." She ducked out from beneath his arm before he could stop her and moved two steps away from him, toward the next set of stairs. "I know why you're here. Because you feel guilty for the way things ended and because you want to make amends, but that's not love."

"Hailey—"

"Two weeks, Shane. It took you two weeks to call me. That's not love, that's guilt."

"There were . . . things I needed to do before I could see you again."

She shook her head. "You're a protector. It's why you made a good cop. Why you make a great brother and son. You'd do anything for the people you care about, and I know I fall into that category because we have this . . . connection. But that's not love. Not the kind I want or need."

His heart squeezed tight, and for the first time since he'd hatched this plan, a sliver of doubt crept in. "You're wrong—"

"No, I'm not. We both know you don't want a wife or a child, not really, and this is starting to feel way too much like Jamaica, like you swooping in to save the girl. Well, that's not love, either, and it's not any reason to get married. I don't need you to save me. I never did. I've spent my whole life settling for things, and I'm not going to do it anymore.

I'm not going to sit around and pretend you love me, then wait for the day you realize you made a mistake and walk. I deserve more." She put a hand on her belly. "We deserve more."

Panic rose in his chest. "Hailey, wait—"

She took a step away. "I won't try to stop you from being involved with this baby when it's born, if that's really what you want. But we both know it's not. So I'm hoping you'll just make things easier for all of us and go now. If you care about me at all, Shane, you'll do this one small thing for me."

He should have gone after her, but he was still too stunned to move, even after she disappeared up the steps and around the corner. One floor up, the stairwell door opened and snapped shut with a deafening clap.

The heat he'd felt at seeing her flickered and went out. All that hope he'd been carrying around the last few weeks crumbled at his feet. He'd waited too long, spent too much time getting himself and his shit together before coming after her, and now it was too late.

*Baby.* She was having his baby. And he'd screwed things up so bad with her, she didn't want him to be involved. Ever.

He stood where he was for a moment, just listening to the sounds around him as an empty, cold space grew in his chest. Finally, because he didn't know what else to do, he made his way down the stairs and out into the early morning sunlight.

He'd left his sunglasses in his car, but he barely noticed the glare. As he took his time crossing the parking lot and slipped his hands into his pockets, he realized he didn't itch for a Tic Tac or hear that irritating voice in his head anymore. She'd changed all that for him, too, and she didn't even know it.

"Maxwell, hold up."

The sound of her voice hit him like a blast, but he didn't turn. Really wasn't up to seeing the hurt on her face again. At least not until he figured out what he was going to do next. "Yeah, I know. I'm leaving, don't worry."

"Who's Dr. Robinson?"

That stopped him. He turned slowly to look at her. "Who?"

She crossed her arms over her chest, looking pissed and sexy all at the same time. "Rafe's planted himself in my office and says he won't leave until I ask you two questions. Since Lisa seems to be backing him up on this one and I want both of them gone, I'm asking. Who's Dr. Robinson?"

"Jackass." Shane glared across the parking lot toward the building. He was gonna kill Rafe. And his meddling twin.

"Well?"

It's not like there was a reason not to tell her now, right? He shrugged. "A counselor."

Silence. Then she said, "You're seeing a shrink? But you . . . I thought you didn't like psychiatrists."

Okay, yeah. Seriously killing his loose-lipped brother-in-law. "I didn't like the one my department used. Guy was always trying to get into my head. This one's all right, I guess. For a head doc."

Her brow drew together, and she dropped her arms. "What . . . what did he say?"

He took a deep breath and figured *what the hell?* It wasn't like any of this was going to change anything. "He says I've got some form of post-traumatic stress disorder. PTSD. I don't know, I mean, it's not the same as what the guys coming back from the Gulf are dealing with, but apparently it only takes one event to trigger this kind of thing and after everything that happened with Julie . . ."

He let the words trail off because he didn't know what else to say. And when she didn't respond he knew, yep, it didn't change a thing. "Look, I'm just gonna go—"

"Hold on," she said. "Who are you doing investigative work for?"

His irritation rose. He'd pretty much spilled his heart at her feet, and she'd made it completely clear she didn't want him, but now she was peppering him with questions just to ease her curiosity? "Why the hell are you asking me this? If Rafe's up in your office, then you damn well know I'm working at Odyssey doing background research. Not much different from what I used to do, except now I'm working with antiquities instead of dead bodies."

The color drained from her face. "Oh, my God."

His frustration had reached its peak, but it ebbed when she reached for the hood of a car to steady herself. That protective instinct of his she hated so much clicked into gear. "What's wrong?"

"You . . . You're working at Odyssey? With a crook and a thief?"

"They're reformed. Or so they say. Do you feel all right? Is it the baby?"

"No. I . . . oh, my God." Her eyes shot to his. "You really do love me."

His brow wrinkled. "I told you that already."

"Yeah, but I didn't really believe it. You don't even *like* Rafe."

"Not anymore," he said with a scowl. Her color was still pale, but she didn't look sick, just shell-shocked. But why—

"Why didn't you tell me? About Odyssey and the counselor?"

"Because it doesn't have anything to do with you and me."

"Yes, it does. It has everything to do with us. I thought you were here out of guilt. And that you were avoiding me after what happened in Jamaica because I didn't really mean anything to you. And that you only offered to marry me because I told you I was pregnant. But this . . ." She lifted her hand. "This proves I was wrong."

A flicker of hope ignited in his chest. "It does?"

She eased forward to stand in front of him. "Are you really working for Rafe and Pete?"

"*With* them. I refuse to admit I'm working for either one of those guys."

Slowly, her lips curved into the sweetest smile. One that sent warmth through his chest and into his limbs. And that flicker flared into a full-blown flame. "I don't want you leaving law enforcement, not for me."

His heart thumped so hard, he was sure she had to hear it. "I'm not. I left for me. And just so we're clear on something else, I'm not seeing the shrink for you, either. I'm going for me."

He shifted uncomfortably, but knew this was important, and part of the reason he hadn't told her about his sessions in the first place. "I've got a long way to go, and I was a hot-head before, so there's no telling if I'll ever be completely right in the head, but . . . I'm working on it. I didn't stay away from you because I wanted to, Hailey. I stayed away because I didn't know if I could make this work. And because I didn't want to hurt you any more than I already had."

Her eyes softened. "The only thing that hurts me is when you shut me out. Don't you know that?"

"I do now. I'm working on the rest of it. That's why I came here now rather than waiting until my treatment's done."

She moved into him so suddenly, it stole his breath. Then her arms were sliding around his waist, her chest brushing his, her fingertips grazing the scar on his side. But the only memory her touch ignited was the one from Puerto Rico where she'd used her lips and tongue to kiss each of his scars and every inch of his body. Not the one from Chicago, not the one with Malcolm that had haunted him so long.

He slid his fingers into her hair and tipped her face up to his, just before lowering to take her lips in a kiss he hoped she knew came from the very soul of him. And when he eased back to look down, his heart swelled to find her smiling.

"I want a prenup, Shane."

"I don't want your money, Roarke."

"Not like that," she said. "I want a prenup that says if you do decide to bail on us, I get one free shot at you."

He barked out a laugh, pulled her close. Snarky, smart and so damn tough she could hold her own with him and anyone else. Had he thought she needed him to save her? Man, he'd been so wrong. She'd saved him. Right from the very beginning. "Stop it, would ya? You're turning me on. We're in public."

She smiled against his neck. "It's only my employees. And my family. And your bosses. No one will get the wrong idea."

"Everyone's had the wrong idea about us from the very beginning," he said into her hair, loving the way she said his name. "But not me. Not anymore." He pressed his lips against the soft, soft skin of her neck. "I've finally got the right one. I've finally got you."

"You do," she whispered. "For as long as you want me. Us," she corrected, reminding him he was getting a package deal.

He slid one hand down to her tummy. "What do you think about the names Tommy and Gina? Seems fitting, don't you think?"

She laughed so hard, he felt it all the way in his toes, then up into his chest to melt the last bit of ice around his heart. "I think . . . I've never loved anyone more than I do right now."

He knew he hadn't. Ever. He squeezed her tight. "Tommy and Gina it is, then."

# ☐ **YES!**

Sign me up for the Love Spell Book Club and send my FREE BOOKS! If I choose to stay in the club, I will pay only $8.50* each month, a savings of $6.48!

NAME: _____

ADDRESS: _____

TELEPHONE: _____

EMAIL: _____

☐ I want to pay by credit card.

☐ **VISA**    ☐ MasterCard.    ☐ DISCOVER

ACCOUNT #: _____

EXPIRATION DATE: _____

SIGNATURE: _____

Mail this page along with $2.00 shipping and handling to:
**Love Spell Book Club**
**PO Box 6640**
**Wayne, PA 19087**
Or fax (must include credit card information) to:
**610-995-9274**
You can also sign up online at **www.dorchesterpub.com**.

*Plus $2.00 for shipping. Offer open to residents of the U.S. and Canada only. Canadian residents please call 1-800-481-9191 for pricing information.

If under 18, a parent or guardian must sign. Terms, prices and conditions subject to change. Subscription subject to acceptance. Dorchester Publishing reserves the right to reject any order or cancel any subscription.